my stubborn heart

my stubborn heart

a novel

BECKY WADE

BETHANY HOUSE PUBLISHERS

a division of Baker Publishing Group
Minneapolis, Minnesota

Published by Bethany House Publishers
11400 Hampshire Avenue South
Bloomington, Minnesota 55438
www.bethanyhouse.com

Bethany House Publishers is a division of
Baker Publishing Group, Grand Rapids, Michigan

Printed in the United States of America

Library of Congress Cataloging-in-Publication Data
Wade, Becky.
    My stubborn heart / Becky Wade.
        p.   cm.
    ISBN 978-0-7642-0974-1 (pbk.)
    I. Title.
PS3623.A33M9 2012
813'.6—dc23   2012000972

Cover design by Jennifer Parker

Cover photography by Photolibrary/Cusp Images, Richard Leo Johnson/Beateworks/ Corbis

12   13   14   15   16   17   18   7   6   5   4   3   2   1

For Lily, Colin, and Corinne.
Mommy loves you very much.

prologue

There once was a girl who'd been praying for a husband since the fourth grade. Over the years she'd prayed for his health, his happiness, his protection, and—okay—sometimes for his good looks. She'd prayed that she would meet him when she was meant to.

Except that she hadn't.

She'd been avidly expecting and watching for him all this time, from the fourth grade straight up to the age of thirty-one. And though she tried hard to be positive, the truth was that she'd grown tired of waiting. Tired of dating. Tired of breaking off just two bananas from the bunch at the grocery store. Tired of the singles group at church. Tired of living alone.

Worse, she was beginning to doubt that her nameless, faceless husband existed at all. Maybe, late at night in her kid bed, her college bed, her adult single woman bed, she'd been praying for someone who wasn't coming. Ever.

Perhaps her husband had run in front of a bus as a child. What did God do in that situation? Swap in an understudy? Or maybe she'd missed her husband during the bustle of her college years, never knowing that the shy guy from physics class was *the one*. Or perhaps, right from the start, God had never intended for her to marry.

Or maybe, just maybe—and this was the hope she still clung to despite the evidence to the contrary—her husband was still on his way.

There once was a mother who'd been praying double hard for her son ever since he'd stopped praying for himself.

From earliest childhood, he'd been extraordinary—a perfect, miraculous blend of athletic ability and focused determination. She and her husband had supported and loved him, but never expected of him what he'd made of himself. How could it even have entered her mind to dream a dream that big? She'd watched with a mixture of sentimental pride and stunned surprise as he'd climbed up every level of the sport of hockey.

By the age of eighteen he was playing professionally. From there, at what she'd thought would be the pinnacle, his star had only continued to rise. He'd been photographed for grocery store magazines. He'd moved into a house surrounded by a wall of security. He'd married a beautiful girl in a grand wedding ceremony filled with the flashes of cameras, wedding planners, and peach-colored roses.

Her son had accomplished it all. The height of success in his career. National fame. Wealth. Personal happiness with his wife.

And then it had all come apart, crashing and rolling out of reach like a handful of spilled marbles. His wife had been diagnosed with cancer and nothing—not money, not the best doctors—had been able to save her. When she'd died, he'd walked away from his sport, from the big house with the wall, from the fame.

In the years since, he'd retreated inside himself to a place where none of his family or friends could reach him. So his mother prayed. She prayed that God wouldn't forget about him, this son of hers, who'd gained and lost the world in just a third of his lifetime. She prayed that God would send someone who could find him and save him from his prison of grief. And she prayed that maybe, somehow, in time, his heart would soften and he'd find love again.

Funny thing about prayers. God hears them. But you just never know if, when, or how He's going to answer them.

chapter one

Kate Donovan entered the town of Redbud, Pennsylvania, for the first time driving a car packed with her seventy-six-year-old grandmother, a comprehensive set of encyclopedias on American antiques, three sacks of nonperishable groceries, and enough pink luggage to give Mary Kay fits of jealousy. It was the end of their three-day car trip from Dallas but only the beginning of their big adventure together.

"Look at this town." Gran lowered the passenger window. "Look at it! Just try to tell me this isn't the sweetest town you've ever seen." The afternoon breeze blew into the car, mussing Gran's stylishly short white hair and sending Kate's long red ponytail flying. "Didn't I tell you it was sweet?"

"You did. And it is." Quaint brick buildings holding shops and restaurants lined Main Street. Kate spotted one adorable B&B and then a painted wooden sign advertising another. The trees dotting the edge of the sidewalk grew above and across the street, forming a tunnel of branches. Gran pointed left and right, telling Kate who'd owned this building when she'd been young, how that one had been a candy store in 1940, and how so-and-so had burned this one to the ground with a cigarette butt.

Before Kate could manage a single good look at anything, the glossy storefronts ended and neighborhoods began.

"Oh, Kate," Gran said, "we're almost there!"

After the endless highways, the endless sitting, and the endless fast food, Kate was finally going to see Chapel Bluff. The house where Gran had been raised had belonged to their family since it was built in 1820. Kate had heard stories of it and its generations of occupants since infancy.

"Take a right here, sweetie."

Kate turned right and followed the lane as it climbed. Charmingly boxy homes with doors painted red and green and black sat back from the road on lots of an acre or more each. The plots grew bigger still until the houses disappeared and countryside took over.

"It's beautiful here," Kate said.

"It is, isn't it?"

Kate punched a button and the sunroof slid open. The air seemed fresher here, clearer. Leaves, bronzed by the Saturday afternoon sunlight, waved and chattered at them from their branches.

"This is it," Gran said with hushed anticipation. She motioned toward the shady private drive on their left. "Just here."

Gravel crunched as Kate maneuvered her Explorer upward along the road. The forest cleared and she suddenly got her first sweeping view of the house.

"Chapel Bluff," Gran said reverently.

Chapel Bluff. Kate released a whistling breath of appreciation and promptly fell in love with it.

Though the drive continued on to what looked like a barn, Kate stopped next to the house and killed the engine. The two of them sat in silence, simply staring.

The three-story house had been constructed of brown and beige stone. A white door covered by a little pointed portico sat squarely in the center, flanked on either side and above by gleaming windows trimmed with white paint and black shutters. Recessed from the middle section of the house, two wings jutted outward. Both were built of the same stone and graced with the same glinting windows. Two dormer windows and no less than three brick chimneys marked the slate roofline.

It looked like something straight out of the English countryside. All it needed was hedgerows and climbing roses.

It would have been one of the prettiest houses Kate had ever seen, except that it had a scruffy, abandoned air about it. There were no flowers, no bikes propped out front, no flags, hay bales with scarecrows on top, or wreaths. Just slightly weedy planting beds, drawn curtains, and the lonely sound of crickets.

Kate gazed past the house to the barn, and then to what appeared to be a small clapboard chapel in the distance. All three buildings stood on a wide meadow. Where the meadow ended, the forest began, rising hill upon hill into the distance. And all of it, as far as the eye could see, Gran always said, was Chapel Bluff land.

It was more, really, than a house on a big chunk of property. It was too rambling and old to be just a house. An estate, maybe.

"Thank you, Kate." Gran's voice wavered, and Kate turned to see her grandmother smiling tearfully at her. "For coming with me. It means so much to me."

Kate leaned over and hugged her. "I'm glad I could bring you. Glad to be here."

They clambered out of the car and were greeted by a cool mid-September breeze. Gran struck out ahead of Kate, the hem of her long shirt fluttering. Today Gran had on a black turtleneck, black matte jersey pants, and a wine-colored Asian print shirt. She'd accented the outfit with four bracelets, two enormous rings, one necklace of burgundy stones, and her rectangular rimless glasses.

They paused on the porch while Gran fumbled the key into the lock and attempted to turn it.

Nothing.

Kate tried. Gran tried again. Kate tried and finally, after some serious arm wrestling, got the bolt to unclick. The door swung inward with a rusty squeak.

The smell hit Kate first. Mothballs, must, and stale air.

The dimness hit second. She squinted and made her way inside behind Gran. In the murky light she could just make out heavy pieces of furniture, art, and accessories all so unbelievably retro that it would have been funny if it hadn't been so tacky. "Whoa," Kate said. "I thought you were half kidding about the furniture."

"No. It's been exactly like this since 1955, when Mother had it redecorated."

They moved around the room opening curtains, letting in light. "Matt brought people out to fix the pipes and make sure the heat's working," Gran said. "The electricity *should* be on." Experimentally, she turned the knob of a lamp, and amazingly it switched on. "Ah, good." Hands on her hips, Gran looked about her. "Velma recommended a housekeeper who came by yesterday. The poor woman probably had a fit when she saw the place."

Kate had taken a three-month leave of absence from her job as a social worker to help Gran renovate Chapel Bluff. Now that she was getting her first good look at the place, she supposed she should feel overwhelmed at the thought of three straight months of work fixing up this *Leave It to Beaver* time capsule. But instead, as she took in the hideous brown carpet, the ugly maroon sofas, and the dingy beige wallpaper, something like delight rose inside her. This house was begging for help. *Begging.* More than any house on any HGTV makeover show she'd ever watched. Three months off work to renovate the place? Heaven.

Her fascination grew as Gran took her on a tour of the bottom floor, which held a mammoth den in one wing and an office in the other. A door set at the back of the living room issued them into the dining room, which had picturesque low ceilings, exposed beams, and a long fireplace. A short hallway from there led to an airy kitchen with windows on three sides. Clearly, the kitchen had originally been built as a separate structure from the main house, then joined later by the hallway.

Like the rest of the house, the floor in the kitchen was wide-planked pine, marked with time and wear. And though the outdated curtains and wallpaper had to go, the bright red '50s-style oven and refrigerator were quirky but cheery. White tiles stretched across the countertops, and a terrific French butcher block sat in the center of the room.

"The kitchen's actually pretty cute," Kate remarked.

"I agree. It's the best of the lot. Matt got the appliances working for us."

Kate opened the fridge and, sure enough, cold air rushed out.

"He's a gem, that boy," Gran said, "and even though I haven't see him since he was knee high . . . C'mon, sweetie, let me show you the upstairs." They made their way back to the living room and up the staircase.

". . . Even though you haven't seen him since he was knee high," Kate prompted.

"Even so, I'll tell you two things I know about Matt Jarreau." Gran gained the second-story landing and regarded Kate with twinkling eyes. "He's single. And he's a hunk."

Kate laughed. "You think he's a hunk based on what you remember of him from twenty years ago?"

"Twenty-five. And also the phone conversations we've had about the work he'll be doing for us. I could tell by his voice."

"I don't know, Gran. Casey Kasem has a good voice."

"No, I'm sure of it. We're the luckiest two women in this town, because I'm telling you, and mark my words, our contractor is a hunk."

Kate woke the next morning beneath a mound of quilts. She snuggled down deeper, flexed her toes, and for long minutes simply lay there, luxuriating. Chapel Bluff, like all houses, had its own kind of hum. She listened to the creaks and the muffled bumps of the plumbing and furnace. She smelled old wood in the air and Bounty fabric softener on her sheets.

Kate had picked the third-floor attic bedroom for herself, and through the four dormer windows, two on her right and two on her left, she could see slices of treetops and morning sky. Birds circling and chirping.

As she considered the honey-colored wooden ceiling beams above her, the peeling white wall paint, and the curly brass bed frame, a rush of gratitude filled her chest. She'd needed a break from her rut, from her loneliness, from her job, and God had known. He'd given her three months and this beautiful, beautiful old house.

She showered in a second-story bathroom the color of an avocado, and made her way downstairs. Gran was nowhere to be seen, but in the kitchen she discovered freshly baked apple-cinnamon muffins and coffee. She took her time over breakfast before refilling her coffee mug, pouring one for Gran, and taking both mugs outside.

Kate found her grandmother exactly where she'd known she'd be, on her knees in one of the front flower beds. She wore a turtleneck under her gardening overalls, gloves, plastic magenta clogs, and a straw hat with dangling purple ribbons.

"Morning, Gran."

The hat tilted upward, exposing a wide smile. "Morning! Is that more coffee?"

"I thought you might like another cup."

"Thank you." She pushed to her feet, peeled off the gloves, and accepted the mug.

Minutes later, they were still standing together discussing Gran's plans for the garden when a white truck turned onto their driveway. It was a Ford Super Duty, a few years old and slightly dusty.

"That'll be Matt now," Gran said, waving and making her way forward.

Kate shielded her eyes and watched the driver park, then walk toward them across the lawn. She moved to follow Gran, then slowed.

He wore jeans, scuffed work boots, and a brown and blue flannel shirt that hung open over a white T-shirt. His battered UNC baseball hat was pulled so low that shade slanted across his face.

Uh-oh for her, because Gran had been right.

He was a hunk.

Not only that, but something deep inside her almost seemed to—to *recognize* him. Which was ridiculous. Kate faltered and stopped.

Gran greeted the man with her trademark affection, hugging him, exclaiming, and smiling. "Kate." Gran drew him over to her. "This is Matt Jarreau. Matt, my granddaughter Kate Donovan."

"Nice to meet you," Kate said.

"You too."

"Thank you so much," Gran said to him, "for taking care of the electrical issues and the plumbing and all the rest so that we could move right in."

"Sure."

"We've certainly got a lot of work ahead of us, don't we?"

"Yes, ma'am."

"Is it still all right with you to begin by painting the bedrooms where Kate and I are staying? We'd so like to enjoy those rooms during the renovation. . . ."

Gran's voice went on, but Kate hardly heard. Matt had a fascinating face. Hard, handsome, and grave. A clean jawline and a firm, serious mouth. His nose looked like it had been broken and expertly reset, and faint scars marked the skin below his bottom lip and above an eyebrow. He had dark brown hair, slightly overlong so that it curled out from under the back of his hat.

What took Kate's breath away, though, were his eyes. They were dark, dark, dark, almost liquid brown. Thoughtful, long-lashed, shielded, and somehow . . . somehow wounded. All the more startling for being set in such a masculine face.

She studied those eyes as he spoke to her grandmother and she thought, *Tragedy*.

The conversation between Matt and Gran continued. She stood there feeling vaguely idiotic, holding her coffee mug and finding it hard to look away from him. It was as if something within her had been sleeping and now—the longer she was near him—the more it was waking, becoming alert, jangling. That something seemed to be saying, *It's you.*

Finally.

I've been waiting.

For you.

Which was crazy. Crazy! Yet her heart, as if it knew something her brain didn't, executed an awkward double beat, and then started pounding anyway.

". . . Kate and I have already picked out the paint colors for our rooms," Gran was saying, "but we didn't know how much you'd need and so we haven't purchased it yet."

"I'll get it for you," he replied.

"Oh, would you? That would be wonderful." Gran led the way up the front walk. "Come on inside, and I'll get the paint swatches."

Kate and Matt followed Gran into the house. He was over six feet tall and moved like an athlete. She could sense his coordination and strength. She'd bet money that he had some serious muscle, and that the straight fall of his shirt hid a washboard stomach.

"Can I get you something to drink, Matt?" Gran motioned to the kitchen. "We have coffee."

"I'm fine. Thanks."

"A muffin?"

"No. Thank you."

"All right, then. Here are the swatches." She swept them off the coffee table and handed them over with the musical click of bracelets. "Do you need to go up and have a look at our bedrooms?"

"I've already measured them so I know how much I'll need."

"Oh, good." Gran crossed her arms, tucking her coffee cup into an elbow. "So tell us about yourself, Matt."

"Not much to tell." Even at that innocuous question, Kate could sense him retreating.

"I remember you coming over here to play as a boy. Your parents were just about Mother and Daddy's closest neighbors. Have you lived in town all your life?"

"I lived in New York a while."

"Oh, did you? Manhattan is such an interesting place. . . ."

As Gran chatted about a recent trip she'd taken to New York, Kate watched Matt move smoothly to the door and take hold of the handle.

In Kate's experience, men as hot looking as he was had an ego to match. But Matt seemed strangely guarded, almost introverted. He hadn't smiled, he'd answered all Gran's questions politely but with few words, and he'd used his posture and expression like a shield.

"Have you been back in Redbud long?" Gran asked him.

"A couple of years. I'd best be going." He opened the door and walked off the front porch.

"Certainly. We'll see you later." Gran waved cheerfully.

They stood watching until his truck pulled out of sight.

"I told you he was a hunk," Gran said.

"You were right."

They made their way to the kitchen and went to work cleaning up breakfast. "I get the feeling that something happened to him," Kate said.

Gran washed off plates and slotted them into the relic of a dishwasher. "To Matt?"

"Yes. Something . . ." Kate stilled, a dish towel dangling from her shoulder. "Something terrible."

"What gives you that impression?"

"I'm not sure. I just know."

"You do?"

"I could see it in his eyes."

Gran stopped, her wet hands dripping water into the sink, and studied Kate shrewdly. "You were unusually quiet around him."

"I was dumbfounded by him! I couldn't think of a thing to say."

"Well, as previously noted, he is a *very* nice-looking young man."

To say the least. Matt Jarreau was in-your-face, big-screen, major-league handsome. But there was something more about him than his mere handsomeness . . . something intangible, that had her by the throat. Her stomach *still* felt fluttery. Which was not good for her. Not. Good. She'd sworn off the really good-looking ones. Absolutely couldn't go there again.

They resumed their cleaning.

"I'm an excellent matchmaker," Gran stated. "Very subtle."

"Oh yes. You were very subtle when you threw me together with Barry Markman at the Fourth of July picnic."

"It's just that his grandmother and I are such close friends. We'd hoped . . . Well, how was I to know he had bad breath?"

"Listen, *no one* is going to make any romantic overtures toward Matt Jarreau."

"Why?"

"He's way out of my league."

"No!"

"Yes." She was ordinary. A thirty-one-year-old redheaded virgin with asthma and genetics that didn't include either hips or boobs. "Even if by some chance he did want to ask me out, I no longer date guys that look like that. I decided a couple of years ago to save myself the anguish." Everyone knew—and her own experience had confirmed—that good-looking men were usually taken, emotionally unavailable, or narcissists. "Okay?"

"Okay," Gran sighed.

With a pang of dread, Kate imagined Gran cornering Matt at every turn, begging him to take her poor, forlorn granddaughter on a date.

"Gran, I'm serious."

"I am, too," she answered. "You know I'd never do anything to embarrass you."

Kate could think of dozens of times when Gran had, nevertheless, done exactly that.

Gran dropped two dirty knives into the dishwasher. "However,

I do think you and I need to invite him to dinner. Single men don't eat well. He probably hasn't had a home-cooked meal in weeks. His mother and father live in Florida now, you know."

"Inviting him to dinner is fine."

"Good. Then that's settled." Gran rinsed out the sink and dried her hands. "What's on the agenda today?"

"Today we've got to start sorting through everything. We need to decide what to sell at the garage sale, what to sell on eBay, what to toss, and what to keep."

"And tomorrow?"

"Hmm." She wasn't going to nurture a single romantic feeling toward Matt and yet . . . she was painfully curious about him. She wanted—it surprised her how much she wanted—to get to know him, to find out what had made him so sad, and hopefully to establish a friendship so that she'd have some company her own age over the coming weeks.

Everyone who knew her knew she had a wide streak of stubbornness running through her. When something got into her head and took root, she couldn't get it out. And Matt Jarreau had gotten into her head and taken root. He didn't know it yet, but she was going to find out his secrets and they were going to be friends. "Tomorrow I'm going to help Matt paint."

chapter two

The next afternoon Matt Jarreau wiped his hands on his jeans and surveyed the paint job he'd just finished in Mrs. Donovan's bedroom. The light purple color was a long shot from anything he'd have chosen. Sleeping in here would be like sleeping inside a purple carnation. Still, the room looked a heck of a lot better without the water stains, cracks, and faded paper that had covered the walls and ceiling before he'd started.

He set about cleaning and putting away the supplies he'd used. Other than the paint colors that she and her granddaughter had chosen for their bedrooms, he liked Mrs. Donovan's renovation plans. She seemed to have an eye for preserving the character of the old house.

Carrying the paint and tarp with one arm and a fresh paint pan and roller brush with the other, he made his way upstairs to the attic room. Yesterday he'd covered the layers of aging wallpaper with a light plaster texture, and this morning he'd taped off the floorboards and the crown moldings. With that done, painting the attic room wouldn't take long—

He stopped abruptly in the doorway.

Mrs. Donovan's granddaughter glanced up at him from where she stood in the center of the room.

He waited for her to murmur something about getting out of his way, and then leave.

Instead, she simply stood there.

"I don't mean to inconvenience you," he said after a few moments of strained silence, "but I was going to paint in here now."

"No inconvenience," she said. "I'm going to help." She bent and lifted a brand-new roller brush off the floor.

He liked to work alone. In fact, almost everything he did in a day—eat, workout, buy food, watch TV—he did by himself. The people in this town knew that and left him alone. It unsettled him that this stranger wanted to paint with him, that he was trapped in here with her.

Without letting his irritation show, Matt spread out the tarp, wedged the lid off the first can of paint, and stirred it carefully. The pale pink color she'd picked looked like chewed bubble gum.

"Oh, I love it," she said.

Matt glanced at her and frowned. "Is it Kate?"

"Yep, it's Kate."

"You might not want to paint in that outfit." She had on a white tank top and black pants, the kind that ended above the ankle. He couldn't remember what women called those. On her feet she was wearing what looked like black ballet shoes.

"This is my painting outfit," she replied. "See?" She pulled the shirt to the side and pointed to a few flecks of paint on the fabric. "It's all right."

He wanted to tell her to take her roller brush and her crazy painting clothes downstairs and out of his space, but she was his client. So instead he nodded, poured the paint, rolled his brush, and went to work.

Out of the corner of his eye he watched her paint a big *N* on the wall, and then use her roller to fill the space between the two

uprights. "I saw them do it like this on *Designed to Sell* one time."
She smiled.

He grunted and tried to ignore her.

After a while she paused, and he could feel her attention on
him. He kept on painting.

"I'm really glad you're able to help us with this renovation."

He nodded.

"Gran has been wanting to update this place for a long time."

He didn't say anything.

"How long have you been doing this kind of work?"

"Three years."

A few moments of quiet. "So you knew my great-grandparents?"

"I did. They were nice people."

"Yes, they were. I miss them."

He kept on painting, hoping she'd drop the small talk.

"You grew up in Redbud?" she asked.

He nodded.

"Just down the road from here?"

He nodded again.

"You know . . ." She paused, studying him. "Having a conversation with you is a lot like having one with myself."

He met her gaze, frowning.

Her lips twitched, then spread into a big, wide smile. Genuine
warmth glittered in her eyes.

He . . . he wasn't sure what to make of her. He was accustomed,
in a way, to women hitting on him. But she wasn't hitting on him.
Teasing him, maybe. Whatever she was doing, he didn't like it.
Didn't like her questions or the directness of her gaze.

"You seem to be a pretty serious person," she observed.

He refocused his attention on the wall and resumed painting.
"I guess I am."

"Do you smile much?"

Pain took a slice at his heart, but he managed to deflect the blow so that it only scored a glancing hit. "I don't know."

"Hmm. What would it take to make you smile, I wonder? Have you ever seen a skinny girl do jumping jacks? I look like a praying mantis when I do them. But I'm willing to embarrass myself and give it a try."

"Thanks for the offer. I think I'll pass."

"You've no *idea* what you're missing."

"I'm sure I don't."

She threw back her head and laughed. "Okay, we're doing better. We're sort of talking back and forth."

The squishy sounds of dipping brushes and rolling paint filled the room. He was used to those sounds, familiar with their kind of silence.

He couldn't remember Kate saying anything at all when they'd met yesterday. She'd been so quiet he'd hardly noticed her. What had happened? He'd liked her better quiet.

Matt shot a glance at her. She reminded him of that movie star from way back . . . the one who was famous for wearing the tiara and shopping at Tiffany's or something. Audrey? Yeah, Audrey Hepburn. Kate had long dark red hair pulled into a low ponytail, but otherwise they looked alike. She was slim like Audrey Hepburn, with little features and big eyes.

"What do you do for fun?" she asked.

Good grief. "Not much."

"Well, since you seem so fascinated by the subject, I'll tell you what I like to do." She squatted to roll a section near the baseboard. "I'm into antiques. I like going to flea markets. I read. I go to movies and dinners with friends. So . . . now you have to tell me what you do for fun."

"I work out."

He caught a glimpse of her wrinkled nose. "Doesn't that fall more under the category of agony?"

"Maybe."

"What else?"

"I watch sports."

She tucked a long strand of red hair behind her ear. "If there's not a game on tonight, Gran and I would love for you to stay and have dinner with us."

"Thanks, but I can't."

"She's a great cook."

"I've got plans," he lied.

"Maybe another night." After about thirty seconds of peace, she continued. "So you're wearing a UNC hat. Did you go to college there?"

"Listen, no offense"—he'd had all of her chatter that he could take—"but I like to work with it quiet."

She studied him with those eyes of hers—they were hazel with long lashes. He didn't see any anger in her expression, just curiosity and something that looked like understanding. "Okay," she said, a dimple flashing in one cheek. "I hear you." Then she amazed him by returning to work.

She wasn't going to leave? He watched, frustrated, as she continued painting. A redheaded Audrey Hepburn in ballet shoes, concentrating hard on covering her walls with pink paint.

Kate sat in the middle of the downstairs library the following afternoon, surveying the piles that encircled her. She deposited a folder of what looked like ancient receipts into the throwaway pile, and then set a porcelain sculpture of a milk cow with a daisy behind its ear in the garage sale pile.

As expected, the job of organizing the contents of Chapel Bluff was huge. Huge! Because she and Gran were so thorough, leaving no drawer uninspected, they were making painfully slow progress. First thing this morning, Gran had called Velma Armstrong and Peg Lawrence and enlisted their help.

Velma and Peg had been close friends of Gran's since their days together at Redbud Elementary. Gran always referred to them as "the girls," a term that had, in Velma and Peg's case, long ago expired.

"Good gracious, Beverly, this job is overwhelming!" Velma emerged scowling from the closet where she'd been buried. Dust hovered in the air around her, sparkling in the sunlight.

Gran looked up from her spot at the desk. "I know. That's why I called you."

"I'm about to choke to death on all this dust!" Velma marched over to a window and forced it open. She was dressed for the day's work in a teal and white velour sweat suit. Her white high-top Reeboks looked like they'd come straight out of 1985 but didn't have a scratch on them. She'd twisted her long hair, an unlikely shade of nut brown for a seventy-something woman, into a rectangular bun secured with white plastic combs encrusted with rhinestones.

Crisp afternoon air flushed into the room, and they all sighed with relief.

"How much more have we got?" Velma asked, eyeing the stacks venomously.

"We haven't even started on those," Gran said, pointing to a wall of shelves.

"Good gracious," Velma muttered.

Gran laughed and slowly pushed herself to standing. "I think we could all use a break. C'mon ladies, the cookies should be just about ready."

Gran led them into the kitchen, then bustled around, scooping cookies off the cookie sheet with a spatula and giving them each something to carry back into the dining room for high tea.

Velma, Peg, and Kate settled at the table, which was set with china teacups and saucers, tea plates, napkins, silverware, and a tiny crystal vase filled with flowers.

Velma eyed Kate assessingly. She swiped at her hairline with fingers decorated with several diamond-studded gold rings and long nails shellacked with opalescent pearl polish. "Kate," she said in an ominous tone, "how old are you now?"

Ah, Kate thought. *Here it comes.* Though Velma and Peg had spent their entire lives in Redbud, Kate knew them well from their annual trips to Dallas to see Gran. "I'm thirty-one."

"Why in the world haven't you married anyone yet?"

"Well . . ." *I'm holding out for Prince Harry. I have cooties, so that makes it hard. Shark attack killed the last prospect.*

"What's the holdup? I mean, you're a pretty girl; there must be plenty of men who are interested in you."

"There've been a few."

"So?"

"So none of them worked out."

"What ever happened to that big, tall, handsome boy from way back?"

"Rick?"

"Yeah."

In the past ten years, she'd had two major and a handful of minor boyfriends. The first major one, Rick, Kate had met her senior year in college and taken with her into the working world. She'd thought they were on the same page, that they'd wanted the same things. But three years in, when she'd finally made the merest and most casual mention of marriage, he'd bailed instantly. She'd felt like a fool for not realizing that he'd been with her strictly because it had been convenient and fun for the short term. "Unwilling to commit," Kate answered.

"How about the nice-looking blond one we met in Dallas a few years ago?"

Her second major boyfriend, Trevor, had seemed great on the surface. After being together two years, right at the point when she'd started dreaming of a diamond ring and a white dress, she'd found out that he'd been cheating on her. Multiple times. Multiple people. "Unfaithful," Kate replied.

"So you broke up with both of them?" Velma frowned.

"Rick broke up with me and I broke up with Trevor." A simple explanation that didn't come close to the iceberg-sized contents of what lay beneath. She'd thought herself in love with each of them. The ending of both romances had completely and thoroughly broken her heart.

Velma grunted. "Well, Rick and Trevor are bad names anyway. You're never going to find a husband dating men with names like that. Look for a man with a good name." Her heavily penciled eyebrows lowered. "And look fast, because if you ever want to have children you need to find someone soon."

Ouch. Kate wished she could shrug off Velma's words. She tried. But despite her efforts, the words stung and stung hard. "I'll try to get a move on," she said dryly.

Gran breezed in with a plate full of oatmeal chocolate chunk cookies. "Hats, everyone!" She lifted the top of a nearby window seat. From the storage compartment beneath, she pulled out four of the many hats they'd uncovered in an upstairs bedroom yesterday.

No one expressed surprise. Gran frequently served high tea. And she almost always insisted on wearing big, gaudy hats.

After some debate about who looked best in which, they started in on the tea. "It's Victorian Garden," Gran pronounced as she poured, "and it tastes like a flower."

Kate watched Peg take a delicate sip of tea, then set her cup back on its saucer with an inaudible click. Peg was, and always had been, a beauty. Her makeup was impeccable, her pale gray bob beautifully cut and styled. Today she looked almost casual in leather loafers, gray slacks, a white collared shirt, and a red knit sweater tied around her shoulders. The gold charm hanging from her necklace exactly matched the gold charms on her earrings.

"You look thoughtful, Peg," Gran commented.

"Peg's always thoughtful," Velma said.

Peg laid her napkin gracefully in her lap, taking her time. "When you were in the kitchen, Beverly, Velma was telling Kate to hurry up and get married. I've been sitting here ever since trying to think of one good reason why Kate would want to."

"What?" Velma squawked.

"Girls these days don't need to get married, Velma," Peg said steadily. "They have their own careers and make their own money. They can adopt a baby from China if they want a child. Why do they need a husband?"

"Exactly!" Kate said gamely, though she didn't feel the least bit excited about a life of singlehood and a Chinese baby.

"Why would they want a husband?" Velma repeated incredulously. "Why, Peggy Elizabeth—"

"Men are messy," Peg serenely interrupted. "And bossy. And *sometimes* they refuse to go on a cruise to Alaska and instead insist on taking a cruise to the Caribbean for the sixteenth time."

"Ah," Velma said. "So that's the bee in your bonnet."

"Well . . . yes. I simply can't understand what William has against Alaska." Peg gently squeezed Kate's forearm and smiled. "You have to understand, Kate, my husband is still around, so I'm allowed to complain about him."

Velma let out a hoot of laughter.

"They become saints, of course, once they're gone," Peg said. "But let me tell you, the reality of a husband is at times very trying."

"Of course husbands are trying! But Kate should still marry." Velma peered at Kate through her big glasses, the kind with earpieces that started at the outside bottom of the lenses and swirled back over the ears. "Herb was a nincompoop. I divorced him after fifteen years of his nonsense, and I've been a single gal ever since. Even so, I'm glad I married the big dope because he gave me four sons." Her attention swung to Gran. "You adored Arthur."

"Yes, I did," Gran agreed.

It had been obvious to everyone who'd known them that Kate's gran and grandad had indeed adored each other. They'd been happily married for more than fifty years. At the end of his life, her grandad had fought valiantly against leukemia before God took him home a year and a half ago.

Losing him had made Kate more determined than ever to bring Gran here before it was too late, to embark on something new and promising together, and to fulfill Gran's lifelong dream of restoring her beloved Chapel Bluff.

"And Peg," Velma continued, "might complain about William, but that man has loved her since the day they met our junior year at Westfield High. He spoils her rotten and just about lives to make her happy. If she wants to go on a cruise to Alaska, that's exactly where he'll end up taking her."

Peg glanced at Kate. "I'm *still* tired of picking up his dirty socks."

Just then footsteps sounded and they all looked up as Matt filled the dining room doorway.

Goose bumps slid down the back of Kate's neck and all the way along her arms. She'd spent time chatting with him again this morning. It had gone about as poorly as their conversation yesterday. She'd tried to be warm and charming, but she'd felt the whole time like she was annoying him royally.

He didn't so much as raise an eyebrow at the sight of the four of them in their enormous hats.

"Matt!" Gran exclaimed. "Please join us. It'll only take me a second to get you a cup."

"No, thank you, though. I came to tell you that I'm finished for the day, Mrs. Donovan."

"Beverly, please."

"Beverly. I'll be back in the morning."

"I'm going to fry chicken tonight. Would you like to join us for dinner?"

"Thanks for the offer. I can't tonight." He nodded to them, turned, and left.

The four ladies listened until the front door closed and his truck engine turned over. Velma leaned forward. "Now, I *have* told you about Matt Jarreau, haven't I?"

Kate shook her head.

"Tell us what?" Gran asked.

"I didn't tell you about his history, Beverly? That time on the phone when I recommended him to you?"

"No, I don't believe so," Gran answered.

"You've heard of him, though? Our local celebrity?"

Celebrity? Unease trickled through Kate. "No," she said slowly. "All we know is that he grew up down the hill from here and that he knew Great-Grandma and Grandpa."

"Good gracious! They don't know who he is, Peg."

"I'm as surprised as you are."

"Matt Jarreau," Velma said, looking at them gravely, as if imparting a momentous secret, "is famous. Certainly the most famous person ever to come out of Redbud, Pennsylvania."

"Famous for what?" Kate asked. *Drywall?*

"Hockey. He was a great hockey player for the New York Barons in the . . . what's the name of that professional league?" she asked Peg.

"The NHL."

"Right, the NHL. When he was with the Barons, they won two of those . . ." She shook her fingers impatiently. "The big trophy?"

"The Stanley Cup," Peg supplied.

"And he was their leading score person the times they won it. Their star." Velma leaned back, looking pleased with herself, and took a triumphant sip of tea.

Kate just stared at her, frozen with surprise. Their *contractor* was a hockey legend?

"What happened?" Gran asked. "Why isn't he playing anymore?"

"Well, that's the sad part," Peg said. "About five years ago he married a former Miss America. Beautiful girl named Beth Andrews."

"It was about ten years ago that she won Miss America," Velma added. "Any chance you remember the tall, gorgeous blonde who did the ballet act?"

Kate and Gran shook their heads.

"Had hair down to here?" Velma indicated the middle of her back. "Lovely, *lovely* girl. And sweet, too."

"Wait, wait, wait," Kate said. "You're telling me that he married an actual *Miss America*?"

Peg nodded. "That's right."

"Of course, she'd completed her reign by the time they met and married," Velma said. "Can't remember what her cause was now. Blind people, maybe? Anyway, she and Matt had a big society wedding down where she was from. Georgia, wasn't it?"

"Yes. There were pictures of it in *People* magazine," Peg said.

"At the time it was a big to-do. Ritzy, you know." Velma popped a section of cookie into her mouth, chewed. "Anyway, they were only married a couple of years. And the last six months or so of that Beth was very sick."

"Sick with what?" Gran asked worriedly.

"With brain cancer," Velma answered. "Poor thing. It was awful. Here's this beautiful young girl with so much to live for, and she's diagnosed with brain cancer. She was only twenty-seven years old when she died."

"I'm so sorry to hear that," Gran murmured.

Kate's heart sank for Matt. She'd wanted to uncover his secrets, to know what had caused the tragedy she'd seen in his eyes. But now that she did know, she was sorry she knew, and terribly, *terribly* sorry about what he'd been through. She couldn't believe she'd had the gall yesterday to tease him for not smiling, for being so serious.

"When she died, Matt quit playing hockey," Velma said. "Right there at the top of his career. Nobody knows why. Most people thought he'd want to keep playing even harder afterward, you know, to take his mind off things. But nope. He just left it. Then he came back to Redbud, I think, because he knew nobody here would bother him."

"He's not seen much around town," Peg said. "He concentrates on his work."

"But he must not need to work." Kate was struggling to understand. "He must have a fortune."

"Oh, indeed," Peg answered. "A fortune."

Velma made a *tsk*ing sound. "For all the happiness it's brought him. I wouldn't want to speculate. . . . Oh, who am I kidding? I'll speculate. I think he needs something to do with himself. He likes fixing up old houses, so he works."

Silence descended over the ladies like spring rain. They were all somber faced, considering Matt and his young and lovely dead wife.

Kate looked at her tea and the remains of her cookie.

She no longer felt like eating.

Ordinarily, *Antiques Roadshow* and an open bag of peppermint taffy cured all Kate's ills. But not tonight.

She lay sprawled on her bed wearing a tank and drawstring pajama bottoms, watching the only TV in the house. It had been loaned to her by Peg, and thanks to today's visit from the cable company, both it and the Internet connection on her laptop were up and running.

She'd seen this *Roadshow* episode before. They were in Tucson *ooh*ing and *ahh*ing over Native American finds.

She tapped the brass footboard with her big toe and popped another taffy into her mouth, trying hard to find enjoyment in it. Her romantic's soul was still reeling with sadness for Matt and his wife. Imagining the realities of what losing his wife must have been like for him made her shiver with sorrow.

The longer she contemplated his grief, the more it mingled into her own personal grief. If he, of all people, wasn't enjoying happily-ever-after with someone, then what earthly chance did she have?

Over the years, she'd developed a pretty thick skin. People's comments about her singlehood ordinarily rolled right off her back. But Velma's words from earlier today hadn't.

"Look fast, because if you ever want to have children you need to find someone soon."

Velma had merely stated the obvious fact that Kate, and everyone else in the world, already knew. At thirty-one she wasn't old, not by a long shot. But she, her ovaries, and her eggs were all older than they used to be.

She let her head sink into the jumbled quilts and lay staring blindly at the ceiling. It was un-P.C., but she wanted—had always wanted—to be married and to have children. Maybe because her grandparents on both sides and her parents had such great marriages. To this day her mom and dad did everything together—grocery shopping, tennis, movies, trips. They still held hands, they still whispered secrets. They were partners and best friends. They were the fairy tale.

There had been lots of times when Kate, as a knobby-kneed kid and then as an awkward teenager, had watched them together and felt left out of their little circle of two. All those times she'd thought, *Someday. I want that for me someday.*

As a girl she'd forced her younger sister to play Ken and Barbie with her, inventing elaborate stories of their devotion to each other, their happy house, their numerous children. As a young teen, she'd read dozens of those skinny romance novels in the juvenile fiction section. As an older teen she'd made trips to the video store to rent and re-rent movie love stories.

Fall in love. Marry. Be blissful. Have babies. That had always been her plan. The fact that she was thirty-one and single left her feeling in weak moments like this one as if she'd somehow missed the train going where she'd wanted to go in life.

Part of the problem? She had the most disastrous penchant for liking the wrong guys. Why couldn't she just fall head over heels for someone from the singles group at church? What was wrong with her that she couldn't go for someone open and wholesome— someone who was attending seminary or who carried their Bible to church in the little leather case with the handles? *Why?!* Was she self-destructive and didn't know it? Horribly shallow?

She'd always been the responsible eldest child. Outgoing, yes. But never one to swerve from the Road of Right Priorities. No booze, no drugs, no promiscuity.

Yet in this one area of her life, the arena of men, she didn't understand herself. In the two years since she and Trevor had broken up, she couldn't figure out why her heart remained unswayed by guys who were obviously the right, smart, practical choice. She desperately wanted to fall in love with a good guy. But try as she might, her stubborn heart resisted every candidate. And as long as this trend continued, she knew very well that she was going to stay single.

Loneliness, her old enemy and companion, slithered around her middle and squeezed.

Kate sat up, frustrated with herself. She'd learned today that Matt had lost his wife, and she was still managing to throw *herself* a pity party. She shoved her feet into her pink UGG slippers and made her way downstairs. She let herself out the back door and walked across the grass in the moonlight, taking deep breaths of the woodsmoke-scented night air. In the distance, the chapel gleamed. Her ancestor, the one who'd built Chapel Bluff, had taken care to put that little building with the cross on top right at the heart of their property. It reminded her that this family had been founded on what was important. Every generation had carefully instilled their faith in the next, right on down to her. She'd been raised in the church, and her relationship with God was long-standing, close, and easy. He should be enough for her. She knew He *was* enough. She was only sorry and guilty that at times like this He didn't feel like enough.

She crossed her arms, slowly drinking in her surroundings. The stone bulk of the house. The building doggedly known as the "barn," though it contained parking spaces for several cars but not a single animal. The black hills in the distance. The starry sky. And again, the white-washed chapel in the center of it all.

She began to walk, enjoying the crunch of the driveway and then grass under her slippers. She could feel God in the night.

Jesus' words in Matthew popped into her mind. **If you have faith as small as a mustard seed, nothing will be impossible for you.**

It was humbling to have faith tinier than a mustard seed. Kate stopped walking, sighed, and let her eyes close.

I have a plan for you, God seemed to say.

It would be nice, Lord, if it could include a man.

Silence answered.

The hardest and the truest thing was the supremacy of God's will, which meant that no matter how much she prayed for a husband and a family, she wasn't guaranteed that she'd ever receive what she asked for.

She began to stride forward again, praying, feeling the cool air on her skin, in her lungs. Her mind drifted to Matt.

Okay, so there was a magnificent-looking hockey legend currently renovating her grandmother's house. Okay. She could handle it. She could absolutely resist the temptation he presented.

She was a social worker and it was in her DNA to reach out to people who were hurting and do her best to make things better. Now that she knew what he'd been through, she was even more firmly set on befriending him.

It wouldn't be easy.

But she could try.

If she stuck with it, maybe she could eventually force him to smile. Bring a little bit of fun into his workweek. Nothing that would begin to ease his loss, of course. But something.

She took a deep breath.

She could try.

She found him the next morning at work in one of the second-story guest bedrooms. He'd ripped away a section of the wall, revealing the wooden framework beneath. Brittle plaster lay around his feet like rubble.

"Wow," Kate said, taking in the mess.

Matt stopped what he was doing and glanced at her. He was wearing khaki cargo pants and a long-sleeved cotton T-shirt that said *Abercrombie and Fitch* across the chest. His baseball hat rode low over his eyes.

"I brought you a bottled water," she said. "Thirsty?"

He hesitated. "Sure."

She picked her way through the clutter and handed it to him.

"Thanks."

"What're you working on?" she asked.

"There was a leak." He pointed to a crack in the metal plumbing line.

"Looks like it rotted all the wood around it."

"Yeah."

"And your plan is . . . ?"

"I've got to replace this section of plumbing. Frame in new wood. Put up drywall."

"Could you use some help?"

He eyed her critically. "Not really."

She couldn't resist. She had to smile. He was intimidating, he truly was. Big and brooding with eyes like a blade when you irritated him. She was certain that he scared off almost everyone. Yet for some reason, he didn't scare her. "I understand. I'd probably just get in your way." She went and sat cross-legged on a clean patch of floor. "I'm taking a break, so if you don't mind I'll just sit and hang out for a little bit."

He didn't give her permission to stay, but he didn't tell her to get out, either. She took that as a promising sign. "I love working on old houses," she said. "I have a duplex back in Dallas, and I did some of the work on my half when I bought it."

He concentrated on peeling off plaster.

"Even though Gran's told me about it for years, this is my first time to visit Chapel Bluff."

More silence.

"I'm glad I was able to get the time off from my job," she said, "so that I could come here."

He still wasn't responding. She racked her brain for something else to say.

"Where do you work?" he asked without looking at her. "Back in Dallas."

She felt absurdly pleased at his question. It was the first one he'd asked her about herself. "I work at a place called Christopher's House. We provide a temporary home to kids who've been abused or abandoned."

He took that in for a few moments. "Kids who've been removed from their homes?"

"Right, by Child Protective Services. We're called an emergency residential shelter. We give the kids a place to stay and recover until they're placed with a foster family."

"What do you do there?"

"My official title is case manager. I'm assigned to children as they enter Christopher's House, and I manage their cases until they're taken away."

"Manage their cases?"

"I spend time putting together welcome baskets, talking with the child, arranging for clothing, organizing a doctor's or a psychologist's care if they need it, planning how long they'll stay and where they'll go next. That kind of thing. I'm in touch a lot with their CPS case workers and the foster families."

He used a saw to cut through the leaky pipe, removed the broken section, then took out his tape measure and noted how long the new pipe would need to be. "How many kids do you handle a month?"

He was actually talking to her! "Well, I work with another woman who's also a case manager. It varies, but between us we do about sixty every month."

He gazed at her then, looking grim. "Sixty kids a month?"

"Yeah."

"How young?"

"Newborn on up. We have a nursery with cribs for the littlest ones."

His chocolate brown eyes, always so sad, seemed to ask her the questions she'd asked herself for years. Who would hurt a baby? Who would leave a little boy or girl alone to fend for themselves? Who would beat a child?

She had no trite reassurances to offer.

He went back to work and she watched him, her thoughts on her office back home, her co-workers, the kids, and what they'd be doing this morning.

Despite the depressing aspects of her job, she'd managed to stay positive about it year after year. It had been clear in her mind that while she couldn't change the past for the children she worked with, she could influence their future for the better.

No matter how boring or lonely her personal life had been, she'd always believed her job was something she'd gotten right. She'd known she was exactly where God wanted her to be. Then about six months ago a girl named Gabriella had committed suicide.

Just the thought of it caused Kate's heart to twist. She looked down, picking at a bumpy thread in her jeans. She could clearly picture Gabriella's curly dark hair, her glittering eyes, her expression—so tentative and so sensitive despite everything she'd been through.

Gabriella had stayed at Christopher's House twice: once when she'd been an elementary student and Kate had been a new employee there, fresh off her degree, and then again a year ago when Gabriella had been fourteen. Both times Kate had managed her case. After Gabriella's first stint at Christopher's House she'd eventually been returned to her father. After the second stint, Gabriella had been placed with a foster family. Outwardly, it had looked like things were stabilizing and improving for the girl.

And then, in the middle of the night one night, she'd swallowed a bottle full of pills.

Her suicide had struck Kate like an earthquake. She'd stood graveside as the girl was lowered into the earth, asking herself then and a million times since if she could have done more. If she *should* have done more.

After Gabriella's death Kate had started to lose her joy in her job. At first she thought she'd just misplaced it, like a set of keys, and that she'd find it again shortly. But her enjoyment of her job had stayed lost. Every scared young face, every terrible story, every mental picture of the circumstances the child had come from weighed heavily on her. She began to feel powerless to help them—any of them. For the last six months she'd been going through the motions of her job out of habit instead of real motivation.

When Gran had asked her to come away with her to Chapel Bluff for three whole months, Kate had known God was offering her a lifeline. She'd taken it.

She glanced up and found Matt watching her.

She met his gaze directly, which sent her heart thumping. *Just a friend!* she reprimanded her heart. *Just a friend!* "Well . . ." She stood up and dusted off her butt. "I better get back to work. Would you like to join us for dinner tonight? If Gran could cook for you she'd think she'd died and gone to heaven."

"Can't. Thanks, though."

"No problem." She made her way downstairs. Her pulse was still speeding. *Just a friend! Just a friend!*

On Thursday Kate sorted through three closets and the fourth of Chapel Bluff's five bedrooms. She pried some small talk out of Matt and invited him to stay for dinner. He declined.

On Friday morning Kate sweated through a yoga class. She organized the entire contents of the kitchen. She forced Matt into more conversation.

On Friday afternoon Kate finished categorizing the house. Much had been thrown away. Much was waiting for their upcoming yard sale. Kate worked to post the remaining twenty-three items on eBay. She invited Matt to stay for dinner. He declined.

On Saturday Kate and Gran slept late, then toured the town. Kate convinced Gran to buy a watercolor by a local artist to hang above the fireplace mantel in the den. They had bowls of soup and French bread at a restaurant called The Grapevine on Main

Street. They visited some of Gran's old friends in the afternoon. Matt wasn't around to invite to dinner.

On Sunday they went to church at First Baptist, then to lunch at Peg's house. Peg's husband, William, was there—distinguished and adorable in Ralph Lauren from head to toe. Someone named Morty was also present. Kate couldn't divine his connection to the group except that he was a retired Redbud police officer and clearly had the hots for Velma. Matt still wasn't around to invite to dinner.

On Monday morning Matt showed up right on time in faded jeans, a flannel shirt, and his UNC cap. Kate ruthlessly refused to be moved by the sight of him. She stripped all the dingy curtains throughout the house and began the arduous process of removing the wallpaper in the kitchen and dining room. Gran made enchiladas for dinner. Kate invited Matt. He declined.

On Tuesday Gran informed Kate that Gran's mother and grandmother had used the attic of the barn for storage. Sick of sorting and organizing, Kate decided to procrastinate on the barn for a few more days and continued battling the wallpaper. She invited Matt to stay for dinner. He declined.

On Wednesday Kate strained and stretched through another yoga class. Upon her return to Chapel Bluff, she was squeezing conversation out of Matt while he was installing drywall in one of the upstairs bathrooms. She invited him to stay for dinner. And wonder of wonders. Miracle of miracles! On what had seemed like an ordinary day until that very moment . . .

He said yes.

chapter three

Matt wasn't sure why he'd said yes. He'd never made the conscious, thought-out decision to agree to dinner with Kate and Beverly. In fact, in his head, he'd made the opposite decision. The decision to stay away from them.

Today when Kate had come to talk with him, she'd been wearing her yoga clothes and flip-flops, with her red hair up in a ponytail. She leaned against the doorjamb of the room where he was working. "How's it going?"

"It's going okay." Her frequent visits no longer annoyed him as much as they once had. With a bolt of shock, he realized that he must have actually come to like her a little bit.

She chatted for a while about the renovation, the town, the TV show she'd watched last night. Then she invited him—again—to dinner. Any regular person would have taken the hint and stopped inviting him days ago. But Kate asked him every single day. She might be petite and friendly, but she was also unbelievably persistent.

"C'mon," she said. Threading her fingers together, she raised her joined hands to him, mock begging. "Please." She cocked her head and smiled persuasively. "Just one little dinner, Matt. It would make Gran so happy. What do you say? Just one dinner? Please?"

In that moment, looking into her hopeful expression, he'd been unable to say no. His vocal cords had agreed before his brain had any say.

Afterward, he couldn't believe he'd said yes. Just thinking about eating dinner with them made him uncomfortable. Should he dress up? Bring something? Were they going to ask him questions he didn't want to answer? He'd much rather stay home and eat a sandwich.

But it was too late for that. He had to go.

When Matt knocked on the kitchen door that night, Kate hurried over to answer it and found him on the threshold, holding a bouquet of flowers and looking completely unsure of himself.

Tenderness stirred within her. "Hi," she said, trying to act like having him over for dinner wasn't the huge deal that it was. "C'mon in."

"Matt!" Gran bustled over to greet him. "Welcome, welcome. My fingers are covered with food, but here," she leaned into him and wrapped her upper arms around him while keeping her hands safely splayed in midair, "let me hug you." She pulled back, beaming.

Without his ball cap he looked different to Kate, more formal. The cheery kitchen light picked out glossy strands in his dark hair, still damp from a shower. He was wearing a brown knit sweater that had a short zipper at the neck. Through the V of the zipper Kate could see the neckline of a white T-shirt underneath. "Umm . . . these are for you both," he said, extending the flowers.

Because Gran's fingers had crepe stuffing on them, Kate moved forward and took the flowers from him. "Thank you. Wow, they're beautiful. I'll find a vase."

"Oh, they're *lovely*," Gran said. "Just lovely! Thank you so much."

He nodded, put his hands in his pockets.

"Well, come on." Gran motioned for him to follow her to the kitchen counter, where she was fully in the throes of cooking. "Wash your hands so I can put you to work."

He hesitated for a moment, but did as he was told.

Kate smiled to herself. Poor, poor Matt. He may once have been a warrior on the ice, accustomed to body-slamming giant men, but he wasn't equal to the coming onslaught from Gran. He was going down.

She located a crystal vase, filled it with water, and pretended she knew how to arrange the bouquet of ivory hydrangeas and white roses.

Gran resumed stuffing crepes with a mixture of sautéed mushrooms in a creamy sauce, chicken strips, and Monterey Jack cheese. Her two stone bracelets clicked together rhythmically. Just this week she'd made herself a long string of mauve and purple beads, which she wore behind her neck, the ends attached to the earpieces of her glasses. She'd taken to whipping her glasses off and letting them drop down, only to slide them back on a half second later. At the moment the glasses were in the "on" position and the beads were swinging from side to side. "I could use three or so more crepes, Matt. Would you mind cooking them up for me? The batter's just there."

Matt paused in the act of drying his hands. He eyed the oiled skillet, the spoonula, and the mixing bowl of batter the way a kindergartner might an algebra problem.

Kate swallowed an unkind giggle and went to work setting the kitchen table.

"I . . . uh . . . I don't cook," he finally said.

Gran whirled on him. "Don't cook?"

"No."

"Whatever do you eat?"

"Uh, sandwiches and frozen meals, mostly."

"For dinner?"

He tilted his head as if trying to understand. "Yes, ma'am."

"Not while I'm living at Chapel Bluff you're not."

He just stared.

"You're going to be eating dinner here from now on, and mark my words, young man, I'm going to teach you to cook!" Gran's white hair stuck up in artful tufts. Her blue eyes narrowed. "I will not take no for an answer."

"I . . ."

"I insist." Gran turned back to her cooking.

Matt glanced at Kate. "Uh . . . Maybe Kate could handle the crepes."

"Don't look at me," Kate said. "I don't cook."

"Blasphemy!" Gran said.

"I'm the person at family meals that sets the table and puts ice in glasses and takes drink orders," she explained.

"How about I be that person tonight?" Matt said.

"No, no, no, no, *no,*" Gran replied vehemently. "Despite years of effort on my part, I've resigned myself to the truth that Kate's talents lie in areas other than cooking. I haven't even begun to work on you, however."

He knit his brow and faced the stove.

"Now, Matt," Gran continued, her eyeglass beads a-swaying, "begin by warming up the skillet. . . ." She kept up a steady stream of chatter, talking him through the meal's preparation step by step.

Three times in a row Matt poured too much crepe batter into the skillet. But to his credit, he tried a fourth time, saying little, clearly concentrating hard. Kate watched him surreptitiously as she opened windows to let in the evening breeze, set the table, and made iced tea. The only mishap came when Gran asked him to slice a tomato for the salad. His knife slipped off the tomato's smooth skin, which sent it skittering along the countertop and over the edge of the sink. It plopped into a dirty mixing bowl full of suds.

"Shoot," he whispered.

Kate couldn't help herself. She laughed.

He glared at her.

"I'm only laughing because that's exactly the kind of thing I'd have done," she said.

"Care to try your luck?" He extended the knife to her, one eyebrow raised menacingly.

"When I'm having so much fun watching you? No thanks."

He actually ground his teeth.

More laughter burst from her. She swiped a fresh tomato from the bowl on the chopping block and placed it in front of him. "See? No harm done."

"You wouldn't say that if you were that last tomato," he muttered darkly.

Matt had stopped enjoying food. He hadn't meant to. But somewhere along the way he'd gotten out of the habit of eating a good meal, apparently. Because tonight's dinner—the stuffed crepes, the homemade bread rolls, the salad, the asparagus with butter and salt on top—was the best-tasting food he could remember having in months.

Years?

And now, after all that, Mrs. Donovan leaned over his shoulder and placed a dish of blackberry cobbler in front of him. Straight out of the oven, a scoop of vanilla ice cream melting in white rivers on its crusty top. Kate poured a mug of steaming coffee for him and set it next to his cobbler.

As stuffed as he was, he couldn't make himself stop. He waited for them to find their seats, then followed their lead by picking up his spoon and digging in. Eating this food in this old-fashioned kitchen was like visiting a land he'd loved once but hadn't been back to in a long, long time. As pained as social interaction had become for him, it surprised him to admit that he didn't hate being here as much as he'd thought he would. It was hard to hate an evening filled with such amazing food.

"This is delicious, Gran," Kate said.

"Yes, it is." Matt put down his spoon, trying to pace himself. "Thank you."

"You're welcome." Mrs. Donovan reached across the table and squeezed his hand. "I'm glad you like it. And I'm glad you'll be joining us from now on." Before he could correct her on that, she pushed back her chair and went to set her dish in the sink. "And with that," she said, "I'm off to bed. Early to bed and early to rise." She winked at him. "Another reason to learn to cook, Matt. Then, by rights, you shouldn't have to clean." She sailed toward the dining room. "Night, Kate."

"Night, Gran."

"Night, Matt."

He rose to his feet. "Good night."

Mrs. Donovan shot him a parting smile and disappeared.

Kate went back to work on her dessert.

He lowered to his seat, took a few more bites. What had just happened? Mrs. Donovan had left and now he was alone in the kitchen with Kate, eating together. It felt a bit like a date.

A date. Just the thought tightened his gut with dread.

He didn't like her like that. Mostly what he felt toward Kate was caution. And yet . . . he was here, wasn't he? He'd admitted to himself earlier that there was something about her that he liked a little.

He studied her bent head. So what was it? What was it that he liked?

To look at her, you'd think she'd come from old money. She was understated and sophisticated like that. Except her watch wasn't Rolex and her diamond earrings, though probably real, were tiny. She was an unusual mixture of other things, too. . . . She was no bigger around than his wrist, yet he'd seen her work all day stripping wallpaper and hauling boxes. She laughed easily, yet he could sense that she'd dealt with sadness. At first he'd guessed that she had an event planner kind of job, but instead she was a social worker who spent her time with struggling kids.

He admired some of those things about her. But still, none of them was *the* thing that drew him.

Since Beth died, he'd been living with a cold ball of grief square in the center of his chest. He took it with him everywhere he went. It clouded every thought he had. It motivated every decision he made. The people in his life couldn't touch that cold ball. Nothing and no one had. Nothing and no one could.

Except maybe . . . her.

He couldn't explain it, but Kate had the power to thaw some of the coldness inside him. Just barely.

He didn't want her to have any effect on him at all. That she did made her dangerous. He was just barely surviving. It was all he could do to simply get through each day, just the way he'd been getting through every awful day since Beth died, by going through the motions. He did the same familiar, necessary things in the same way every day. If he kept everything the same, at least, he trusted that he could make it from morning to night, that he could hold on to his equilibrium. If he stepped away from what he was used to, he might not be able to keep it together.

She happened to look up and caught him staring. "What? Do I have food on my face?" Tentatively, she used a hand to shield her mouth.

"No."

"Are you sure? Please tell me, because I'll be mortified if I look in the mirror later and see blackberries in my teeth."

"I'm sure."

"Okay." She scooted her chair away from the table, leaned back in it. "I'm stuffed. I can't eat another bite."

He ate his last spoonful.

She regarded him with a sympathetic half smile. "Gran's expecting you to eat dinner with us from now on."

"I can't."

"Can't you?"

He didn't answer.

She assessed him for a few moments, the ticking of the kitchen clock loud in the silence, then rose and began stacking dishes and silverware. "So you said earlier that you usually do frozen food and sandwiches for dinner."

"Yeah."

"Me too. Do they have a Potbelly Sandwich Shop in town?"

He nodded. "Over on the south side near Fourth and River-bend."

"Oh good. Have you had their Italian on white bread with the pickles and hot peppers?"

"No."

"You should, it's incredible." She carried their dishes to the sink. "What about cereal? You ever eat that for dinner?"

"About once a week."

"Me too. What about canned vegetable soup?"

"Yeah."

"Same here. Chinese takeout?"

"Sometimes." That was a lie. He didn't want to tell her that even stopping at a restaurant for takeout got him all kinds of attention he didn't want.

She started wiping off the plates with a long-handled scrub brush. "At home in Dallas I'll get Chinese some, but I get Mexican more. We have unbelievable Mexican food in Dallas. There's none here in Redbud, though, right?"

"Right."

Matt took a sip of coffee, torn. He wanted to hightail it out. But just how rude would it be for him to leave her with the entire mess to clean up? He eyed the pile of dishes and could hear his mother in his head, schooling him on manners. She'd be devastated if she knew he'd left without at least offering to help.

Resigned, he walked to the sink and nodded to the dirty dishes she was working on. "I can do this part."

"It's okay, really. You don't have to help me clean up."

"I don't mind." Another lie. And another thing he'd gotten out of the habit of—saying what he really felt.

"You sure?"

"Yeah."

"Well, thanks."

He rolled up his sleeves and began slotting the dishes into the dishwasher while Kate moved around the kitchen putting things away. They worked in companionable silence until the job was done.

As he drove home afterward, he thought back over the evening. Cooking. The way the food had tasted. The things they'd talked about. Mrs. Donovan. Kate. He'd come away from it all okay. But his instincts were telling him that it would be safer, much safer, for him to refuse their dinner invitations from now on.

The two of them were welcome to their nightly dinners, but they were going to have to count him out.

The road to hell is paved with good intentions.

Despite Matt's good intentions, he came for dinner the next night.

And the next.

Mrs. Donovan, a lady he'd thought to be a sweet and gentle person, flatly refused to accept the fact that he wouldn't be coming for more of her cooking lessons. Try as he might, he couldn't convince her otherwise.

On Saturday and Sunday he gratefully retreated to his solitary life. He didn't have to go to Chapel Bluff for two whole days, didn't have to cook, didn't have to speak, didn't have to shield himself from Kate's hazel gaze.

Nothing like a brisk walk in the company of seventy-year-olds to make a person feel like a fitness slacker.

It was Sunday, and Kate and the others had been to church that morning. Gran, Velma, and Peg went to different congregations because they each had to attend, *obviously*, the church they'd gone to since babyhood. Next they'd done what any sane Christian rushed to do after worship: They'd changed out of their church clothes. Then they'd met at Peg's for lunch. And now, because it was a pristine day and because the older people got, the more they grumbled after big meals about needing to "walk it off," they'd set out into the woods behind Peg's house. Their party included the regulars: Kate, the three "girls," Peg's husband, William, and the still-haven't-figured-out-how-he-fit-into-the-group Morty.

The weather was painfully pretty. Sunny and clear, with a clean brisk wind that rustled the grass and lifted Kate's hair away from her face. The forest that surrounded them smelled like a Girl Scout campout—damp and woodsy and comforting.

Fall. Kate loved it. Loved the holidays. Loved wearing jeans and her quilted trench coat that she'd saved and saved for. Loved the temperature.

Predictably, Velma had charged into the lead. William, in his good-natured way, was attempting to keep up with her both in pace and conversation. Gran and Peg came next, walking arm in arm, heads bent toward each other. Which left Kate, huffing and puffing ever so slightly, to bring up the rear with Morty.

"So where do you live down there in Dallas? You have a house?" Morty asked.

"I do, actually. It's a duplex I bought four years ago."

"Oh yeah? Who's living in the other side?"

"A really nice lady. She's a librarian at SMU." Her renter had been living in the right half of the duplex for thirty-five years, so Kate had simply inherited her when she'd bought the place. Judy was quiet, scholarly, had two cats and loads of potted plants. Judy'd never been married. As much as Kate liked her, she couldn't help occasionally thinking that their duplex was like a before and after snapshot. Kate was the "before," but frequently felt like she was sliding inexorably toward the exact same fate as Judy. Cats and potted plants.

"Your tenant isn't making meth, is she?"

She glanced abruptly at Morty. "Meth?"

"Yeah. I'm retired from the force, but I keep up with things pretty good. All kinds of people making meth in their kitchens these days. Selling it right from their home."

"Ah . . ."

"Strangers coming and going at all hours?"

"No."

"Suspicious people parked out front?"

"Nope. I'm pretty sure my tenant isn't making meth."

He harrumphed. "Well, good then."

Morty looked like Elvis might have looked at seventy-seven. Hair dyed black and glistening with gel. White T-shirt over a barrel chest and a stomach that wasn't quite a potbelly. Ironed jeans. White socks. Black penny loafers. When they'd left the house he'd pulled on a gray Member's Only jacket.

"Do you do much bowling down there in Dallas?" he asked.

"No, I'm afraid not."

"Well, come on out while you're here. Bring Beverly there. I'm at the lanes every Tuesday and Thursday at ten. Be happy to give you some pointers."

"Thanks, Morty."

They walked, shoes crunching over twigs and leaves.

"Play any poker?" he asked.

"Not much these days."

"Well, these here and I," he motioned to the group ahead, "we get together on Friday nights for poker."

"Was that your idea?" She couldn't imagine anyone else in the group coming up with it.

"Yeah. But the rest of 'em are getting pretty good."

Kate nodded.

"I talked with Beverly about it at lunch, told her to come and bring you this Friday, but she said Matt Jarreau eats with you on Fridays and she didn't want to leave him." He dug his hands into the pockets of his jacket. "So I was thinking that if you and your grandmother are interested in playin', we could all meet up over at your place there at Chapel Bluff on Fridays."

"Sure, that would be fine." Sorry social life when this prospect excited her. "What do ya'll play for?"

"Money. But the buy-in's just five dollars each." He nodded disdainfully toward the others. "These here don't want to play for big money."

"I see."

Quiet stretched as they ambled along the dirt path. In the distance, Kate could hear the gurgle of a stream.

"So, Kate."

"Yes, Morty?"

"There's something I've been wanting to talk to you about."

She couldn't imagine what, since they'd already covered meth, bowling, and poker. "Okay."

"You're young. You know all about romance and such."

Who did Morty have to offer, she wondered. Commitment-phobe grandson? Geeky neighbor? Self-obsessed nephew? "I'm not sure I do know that much about it, unfortunately."

"Well, I . . ." He scowled. Alongside the trail, the creek came into view—clear and cold looking with a few leaves floating on top. "Young girls your age—you like going to the, what do you call it? Spa? Getting your nails done?"

She looked at him, befuddled.

"What I'm trying to say— What I mean is—" He growled in frustration, stopped walking, and turned to face her. "I love Velma."

"Ah."

His faded green eyes filled with earnest sadness. "She won't have me, though. Won't even agree to a date."

Kate winced. "I'm sorry."

"And I'm sick of waiting for that woman." He began to gesture, warming to his subject. "My wife's been gone twenty years and a man has needs. . . ."

If he finished that thought, Kate was going to hurl herself into the stream.

"Velma's a spirited one," he continued. "I know that. Heck, I like fire in a lady. But I must've asked her out fifty times now and still nothing. Nothing!"

"I see."

"I have my pride, you know."

"Yes, of course."

"I've about had it up to here with her." He vehemently indicated his forehead.

"Got it."

He stared moodily at the stream, cracked a few knobby knuckles. "I've got a couple of tricks left up my sleeve, though."

Kate waited, curling and uncurling her toes in her sneakers.

He indicated the path ahead. "Shall we?"

"Sure."

They began forward. "I'd like to offer you a deal," he said. "I'd like you to help along my pursuit of Velma. You know, get her to go on some proper dates with me."

"I don't think I have much influence with her, Morty."

"Oh, I reckon you do. I can tell that she thinks highly of you."

This was news to Kate. Apparently affection and grim acceptance were, coming from Velma, indistinguishable.

"She only has sons and grandsons, you know. Freeloaders, the lot of them. Compared to them, you're a peach."

"Oh."

"So here's the thing. Bring her around to me, and I'll give you some certificates—gift certificates, you know—to the spa."

Now he was talking her language. "How many gift certificates?"

"One for each date."

"How much would each of these certificates be worth?"

He peered at her, eyebrows lowered.

She grinned at him, shrugged. "Velma's not going to be easy to convince."

"Fifty dollars per certificate and not a penny more."

"Done." She extended her hand.

He received it with a firm shake.

chapter four

Apparently Gran didn't think Kate could fit a key into a lock without help. Or perhaps Gran worried that the barn was infested with spiders and didn't want Kate bitten without company. Or maybe—and with a sinking sensation, Kate acknowledged this possibility most likely—Gran was attempting some matchmaking. She'd insisted that Matt accompany Kate to the upper floor of the barn so that he could "help her" investigate whatever was stored within.

Matt, who was wearing worn jeans, boots, his ball cap, and another soft-looking flannel shirt over another long-sleeved shirt, had agreed to Gran's request. But he'd agreed with an air of long-suffering resignation, which was hardly flattering.

Matt tolerated her. God knew she'd been trying to establish rapport with him, to loosen him up, to make him smile. But the very best that could be said was that he *tolerated* her in return.

The lower story of the barn was easily accessible through enormous garage doors. But a doorway located at the top of a rickety wooden staircase, which clung to the furthest outer wall of the barn, provided the only entrance to the second story. After unlocking the bolt, Matt shouldered the door open and held it for her.

Kate clicked on the flashlight she'd brought and entered the cavernous storage area. Gritty, heavy air swirled around her like fog. She wrinkled her nose and made her way further inside. The smell reminded her of the churches she'd been to on a trip to England a few years back. Closed up, damp, and old.

"What do you think?" Matt asked.

"I'm not sure yet."

She recognized a few hope chests together near the center of the space, but almost everything else had been covered with fabric and secured with ties. Furniture? It looked like the fabric might be covering furniture. She approached a medium-sized something that was perhaps a chair.

She could hear Matt's footsteps behind her.

Kate set her flashlight on the ground and aimed it at the chair. It took her a minute to free the first knotted tie, and she was grateful when Matt knelt near her feet and went to work on the tie beneath. They were very close to each other, so close that she could almost hear him breathing. Her senses swam.

Just friends, she reminded herself firmly, struggling to get her stupid body's response in check.

When they'd unraveled the knots, Kate pulled away the filthy cover and tossed it aside.

Recognition flooded through her in a singing rush. She lifted her hands to cover her mouth. "Oh," she murmured, staring with disbelief at the chair they'd revealed.

After a few beats of silence, Matt asked, "Does that mean it's good?"

She nodded dumbly.

The wooden chair was illuminated by the flashlight, but also by a wash of sunlight that had managed to fight past a grimy window. The chair stood in a reverent halo of dust motes. Gleaming. Seeming to say, *It's about time someone found me.*

Kate swallowed. Licked her lips. "This is a . . ." She glanced at Matt. He was looking at her strangely, waiting. "This is a Windsor chair." She gestured vaguely. "It has a comb-back and armrests . . . and—" she gripped the wooden piece that ran along the top—"a serpentine crest rail."

"How old is it?"

"Probably about two hundred years."

His eyebrows lifted slightly. "Was it made in America?"

"Yes. New England. This," Kate pronounced, "is a *fabulous* chair."

They stood together for a full minute saying nothing, simply looking. It was a beautiful piece of workmanship. Full of history. Worn, but perfectly so for its age. An extraordinary find.

"How do you know it's not a fake?" he asked.

She made herself move past her shock to tilt it up, then peer below the armrests to see how the wooden slats fit in. "An expert will have to come and look at it before we'll know for sure. But I think it's the real thing."

"You know a lot about antiques."

"Yeah, I love antiques." She ran her fingers down the chair's tapered leg. "I cannot *believe* we just discovered this chair up here!" She grinned at him.

He met her gaze. Not smiling, but not frowning, either. He extended his hand to her, she accepted it, and he pulled her to her feet.

"Do you think there could be more furniture like this up here?" Kate assessed all the other hulking objects filling the loft.

"We can look," Matt answered.

There were at least twenty more fabric-covered pieces. Plus the hope chests, plus wooden boxes of every size. What had seemed like a chore five minutes ago now seemed like an odyssey.

Kate made her way to another nearby piece of covered furniture, something about six feet tall and four feet wide, and started in on one of the four ties.

Matt joined her again, his big hands graceful and sure on the time-crusted knots. Again, she tried hard to squelch the effect his nearness had on her. She couldn't quite do it. Couldn't quite steady herself.

"Care to do the honors?" Kate asked when they'd finished, motioning to the fabric cover.

"It's all you."

Kate whipped the cover off. This time they'd unearthed a corner cupboard. The bottom half contained two wooden doors topped with two drawers. The top half held three shelves visible behind two paned-glass doors that opened outward from the center.

Kate touched one of the knobs on the upper door, then gently ran her fingertips along the glass.

"Well?" Matt asked.

"I think it's even older than the Windsor chair." She laughed with disbelief at this outrageous streak of good fortune, then opened one of the cupboard doors and peered inside. "Second half of the 1700s, maybe."

"Is the paint supposed to look like that?"

"Yes." What had been cream-colored paint when applied had faded, scratched, and worn away to almost nothing. "It's perfect. It should look exactly like this." She gazed at him. "If I'd known there was furniture like this up here, I'd have been here the first day I arrived at Chapel Bluff. The first minute! Gran thought it was mostly junk. Instead, it's . . . it's amazing. We're going to need an appraiser. And someone to clean everything properly. And more fire detectors."

"Fire detectors?"

"All through the house, once we move these things in. Imagine if these were destroyed."

"Imagine."

"Who can we get to move these pieces into the house?" Kate asked.

"I know a few people."

"Good, because as soon as we have our garage sale on Saturday and move all the shabby furniture out of the house, we can move this stuff in."

"You might want to paint first."

"Oh right."

"And refinish the floors."

"Oh right."

"And then you can probably move this stuff over."

She put her hands on her hips and blew a strand of red hair out of her eyes. "I think I better go get Gran."

Her ancestors had had some kind of incredible taste in furniture. About half of the items left forgotten for decades in the barn were extremely valuable. As in, they could have been featured on *Antiques Roadshow* valuable. The mix was eclectic: a Federal mahogany sideboard; a Chippendale—Chippendale!—desk; a walnut Queen Anne dining room set; some Shaker furniture; and a table that Kate suspected might have been made by Gustav Stickley.

Matt had stayed with Gran and Kate all day, saying little in the face of their squeals and exclamations, doing all the hardest work. He'd wielded a crowbar for them, lifted crates, dragged things out of their way, and taken loads of trash to the Dumpster.

Out of splintering wooden boxes they'd uncovered quilts, journals, aged Bibles, three wonderful Hudson River School–era paintings, some pottery, and an extensive collection of Depression glass.

That night after dinner, Kate curled up in the den with a cup of tea, too excited to go to bed. She stared into the empty fireplace and saw lustrous wooden drawers, the clean planed top of a desk, the curving linear beauty of an armrest. She'd made finds today that took her breath away. More finds in a day than she'd dreamed of making in a lifetime. All the better because they were part of her family's history, because they'd find a home again here inside the walls of Chapel Bluff, where they belonged.

She took a long sip of tea, savoring its minty smell. It was all much, much too good to be true.

She found Gran's Bible in the basket by the foot of the sofa and managed to locate the verse she wanted with some help from the concordance. *Every good and perfect gift is from above, coming down from the Father of the heavenly lights, who does not change like shifting shadows.*

Thank you, she prayed. *Thank you, God.*

Tonight, with the stars visible through the den's windows, she couldn't help but brim with hope. Hope for this old house, hope for her future, hope for her job, hope even for their heartbroken recluse of a contractor.

On Friday, the geriatric gang showed up early for poker night.

Dinner wasn't until 6:30, but Kate spotted Peg and William's silver BMW cruising up the driveway at 5:43. Morty's Oldsmobile at 5:48. And Velma's *Smokey and the Bandit* black Trans Am, complete with the big gold bird on the hood, at 5:55.

Kate, upstairs in her terry-cloth bathrobe with wet hair, quickly went to work with the blow-dryer.

Over this past week, and against all odds, she and Matt and Gran had settled into a nightly routine. Every weeknight Matt left work, went home to shower, then came back for Gran's cooking lessons. If the dinner of the night needed time in the oven, they'd sit at the table while it baked, snacking on cheese and crackers or hummus and pita chips. Over dinner they'd chat about upcoming community events, memories from Gran's childhood, movies, books. Everything but Matt himself. Sometimes, he'd help Kate clean. Always, he was out the door by 8:15 to go home and do . . . she wondered what.

Kate sensed that the dinners were hard for him. Simply showing up forced him to extend himself much further than he wanted to. She hadn't told him about poker night, because she'd known if she did that he wouldn't come. But now she was second-guessing herself, thinking that she should have warned him. He might not deal well with Gran's friends, and the last thing she wanted at this point was to push him too hard and scare him off.

By the time she arrived downstairs, the seniors' mealtime gender role-play was well under way. She'd watched this dance since childhood. Amazing how it differed so little from state to state, decade to decade, or with the inclusion of these new participants.

William and Morty were sitting at the kitchen table, doing nothing. In fact, had there been a TV available anywhere downstairs, she was certain they'd have been stationed in front of it watching sports. As it was, they were simply sitting, looking slightly awkward.

The women, on the other hand, were moving at double speed. Stirring green beans, spooning pot roast onto a serving platter, whisking butter out of the refrigerator, and seventeen other things at once.

These two very different time-to-get-food-on-the-table roles had always confounded Kate. How odd and vaguely insulting that she was expected to plunge into meal preparation because she had breasts, while those without were clearly expected to do nothing more than notch back their La-Z-Boys.

Of course, she wasn't exactly in a place to criticize Morty and William. Those Who Filled Glasses With Ice had precious little elevation on their high horse.

After greeting everyone, Kate walked dutifully to the cabinet with the glasses. She was still twisting ice cube trays when she heard Matt's truck pull up outside. She paused, waiting to hear him kill the engine.

He kept it running.

Still running.

He'd seen the other cars and was about to drive home without coming in. She glanced up and found Gran already looking at her. Kate widened her eyes in silent communication.

"Excuse me for a second." Gran dried her hands on her apron and hurried out the kitchen door. Gran could persuade flowers to bloom in January, so Kate had high hopes.

Sure enough, a minute later Matt appeared in the doorway with Gran. Everyone in the kitchen broke off their conversations and regarded him with fascination.

Matt stood with the kind of stillness that held suppressed motion, as if he were on the verge of turning and heading back to his truck. He'd made his face carefully expressionless. For all his physical beauty and strength, he looked vulnerable to her, standing there.

Her heart squeezed. *Shoot!* He was miserable around strangers. She knew this, and she should have warned him about tonight.

"Everyone," Gran said, wrapping her hand affectionately around his forearm, "this is Matt Jarreau. Of course you know he's our marvelous contractor."

He had on a fitted navy sweater and flat-front khakis. She'd bet that he was one of those guys who hardly gave a thought to his clothing. He probably just wore whatever was clean. Yet his casual, sometimes ever-so-slightly-rumpled appearance never failed to make him look like a J.Crew model.

"Matt," Gran continued, "this is William, Morty, Peg, and Velma. Friends of mine."

Matt lowered his chin a fraction. "Nice to meet you."

Velma walked up to him, still holding, with two frayed potholders, the dish of glazed carrots she'd been taking to the dining room when he'd arrived. "Good gracious, you're taller than I realized. How tall are you?"

"Six two."

"Hmm." She scrutinized him from behind her enormous glasses, as if trying to decide whether she'd deign to let him stay.

Kate felt ridiculously protective of Matt, a sentiment he wouldn't thank her for. Still. If Velma started needling him, she was going to have to intercede.

"You're tall *and* you're good-lookin,'" Velma announced. "Nice to have a hottie over for dinner, isn't it, girls?"

Disaster. Kate expected Matt to break for the door. But he stayed where he was, apparently speechless.

Peg blushed and nodded faintly.

"Indeed!" Gran smiled up at Matt, her blue eyes twinkling. "Always nice to have hotties over."

Velma's attention swooped to Kate like a hawk catching sight of a canary. "It sure is, isn't it, Kate?"

"Yes," Kate said lamely. "It is."

And that's how Matt Jarreau was ushered into the kitchen, swept along to the dining room table, and firmly caught in the center of poker night.

After dinner, Morty—who took his poker very seriously—hauled out an enormous case of gambling chips and a small sign stating the worth of each color of chip. While Morty was setting up at the dining room table, Velma made her way to the bathroom. Kate followed her surreptitiously and waited in the hallway outside the bathroom for Velma to come out.

When Velma exited, she caught sight of Kate and halted. "Wouldn't go in there for a few minutes if I were you," she warned. "Stinks."

"Ahh . . ." All Kate's preplanned sentences evaporated, and she had to scramble after them. "It's okay. I wanted to ask you something anyway."

One penciled eyebrow rose. Velma was wearing a black cowboy-cut shirt and tapered jeans tucked into flat ankle boots with fringe on the side. It appeared she'd fallen for an infomercial and shelled out $19.99 in exchange for a machine that punched silver studs into fabric, because she'd punctured her shirt with dozens of them. Her shirt positively gleamed. Brighter than the tin man.

Kate had a vision of Velma attempting to pass through airport security in that thing—metal detectors up and down the terminal shrieking and wailing.

"Morty likes you," Kate said. "And I wondered if you'd reconsider going out with him."

Velma rolled her pink lips into a sour expression. "No. Morty and I get along fine as it is. I'm not interested in anything romantic."

"Why not? I mean, he seems like a good person."

Velma regarded her skeptically.

"He's a nice-looking man," Kate said. *If you like really old Elvises.*

"Nice-looking?" Velma grunted. "In what way?"

"Ah . . ." Kate put her hands in her pockets and thought ferociously. "He's a masculine sort of guy, large, but not too large. And he has an interesting face. Strong. And," with a surge of triumph, "he has lots of hair."

"The hair is a problem for me."

"How so?"

"That black color. It reminds me of a greased-up car tire. You know what I'm talking about? What your tires look like right after you pay extra to get them cleaned?"

"I do know." And Kate had to admit, Morty's hair *was* bad. "What if he did something about his hair? Would you reconsider?"

Velma's mascara-clad eyes studied her without blinking. "Have you appointed yourself his pimp?"

"No! I'm just trying to help him out, I guess."

"Why?"

"I have my reasons. Now, about the hair. If he fixed it, would you go on a date with him?"

"Probably not."

"But maybe?" Kate pressed. "All that admiration has to be flattering, doesn't it, Velma?"

Velma pushed her glasses up her nose, blew out an impatient breath, and turned to saunter down the hall. The rhinestones stuck to her banana clip glittered in the dull light. "I'll think about it."

"Raise," Matt said, and idly thumbed the edges of his two cards before tossing a few chips forward.

William folded. When it came to Kate she again consulted the little piece of paper Morty had given her. It listed the pictures and names of all the different poker hands from best to worst.

71

"I'll . . . reraise?" She looked to Morty and lifted a brow for confirmation that she'd used the right term.

Morty nodded.

Kate pushed a stack of chips to the center of the table.

Matt frowned. He had two pair, but he didn't know if they would hold up against her beginner's luck. Kate knew nothing about poker, but impossibly had maintained the chip lead almost from the time they'd started.

Matt was no serious poker player. But like all self-respecting men, he knew enough about the game to get by. And like all competitive athletes, he didn't like to lose. Especially against a total rookie who kept consulting her cheat sheet and throwing down her cards and saying, "Nothing there!" each time she had a weak hand. It made him pretty darn sure that she had a good hand whenever she started raising like this.

He suspected his hand was better, though. This time. He pushed enough chips forward to equal hers.

The remaining players folded. Morty turned over the fifth card.

Matt checked. Kate peeked at her hand and smiled with transparent excitement. She shoved another tower of chips forward. "Raise."

She must have a royal flush. If he lost this hand, he'd be all but dead. He looked down at the table, scratched the side of his forehead. He should probably fold. At least he could safeguard the chips he had left. And yet . . . stubborn confidence in his cards tugged at him.

What the heck. He met her bet and then some.

She raised again.

To meet her this time would take all he had, and only empty her down to half her chips. He'd be out of the game and forced to go hang out in the kitchen with the other early losers—Beverly and Velma.

What was he, a pansy?

He slid his remaining chips to the center. "I call."

Kate's jaw tightened almost imperceptibly.

"Let's see what you've got."

She wrinkled her nose and revealed her hand. He, too, turned over his cards.

She had . . . She had nothing. He furrowed his brow, trying to understand what she'd been thinking.

Morty leaned toward her. "Now, Kate, you shouldn't have bet on this hand. You don't have anything here. Not even a pair, see?" As Morty's voice continued on with exaggerated patience, Kate's gaze flicked to Matt. One corner of her lips lifted knowingly and she winked.

Shock hit Matt square in the chest.

Just as quickly, Kate looked back to her cards, nodding seriously over Morty's instruction.

She knew exactly what she was doing, Matt realized, stunned. She knew good and well that she'd had nothing. She'd been bluffing. Matt thought of previous hands when he'd folded, when they'd all folded, and she'd raked in their chips with her delicate little hands without ever having to reveal her cards.

The antique lover knew how to play poker? The antique lover? It seemed impossible. He'd never seen anyone who looked less like a poker player. She'd parted her long red hair on the side tonight, and tucked it behind her ears. Classy black turtleneck. Classy gray skirt. The odd black ballet shoes.

Slowly, feeling sluggish, he pulled all the chips toward himself.

Kate was an expert at Texas Hold 'Em. The whole beginner thing was an act. The confused expression, the questions, the reliance on the cheat sheet—phony. He felt like a dunce for falling for it. But one glance around the table told him that all of the other players were *still* falling for it. She was going to take them to the cleaners.

He watched her, grudging admiration sifting through him. He had to hand it to her. The clever little thing knew she only had so long before they realized her charade, so she was running with her chance.

It was William's turn to deal. He shuffled and began sliding cards to each player. As Kate accepted her first card, she looked up at Matt and their gazes locked. She lifted one eyebrow, her hazel eyes glinting with amusement. *So?* she seemed to ask him.

I'm on to you. He mouthed the words silently.

She nodded at him, smiled. Didn't appear the slightest bit worried.

Now that he was wise to her, boy, he was bringing his A game. It was on like Donkey Kong. She was destined to lose.

But, as it turned out, she didn't lose. She won. By custom, they stopped for the night when only three players remained, then divvied up the prize money to each of those people based on their chip count. Kate had twice as many chips as anyone else, then came Morty and then Peg, which was downright embarrassing. Even Peg had beaten him. Matt had made it to the final four, then lost fair and square.

If he did nothing else this week, he was going to study up on poker. His name wasn't engraved on the Stanley Cup for nothing.

After suffering through some mandatory small talk, Matt said his good-byes and let himself out the kitchen door.

Kate slipped out beside him, sliding gracefully into her coat. "I'll walk you out."

They made their way through the dark side by side, hands in their pockets, shoes crunching.

"You had me going in there," he said.

"Did I?"

"You know you did."

She laughed—a soft, easy sound. "Yeah. I know I did. That was terrible of me. Terrible! I shouldn't have done it, but Morty just assumed right from the start that I didn't know anything about poker, and you kept giving me those impatient and pitying looks—"

"Hey," he protested.

"They were *definitely* pitying." She glanced teasingly at him. "I couldn't resist."

He snorted. "Where'd you learn to play?"

"From my dad. He loves the game." She bent her head a little against the fierce wind. "Most families played Scrabble or Pictionary or Uno on family vacations. We played poker."

"I'm going to work on my game before next week."

"Is that right?"

"Well, yeah. I've got to redeem myself." They reached his truck and stood facing each other.

"I'm glad you'll be back," she said. "I'll be happy to take more of your money. There's this Coach purse I've been wanting. . . ." The edges of her mouth lifted until she was grinning in outright challenge.

"Better plan on paying for the purse with your own money."

"I'd rather spend yours."

He glared.

"Bring it on," she said.

"I will."

"I'll have to see it to believe it, mister."

He shook his head. The antique lover was a card shark who also liked trash talking? He moved to get into his truck, then paused, gripping the door handle. "Do you have any other abilities I should know about before I go and make a fool of myself again?"

"I can play golf."

"Seriously?"

She shrugged, as if to say, *Try me and see.* She didn't look strong enough to drive the ball farther than fifty yards. But after tonight . . . well, he supposed it was possible.

He climbed into his truck. "G'night."

"Good night, Matt."

He started the car, turned on the lights, and eased down the driveway. In his rearview mirror he could see Kate standing where he'd left her, shoulders hunched against the cold. Strange woman. It kept him off-balance, this ability she had to surprise him. The way she was still knee-deep in his business every time he turned around. How she looked at him without ever seeming frightened, without ever giving the indication that she was willing to back off and leave him alone.

He wished she'd go inside and get out of the cold. She was small and the air must be cutting right through her. He kept watching her in the rearview mirror, but she still hadn't moved. She just stood there in the dark, long hair blowing, until the bend in the road stole her from view.

chapter five

Kate showed up for sleep that night and found sleep absent. She snuggled deeper under the covers and curled into a near-fetal position. She tried her yoga breathing techniques. She forced all her large muscle groups to relax. When none of that worked, she did what every Generation Xer does with the unanswered questions keeping them up at night.

She Googled them.

After clicking on her bedside lamp, she settled her laptop above the mound of her quilt-covered thighs. As if in greeting, it bathed her in green computer-screen light while it booted up.

The longer she lived at Chapel Bluff, the less she used her computer. Email, the news and information online, and even her eBay sales kept waning and waning in importance and urgency.

When Google's web page popped up, she typed in *Removing hair dye* and hit Enter. Myriad results surfaced.

The first subheading that caught her eye read *Hair Color Gone Bad?* That would, in Morty's case, be an affirmative. Below that it stated *Correct or remove it at home.*

Well, good. She'd actually thought that hair dye would be impossible to remove and that Morty was destined for an electric shaver.

She followed links, studied various products, and read reviews.

It appeared that bottles full of chemicals, a special brush, and rubber gloves were going to be involved.

High cringe factor ensued when she envisioned herself using said products on Morty. She hardly knew the man. But since she'd sold out to him at the merest mention of the word *spa*, she was undoubtedly going to be the second person in the two-person job of removing his hair dye.

She only hoped she could break the news to Morty that Velma hated his hair and then accomplish the necessary beauty treatments without fatally crushing his ego.

Kate went back to Google's main page, her fingertips hovering on the keys. An image of Matt as he'd looked earlier when she'd walked him to his car flashed into her thoughts, growing in size and focus until she could see every detail diamond-bright and clear. . . . The hard contour of his cheekbones. The moonlight that had caught and glittered in his dark, guarded eyes. The strands of brown hair raked by the wind.

Her fingers twitched eagerly. She knew she shouldn't do it. But she really, really wanted to. Would it be so terrible? She'd just take a little tiny peek, just browse around a bit. She shouldn't and yet—

Fingers flying, she typed in *Matt Jarreau* and hit Enter.

Google's response page immediately sprang up, with matches one to ten of over . . . 1,500,000. Her heart sank. She scrolled slowly down. The first hit was an encyclopedia entry about him. He was . . . ah . . . entered in the encyclopedia? Then a hit identifying Matt as one of the legends of hockey. Biographies. Quotes. An article about a famous goal he'd made in the Stanley Cup playoffs. Stats. NHL stuff. Another article. ESPN.com. Pictures that could be viewed.

This was only page one. There were still more than a million other matches.

She tilted her head back, thumping it against the brass headboard. For long moments she simply stared at the pitched ceiling of her attic room.

The words she'd just read—*encyclopedia, legend* for goodness' sake, *Stanley Cup*—were like a bucketful of icy reality in the face.

From the moment she'd met him she'd *known* a romantic relationship with him was never going to happen. So why dredge up more evidence of that fact?

Why? Because her body insisted on getting all jumbled up with excitement every time he walked into a room. That's why.

She felt like a cautionary example in one of those Ten Really Idiotic Things Women Do–type books. There'd be a bad driver's-license-type picture of her with a caption that said, "Don't obsess! Don't drive by your ex's house. Don't read letters from your boyfriend's old girlfriends. Don't stray into bridal websites if you aren't engaged. And *definitely don't pine after your gorgeous contractor who's out of your league.* These behaviors are futile! You're inflicting pain on yourself! Stop!"

She should close down the Internet immediately. But she still—stupidly—wanted to read more. The biographies, at least. Before her traitorous fingertips could act, she lifted her hands up and out of the danger zone.

The Matt she knew—their contractor, the man who cooked dinner in their kitchen, the loner—that guy was already intimidating and daunting enough. She didn't need all these websites to heap amazing upon amazing upon amazing. Better to let him tell her his own version of his biography, if he ever wanted to.

With tremendous self-control, she shut down her computer and slid it under her bed, out of reach. Once she'd killed the light, she burrowed deep under her quilts. For long quiet minutes she lay there, watching the black trees sway against the night sky beyond her windows. All right. So he'd once been an over-the-top famous hockey player. These days he was a grumpy hermit. Maybe that brought him out of the category of men who only dated supermodels into the category of men who dated regular human women.

She snorted at herself, at the foolish bent of her thoughts. Angrily, she socked her pillow and then rolled onto her opposite side.

She might be a hopeless romantic, but she wasn't a stupid one. Matt Jarreau didn't even exist in the same stratosphere that she did. He was *way* more talented, rich, and famous. Plus, he was fatally handsome and she no longer let herself harbor crushes on guys that looked like he did.

They were just friends!

She intended to continue working hard every day to keep her feelings for him strictly platonic. But the more she was around him, the better she got to know him, the more difficult it was.

The next day was the day of The Big Garage Sale, the day when one man's trash would become another man's trash.

They'd been sorting items for days. They'd borrowed card tables on which to display their wares. They had a money box ready for making change. They had color-coded price tags. They'd advertised. They were as prepared for their sale as any aspiring garage sale hostesses since the beginning of time.

Congratulating themselves on their savvy, they'd scheduled the sale to start at eight but knew to expect the avid treasure-trollers to arrive at seven.

They came at six. From that moment on, their perfectly planned garage sale descended into anarchy.

As one exhausting hour tumbled headlong into the next, the respective jobs of Kate and "the girls" grew more distinct. Gran welcomed everyone with smiles and cheerfully answered questions about the merchandise. Kate and Velma haggled over prices. Peg ran the cash box.

The best things they had went fast. But the worst things went, too. Pairs of old and battered high heels. A grimy can opener too nasty to be believed. A toilet plunger circa 1960. It was the perfectly fine middle-of-the-road stuff that was passed over as if it had cooties. Kate tried valiantly not to view this odd circumstance as a metaphor for her dating life.

They'd planned to close things down at four, but the hands on her watch clicked all the way to five before the final stragglers drifted off.

She, Gran, Velma, and Peg were left surrounded by a minefield of junk. Objects tilted crazily against the barn walls, lay jumbled across the card tables, and littered the lawn like soldiers felled in battle.

Looking at the enormity of the mess, Kate's emotions sagged with exhaustion. Had she sat down at some point today? Not that she could recall. Had she eaten anything? She vaguely remembered a few Styrofoam cups of coffee, two donuts, and a bottled water.

"I think we put on a fantastic sale," Gran said.

"It went really well," Kate agreed.

"Some of those people were so gosh darn *cheap!*" Velma looked deeply offended. "I wanted to tell a few of them to take their dollar ninety-nine and shove it!"

"Well, we raised a wonderful amount of money." Peg counted out the last few bills and made a notation on her pad of paper. Somehow, Peg's gray bob still fell in a sleek and orderly line and her pale peach lipstick still shone. Which was some kind of miracle, because Kate knew she looked like she'd been dragged behind an eighteen-wheeler.

"Three thousand four hundred and sixty-two dollars," Peg announced.

"That's marvelous!" Gran clasped her hands together, big rings clacking. "Thank you, everyone." She went around, teary-eyed, hugging them all, telling them that she couldn't have done it without them, murmuring about all the extras she could now afford for the renovation.

In the distance, Kate heard a car approaching. She'd tell whoever it was that the sale was over. They were all beat and they just couldn't—

The car rounded the bend and she saw that it wasn't a car at all, but a white Ford truck.

Her heartbeat did a crazy little hitch and leap. *Matt.* It was Saturday and she never saw Matt on Saturdays or Sundays.

"Why, it's Matt coming," Gran said.

"Well, thank goodness," Velma said. "Looking at that boy always gives me a little pick-me-up, and I sure could use one right now."

All of them watched as he turned the truck around and backed in so that the bed was nearest the mess. With easy grace, he swung down from the cab wearing a black long-sleeved Dri-Fit shirt, jeans, and dark gray running shoes.

"Matt!" Gran greeted him with a brief hug. "How nice to see you."

"Beverly." He nodded to the rest of them. "How'd it go?"

"It went beautifully," Gran answered. "The last of the buyers left just a few minutes ago so we were able to total up all the money. And we did very well. Better than I could have hoped."

"Good. I'm glad." He gave the remnants of their sale a long, evaluating look. "You planning on donating all this?"

"Kate, what was it we'd decided?" Gran asked.

82

"We thought we'd give it to the Salvation Army," Kate answered. "They have a truck and you can schedule a pickup."

"I'll take it over there for you," he said. "That'll get it out of your way."

"Are you sure?" Gran asked. "I wouldn't want to trouble you."

"I'm sure."

"You already work so hard for us, I certainly don't expect you to work on the weekends."

He shrugged. "I know."

"Tall, a hottie, *and* willing to lend a hand!" Velma crowed.

Matt glanced at Velma, his brow knit with a mixture of confusion and distaste, as if she'd just announced *I'm a transvestite* or *Bend over and moon us.*

As the older ladies giggled and continued to dote on him, Kate watched Matt's discomfort grow. He shifted from foot to foot. Looked at his watch. Glared at the ground. Finally, long before the ladies were done fussing over him, he turned and simply went to work taking flattened cardboard boxes out of his truck bed. "All right, all right," he grumbled. "Now all of you go inside and let me do this."

"Thank you again," Gran said.

"Sure."

"Maybe we can just help pack up—"

"*Go.*"

"But—"

His head came up, his eyes blazing. "Go inside," he growled. "Take a break. And let me load my truck in peace."

That sent them all, except Kate, scurrying.

She watched him pop open more boxes. Maybe because she was so tired, so hungry, and so desiring of nothing but a hot bath, the sight of him extending help to them struck her with an enormous wave of gratitude.

"You too." Without looking at her, Matt motioned with his head toward the house.

"Yeah, right." She grabbed the nearest empty box and started filling it. "You should know me better than that."

He stopped what he was doing to frown at her. "You look worn out."

She raised her eyebrows, nearly disintegrating into hysterical laughter. "That's a shame, since I spent the day splurging on beauty treatments."

His expression didn't even flicker.

"Maybe I should ask for my money back."

"Come on, Kate, you know I like to work alone. Go on." Again, that emphatic motion of his head toward the house, as if he were shooing an annoying dog.

Sometimes it was embarrassing to be so stubborn, but she couldn't trot off and let him clean up their garage sale alone. She just flat *couldn't.* "Nope, I'm helping. I may look terrible, but I'm fine." Before he could say anything else she went back to work, quickly reaching for things and stuffing them into her cardboard box. "See, I'm catching a second wind. You're stuck with me."

"Okay, so here's what I wonder." Kate sat beside Matt in his truck as they made their second and final trip from Chapel Bluff to the Salvation Army drop-off location.

When Matt didn't respond she prompted him with, "What's that, Kate?"

"What's that, Kate?" he said.

"Everyone has garage sales on the weekends. And then right afterward everyone does what we're doing and hauls the stuff that didn't sell to Goodwill or the Salvation Army, right?"

"Right."

"So I wonder what the people who work at the Salvation Army are really thinking when they see this stuff coming."

"Meaning?"

"Well, they must look at all the trucks stuffed with all these garage sale leftovers and think, 'You know what, people, thanks—but we'd be a lot better off without all your crap.'"

There was a beat of silence, and then Matt looked across at her and smiled.

He smiled. An easy smile, genuine with amusement. Quickly come and gone, and yet it dazzled her completely. It was the first smile she'd ever seen him give anyone.

"I mean," she said, fumbling for her line of thought, "I mean this is stuff so . . . so *unpalatable* that no one wanted to pay a dollar for it."

"In some cases no one wanted to pay twenty-five cents for it," he said.

"Exactly."

"Something to think about."

"Something to think about," she murmured.

"Kind of kills the sense of charity I'd been feeling."

Kate laughed.

He smiled again, this time straight ahead at the road.

They lapsed into silence, which left Kate time to marvel over those two smiles. She'd made him smile. Twice!

Strange, that amid that proud feeling of accomplishment, she suddenly felt God nudge her to say something to him about his wife.

Terrible idea, she thought. *I've only just got him smiling!*

Go on, God seemed to be saying. **Bring it up.**

It had become more and more difficult for her recently to talk to him and pretend she didn't know anything about the tragedy he'd been through. It reminded her of the elephant jokes she and her dad had told each other when she was little. . . .

How do you know there's an elephant in your refrigerator?
The footprints in the Jell-O.

Well, his past had become the elephant in the room with Kate every time she spoke with him. Big and hard to ignore.

She was too scared to attempt to talk to him about it while looking at him face-to-face. But the two of them were driving along together facing forward with the hum of the engine between them. Talking about it seemed like a possibility. The nudge gradually became an urge. Another few miles passed under the tires until the urge became an almost physical pressure pushing its way up her throat.

Say it, God insisted.

"I heard about what happened to your wife." She didn't blurt it out. Still, without preamble or anything else to cushion them, the words sounded impossibly abrupt. They fell like pieces of sharp metal between them, bald and heavy.

Matt's jaw tensed and his fingers tightened on the steering wheel.

She waited, but he didn't say anything. "I wanted you to know that I'm so sorry," she said.

He didn't respond for a full minute. Kate's chest got tighter and tighter with each painfully awkward second. She was tempted to rush into the void and fill it with words, but she forced herself to wait.

"Who told you?" he finally said.

"Velma and Peg told Gran and me."

She could guess how much he hated being talked about. "You don't like being discussed," she stated.

"No. I don't."

"I know you don't, and I apologize. It wasn't malicious. They asked us if we knew about your past and of course we didn't, so they told us."

He gave a terse half nod.

Might as well just rip the Band-Aid the rest of the way off. "They also told us about your hockey career."

"Former hockey career."

"Right."

She waited, but apparently he didn't have any more to say on the subject. "Well . . . I can't imagine what you've been though, how hard it's been. I'm here if you ever want to talk about it."

He angled his head away, put on his blinker, made the last few turns that would take them to the drop-off spot.

Kate's confidence fizzled and sank.

The Salvation Army came into view. Beyond open double doors an attendant waited. "Well," Matt said quietly as he pulled in, "sorry, buddy, but we're here with our second truckload of crap."

Kate erupted with laughter.

Matt glanced over at her, eyes shining with subtle humor.

"See?" she said. "I offer a whole new spin on things. Aren't you glad you let me come along?"

"Very glad," he said sarcastically.

Relief tumbled through her like a yo-yo unfurling. It was okay. He hadn't liked what she'd said about his wife and his hockey. But he'd survived. She'd survived.

They got out of the truck and began unloading.

She'd said what she'd needed to. He knew that she knew. And now they could proceed without elephants.

Chapel Bluff was bearing her makeover well. Like a stately grande dame, she acquiesced to their ministrations. It was as if she recognized them, Kate often thought, as if she put up with them because they were, after all, *family*.

Now that they'd gotten rid of all the old clutter, Chapel Bluff's interior had become a mostly blank canvas. Room after room held little or no furniture. The old carpets were gone. In their place, plain hardwood floor awaited refinishing. Walls naked of wallpaper, their surfaces carefully repaired, called out for paint.

Kate and Gran had picked a warm yellow for the kitchen and a buttery cream color for the walls in the rest of the house. When they weren't making slow progress through the dining room, living room, library, and den with rollers and brushes, they were working on trim. Kate wanted the window trim, doorway trim, and baseboards resurfaced so that the patina of the wood showed through again. Which meant grueling work removing layers of paint, grime, and years.

But all of it, every hour Kate put into the house, was worth the effort. Because the grande dame, the lady who'd been treasured by their family for almost two hundred years, was beginning to shine.

chapter six

"Morty." Kate gripped the phone and forced herself to break the news. "Velma told me that she might consider a date with you if you change your hair."

Silence yawned across the phone lines without a single crackle. "My hair?" Morty finally asked, clearly confused.

"Yes."

"What does she want me to change about my hair?"

"The color. She'd like you to take out the dye." Kate winced.

"The hair dye?"

"I'm afraid so."

Another protracted pause and then, "That confounded woman! What does she know about style?"

An outstanding point. Velma had wretched fashion sense, and even more ironically, a head full of dyed hair.

"That woman will be the death of me!" he blustered. "Ordering me around. Free with her opinions. Telling me to take out my hair dye. Just who does she think she is? I've worn my hair this way for fifty years!"

Kate murmured sympathetically.

"My wife loved my hair this way."

"Um, Morty . . ." He had, after all, appointed her as his dating advisor. "It might not be such a good idea in general to compare Velma to your late wife."

He harrumphed. She could practically hear him scowling.

"Dye can't even be removed, can it?" he asked. "Isn't that why it's called 'permanent'?"

"Actually, I did a little checking and it seems it can be removed with the right products. I'd be happy to pick them up for you if you'd like."

She could hear muffled footsteps. He was pacing.

"Morty?"

"I'm thinking."

She waited. It touched her, the sound of those footsteps treading back and forth, back and forth. He was considering it, this gruff ex-policeman. Considering the sacrifice of pride, familiarity, and hairstyle for a chance at love.

"I'll do it," he said at last. "Darn her."

Wow. She was struck anew by the fact that love held incredible power for change. "How's Thursday afternoon for you? I'll bring the dye remover over to your house and help you apply it."

"I don't need help with my own hair."

"Unfortunately, the dye removal process takes two people. But if you'd rather have someone else . . ."

"No. You'll do." She heard a distinct grinding of teeth before he hung up.

Kate felt a pang of pity. A relationship with Velma guaranteed him a future of teeth grinding. Morty'd go down to the grave with a mouthful of nubs.

Kate walked into the kitchen at dinnertime that night to find Gran and Matt in a heated argument over aprons. She paused in the doorway, watching, as Gran brandished an apron in her ring-encrusted fingers. It was a white canvas number, with a loop for the neck and two dangling ties to secure behind the back. "Matt, I'm telling you that you need to put this on."

"No way."

"You're about to use an electric handheld mixer," Gran gestured to the appliance already plugged in and waiting on the countertop, "and it's going to get messy."

Matt's hard features took on a defiant cast. "Look, Beverly, I'll cook but I am not going to wear an *apron*."

"Your sweater is cashmere!"

He shrugged.

"Cashmere!"

"I'd rather throw it away after this," he motioned toward the apron, "than wear that."

Gran glared at him as if he'd insulted her.

He returned her glare, not backing down an inch.

"Matthew Jarreau! If I knew your middle name, I'd use it!"

Still nothing. He set his mouth in an endearingly mulish line.

They faced off for several charged seconds before Gran hefted an enormous sigh, shook her head, and went to hang the apron on its peg in the pantry. "Men!"

Matt glanced at Kate.

"No fair of you to start the fun without me," she said.

He grunted, pushed up the sleeves of his beige sweater, and started washing his hands.

Gran took up her position at the counter, her expression disgruntled. "I didn't think your masculinity could be so easily threatened."

"You thought wrong." He dried his hands with a dish towel. "It's David."

"What is?"

He lifted one eyebrow. "My middle name."

"Matthew David Jarreau?" she asked.

"Yes."

"Well, good." She gave a haughty sniff. "The next time I need to use it, I will."

One side of his lips twitched upward, and just that quickly, animosity disappeared and contentment hummed through the kitchen as the two of them launched into their cooking lesson.

Kate had dressed in clothes appropriate for treading through the detonation site of a nuclear bomb. She'd tugged on plastic gloves. She'd mixed chemicals like a scientist. And she'd just shoveled an appropriate amount of something called *color remover* onto something called a *tint brush*.

Operation Correct-Morty's-Hair-Dye-Blunder was about to commence.

The object of her charity was sitting on a vinyl chair in the center of his kitchen, eyeing her grumpily.

She wondered if he'd take offense if she snapped on a pair of goggles and a gas mask.

"Is it ready?" he asked.

"Ready." Kate approached him, centered herself directly behind him, and shellacked the first brushful of goo onto the crown of his head. Whatever unseen "personal space" boundaries they'd had between them evaporated. Discomfort crashed over Kate and she paused momentarily, deeply tempted to pound out the back door at a dead sprint.

Massages, she reminded herself. Facials. Manicures. Spa pedicures! She dove in grimly with both plastic-covered hands, meticulously raking the goo through his hair.

"So," Morty said, "how about those Dallas Cowboys?"

Kate laughed. The tension began to deflate. "How about them."

"They won their preseason games and now they're three and one. They're up against the Eagles, though, on Sunday. . . ."

He continued chatting about football, and Kate continued with the goo and the brush. Like many things in life that made one painfully self-conscious at the outset, like wearing your swimsuit on the first day of summer, time and practice helped one adjust.

When she finished with the solution, he looked like a geriatric rock star with a fetish for hair gel. Some of the black strands stuck directly up, and some lay in matted surrender.

Kate consulted the directions for the hundredth time, then snapped a shower cap onto him.

"What now?" he asked.

"Now it has to process for twenty minutes."

"What does that mean?"

"We let it sit for twenty minutes. It says that I can use a hair dryer on the shower cap to help it along."

His eyebrows lowered skeptically.

Kate grinned at the picture he presented. This burly frowning grandfather, his hair glistening under a shower cap.

"Can we at least move into the den so I can watch TV?" he asked.

"Sure. And then we'll need to come back in here to rinse, shampoo it, and put on the—" she consulted the directions again— "processing lotion."

"Fine."

She followed him into his den. He settled into an old brown

fabric recliner that had a concave back and butt indentions. He'd placed the recliner, without creativity, directly in front of his television. Apparently they still made the this-TV-is-a-piece-of-furniture! televisions, because that's what his was. A TV, surrounded by wood, with a top like a buffet table.

She thought of Peg and William's lovely, tasteful, magazine-worthy home. She thought of Gran's snug ranch-style house in Dallas. She thought of Velma's scruffy house, with its debris-stuffed carport, peeling paint, and six acres of property. They all had homes that suited them. But somehow this two-bedroom condo on the edge of town didn't seem right for Morty.

He kept it neat, but the place was worn and stark, filled with outdated furniture. After a lifetime of police work in this town, children raised, and grandchildren grown, it seemed to Kate that Morty ought to be entitled to more. To a place less lonely.

Kate plugged in her blow-dryer and managed to unfurl it just far enough to reach Morty with the warm air. Morty responded to the noise by turning up the TV volume, so Kate found herself blow-drying Morty's shower cap while the four o'clock local news blared in the background.

Twenty minutes had seldom passed so slowly.

When the time was up, they returned to the kitchen and Morty ducked over the sink. Kate stood on a footstool and leaned over him, rinsing, then shampooing his hair.

The color had faded from inky opaque black to . . . plain dull black.

Kate's hopes sank.

"How's it look?" Morty asked the sink drain.

"Well . . . it didn't change much." She grabbed the towel and wrapped it around his head.

"What's that you said?" He straightened with two joint pops, dried his hair vigorously, then draped the towel around his shoulders. He looked at her questioningly. "Didn't change much?"

"No, but the directions say we can repeat the process two or three more times today."

"Let me go look in the mirror." He disappeared around the corner into the hall bathroom. After a moment he called, "And what if it still doesn't change after two or three more times?"

"Then we'll have to wait a few days and try again. We've got enough product"—Kate's voice and courage were shrinking—"for ten applications," she finished faintly.

He returned and planted himself back into the vinyl chair. "Confounded Velma."

She half expected him to launch into a string of curses, but instead he gave a rusty laugh and shook his head. "Let's try it again, then."

At seven o'clock that night Kate stood above the brown recliner blow-drying Morty's shower cap for the fourth time that day. The television shows had changed each time around. This time he had the volume at max for a cable offering of *The Rockford Files*.

Her mind drifted in circles of bored contemplation. She was thinking how glad she was that she hadn't pursued a degree in cosmetology when something caught her attention. She straightened and stared.

A section of Morty's hair actually looked . . . gray.

Gray!

She checked her watch. Time to shampoo. She shepherded him into the kitchen. He bent over the sink without being asked, well familiar with the routine by now, and she started to wash his hair.

Yes. It truly was gray. A beautiful gun-metal color, slightly darker near the temples, slightly lighter in a streak over his right eye.

"Morty!" She rinsed the suds out, practically bouncing on the footstool with excitement. "It worked!"

"It did?"

"It did!"

And then, before he'd even had a chance to see it, or form his own opinion about it, he asked, "Do you think Velma will like it?"

"Oh, Morty," Kate replied. "She better."

Feeling like a CIA operative, Kate covertly tailed Velma to the bathroom. It was Friday again. Poker night. She waited in the shadows of the hallway.

A few minutes later, Velma exited the bathroom, spotted Kate waiting, and frowned. "Is this going to become a regular thing? Me using the ladies' and coming out to find you here? Because I don't exactly like the idea of somebody listening to me pee."

"Completely understood."

"From now on if you want to talk to me, just tell me you want to talk to me."

"Got it."

"Good." Velma sniffed, then crossed her arms over an orange turtleneck and a black vest decorated with iron-on Halloween characters. Ghosts, pumpkins, witches, and black cats gazed at Kate with surprised eyes. "You wanting to talk to me about Morty?"

"I am." Kate smiled hopefully. "Doesn't his hair look great?"

"His hair looks . . . nice." Velma inclined her head like a queen granting a serf a concession.

"So? Will you go on a date with him?"

"No."

Kate furrowed her brow. *No?* No!

"His hair's better," Velma said, "but his clothes are still a problem."

Kate just stared.

"You know, the white T-shirts and the jeans and the penny loafers. I married my sorry husband when I was twenty years old and that's exactly how he dressed back then. Lord knows, that man was a disappointment." She wrinkled her nose. "I don't cotton to Morty reminding me of Herb every time he walks into a room."

"O-kay," Kate replied slowly. She wanted to shout, *Do you know how many hours it took to remove that hair dye?* Instead, she marshaled her thoughts and managed to ask in a level voice, "What kind of men's clothing do you like?"

"I like a man to look stylish, you know. Maybe some of that Italian fashion."

A mental image of the mobsters from *The Sopranos* popped into Kate's head. She grimaced. "Ah . . ."

"I also like those shirts, those . . ."—Velma waved fingers painted with her trademark pearl polish—"Tommy Bermuda's shirts."

"Tommy Bahama?"

"Yes, Tommy Bahama. I think they sell them in Philadelphia."

Great. Philadelphia. A mere two-hour drive round trip.

"I like slacks," Velma said. "And boots with a nice heel on them. And a spiffy looking burgundy leather jacket would be nice."

Velma had been giving this some thought, Kate noticed, and tried to take that as a promising sign. "So . . . if Morty buys some new clothes, will you agree to a date?"

"I'll think about it."

"I'm going to need a firmer commitment," Kate replied. "If he spends money on new clothes just to please you, then I'm going to need your promise that you'll go on a date with him."

Velma regarded her with a steely gaze.

In the background Kate could hear the others talking, the clack of the poker chips as Morty stacked them into piles.

Velma gave Kate an airy shrug. "Well, you're not going to get a promise. I've been living on my own for forty years, and to tell you the truth, I like it just fine that way."

Kate blew out a defeated breath.

"The only thing I'll say is that I might, *might*, be tempted to accept a date with a man wearing a Tommy Bermuda's shirt."

"These seniors know how to eat." Matt scooped up a second handful of Beverly's caramel corn. They'd been playing poker for an hour and a half and were taking a break before starting up again. He and Kate stood side by side at the butcher block in the kitchen.

"This is very true," Kate agreed, popping some into her mouth.

Man, it was good, he thought. Sticky and buttery with lots of nuts in it. He hadn't stopped appreciating Beverly's cooking. Still couldn't get over it. In the years since he'd moved to Redbud, he'd eaten lousy food either over the sink or in front of the TV. But for more than two weeks now he'd been eating Beverly's home-cooked meals at her kitchen table every weeknight.

"I'm going to have to step up my workouts," he commented.

"What, from two hours a day to three?"

He peered down at Kate and lifted an eyebrow.

She laughed, ate more caramel corn. "On an entirely different subject . . ."

"Yes?"

"I've been thinking that it might be less painful for you if you just went out and bought me the Coach purse I want."

"Really?" he asked dryly.

"Really. That way I won't be forced to win money from you at poker every Friday."

She'd been saying things like this to him all week. It amused him. Trash talking from this fashionable little person he could crush with one finger. He found himself actually looking forward to hearing whatever outrageous thing she'd say next. "Thanks," he answered, "but I prefer this painful method."

She shrugged. "Your choice."

"You know," he said, refilling his glass with water from the tap, "it's going to be very embarrassing for you when I beat you."

"Beat *me*?" she asked with exaggerated disbelief. "At poker?"

"Pride goes before a fall."

"Are you quoting the Bible to me now?"

"I guess I am."

"I love it! As you know, I'm very pro-Bible." She looked delighted with him. "You realize what else it says in there?"

"Enlighten me."

"Those more experienced at poker shall beat those of lesser experience, regardless of gender."

She beat him again.

When it was down to three and they called it a night, Kate had a towering stack of chips. Morty had a respectable pile. Matt had managed to hold on to third place with a lame number of chips. So much for all the World Poker Tour he'd watched and all the poker strategy he'd researched online. It hadn't helped.

He studied Kate with equal parts admiration and irritation as Morty counted out her winnings.

She was good. Perfect strategy, risking when she should and protecting when she should. Excellent at bluffing, because he knew she had to be doing it, but couldn't tell when. Surprisingly gracious. For all their banter, whenever she won a hand she pulled the chips toward herself with nothing more obnoxious than a half smile.

Morty took Matt's chips and exchanged them for five dollars and thirty-five cents of winnings.

Matt's gaze drifted over Kate's profile.

Long ago, before Beth, he'd run across plenty of women who'd started out looking beautiful to him, but had grown less so the better he got to know them and the closer he looked at them.

With Kate, somehow the opposite was happening. Her appearance, the blazing hair and the delicate features, had started out looking plain to him. But over time, so slowly he wasn't sure when his opinion had started to change, her face was becoming . . . interesting to him. He liked her expressions. When she lifted her eyebrows. When she threw back her head and laughed. When she shot him a sideways glance.

Matt stared at the ice cubes in his glass as he swirled them. He'd come to depend on her to make these social evenings—which, let's face it, he was lousy at—bearable. He'd been avoiding attention and conversation for years, and as a result he was rusty at interacting with people. Kate had a way of smoothing the way for him and making it all okay.

"Brooding, Matt?" she asked lightly.

He glanced up. She was standing, regarding him with a joking light in her eyes as she collected napkins and empty cups.

"Nope. Not when I have"—he flicked a finger toward his puny pile of dollars and coins—"this tower of money here to comfort me."

"Yes indeed. What are you going to splurge on?"

"Maybe a sandwich, chips, and a drink at Subway?"

"You wish! Probably just chips and a drink."

"Bummer."

She drifted off, carrying the dirty dishes toward the kitchen.

It wasn't easy for him to come here, to be a part of this group. *Her* group. But at the same time, he couldn't help but feel just a little bit . . .

Glad.

chapter seven

Kate stopped in the doorway of the upstairs bathroom, where Matt was working. "Exciting news," she said.

Matt looked up from stirring what appeared to be a bucket of white grout.

"Wayne Gretzky's on his way over for high tea!" she exclaimed.

He regarded her with skeptical amusement.

"Okay," she said. "So, not really."

"That's a shame. Wayne and I love high tea."

She grinned. "Well, my actual news is only a little less exciting. Gran and I just finished painting. Every room. The whole house. Done!"

"Congratulations."

"Thank you very much." She grabbed an empty orange plastic Home Depot bucket, turned it over, and took a seat.

She watched Matt finish stirring the grout, then apply it to the wall above the bathtub with a triangular metal spatula. Once he'd spread the grout, he used the teeth on the end of the spatula to score it in preparation for the tile. She and Gran had picked white subway tiles that matched the white of the whirlpool tub he'd installed.

"I can hardly wait to use that bathtub," Kate said.

"Something you remind me of daily."

"That's rude."

"What?"

"To remind me of my own repetitiveness."

He cocked a half smile. "What am I supposed to do? Listen to you drone on and on about the same things day after day?"

"Of course."

"Then you're not paying me enough."

Kate chuckled. Silence drifted between them as he continued to work. She watched his hands as they moved. Big, strong, muscular hands. Marked with small scars. Graceful and competently assured.

When he finally had the grout how he wanted it, he reached down for a tile. Kate scooted her bucket near the stack of them, lifted one, and handed it to him. "Since Gran and I are done painting, it's time to refinish the floors."

He nodded.

"We called the floor guy you recommended, and he said his crew could come later this week. It'll take them three days, and we're supposed to stay out of the house while they're here because of the dust. Will that work with your schedule?"

"Yes."

"Do you think we can move the antiques from the barn into the house next Monday then?"

"Yeah."

"Should I hire movers? To get it all from there to here?"

"Nah, I'll call a few of the guys that work with me sometimes and get them to help me move it over."

"Perfect."

Quiet settled.

"Gran and I thought we'd take a trip to Philadelphia while the floor is being refinished," Kate said. "Go see the sights. The Liberty Bell, Independence Hall, and all that. We leave tomorrow." She watched closely for any sign of a reaction, any slight indication that he cared whether they stayed or left, that he'd miss them. Nothing came. He just continued with the tiles, completely indifferent.

What had she expected?

She wasn't sure how to broach the next subject. She picked at the speckles of paint on her fingernails, mentally debating her tactics, then finally deciding to be blunt. "Morty loves Velma."

Matt lifted his head, gazing at her with those fathomless chocolate brown eyes framed by long, dark lashes. "Come again?"

"Morty loves Velma."

"Are you serious?"

"Yes. I'm telling you because I need your help," Kate said.

"My help?"

"Yes."

He held out a hand. "Tile."

She handed him another.

He stuck it into place. "My help with what?"

"With persuading Velma to go on a date with Morty."

He paused momentarily, then placed a little X-shaped spacer next to the tile. "I can't wait to hear how you think I could help with that."

"Velma said she'd consider Morty if we did something about his hair. So we did. But now she wants him to change the way he dresses."

"I've got a suggestion."

"Which is?"

"Morty should tell Velma to jump off a cliff."

"He can't because, as previously noted, he loves her."

Matt grunted disdainfully.

"Velma told me she likes Tommy Bahama shirts on men."

He rolled his eyes. "It's October. Aren't those for like—" he made a vague gesture—"trips to the Caribbean in July?"

"Exactly. But she wants what she wants, so Morty has given me permission to buy a Tommy Bahama shirt for him when I'm in Philadelphia. I wondered if there's any chance, any small chance at all, that you'd be willing to take Morty shopping while I'm gone for the rest of the clothes he needs."

He stared at her incredulously.

"Just a few pairs of pants. Some boots. A leather jacket. And some extra shirts," she said in a rush.

"Kate."

"I think he's too embarrassed to tell William or any of his other friends about this. And it would be way too awkward for me to shop with him." She gazed at him beseechingly. "You know something about men's clothing and Morty has a man crush on you, of course, because of your athletic superpowers, so I think he might let you advise him."

"Man crush?" he growled.

Kate laughed and dropped her face into her hands. "In a matter of speaking." How did she get herself involved in these dramas? She waited for him to shoot her down.

"I don't really go shopping for clothes with other men."

She lifted her face. "I know." She shouldn't have asked him. It had been such a long shot, but she'd irrationally hoped—

"I'll do it." He sighed.

"Really?"

"Yes."

She gaped at him, absurdly grateful. "Thank you."

He shrugged.

"No, really, Matt. Thank you. I appreciate it."

He returned his attention to the tile. "So what other old-people activities do you have planned for Philadelphia? You going to ride around on a tour bus? Eat dinner at four-thirty?"

"Very funny."

"How old are you?"

"Do you ask because I seem like a seventy-year-old?"

"I ask because you hang out with seventy-year-olds."

"How old do you think I am?" Just as soon as the words left her mouth, she wished she could stuff them back in. *How old do you think I am?* Every woman—including herself—knew to avoid that question like the plague. It had popped out accidentally. Talk about setting yourself up for devastation.

"I wasn't born yesterday, Kate. There's no way I'm guessing your age."

Smart man! "I'm thirty-one."

He gave her a doubtful expression.

"I am."

"You look younger than that."

People frequently assumed that because she had no curves. "How old are you?" she asked.

"Thirty-two."

Huge internal sigh of relief. She *really* hadn't wanted to be older than he was.

"So if you're thirty-one," he said, looking across his shoulder at her and lifting one eyebrow, "shouldn't you be married by now?"

She glared. "Not you, too."

His lips twitched, and she could tell by the sudden glint in his eyes that he was teasing her. Ah. Uproarious!

"Tile," he said.

She passed one over.

"Where'd you go to school?" he asked. "I'm guessing it was a four-year Christian university."

"Baylor."

"Uh-huh. And you must have been in a sorority there."

"Must have been?"

"Am I right?"

"Yes."

"And you must have been popular with the fraternity brothers."

She shot him a not-very-ferocious scowl.

"And you attend church on Sundays."

"Yes," she said.

"So what's the deal?" he asked. "Women on that track marry by twenty-five."

"Not this woman."

"Is there a boyfriend I don't know about? An engagement?"

"Negative."

"How come?"

She let the silence stretch. "Are you looking for a joking answer or an honest one?"

He adjusted a tile until it was perfectly aligned, then straightened away from the wall. He regarded her evenly, serious suddenly. "An honest one."

"Well . . ." She tried to decide how to phrase it without sounding pathetic. "The honest answer is that I've had some short-term and long-term boyfriends over the years but none of them have worked out."

"Because . . ."

"Well, for example, the last short-termer was reckless, um . . . selfish, and generally unkind."

"Is that all?"

"Alas, no. That's just the beginning of the list."

She expected him to smile, but instead he acknowledged her words with a frown.

Kate attempted a lighthearted shrug. "My romantic story is just the common, boring story. Nice girl who hasn't met the right guy."

He continued to measure her.

"That's if there *is* a guy out there for me somewhere," she added.

"Of course there is."

Spoken like someone who was totally disconnected from the realities of her dating life. He'd been a rich and famous hockey star, since what, teenagerhood? And she was quite sure he'd been gorgeous since birth. The acquisition of eligible women had probably been the simplest thing in his life.

He stretched out a hand. "Tile."

She placed one in his palm. A visual image of match.com's office building back in Dallas popped to the front of her mind. An enormous gray mirrored structure a block wide and at least three stories tall. All those employees, all that square footage, dedicated to singles in search of matches. Every time she drove past that building, the sight of it bummed her out. Reminded her how looming and impossible that search could be. *Was*, in her case.

Where had she put her bag of peppermint taffies? Suddenly she needed some urgently. She pushed to her feet, brushed off her jeans. "I know how you like to work with it quiet, so I'll leave you to it."

His brows knit. "When has my desire to work with it quiet ever stopped you before?"

She grinned. "There's a first time for everything."

He glowered.

What was wrong with her? Something. Because even his glowers struck her as adorable.

Thank goodness for blockbuster.com, because he wouldn't be caught dead renting these movies in public.

Matt looked over the selection that had come up on his computer screen in response to his search for Audrey Hepburn. Yep, there was *Breakfast at Tiffany's*, which he'd heard of. He ordered it, then studied the rest of the movies. He wasn't the slightest bit familiar with any of them.

After some scrolling and clicking, he ended up also choosing something called *Charade* and something called *My Fair Lady* because the blockbuster.com users had rated them with the most stars.

Matt submitted the order and leaned back in his desk chair. He'd been wondering more and more the past few days if Kate really did look anything like Audrey Hepburn. Now he'd be able to see for himself.

He glanced at his desk clock. It was late. No doubt she and Beverly, on their old folks' schedule, were long asleep. The two of them had loaded up the Explorer and left for Philadelphia yesterday, Tuesday, around noon.

He'd enjoyed being alone yesterday and today. It was nice to have some time off from Chapel Bluff, from all that talking, from the constant female scrutiny. He could breathe easier holed up here in his house by himself. He liked it best this way. Preferred to be alone.

At least it used to be true that he preferred to be alone. But as time passed, a bad thing began to happen. The longer Kate and Beverly were away, the slower the hours went. Thursday stretched long before finally dragging into Friday.

On Friday Matt worked out, ran errands, and fixed everything that needed fixing around his house. Did stuff for his business. Peg called and invited him to poker night at her house but Kate wouldn't be there, so he invented an excuse and turned her down. He did laundry, then watched a wussy Audrey Hepburn movie. In bed that night he lay awake staring at the ceiling when he should have been sleeping. Friday crawled into Saturday.

On Saturday he took Morty shopping. Feeling like a total idiot, he sat outside the dressing room and commented on the clothes Morty tried on. When he wracked his brain to remember why he'd agreed to help Morty pick out a new wardrobe, all he could recall was the way Kate had looked at him. Those hazel eyes pleading. He watched another extra-wussy Audrey Hepburn movie, then spent another night staring at the ceiling. Saturday clicked second by second into Sunday.

On Sunday he worked on his lawn until every leaf had been raked, every flower bed weeded, every bush trimmed, every blade of grass cut. He surfed on the computer, caught up on email. Then he kicked back on his sofa and took in hours of sports on his big screen. When he couldn't watch another minute, when the noise became unbearable, he clicked off the TV and padded into the kitchen. Matt used some of the skills Beverly had taught him and cooked his own dinner. Grilled chicken, salad, and steamed broccoli. He did a pretty decent job, except food didn't taste as good when you ate it sitting alone at your kitchen table. He cleaned up all the dishes and checked his watch. When he saw that it was only seven o'clock, something like despair plunged through him.

He took another shower, even though he didn't need one, and pulled on pajama bottoms and a T-shirt. He lay on his bed, with pillows propping up his head, the light angled just right, and his feet crossed at the ankles. He tried to read. Tried. Tried. Checked his watch. Seven thirty-four.

One athletic move and he was back on his feet. He found himself stalking through his house, impossibly restless, discontent.

What was wrong with him?

Since Beth . . . he didn't get out much. He worked, exercised, and watched sports on TV. The rest of the stops he made—the grocery store, the gas station, Home Depot—he only made when necessary.

It had been his choice to live this way. After she died, and for the years since, he hadn't felt up to being social. He hadn't had the heart or the energy to return phone calls, go to bars or restaurants, or hang with friends at their houses.

Pacing, Matt made a circuit through the kitchen, dining room, den. Kitchen, dining room, den.

He couldn't remember now though exactly why he'd isolated himself to this degree. He'd always been reserved. Concentrated. Preferring to let his play on the ice do his talking. He'd never been the laughing, kidding, life-of-the-party type. But before Beth died, he'd loved going places with her. He'd had friends. He'd been able to talk to people.

He wished he could go somewhere—anywhere—now.

But he was a freak. People made him feel uncomfortable, and he knew he made people feel uncomfortable. He was the guy whose wife had died tragically and who'd then quit his career as a professional athlete. How did a person make conversation with *that* guy? He couldn't blame them. He could hardly make conversation with himself.

He shoved his hands through his hair. To hold together what remained of his sanity back then, after Beth's funeral, he'd pushed everyone away. But the aloneness he'd grown accustomed to—*welcomed*—over the past three years now felt heavy to him. Like a burden.

He stopped before his front window, crossed his arms over his chest, and glared at the view of black woods against a dark gray sky. So what had changed?

He knew exactly what had changed.

Kate.

He'd agreed to that first dinner with her and Beverly at Chapel Bluff. Probably a mistake. But not a terrible one if he'd insisted that it be a one-time thing. That's what he should have done. Instead, like a dupe, he'd waded in up to his neck. So deep that he now found himself sucked in to the dinners and the poker nights, hauling truckloads to the Salvation Army, watching Audrey Hepburn movies, and helping someone's grandfather pick out pants. Until he couldn't spend five days by himself.

Until he was lonely without her.

Panic seized him. He couldn't be lonely without her. How long had he known her? He thought back over the calendar. He'd known Kate a month. One lousy month! He blew out a scoffing, disgusted breath.

With unswerving purpose, he walked to Beth's picture. He kept it in a silver frame, sitting on the high granite bar that ran between his kitchen and den.

There had been so many pictures in their Manhattan apartment. Framed. Hanging. Whole albums of them. He hadn't been able to bear looking at them, after. He'd put the entire contents of their home in storage when he'd moved back to Redbud. Except for this one picture.

His physical, tangible memories of Beth herself . . . the texture of her hair, the smell of her perfume, the sound of her voice . . . had grown hazy. But he knew every square inch of this one-dimensional image of her by heart.

The snapshot had been taken at their wedding. Her upper body was turned to the side, but her face was looking back, her eyes gazing directly at the camera. She was laughing with joy, her long blond hair falling down her back.

She'd been beautiful in the best all-American way. Almond-shaped eyes. Slim, sloping nose that turned up just a bit at the tip. Tall and curvy with mile-long legs. People had called her a Barbie doll, and it had annoyed him at the time. But looking back, he could understand why they'd said it. She'd been that pretty, that smooth, that perfect.

And sweet. A tenderhearted Georgia girl with a Southern accent and a genuine interest in everyone she met. She'd worked for the Leukemia and Lymphoma Society for as long as he'd known her. She'd cried at Hallmark commercials, had carried bugs outdoors on pieces of paper rather than smash them, and had wanted nothing more than to be a mother.

And this was the girl, *his girl*, who'd died of brain cancer at twenty-seven. His vision of her picture wavered as tears pooled in his eyes. He'd been missing her so long and so exclusively. How could he do this to her? How could he betray her by missing someone else?

He'd let her down in life, and now he was letting her down in death.

The old familiar waking nightmares streaked through his memory. Visions of sitting side by side in the doctor's office when they'd been given her diagnosis. Beth crying in his arms late at night, terrified and devastated. Her lying swathed in sheets and blankets. Dying.

Chills and fury raced down the back of his neck, across his shoulders, along his arms. He strode into his bedroom. Yanked off his pajama bottoms and pulled on jeans. Stuffed his feet into his Adidas. Grabbed an athletic jacket out of the closet and shoul-dered into it. He palmed his keys and garage door opener as he passed through the kitchen and banged out the back door. Five strides and he reached his garage.

He hadn't done this in months. He always drove the truck. He punched the second button on his garage door opener and stood with his legs braced apart against the cold and the night, watching as the door slotted upward, revealing his Lamborghini Murcielago.

He slid inside the low car, turned the key, and listened with satisfaction as the engine roared to life. She was black on black. Six-speed manual transmission. A vicious, beautiful tyrant of a car that suited his mood perfectly.

Matt kept his speed carefully slow as he made his way along the narrow roads leading out of town. When he reached the high-way, he eased into the fast lane, downshifted, then went streaking forward into the endless cement pathway striped with light. Fast. Faster. The rear spoiler rose, and the side mirrors folded into the body of the car. The snarling of the engine consumed his hearing.

He couldn't let himself grow attached to Kate and Beverly. For so many reasons. They were only in Redbud temporarily. Two more months at most. If he allowed himself to care about them, where would that leave him when they left? Worse off than he already was.

He couldn't afford to be any worse off. Not when he was already in such sorry shape . . . just barely functioning.

He had a job to do at Chapel Bluff. No more and no less. Just that. Just the work. For the sake of his sanity, he needed to step back from all the rest.

Matt watched with savage approval as the red needle of the speedometer climbed. Light posts whipped past. Roadside trees blurred by. The dotted yellow line on the asphalt zipped below him into infinity.

chapter eight

Life truth: Never put on makeup in dim light. The repercussions, once you got a look at yourself in daylight, could be terrifying. Stray eyebrow hairs. Foundation smears. Garish blush. Unfortunately, a second life truth about makeup was that the strong light required to do a good job of it was also an ego shredder.

It was finally Monday. Kate had finally returned from Philadelphia to Chapel Bluff and was eager to finally see Matt again. Foolishly eager.

"Foolishly," she whispered to herself. But try as she might, she couldn't seem to squelch her excitement. Like a fourteen-year-old getting ready for a school dance, she was taking extra, fastidious care with her makeup.

Kate leaned back, squinted at herself in the mirror, then leaned forward and swept on more eye shadow.

She'd thought about Matt the whole time she and Gran had been in Philadelphia. What was he doing with his time? Had he met some gorgeous socialite while they were away, taken her on a date, and instantaneously fallen in love? Was he eating well? Had his shopping expedition with Morty gone okay?

She'd even eyeballed the phone in their hotel room a couple of times, contemplating the possibility of calling him. She'd longed to call him. *Longed*. But in the month of their acquaintance, she'd never once talked to him on the phone. Their entire system of communication existed inside the sphere of Chapel Bluff. It would have been too weird, too jarring, for her to call him.

Gran had talked to Velma and Peg, however, and through them Kate had learned that Matt had declined poker night on Friday. Which had set off a whole new string of questions. Without them, did Matt have anyone to talk to? Was anyone checking on him? Was he sitting home alone?

Which was nuts! He had family. Parents who lived in Florida, and an older brother somewhere. He surely had lifelong friends. All kinds of people who cared about him, probably.

She set her makeup back in its drawer. Glanced at her reflection one last time. Face and hair were as good as they were going to be. She had on a new fitted V-neck sweater in sage green, and her most flattering pair of jeans. They planned to move the antiques from the barn into the main house today, and she didn't want to look like she was trying way too hard to be cute for a man she'd decided a thousand times was nothing more to her than a friend.

She bolstered her courage, strove for a casual air, and went in search of him. He wasn't in the bathroom he'd tiled last week, or any of the downstairs rooms. As she neared the kitchen, Gran's happy chatter floated toward her, which meant that Gran must already have Matt in her clutches. Kate knew just how she'd be feeling, pleased like a bear with a trout in its paws at having caught him.

Kate walked into the kitchen and sure enough, found Matt sitting at the breakfast table with several plates of food arranged in front of him. Gran was flitting about the room, talking and gesturing with animation.

Matt's gaze cut to Kate's.

"Hey." She smiled. "Good to see you."

"You too," he said without enthusiasm, as if he'd said it because it was the requisite response. If he'd risen at all, she'd have given him a friendly hug, but he stayed right where he was, planted in his chair. Baseball cap pulled low over his eyes. Expression solemn.

Something was wrong.

"Morning, sweetie," Gran said. "Sit, sit. When Matt showed up for work I asked him if he'd had breakfast and he hadn't, so of course I couldn't let him go to work on an empty stomach. Gave me a good reason to cook something."

Kate looked at the spread. "Wow."

"Bacon. Sausage. Eggs. Pancakes." Gran pointed at each in turn. She was wearing her jade rings and bracelets, Kate noted. The ones she liked to pair with her green Naturalizer flats. She had on her wide jean skirt and a black tunic-style shirt. The colorful beads that draped behind her neck from the sides of her glasses swung rhythmically.

"The food looks delicious," Kate said.

"Coffee?" Gran asked.

"Please."

Gran bustled to the other side of the kitchen. Kate returned her attention to Matt.

He was still looking at her. His expression was intense, but guarded. There was no shine of camaraderie there anymore.

Her chest tightened with intuition. "Study any poker while we were away?" she asked, hoping to thaw him out and bring him around.

"Nope."

"Well, good then. That Coach purse is looking more and more like a sure thing." She smiled.

He didn't smile back. Instead, he held her gaze for a few beats, then looked downward at his half-eaten food as if unsure what it was doing on his plate.

Kate glanced at Gran.

Gran gave her a troubled frown, lifted her hands and mouthed the words *I don't know.*

Kate's heart started to pound with hollow thumps. Through dint of will, she helped herself to breakfast. Her hands felt a little wobbly and her stomach started tightening. Her thoughts spun around, descending at the center like a whirlpool.

Pull yourself together! she told herself. He might just be having a bad day. "Don't the floors look great?" she asked him.

"Yeah," he said.

The single syllable was followed by uncomfortable silence.

"I think they do, too!" Gran said. "I just knew we made the right choice, to go with that honey-colored stain. It looks so nice with the paint we picked."

Gran, bless her, could fill silence with the best of them. Her voice bubbled on, like a cheery brook, lending an odd backdrop to the sadness strangling Kate's throat like a vise. She gave up the pretense of eating and just looked at Matt, who was similarly still, staring out the window.

She'd seen it happen plenty of times with traumatized kids at work. And it always broke her heart.

He'd regressed. During the five days they'd been gone, he'd retreated from them to somewhere he perceived as safer. He'd slid back to the bottom of the mountain he'd been climbing. The mountain she'd been pushing him up since the day they met.

Tears stung the back of her eyes.

He hadn't asked for and didn't want her help. He wasn't her responsibility. She was a social worker who specialized in mistreated children. She knew nothing about wounded men who still loved their dead wives. Even so, she'd been really pleased with the way their friendship had been going. It had taken a month of effort to get him to banter back and forth with her, to tease, to occasionally smile. It devastated her to see him like this again, so distant and shuttered.

She didn't know . . . she blinked a couple times to clear the moisture from her eyes . . . if she had the heart to push him up the mountain again. To start over at the bottom. Not when he could decide to slide down again at any time. Not when it hurt this much to see him slide.

She shouldn't have gone to Philadelphia. . . .

But, no. She wouldn't let herself wallow in guilt when this wasn't her fault. The men who'd refinished the floors had ordered her and Gran to leave, so they had. Their absence might have played a role in whatever was going on in Matt's mind, or it might not have. What she knew for sure was that pulling back had been his decision.

Oh, Lord. What a loss. She thought of the conversations the three of them had been having lately over dinner. The way he'd smiled at her inside his pickup truck the day they'd driven to Salvation Army. Sitting on top of a Home Depot bucket watching him work.

Matt had eased her loneliness.

Looking now at his tense profile caused that chronic loneliness, which always circled above her like a vulture, to rush in on her horribly. She didn't want to rattle around in this house with him for the next two months, neither of them talking to the other.

What was she going to do?

The only thing she could do. Pretend to act cheerful and focus on moving antiques.

Let it be said that God is kind.

Because when Kate arrived at the barn later that morning, she found Matt and two strangers already within. And one of the strangers was indisputably, in-your-face, *fine looking*.

Matt stopped work and straightened when she entered the barn, as did the other two. "Kate," he said, motioning with his hand, "this is Tyler and this is Ryan."

Ryan was a huge teddy bear of a person with a balding forehead and twinkling eyes. "Nice to meet you."

"Nice to meet you, too." He and Matt went back to work.

Tyler, the fine-looking one, approached her with a forthright grin. "Oh man, this job just got a heckuva lot better." He extended a hand, and when she placed hers in his, he enclosed it with a firm grip. After an extra long shake, he stepped back and gave a low whistle. "You're gorgeous, young lady."

"Why, thank you. You're not half-bad yourself."

An understatement. He had the whole bit going for him: Deep dimples. Squarish face. Light blue eyes. Dark blond surfer hair. One of those leather tool belts the carpenters on HGTV were so fond of. He wore baggy low-slung jeans, hiking boots, and a brown and beige collared Op shirt, the likes of which Kate hadn't seen since fifth grade. They still made those?

"Man," Tyler said, "if I'd known you were living here— It's Kate, right?"

"Right."

"I'd have been over here weeks ago working on your house for you for free. But of course my friend Matt didn't say a word about you. Obviously wanted to keep you to himself." He gave her an amused wink, and they both glanced at Matt.

Matt was staring at them. He looked like he'd swallowed a frog. Stunned and displeased.

Ha! Kate thought, with a surge of satisfaction. How terrible, very wrong, of her to feel so delighted. But, *ha! Maybe I won't bother pushing you up the mountain again, you big, dumb lump!*

"That's Matt for you," Tyler said. "A man of few words."

"Very few," Kate agreed.

"Hopefully you're a talker," Tyler said. "Ryan and I like to talk it up while we're working."

"I'm a talker."

"Well, double good, then." The dimples plunged into his cheeks. "Where are you from? You've got an accent."

"I'm from Dallas."

"I should have guessed. Have you ever been to Big D, Ryan?" he called.

"Nope," Ryan answered, poking his head out from behind an armoire.

"You need to go, man. Like eighty percent of the women there are beautiful. It's crazy! They all look like Dallas Cowboy cheerleaders."

"Sweet," said Ryan. "Of course . . . I'm married."

"Oh, right. Then don't go. It'd only bum you out." Tyler looked down at Kate with an unrepentant expression. "I can go, though."

"Single?"

"Oh yeah. You?"

"Yep."

"Excellent. Then I've got all day to twist your arm into going on a date with me."

Matt made a disgusted sound.

Tyler glanced at him. "Dude, don't embarrass me in front of the lady. I was on a roll."

"Yeah," Matt muttered, "real impressive."

Tyler gave her a comically long-suffering look. "See what I have to put up with?"

"Terrible," she said.

"Horrible." He swept his arm outward toward the massive space. "So, young lady, how would you like us to tackle this job?"

"Well, I know where in the house we want the furniture to go, if that's any help."

"Maybe you could get some of those . . . whadda'ya call 'em? Sticky notes? . . . and put them on the furniture. You could write on them telling us where you want us to take each one."

"Okay, sure."

"And you'll have to promise me that you won't try to move anything heavy yourself."

She lifted her brows.

"No way, princess. No heavy stuff for you. Wouldn't want you to strain a single pretty muscle."

Matt groaned aloud.

Despite all the good things in Kate's current reality—Gran, her work restoring Chapel Bluff, Tyler's flirting, the vacation from her job in Dallas—she found herself lying in bed that night and staring up at the ceiling while tears eased out the sides of her eyes and coasted silently down her temples.

Matt.

Infuriating man!

Now that he'd yanked his companionship away, she felt shamefully . . . bereft.

It had been awful to exist in the same house with him today, trying to act normal, struggling not to show how much his coldness hurt.

She'd attempted to ignore him, but attempting to ignore Matt was like trying to ignore a searchlight. The light might be quiet, but it blasted white color and incredible heat. That's how ridiculously aware of him she always was. Ridiculously aware and, for today anyway, inwardly churning with hostility. Because in truth, she was deeply, *deeply* irritated with him.

His wife had died. And he'd loved her so much that her death had left him devastated and broken. She got it. And yet it wasn't okay to be rude to people. Especially them! She and Gran a) were technically his employers and b) cared about him.

She heaved a sigh, then swiped away her tears with her index fingers.

A big part of her wanted to write Matt off. It would be simpler and a lot less painful. She could stop trying so hard. She could stop torturing him. She could just let him go.

But every time the idea crossed her mind, she envisioned him coming across the lawn the first day she'd met him. She'd looked into his face and seen tragedy in his eyes. She could clearly picture him, looking at her as he'd looked at her that day from under the brim of his hat, with those grave, sad eyes.

He was injured, and he needed her help. She was probably flattering herself dangerously to presume that, but she couldn't shake the idea. And as long as she felt that he needed her, she refused to give up on him. No matter how maddening he could be.

The furnace came clonking, then whirring, to life. A tree branch scratched against the roof. Through her tears, Kate contemplated the moon visible through the window.

I am weary, God. Give me your rest.

It was a breath prayer. She didn't have the emotional strength to form a long, coherent prayer at the moment. So she simply breathed in, held her breath for a few beats, and then whispered, "I am weary, God. Give me your rest," as she breathed out.

Breathe in. Silent tears. Breathe out.

I am weary, God. Give me your rest.

The next day, Kate entered heaven.

Heaven on earth in the form of an antique shop named The Plaid Attic. Not immaculate heaven, like the antique shops on Redbud's Main Street. In those stores, Kate was afraid to turn around for fear that her purse might smash something over-priced. Instead, The Plaid Attic offered a cluttered, cozy, inviting heaven.

Outside, the October day swirled with cold, but the inside of the shop welcomed her with warmth. Kate unwrapped her scarf and made her way deeper inside. She smelled brewing coffee, a citrus candle, and that familiar woody, dusty smell that always meant deliriously wonderful *old stuff.*

"I'll be out in a second" came a woman's voice from some unseen back room.

"No hurry," Kate called.

The furniture wasn't displayed bare, but neither had it been overly accessorized. A whole collection of blue stoneware pottery reclined inside a rustic bookcase. White tulips flopped out of a ceramic jug, scissors and cellophane still lying next to it on top of a mahogany sideboard. Beautifully framed sketches stood propped up on a walnut bachelor's chest. A Spiderman action figure peeked out of a bureau drawer.

Kate noticed with some admiration that the owner of the place had actually managed to paint the walls plaid. A pale blue, white, and green plaid, with ribbons of pink running through it. The colors on the walls echoed the long rectangular rug of periwinkle blue and sage green gingham.

A woman emerged from the rear of the shop wearing a bright pink fleece, jeans, and pink Crocs. "I was attempting to organize the back room. Like that'll ever happen." She rolled her eyes and smiled. "Can I help you?"

"Yes. I'm Kate Donovan."

"Theresa Kickenbach. Nice to meet you."

"Nice to meet you."

Theresa had a head full of pale blond curls that sprang upward and outward from her scalp, ending in a bouncy line just above her shoulders. Though her hair had tons of volume, it looked fine and fluffy. Like if she pulled the whole thing into a ponytail she could probably secure it with an orthodontic rubber band. Kate could see that she'd attempted to tame a section of bangs with a tiny—no bigger than an M&M—yellow clippie.

"A gentleman at one of the other antique shops told me where to find you," Kate said. The Plaid Attic was two streets off Main, tucked into a quiet block. "He said you're an antiques appraiser."

"I am—I was . . . No, I *am*, I just don't do many anymore. Come in, come in." Kate followed her to the back, where an Arts and Crafts table served as a desk. "Here . . ." Theresa cleared a stack of magazines, mail, and files from the wing back that faced the table. "Have a seat."

"Thanks."

Theresa bustled around the opposite side and settled on a rolling desk chair. Behind her, an enormous cork bulletin board bristled with photos, Post-it notes, and children's art.

"Are you from here?" Theresa asked.

"I'm from Dallas, actually. I'm here with my grandmother for three months to renovate Chapel Bluff."

"Oh, sure." Realization lit her gray eyes. "I came to your garage sale."

"You did?"

"Yep, and I bought a few things for some clients of mine to add to their collections. So if you're looking for an appraiser, dare I hope that means that you'd like me to come and appraise Chapel Bluff's antiques?"

"Exactly."

She rubbed her hands together. "What do you have? Furniture? Art? Collectibles?"

"All of the above."

"Mmm. I'd *love* to get a look at everything."

Just then the bell above the door jingled merrily, admitting two women.

"Excuse me a minute?"

"Sure," Kate said.

Kate relaxed into the chair and sighed. Matt had been just as cold toward her this morning as he'd been yesterday, and it felt like a vacation to get away from him and Chapel Bluff for a few hours. If she could drink this place in—like a steaming cup of hot chocolate with whipped cream and sprinkles on top—she would.

Kate glanced over and saw one of the women gesture to the Spiderman action figure in the bureau drawer. "Do you have children?"

"I do," Theresa answered. "A daughter who's seven and a son who's four." She made a wry expression, plucked Spiderman out of the bureau drawer, and shut it with her knee.

Theresa spoke with the customer for a few more minutes, then returned to her desk chair, which squeaked when she sat. She held up Spiderman. "Jack's been looking everywhere for this."

She tossed him into an enormous purse already overflowing with odds and ends. "You don't have kids, do you?"

"No."

"Thank goodness!"

Kate tilted her head. "Thank goodness?"

"You're so thin. If you were that thin *and* a mother, I was going to have to shoot myself."

Kate laughed.

"No, really. You wouldn't believe how many women get pregnant, have babies, and come through it all looking like high school cheerleaders. It's appalling!"

"Appalling."

"I mean, I've tried to lose weight," she said, indicating her chest and wide hips, "but my body isn't budging. And on that note—" Theresa reached under some papers, extracted two Hershey's kisses, and extended them to Kate—"care for some chocolate?"

"Sure." Kate grinned and took one.

"You look too young to have kids anyway," Theresa commented. "I'm forty. *Forty!* That's so depressing. Here. More chocolate." She pushed two more kisses across the desk.

"Thanks."

"So tell me about Chapel Bluff and why you're interested in hiring an appraiser."

"Well, when we were clearing out the second story of the barn, we discovered all these incredible antiques. My grandmother thinks they've been stored there since the fifties."

Theresa nodded.

"We need someone to come and appraise it all so we can get it insured."

"Gotcha. Are the items still in the barn?"

"We just started moving them into the house yesterday."

"What makes you think the things you've found are valuable enough to require insuring?"

"Well, I'm not sure, but I think we might have a Windsor chair, a Federal sideboard, a Chippendale desk, some Hudson River School paintings, and a table that might, just might, be a Stickley."

Theresa regarded her with round eyes for five full seconds. "Wow."

"I know."

"You've been doing your research," Theresa said.

"I'm crazy about antiques. I'm strictly an amateur, but they've been a hobby of mine for years."

"It's official then, we're going to be friends. You're here temporarily?"

"Until mid-December."

"Perfect. That's just enough time for me to fall in love with you and be left brokenhearted when you leave." Theresa shot her a mock grimace, then extracted a file and began paging through it. "I worked for Sotheby's in the city once. Can you believe it? That was a hundred years ago, before my daughter was born, before we moved to Redbud. I'm an Accredited Senior Appraiser, shockingly, and the documentation is in here somewhere. Hmm." More distracted flipping. "At least I thought it was . . ."

"That's all right, I believe you."

"Well, look me up online and verify my credentials." She closed the file and set it aside. "I only work when my son's at preschool. But I really enjoy this shop and appraising, and as I tell Doug— that's my husband—even though I don't work lots of hours or make much money, this job is worth the price of my sanity. Sanity, you understand, is in short supply when you're the mother of young children."

"I'm all for sanity."

"I'm afraid, though, because of my hours, that as an appraiser I'm going to be slow."

"Are there any other Accredited Senior Appraisers in town?" A smile tugged at Kate's lips.

"No."

"Then I guess I'll put up with you."

"Good." Theresa tilted back her chair, looking satisfied. "I can hopefully pull in the grandparents to help with the kids, and there's a lady in town who can work some hours for me here."

"Perfect."

"Perfect!"

"When can you start?"

Who would have guessed that Tyler was some kind of idiotic, annoying Don Juan?

Not Matt, that's for sure. He'd worked with Tyler on and off for over a year. He was a good electrician, and Matt had called him in on several of his jobs. On those other occasions Tyler had been punctual, easygoing, and hardworking. But Matt would never have booked him for this job if he'd known the guy was such a pathetic wannabe ladies' man.

He, Tyler, and Ryan had been hauling furniture into Chapel Bluff for two and a half days. And for almost every minute of every hour Matt had had to listen to Tyler prattle on and on and on to Kate. Constant jokes, constant compliments, constant mindless chatter. All of it obviously superficial, like grease smeared on top of a window. But, astonishingly, Kate seemed to be buying it. Smart, quick-witted Kate—who he'd thought had a good head on her shoulders—was actually buying Tyler's shtick. And not just buying it. Lapping it up.

Matt had made an art these past few years out of letting talk swirl around him, circling, but not touching him. But *their* talk, he couldn't seem to tune out.

At this point Matt would have been happy—thrilled—to get in his truck and drive for days to escape having to hear another word between Tyler and Kate. To distract himself he started making a mental list of all the ways he could leave Chapel Bluff.

He could go by train. Plane. Motorcycle.

Last night Beverly had invited all three of them—him, Ryan, and Tyler—to stay for dinner. Matt had refused. Ryan had likewise refused because his wife had dinner waiting for him at home. Tyler had leapt at the chance.

Matt had been the one who'd decided to put distance between himself, Kate, and Beverly. Even so, it rankled that Tyler had slipped right into his empty spot at the dinner table. That Kate had found someone so much more charming than him to talk to. That Kate seemed so delighted to turn her back on him.

He could leave by four-wheeler. Mountain bike. Skateboard.

"You're a design genius, young lady," Tyler said to Kate. "That's a perfect place for that sideboard."

"Why, thank you," Kate replied.

Matt ground his teeth and imagined leaving by Greyhound bus. He'd even have settled for horse.

Hot-air balloon.

Donkey cart.

chapter nine

Never underestimate the effect of outrageous flattery on the ego. Because the effect of it, really, cannot be overstated.

The things Tyler said to Kate! Coming from anyone sleazy, they'd have been a huge turnoff. But coming from him, with his irrepressible good humor and dancing blue eyes, the words soaked in like moisturizing lotion on dry, scaly skin. Perfectly welcome.

Near lunchtime on Thursday, Velma strode through the front door of Chapel Bluff wearing a knee-length sweater knit with pink, purple, and black zigzags, black cotton stirrup pants, and her spotless white Reeboks. She stood in the front room watching, eyes sharp behind the lenses of her glasses, as Matt and Tyler carried a rosewood desk past her. "Two hotties!" she declared. Her gaze sought, and found, Kate's. "When did this happen?"

"Tyler came Monday," Kate answered.

"Good gracious, Kate, I hope you're planning on taking advantage of this situation."

"I . . ."

"Who're you?" Velma demanded of Tyler.

"I'm Tyler Vanzandt. A pleasure to meet you, ma'am."

Matt tugged the other end of the desk up the hallway, pulling Tyler from view.

Velma stared after them for a few beats, then turned and motioned for Kate to follow her toward the kitchen. "This is a good opportunity for you, Kate."

"How so?"

"Don't be dense. To find yourself a husband, of course."

"Of course."

"You may not get many more chances."

Happy thought for the day. Wish she had that one on a plaque. "I'm doing okay."

They reached the kitchen and Velma came to a halt. "Where's Beverly?"

"At the grocery store."

Velma's lips twitched into a frown. "I was thinking she'd have something good going for lunch. Thought I'd stop by for a taste."

"Sorry. I can offer you a sandwich."

Velma considered her diminished options. At length, she gave Kate one of her queenly head tilts of concession. "That'll be fine."

Kate got out all the fixings for deli turkey sandwiches. Velma helped herself to an ice-cold Tab soda, which Gran kept stocked for her. Until coming to Chapel Bluff, Kate would have guessed that they'd ceased production of Tab back in 1984.

Kate started putting the sandwiches together. "I'm glad you're here." Which was a slight overstatement. "I wanted to talk to you about Morty."

"What about him?"

"I haven't seen him since I got back in town, but I understand he went shopping with Matt. Have you seen him in his new clothing?"

"I have."

"And?"

"To be frank . . ."

Kate braced herself.

132

"I like the new clothes. They're an improvement."

Genuine relief flushed through Kate.

"Except," Velma continued, "I haven't seen a Tommy Bermuda shirt."

"No, I bought him one in Philadelphia, but I haven't had a chance to get it to him yet. So. About going on a date with Morty—"

"I'm going to reserve judgment until I see him in the shirt."

Kate rolled her lips inward and bit them to keep from saying something she'd regret. She added pita chips to their plates and carried them over to the table. From the fridge she grabbed a container of hummus and placed it between them.

"What's this?" Velma asked.

"It's hummus."

"Which is . . . ?" She picked up a pita chip, surveyed it critically, then nudged a swirl of hummus with it.

"Ground-up chickpeas."

"Chickpeas!"

"Right."

Velma wrinkled her nose but took a bite. The pita chip crunched loudly inside her mouth. She looked faintly disgruntled. Swallowed. Then let out a grudging "Hmm."

They ate in silence for a few minutes. "You know," Velma said, narrowing her eyes, "in order to catch a husband, I think you're going to need to wear more makeup."

Kate slowly lowered her sandwich, fisted her napkin, and met Velma's gaze head on. "You haven't wanted a husband in all these years. Why are you so interested in finding me one?"

"Why are *you* interested in finding *me* one?" Velma shot back.

"I just want you to go on a date with Morty!"

"Well, I'd be satisfied to get you out on a date, too. Either with Matt Jarreau or that Van whatever-his-name-was person. Good gracious, Kate! If you don't make a move on one of those men, I might have to take matters into my own hands."

"Take matters into your own hands?"

"Well, if you insist on standing around doing nothing, I'll arrange things for you with one or both of them myself."

Kate nearly passed out at the thought. "No. Velma, let's be clear on this: I do *not* want you to set me up with either of them." She could withstand a lot of embarrassment, but she didn't think she could survive Velma Armstrong as her romantic representative.

"Might want to rethink that. I'm a good matchmaker. What do they call them in the Jewish culture? A yenta? I'm a yenta."

Kate wasn't so sure Velma had that definition right. Didn't *yenta* mean a gossipy busybody? "No, thank you. I don't want a matchmaker."

Velma's gaze didn't flicker from Kate's. "Then take this free advice: More makeup, Kate. And you need more jewelry, too." She indicated her own rings, which decorated even her pointer fingers and thumbs. "Men like a little flash."

Kate could only stare.

"I'll just say one more thing."

Kate winced, waited.

"At that Victoria Secrets they've got some of those push-up bras. A really tight one, a really high one, might do you a world of good."

Thankfully the second female visitor of the day didn't come in advocacy of the push-up bra. Theresa came sheerly for the love of antiques.

Kate spent forty-five minutes with her looking over, admiring, and discussing the newly placed furniture and artwork. For days, Kate had been considering where to put what. With just a few exceptions, she was thrilled with how everything looked in the spots she'd picked. They still needed couches, armchairs, rugs, lamps, and a couple of coffee tables. But with the fresh paint, the shiny floors, and the wonderful old furniture standing sentinel in every room—the house had taken a radical turn for the better. It was becoming what it had been meant to become: a graceful, tasteful, impeccably restored, and well-loved country house.

She and Theresa completed their tour in the dining room, gazing appreciatively at the Queen Anne table and chairs.

"Just look," Theresa murmured, "at those cabriole legs and the pad feet. I could just die!"

"I know!"

Theresa slid her hand across the top of the nearest chair's back. "A scrolling crest rail." Then she indicated the carved piece of wood that ran straight up the back of the chair. "Do you know what this is called?" As they'd gone along, Theresa had begun to quiz Kate, clearly pleased by her newfound client's knowledge of antiques.

"I've no idea."

"This, my friend, is a vase-shaped splat."

The sound of approaching footsteps came from the front room and they both looked up as Matt filled the doorway. He was a recipe for heartbreak: powerful body, worn-in jeans, a pale blue long-sleeved Under Armour shirt, and his ball cap pulled low.

He stopped when he saw them. "Excuse me." He dipped his chin slightly and made to continue by on his way to the kitchen.

"Matt," Kate said, holding him up, "this is Theresa. She's going to be appraising all the antiques for Gran and me. Theresa, this is Matt Jarreau. He's restoring Chapel Bluff."

A scalding blush burst to life on Theresa's cheeks, then rolled across the rest of her face. Lamely, she lifted a hand in a kind of half wave. "Hi."

"Nice to meet you," Matt said.

"You too," Theresa answered.

Awkward silence. "Staying for dinner tonight?" Kate asked Matt.

"Can't tonight." He moved toward the kitchen. Kate hated the stilted way he talked to her now, as if every word had been gouged out by a knife. He ducked out of the room.

They both listened as he said good-bye to Gran, who was clanging around in the kitchen preparing high tea, then exited out the back door.

"Kate!" Theresa hissed. "You didn't tell me that Matt Jarreau was working here."

"Was I supposed to have told you?"

"Of course! That's *Matt Jarreau*." She pointed emphatically toward the door he'd left through.

Kate nodded, smiling. "I know."

"Matt Jarreau, for heaven's sake." Her gray eyes rounded. "I have a crush on him. Doug and I joke about it. I've told him that if Matt Jarreau ever asked me to run away with him, I'd be out the door in a heartbeat. And Doug always agrees that yes indeed, if Matt Jarreau ever wants to run away with me, then I'll have his blessing."

"Oh."

"You definitely should have warned me!"

"I'm sorry!"

"I didn't know what to say to him! Am I blushing?"

"Just a little."

Theresa groaned. "I always blush when I'm embarrassed."

"It's almost all gone now."

"Do you have any idea how lucky you are? It's very difficult to run into Matt Jarreau around this town. Since he moved back to

Redbud, I've only seen him a handful of times. Twice I got super lucky and spotted him at the grocery store. . . . Oh no! Look at what I'm wearing."

Theresa had on a gray sweat suit sprinkled with black dog hair along the outside of one leg, a lavender shirt with an overstretched neck hole, and running shoes of medium age. Her curls shot out from her head in seventeen different directions. "How mortifying."

"You look adorable," Kate said, meaning it.

Gran breezed into the room carrying a glazed buttermilk cake.

"I'm going to dress up next time I come, Beverly," Theresa said.

Gran set down the plate. Blinking in confusion, she asked, "On my account?"

"When Kate called to tell me the antiques were in, I just couldn't resist. I had to run by for a quick peek. But next time, when I come to begin the appraisal, I'm going to be looking *très* professional."

"Oh goodness, no," Gran answered. "Just wear whatever you're comfortable in."

"Well . . ." Theresa glanced at Kate. "Maybe I'll go for business casual then, if Matt Jarreau is going to be around, so that I'll look marginally impressive. Will I have a chance to redeem myself with him?"

"Yeah," Kate said. "He'll be around." *Whether he'll be worth talking to is another matter.*

"Is he wonderful?" Theresa looked back and forth between them. "He is, isn't he?"

"He's wonderful," Gran assured her. "A darling, darling boy. So smart and handsome and kind."

Handsome, yes. Smart? Fine. But kind? That wonderful, darling boy isn't even being civil at present.

"He's quiet and reclusive, right? That's what I hear." Theresa sighed dreamily. "I love that whole dark, intense, brooding thing."

This conversation was beginning to annoy Kate. Why was everyone so eager to adore Matt in sunshine or rain, good behavior or bad, happy mood or grouchy?

"Can you join us for tea, Theresa?" Gran asked.

"I wish," Theresa moaned. "I love to ruin my appetite for dinner."

Gran laughed. "A girl after my own heart."

"But I have to go," Theresa said. "I dropped my kids off at my neighbor's, which means I'll have to pay her back by watching her two hyperactive children. This visit's already going to cost me." She patted her pockets, started looking around for her purse. "Next time, I'll definitely stay for tea, and then you'll have to give me an opportunity to return the hospitality." She located her purse, slung it over her shoulder, and straightened. "Halloween's less than a week away. Do you have plans?"

Kate shook her head.

"Then come and spend it with us. My house will be a mess and I'm sure the whole evening will be complete chaos, but I can promise you candy corn."

"Candy corn?" Gran asked delightedly.

"Candy corn," Theresa confirmed.

"We'll be there," Kate said.

Tyler Of The Charm And Cute Surfer Hair had finished his official duties at Chapel Bluff, but stopped back by on Friday morning to ask Kate out.

Kate was upstairs, painstakingly cleaning the inside of a hope chest when he found her. The whole time he was leaning against the bedpost putting in a respectable amount of small talk, the whole time she was wiping down the chest and chatting back, she knew exactly what he was working up to. And she felt . . . fine about it.

Tyler was seriously appealing. But for whatever reason, she didn't have, in her heart of hearts, that mysterious something for him. That something that gave you goose bumps. That made your heart pound when the phone rang. That made you stare at the other person's lips. She liked to affectionately call that something *hormones*. Bummer of bummers, she didn't have hormones for Tyler.

Yet.

Hormones were usually either there from the beginning or not at all. But sometimes, *sometimes*, they came on gradually. So a single girl of any age and experience ought to know better than to turn down a date with an attractive guy strictly based on lack of hormones.

What they did have—she and Tyler—was great rapport. It would be a cinch to talk to him for hours. Isn't that how all the epic marriage-making romances of her friends had begun? With those four pivotal words? *We talked for hours.*

"So, Kate," he said with his dimpled smile. "I'd love to take you to dinner. Any chance I can convince you to go with me sometime?"

Attractiveness + Rapport = Affirmative Answer. "Sure. I'd like to."

He looked surprised and pleased, though she was quite sure that 99.9 percent of the women he asked out agreed. "Great," he said. "I'm going out of town tomorrow on this camping thing with friends and won't get back until Monday. How about Tuesday night?"

"Sounds good."

———

Matt froze when he overheard Tyler and Kate talking. He'd been walking along the upstairs hallway on his way to the stairs when he'd heard their voices. Tyler was asking her out and she was accepting.

In utter silence, he leaned against the hallway wall. A bolt of possessiveness, the fiercest emotion he'd felt in years, stabbed through him. *Mine*, he thought, shocked by his own reaction. Kate was his. *His.*

Wrong. Yet his instincts were screaming at him to do something, to intervene. He wanted Kate to himself. He wanted her to be . . . What?

What she'd been to him before. His friend.

Right, Matt. Then why do you care who she dates?

He held himself immobile, trying to get his feelings under control. His breath rasped tight in his throat.

He'd known since Monday morning that this would happen. He'd been prepared for it. Then Tyler had finished work at Chapel Bluff and left. Matt had been embarrassingly relieved, thinking that maybe he'd been wrong. That Tyler hadn't planned, after all, to take their flirting to the next level.

Silently, Matt forced his body away from the wall and down the hallway back in the direction he'd come so they wouldn't see him. He must be losing his mind, he thought, with a shaft of real fear. Because all he could think was *mine.*

Mine!

chapter ten

"I'm sorry, Beverly. I can't stay."

"You have to! It's Friday. It's poker night! Look, I'm making all your favorites."

Kate arrived in the kitchen in time to see Matt poised near the back door and Gran positioned near the counter, pointing out all the food she had going.

"Lasagna," Gran said. "I've been simmering the meat sauce all afternoon. Big salad. Bread—I'll have it crispy, the way you like it. And the pièce de résistance—cheesecake with a layer of chocolate ganache on top." Gran smiled winningly at Matt. She looked so cute, wearing her apron, a wooden spoon clutched in one hand, and her white pixie hair.

Matt pursed his lips and shifted uncomfortably. He had on an old beige ball cap, frayed at the bill, and Kate's favorite plaid flannel in shades of green. Though the clothes were painfully familiar, the Matt of this week had made himself a stranger. He'd been especially surly today, worse than all the other days this week. Gran had taken Kate aside three times already to worry, fuss, and cluck over him in private.

"You have to stay," Gran said, her confident expression beginning to waver. "We host poker night at Chapel Bluff just so you'll come."

Kate tensed, waiting for Matt's answer. He hadn't joined them for dinner all week, but surely he'd relent tonight. He wouldn't disappoint Gran when she'd gone so far out of her way for him. Would he?

"I can't do the dinners anymore," he said flatly. "Look, I . . . I don't want to impose on you." He reached for his brown leather coat and started shoving his arms into it.

Gran watched him, her expression crestfallen and confused.

Kate's heart thudded dully. He was going to walk away.

"But we love having you," Gran answered. "You're not an imposition."

He stilled, his fingers on the doorknob, his gaze fixed on the floor. "I apologize."

Gran tilted her head to the side, beseeching. "Matt."

"You . . . you've been great. It's nothing to do with you. It's . . ." He shook his head, seeming frustrated with the inadequacy of his words. "Don't trouble with me. And please don't count on me for any more dinners. I just can't."

He shouldered out the door and closed it behind him.

In the ominous quiet of the kitchen Kate could hear the sauce bubbling, the wall clock ticking.

She was suddenly, stunningly furious. With a growl of frustration, she went after him.

"Are you going to talk to him?" Gran asked anxiously.

"Among other things."

"Be gentle, he's—"

But Kate was already out the door and striding hard after him. Gentle? *Gentle?* She was going to kill him.

He was almost to his truck, silhouetted against the gold air of approaching sunset. "What was that?" Kate called after him.

He kept walking.

She closed the distance between them, pulse throbbing hard, breath coming fast. "What was that back there?"

He gripped his truck's door handle. Turned to glare at her.

"Gran made that entire meal for you, and you don't have the courtesy to stay and eat it? Is that really too much to ask?"

"Like I said. I can't do the dinners anymore."

"Why?" She planted her fists on her hips.

He held her gaze for a long, taut moment. "I just can't."

"What? No more explanation than that?"

"Back off, Kate."

His snapping dark eyes warned her to let it drop. But the anger in her rose to meet his warning, then surpass it recklessly. "You know what? No. I've tried backing off all week and it's not working. In fact, it only seems to be making things worse."

With icy silence he opened the truck's door and moved to get in.

"Don't you dare get in that car," Kate snarled. "Don't you dare."

He angled his face downward, holding himself with unnatural stillness, as if trying to overpower his temper. She watched his chest rise and fall.

Kate wanted to shake him, hurt him, scream at him. *Come on*, she thought. *Come on! Confront me. Fight with me!*

Without sparing her so much as a glance, he slammed the truck door and set off across the meadow toward the forest.

She followed, behind and beside him. "Would you just tell me what's going on with you?" she demanded. "Could you do me that favor at least?"

He kept on as if he hadn't heard her question. A continual wall, shutting her out. She'd managed to bear five days of him shutting her out, and she might have been able to put up with more of his bull if it had been solely directed at herself. But Gran? Who'd only ever adored him? Just the thought of Gran's heartbroken expression back in the kitchen made her want to launch herself at his back and strangle him. "Do you think this is the best way to go about your grief, Matt? Forcing everyone away to protect yourself?"

She stopped, tired of keeping up with him. But he didn't slow, so she groaned and went after him again. "This recovery plan working out for you?" she called loudly.

"None of your business."

She could tell that he was furious, and perversely, she was glad.

When they reached the line of trees that marked the woods, he finally slowed. He passed under the outermost branches of a wide elm, then stopped, covered in a blanket of shade. He presented her with his back and stared angrily away from her into the coming darkness of the forest.

Kate gauged him, moving to the side so she could see his profile, the way the muscles in his jaw were working, the tense line of his shoulders.

She looked down at her ballet flats and shifted her weight, causing the carpet of grass and pebbles to crunch underfoot. She waited for him to speak.

Nothing. Still no words.

The trees swished with the wind. She needed to calm down, to say the right thing. But what *was* the right thing to say to him? She had no idea. She could clearly sense the shield he'd put up between him and her, between him and the world. She could scream with the frustration of coming up against it again and again and again! "Does it make you feel better to keep people at arm's length?" she finally asked.

"Kate, just leave me alone." He reached out and gripped a nearby branch so hard his fingers whitened. "Seriously, just go."

She flinched and crossed her arms hard across her chest to

protect herself. He couldn't stand her. He didn't want her any-where near him. The shreds of pride she had left demanded that she turn and stomp back to the house. And yet . . .

"*Go*," he said.

"No." Her brows lowered with implacable determination. "Have your family and friends been content to leave it at that? Did they all run off when you told them to go?"

The defensive cast of his profile answered the question.

"Shame on them," she whispered.

"Because they respected my privacy?" he asked with disbelief, looking across at her. His gaze seared her.

"Maybe they respected your privacy too much. I'm not going to be content with that."

He dropped his hand from the tree branch and turned to face her fully. "Why are you even bothering with me, Kate?"

"Because up until Monday morning I thought we were friends. I liked our friendship. I liked you."

"Past tense."

"I don't know yet. I'm still deciding."

He pulled off his cap and shoved his fingers through his dark hair once, then twice, leaving it in messy disarray.

"Look, here's the deal," she said. "The way you've acted this week has been hard on me and Gran. I can't let you go on treating us like that when we don't deserve it."

He frowned.

"You want to tell me what happened while we were in Phila-delphia that made you pull away?"

"No."

"Well, I'm not a mind reader, but since you're not talking I'm going to take a guess."

A vertical groove formed between his brows.

"We left," Kate said, "and during the time we were gone something happened that made you start wondering why you were wasting your time making friends with a grandmother and her annoying granddaughter from Dallas. I mean, we're only here temporarily. We're maybe more trouble than we're worth. And after what happened with your wife, you'd rather not get attached to anyone ever again. . . . How'm I doing?"

He held her gaze, silent.

"You know, Gran lost her spouse, too." Kate bit her lower lip, an unexpected rush of emotion for her grandad cinching her throat. "My grandad was this wonderful, wonderful man. He was a pediatrician. Gran's mentioned him to you, right?"

He nodded.

"He was so sweet and scholarly. He always wore these"—she motioned vaguely toward her chest—"vests that buttoned down the front and tweed blazers with, you know, those oval patches on the elbows. He and Gran adored each other. They had such a good marriage. They'd been married fifty-four years when he died."

He waited, listening.

"I guess I'm telling you about Grandad to remind you that you're not alone. That other people have suffered through the loss of a spouse. Some of them, like Gran, have still managed to find joy in their lives afterward."

"Beverly's a better person than I am."

"No, she's not. She's great, but so are you."

He didn't reply.

"I think . . ." Kate started, lost her nerve, and started again. "I think that God has blessings He wants to give you but can't until you let Him."

"I'm not going there with you. I'm not going to talk about *God* in all of this."

"Okay."

He worked the brim of his ball cap between his hands, bending it, then finally putting it on his head backward.

"What *can* you talk about with me?" she asked.

"Nothing more tonight. And that's the truth, so stop pushing."

She opened her mouth to argue . . . then thought better of it.

"I'll go back to the house," he said, "and eat dinner."

"Good. Thank you."

"But I'm not promising anything else." He looked her dead in the eyes. "I need you to back off."

"I . . ."

He was standing there, waiting for her to agree, but for the first time since she'd met him, she had no words. Her limbs suddenly felt heavy and cold. The temperature of the air whistled chill across her skin.

He blew out a frustrated breath, then motioned for her to go ahead of him back to the house. Kate started forward, and he followed silently behind her.

Now that her anger had deflated, she was slightly embarrassed by how she'd acted. Why did she have to be so blasted persistent? When she'd been growing up, her mom had often shaken her head at Kate's determination and murmured, "Like a dog with a bone."

That's clearly how Matt viewed her, and why wouldn't he? Anyone with an ounce of dignity would have left him alone when he'd asked. But she hadn't been able to quit because she cared and because her instincts had told her that she needed to press. If she didn't, who else was going to? And if no one else was going to, then how was he ever going to open up to anyone again?

They walked on. The sun had bumped below the line of the horizon, casting palest pink against the undersides of the clouds.

147

Kate could see by the cars parked in the distant driveway that everyone except Morty had already arrived.

When they entered through the kitchen, the seniors greeted their return with exactly what they didn't need—rabid curiosity.

"Matt can stay for dinner after all," Kate told Gran.

"Excellent!"

Kate and Matt went to work setting the table, Kate's mind full of the things they'd just said to each other. When Morty arrived, it took her a few seconds to realize he was wearing the Tommy Bahama shirt.

The shirt's beige, peach, and ivory palm fronds scrolled down each side of his chest. The cut emphasized his broad shoulders, the peach looked terrific against his glinting silver hair, and the collared neck and short sleeves gave him a confident, casual air. He could have been someone's wealthy, distinguished, Hawaii-loving uncle.

The shirt had cost 120 dollars, a sum that must have struck Morty as exorbitant, even though he hadn't batted an eye when he'd reimbursed her.

Everyone buffeted Morty with compliments as soon as he walked in. Kate looked to Velma, who was assessing Morty from head to toe. At first it looked like Velma's verdict could go either way, but gradually her expression settled into lines of approval.

Kate and Morty had scored a potent hit in the game of Battleship for Velma's heart.

Over dinner, conversation and iced tea flowed easily around the Queen Anne dining table. Matt, sitting diagonally across from Kate, was subdued but managed to answer questions politely. When he begged off from poker after helping load the dishwasher, no one hassled him, least of all Kate.

From the kitchen window she watched him walk across the

dark yard toward his truck. His posture and pace reminded her of a convict escaping from prison.

If she hadn't been surrounded by a roomful of observant eyes, she might have succumbed to peppermint taffies and tears. She'd said everything she could think to say to him outside under the big tree. He'd grudgingly agreed to eat Gran's dinner tonight. But beyond that, about all the stuff that really mattered, she couldn't help but feel she'd failed.

He was about to do some serious drinking.

Matt rummaged around in the back of his pantry, hunting for a bottle of Jack Daniels—something he never drank—and a couple cans of Coke—something else he never drank. After dropping a bag of corn chips, spilling the flour, and knocking over a whole row of spices, he located what he was after.

Back in the kitchen, he filled a tall glass with ice and sat himself, the Jack, and the Coke at the kitchen table. He hadn't bothered to turn on any lights except for the one suspended over the table, so the rest of the house remained dark.

This was *such* a bad idea.

He went to work pouring a medium amount of Coke and a huge amount of whiskey into his glass.

Drinking alcohol and competing at peak physical ability didn't go together. He'd been an athlete since, what? Eight? So he'd drunk precious little in his life.

Tonight was about to be an exception. Because, unfortunately, the fact that this was a bad idea suited him at the moment. He wanted to be self-destructive, and he sure as anything couldn't get drunk at one of the town's bars. The entire population of Redbud would know about it by noon tomorrow.

Matt didn't even wait for the ice to make the liquid cold. He just started right in, drinking deeply. Then he sat back in his chair, rested his forearms on the table, and stared blindly at the wall, waiting for it to take effect.

"Do you think this is the best way to go about your grief, Matt? This recovery plan working out for you?"

He looked determinedly away from the wall, as if by doing so he could avoid Kate's words.

He usually came home from the gym after exhausting himself physically and then occupied his mind with TV or the computer until bed so he wouldn't have to think. It was awful uncomfortable to just sit here with his thoughts. He hated his thoughts. Yet he didn't want to watch sports or turn on the computer tonight. He wanted to make himself face his own sorry company.

"Maybe they respected your privacy too much. I'm not going to be content with that."

He took some more pulls on his drink. Ever since Beth died, all his friends and family had bent over backwards to be nice to him, to avoid confronting or upsetting him, to protect him. Even before Beth. He'd been a professional athlete. Nothing but supporters had surrounded him. He could hardly remember a time when people hadn't agreed with him.

Kate had mightily disagreed with him tonight.

He'd thought he'd hated how carefully everyone treated him. But look at him now. One woman had called him out and it had knocked him flat. What's worse, he had a sinking feeling that he'd deserved everything she'd said. Merely remembering the angry way she'd looked at him caused his muscles to contract, tensing up. His heart started to beat loud and painfully. Fear reactions. Because she scared him.

He was afraid she could already see too much and that she'd keep coming at him, demanding more from him than he could give. He was afraid that she would fall in love with Tyler. He was afraid that he'd be desolate without her when she left.

He didn't know what to do. What could he do about her? He felt trapped, like an animal tied to a stake in broad daylight.

He frowned at his empty glass. Without bothering to refresh the ice, he poured more Jack, more Coke. If he could, he'd gladly pay Beverly twice what she was paying him, just to let him quit. Some other poor sucker could finish the house.

Except that in his life, he'd only broken one commitment. He'd broken his contract with the Barons when he'd left the team after Beth's death. Afterward, he'd promised himself that he'd never break a commitment again.

How much longer would the work take? Six weeks? The thought filled him with two kinds of panic. Panic because that was such a long time to protect himself from Kate. Panic because that was such a short time before she'd be gone for good and he'd be completely alone again.

"After what happened with your wife, you'd rather not get attached to anyone ever again."

Well, too late, buddy. Because despite his terror of it, his determination to do the opposite, he'd gone and gotten attached to her anyway.

She was like sunshine. When she was near, the ice inside of him eased. She made him feel warmer, more comfortable, almost whole. Even these past few days when they hadn't been talking, he'd felt it and it drew him undeniably.

When she left, where would he be? He didn't think he could handle any more disappointments.

Really? he asked himself with disgust. *After losing your wife* to brain cancer, you'd think you'd be able to withstand a few small disappointments.

But instead he felt fragile. Like with one misstep, he'd crack.

Maybe he could keep a simple friendship with her going without letting her any further inside his head than she already was. Maybe she'd be satisfied with that. Maybe he could manage not to feel sick to his stomach when Tyler came by to flirt with her.

Right. *Right.*

He drained half his glass.

"I think that God has blessings He wants to give you but can't until you let Him."

She talked frequently about her church back home, and she dropped God's name into conversations as if He were a friend. But suggesting that God had blessings for him that he was refusing? No. That was going too far. He'd had faith in God once and had come away bitterly disappointed. God had nothing but heartache to offer him, and he had nothing but animosity and resentment toward God. They were pitted against each other now, and he never saw that changing.

Exhausted, he dropped his head into his hands. What was he going to do?

He couldn't care about the beautiful redhead with the big heart. And he couldn't not care.

chapter eleven

Holidays back home in Dallas had taken on a *Groundhog Day* quality for Kate in recent years. For Halloween she'd take out the same witch, wooden cat, orange wicker pumpkin, and the wreath with the funky little skeletons hanging off it. For Thanksgiving she'd take out the same pilgrims, Indian corn, caramel-colored leaf-shaped plates, and the fall wreath made of birch branches. For Christmas she'd take out the same nativity set, tree ornaments, and white lights for the bushes out front.

Kate's sister, Lauren, had married three years ago and forged new holiday routines for herself and her husband. Which left Kate—still under the holiday umbrella of her parents—celebrating Halloween and Thanksgiving and Christmas with her mom and dad in the same places, in the exact same ways, year after year.

Kate loved tradition as much as anyone. But the brain-numbing repetitiveness of it all had begun to leech away a lot of the fun.

What a tangible relief to be celebrating Halloween and Thanksgiving at Chapel Bluff this year. She and Gran hadn't brought any of their decorations with them. So, on Halloween afternoon, in a moment of Martha Stewart-inspired fervor, Kate went trudging into the woods in search of nuts, berries, and leaves to use as decorations. She found zero nuts and zero berries. There was an abundance of leaves, however, so she came home from her expedition with a bag full of those and an assortment of pinecones.

Gran, ever creative, arranged the pinecones inside a large glass hurricane on the dining table, then decided that they should make garlands out of the leaves. So Kate and Gran spent two happy hours in the den sipping hot chocolate and stringing fall leaves while gray clouds somersaulted across the sky outside. Once they'd completed their garlands, they hung them in swags across the windows in the front room, dining room, and kitchen.

Finished, they stood together admiring their artistry, feeling pleased with themselves. Especially Kate. The whole thing was so un-*Groundhog Day*!

Theresa's predictions for Halloween night at her house came true.

There was candy corn.

It was chaos.

After they'd all finished feasting on Chinese takeout, the kids rushed to the back of the house to put on their costumes. Gran and Kate helped Theresa clear the table of black and orange ghost-encrusted dinnerware. Theresa's husband, Doug, a tall, long-limbed man with a placid disposition, bundled up the trash and headed out the back door with it.

"You guys really don't have to do this," Theresa said, motioning to the dishes they were in the process of rinsing and placing in the dishwasher.

"Nonsense!" Gran replied. "You have enough to do tonight. Let us help you with this at least."

"Well, if you insist, then I'm not going to turn you down." She gave them a grateful smile. For the festivities, Theresa had dressed in jeans, a black top with a witch on the front, and a pair of black cat ears.

"Thanks for dinner," Kate said.

"You're welcome. I hope you don't mind that it wasn't home-made. I try to avoid cooking as much as is humanly possible."

"Don't say that around Gran," Kate warned. "She'll have you out at Chapel Bluff, taking cooking lessons from her whether you want to or not."

"Exactly!" Gran agreed. "You should see how much Matt has learned."

"Whoa, whoa, whoa. If Matt Jarreau's going to be at these cooking lessons, then maybe I'll consider it."

"What's my wife saying about Matt Jarreau now?" Doug asked, returning from outside.

"Beverly here gives him cooking lessons," Theresa answered, "and I was saying that if Matt's involved, then I might want to learn to cook after all."

Gran looked appalled, but Doug just shook his head, smiling softly, not threatened in the least.

"Well," Theresa said philosophically, "if he wants to run away with me, it would be good if I knew how to cook him dinner, at least."

"Mo-omm!"

Kate and Gran both started at the sound of the high-pitched wail from the other end of the house, but Theresa and Doug appeared immune to it.

"Emma is playing with my Power Ranger nunchuks!" Jack yelled.

"I'm just looking at them" came the defensive reply.

A squeal, a grunt, a shout.

"I don't want her to play with them!" Jack screeched. "She'll break 'em!"

155

"It's okay for her to look," Theresa called wearily.

"No!" Jack screamed. "She's swingin' 'em! No! Give 'em back!"

Emma said something muffled, followed by more howls from Jack.

"Oh, good grief," Theresa muttered. She stalked from the kitchen. "Excuse me, everyone, while I go and throttle my children."

The doorbell rang. Doug didn't make a move.

"Would you like me to do the honors?" Gran asked.

"Please," he said. "I believe Theresa put the bowl of candy by the door."

While Gran periodically opened the door for trick-or-treaters, Kate finished straightening the kitchen and then went to help Theresa get the kids ready.

Kate was sweating and Theresa's cat ears and patience were both askew by the time the two of them had dressed the kids, put their makeup on, arranged Emma's hair, and accomplished a frantic emergency search for Jack's treat bag. They emerged into the den with a short red Power Ranger and a Princess Leia who'd insisted on wearing five pink plastic bracelets and dangly clip-on earrings.

Theresa took lots of photos, then rooted around for flashlights. Doug, still relaxed and seemingly oblivious to the general craziness around him, escorted the kids outside onto the front walkway.

"I want to run ahead," Emma said.

"No!" Jack cried. "She got to run ahead last year and I was always last."

"We'll all go together," Theresa hollered.

"Then who gets to push the doorbells?" Emma asked, her face poised for a meltdown.

"You can take turns," Theresa answered. She finally located two mismatched flashlights. Only one had working batteries.

"Figures," she grumbled. She went and let their black lab in from the backyard, then attached his leash in the foyer while his tail beat Kate and Gran in the knees with rhythmic crushing blows.

Finally, with the dog in one hand and her flashlight in the other, Theresa swiped a curl off her forehead, then stilled to look at Kate and Gran. "Would you ladies like to come with us, or would you rather stay here and man the fort?"

"I'm happy to man the fort," Kate answered, trying not to look too eager at the prospect of a few minutes of quiet.

"Me too," Gran said.

"Okay, we'll see you in a little while then." She bustled out the door and down the porch steps. "Help yourself to candy!"

Kate and Gran stood in the open doorway, watching the four-some take a right at the sidewalk.

"My oh my," Gran breathed. "Being here reminds me of when my boys were little. Such a busy time. Such hard work."

Kate watched Power Ranger and Leia launch into a pushing, shoving sprint toward the neighbor's door. Jack tripped over his own feet and went sprawling. Kate half expected Emma to trample him in her haste to reach the first house, but instead Emma picked him up, dusted him off, and handed him the treat bag he'd dropped.

"Hard work but the best work," Kate said.

"Yes, that's true."

This family's life was rambunctious and tiring and frenzied and . . .

Perfect. It was exactly what she'd always valued and hoped to have herself.

If only I had boobs, she thought ruefully. Boobs probably would have made the difference.

Kate settled onto a corner of the couch in the den with a handful of candy corn. Theresa's comfortable and cluttered house surrounded her with a mishmash of stunning antiques and kid-worn furniture.

Gran lowered into a leather chair with a sigh. "I wonder what Matt's doing with himself tonight."

"I don't know." Matt had negotiated with Gran and they'd compromised. He would still show up for cooking lessons and dinner on Wednesdays and for poker night on Fridays. But the other nights he'd have off. She couldn't imagine him answering the door tonight and passing out candy. He was probably either spending the evening with friends or holed up in his house with the porch light off.

"I hope he's out having a good time," Gran said.

Somehow Kate couldn't picture it. She hoped he wasn't a porch-light-off person. But she worried he was exactly that. A porch-light-off person who wanted to keep it that way.

"So what do you think of those two over there?" Tyler asked Kate. They were ensconced together in a booth, surreptitiously discussing all the couples around them at the restaurant.

"Those two?" Kate asked, inclining her head toward two fifty-somethings.

"Uh-huh."

"They're not even looking at, much less speaking to, each other."

"Exactly."

"I'd say they're empty nesters who don't have anything in common now that their kids are grown and gone."

"Hard times." He looked at her with one edge of his smile hitching upward.

"Hard times," she agreed.

Tyler sure was easy on the eyes. The hip blond hair. The outdoorsy style. The blue eyes.

"What about them?" he asked, indicating a young couple gazing ravenously at each other. Kate watched as the woman squeezed the man's upper arm with her long-nailed fingers. He said something. She laughed with unprecedented gaiety. He launched into a story, gesturing emphatically.

"Hmm." Kate watched more, assessing. "Definitely not married."

"Definitely not. How long would you say they've been a couple?"

"I don't know. What would you give 'em?"

"Two weeks?"

Kate smiled. "I'm inclined to be generous. I might give them two months."

Tyler took a lazy swig of beer. "Is it going to go well for them, do you think?"

"Afraid not. He's doing all the talking. I mean, at some point in their relationship she's got to want to say *something*, right?"

"I'd think so."

"I'm guessing they'll last six, maybe eight months before she realizes that he never shuts up and he realizes that she wears too much makeup."

Tyler looked skeptical. "I've never known anyone who broke up with a girl because of her makeup."

"True. Let's see, what would be more likely?" The woman continued to cling, the man continued to talk. "He'll break up with her because she's too needy. Or because he suddenly comprehends that she's hoping to rope him into a serious relationship."

"There you go, young lady." Dimples flashing, Tyler tipped the edge of his drink toward her. "Now, *that* is more likely."

Kate snorted disparagingly. "Men."

"We've just got one couple left," he said.

"Best for last," Kate murmured. She eyed the nicely dressed couple in their forties. They were attractive and athletic looking. They talked intently, smiled at each other's quips, and enjoyed easy silences. The wife had rested her hand on the table and Kate had watched her husband cover it with his, squeeze, and hold it for long minutes. "They're the happily-ever-after couple," Kate said.

"Married?" Tyler asked.

"Oh yes. Note the wedding rings."

"It's possible they could both be married to other people."

"No way! They're married to each other and probably have been for twenty years."

"So long?"

"Yep. A couple doesn't get to that level of . . ."

"Boredom?"

"Tyler!"

"What?"

"You're terrible."

He looked pleased.

"I was going to say," she continued, "that a couple doesn't get to that level of *ease* unless they've put in some serious years."

"Ah. Ease."

"Right."

"Is that the best a person can shoot for in a long relationship?"

"It's one of the best things. Of course, there's also a small thing called undying love."

"Oh, that."

"Yes." She had to smile. "That."

Tyler's gaze caught on something behind Kate. "Here's our food," he said, watching their waitress approach with appetizers balanced on a round tray. The college-aged girl slid their plates in front of them with effortless efficiency.

"You do that so well," Tyler said to her. "You go to school to learn that?" He grinned at the girl, and she responded with a smile.

"Believe it or not," she replied, "it just comes naturally."

"Thank you so much," he said.

"You're very welcome. Can I get you anything else at the moment?"

"Kate?" Tyler asked.

"No, I'm good. Thanks."

"We're doing just fine," he said to her.

The waitress eyed Tyler appreciatively before heading back toward the kitchen.

So far tonight Tyler had used the same combination of flattery and banter that he used on Kate with: Gran, the pair of women friends he'd held the door for as they'd entered the restaurant, the hostess, and their waitress. All the women—no matter their age or situation—had responded predictably, blossoming to him like a flower to a bee.

Tyler, Master Of The First Date. Since the moment he'd arrived tonight to pick her up, Kate hadn't experienced so much as an instant of awkwardness. He hadn't tried to lunge for her door handle at the same time that she was reaching for it. He hadn't attempted to order anything for her. He hadn't left her languishing in uncomfortable silence. Even the restaurant he'd chosen—perfect first-date fodder. Just the right mixture of posh and cozy.

He was impossibly smooth. Maybe the smoothest guy she'd ever gone out with. Which begged the question: Why wasn't she falling for him?

"So what about us?" he asked. He paused over his Caesar salad, and she paused over her French onion soup.

"Us?"

"Yeah. If you had to give us an evaluation, what would you say?"

"Well, we're smiling and we're talking. Two pluses."

"And let the record show that I'm letting you handle your half of the conversation."

"Duly noted."

"So?"

"So I guess I'd say that anything's possible."

He gazed directly at her, holding her attention. "I like you, Kate."

Unsure how to reply, she turned her attention to scooping up a spoonful of soup, soft bread, and melted cheese.

"If I promise not to expect anything from you except your company, will you go out with me again?"

Ooh, he was *so* good. He'd phrased that in such a way that it would be pressure-free to accept him and witchy to decline him.

Kate glanced up at his ideal face, surrounded by the ideal surroundings of the restaurant, and wondered why in the world he wanted to date her when he could date any available woman in the county. "Sure," she said. "Sounds like fun."

chapter twelve

On poker night, Velma showed up early to begin the women-do-all-the-work-while-the-men-sit-and-watch pre-dinner thing.

Kate was alone in the kitchen snacking on Fritos when Velma arrived, bringing with her the smell of chicken spaghetti casserole. Kate quickly moved to help Velma get her two foil-covered nine-by-thirteens into the oven.

That done, Velma unzipped her jacket, revealing yet another shirt punctured with metal studs. The denim fabric had a slightly lopsided longhorn head pounded across the back and what was maybe a cowboy boot pounded through the upper right chest. Black acid-wash jeans fit snug and high around Velma's belly pooch before tapering close to the ankle and disappearing into her fringed boots.

"So," Kate said, wondering if she'd missed the memo declaring tonight rodeo night, "Morty looked great in the Tommy Bahama shirt."

"He did."

"Are you ready to go on a date with him?"

Velma reached into the Fritos bag and helped herself to a few.

"How about I let Morty know that you're willing," Kate said coaxingly. "Then he can call you and set something up."

"There's one final thing that really bothers me about that man."

163

Kate didn't show the slightest outward reaction, though inwardly her patience pulled thin. "Which is?"

"His car."

His car? "He drives what? An Oldsmobile?"

"Yes, and I hate that old-man car."

Kate gawked at her, incredulous.

"I'd understand, of course, if that were all he had. But Morty has a 1957 Cadillac convertible. Gorgeous. Black with silver trim. He bought it in the early sixties and he's had it ever since. How long ago would that be now?"

"Forty-five years? Fifty?"

"He's had a Cadillac convertible for *fifty years* and he never drives it!"

"Where is the car?"

"He keeps it in a special storage garage. He washes it and waxes it and makes sure it's running perfectly, but he never backs the thing out. Imagine!" Her penciled eyebrows drew downward with irritation.

"All right. I'll talk to him about it."

"You can tell him that Velma Armstrong is only going out on a date with him if he picks me up in the Cadillac. He shouldn't bother even *attempting* to pick me up in that shoddy Oldsmobile. Won't go well for him."

"Okay. Got it."

"Good."

Was it really possible that Velma—*Velma?*—could be this choosy? Were there so many eligible men beating down her door?

Kate tried to imagine herself requiring every prospective guy she met to undergo a hair, clothing, and car makeover before she'd date them. She'd never go out again! So how was it that this crotchety seventy-something managed it?

"I know exactly what you're thinking, Kate." Velma pushed her glasses to the top of her nose, then zeroed in on Kate with squinted eyes. "Now, listen to me and listen well. You ready?"

"Yes."

"Women who've made peace with living alone," she started, counting off one finger, "and women with healthy self-confidence . . ." She counted off a second finger, then cocked her head at Kate. "Are you getting this?"

Kate nodded. "Women who've made peace with living alone and women who have a healthy self-confidence . . ."

"Can always, *but always*, afford to be picky."

To win at poker one needed to be both good and lucky. Kate had been good tonight, but she hadn't been lucky. Matt had beaten her with a flush for a big pot. Later, William had beaten her with pocket aces. She'd had to work hard to build her short stack of chips into a respectable pile. And now, finally, she had a straight. She was about to put the hurt on Morty, William, and Matt.

"The girls," all of whom had already been put out of the game, were chatting happily together on the window seat while the serious players battled it out.

It was Morty's turn, but he appeared to be frozen in vengeful contemplation of his iced-tea glass.

"Morty?" Kate said gently.

He startled, then absently threw in a couple of chips.

Kate frowned. For some reason, Velma's stipulation that Morty liberate his Cadillac from storage, a demand that had seemed to Kate to be the easiest demand of the bunch, had thrown Morty into a tailspin. When she'd pulled him aside earlier and told him, he'd immediately gone into fight mode, the muscles in his shoulders and arms bunching up defensively. He'd spent the evening since vacillating between brooding silences and hateful stares at Velma.

It made for an awkward atmosphere not helped, of course, by Matt and the current state of her friendship with him.

Kate checked her cards again, then feigned indecision over whether or not to fold. Finally, seemingly grudgingly, she threw in some chips.

Since their fight, Matt had changed his ways. He was no longer rude and distant toward her. Now he was polite and distant instead. She talked with him, and he talked back.

He was circumspect. Careful. Respectful.

She'd decided that maybe she'd preferred his rudeness. It had seemed more . . . real. Now, no matter how hard she tried to put herself in his line of vision, he never quite met her eyes. When they'd finish a conversation, she'd be left troubled, staring at him and trying to figure out what on earth was going on inside his head. Which was of no use. She hadn't a clue. And the shield he kept firmly between them certainly wasn't going to let her find out.

Kate told herself to be satisfied. He was giving them as much of himself as he could.

So why did her chest ache every time she looked at him?

She glanced across the table and caught him staring at her. He instantly averted his gaze.

Strange. Kate tilted her head, studying him.

The hand he'd rested on top of his cards tightened into a fist until she could see the veins standing out.

William played. Matt played. Still, she watched him, stubbornly waiting, trying to understand—

His lids flicked up and he looked right at her, his eyes burning with emotion.

An electric current snapped between them, raising the hair on

Kate's arms and causing her heart to jolt. She broke the connection by looking quickly down, flustered. What had just happened? What had she just seen?

She knew exactly what she'd seen. Attraction. But as she went on to put Morty out of the game and win the hand, as they divvied up the winnings and said their good-byes, Matt treated her exactly the way he'd treated her all week. With detached politeness.

Kate began to doubt what she'd seen, to question what had passed between them in those few heated seconds. I mean, seriously. What was she expecting? That Matt was developing the hots for her?

Pigs would sooner fly.

The following morning introduced itself as the most flawless early November Saturday morning in the history of Pennsylvania. Seventy-two degrees, sunny, with just a whisper of breeze. So gorgeous that Kate decided to bypass the yoga studio in favor of a power walk through the neighborhood. She'd been at it about twenty minutes and was following one of the rolling streets, just cresting a hill, when she saw him.

Matt, jogging toward her with an iPod strapped to his bicep. He had on long navy basketball shorts and running shoes, but had taken off his shirt somewhere along the way and was running with it balled in his hand. His lean, hard, muscular chest glimmered with sweat.

She nearly had a heart attack, right there on the side of the road. Her feet stumbled, stopped dumbly. She had to force herself to resume walking out of abject fear that he'd look up and catch her ogling him.

When Matt finally did glance up and spot her, he jerked to a complete halt. For a moment, it looked to Kate like he might turn around and run in the opposite direction. But no, he just stood there, his chest pumping in and out, waiting and watching her as she drew closer. Her own iPod, which she'd clipped to the V-neck of her workout top, chose that moment to launch into ABBA's "Take a Chance on Me."

She almost never saw Matt on Saturdays and Sundays. It jolted her to run into him on the weekend, outside the boundary of Chapel Bluff, *and*—heaven help her—shirtless.

She stopped in front of him. He pulled out his ear buds and she pulled out hers. ABBA cut away, leaving them surrounded by nothing but the murmuring of trees and drops of sunlight.

"Hi," Kate said. It was incredibly hard not to gape at his chest. To attempt to keep her attention on his face.

"Hi."

"Looks like we had the same idea."

"Yeah." He was still breathing hard. His brown hair was completely drenched.

"Except you look like you're working way harder than me. What have you run? Twenty, twenty-five miles this morning?"

His lips twitched slightly. "Only four."

"I'll be stunned if I've made it a half mile yet."

He was doing that thing where he didn't look exactly into her eyes. But he wasn't looking past her this time, either. His attention slid down her throat and along her shoulder.

"What's that?" He nodded toward her hand.

"Oh." She lifted it to show him. "My inhaler. I have asthma, so I keep it close by when I exercise, just in case." She shifted in her running shoes, groped mentally for something to say. All that glistening skin! "So what are you listening to?"

"Oh. Ah . . ." He twisted his arm, glanced distractedly at his iPod. "I think 'Wanted Dead or Alive' was on when you walked up. You?"

"ABBA. I went to see a traveling production of *Mamma Mia* when it came through Dallas, then went right out and bought the soundtrack."

TMI, Kate! Quit babbling. TMI!

A car drove along the street and they both watched it pass, grateful for the diversion. Okay, so that heavy look he'd given her last night hadn't been a complete delusion. There *was* something new between them. An awareness. A tension. It was probably mostly on her side, affecting her emotions. But there had been a shift. She could feel it acutely.

"Is your house near here?" she asked.

"Yeah. It's back down this way and then to the left." He turned to gesture, describing where he lived. With his attention elsewhere, Kate snuck a furtive peek at his nearby shoulder, arm, chest. There were a few faint, pale scars on his upper body. No doubt from the hockey.

They only made him hotter.

She peeled her attention away in the nick of time, nodding at him when he finished as if she'd been listening the whole time.

She gave him a chance to invite her to his house for a breather, a glass of water, a make-out session. But he offered none of the above.

"Well, I don't want to keep you," she said. "Enjoy the rest of your jog."

"Thanks. You too."

"I'm glad I ran into you." It was true. Seeing him shirtless and sweaty was like a shot in the arm. She now felt like she had the hormone power to walk for miles.

She smiled at him and his focus caught on her mouth for a second.

"See you Monday," she said.

"Okay." And with that he nodded to her then ran past, launching into the upward slope of the hill with impressive speed.

She pivoted slowly to watch him.

If you change your mind, I'm the first in line . . .

It was only after he'd disappeared from sight that she realized the refrain from "Take a Chance on Me" had sprung from her own heart. Her ear buds were still dangling from her fingers.

She had to remind herself for the one thousandth time that he was only ever going to be her friend. She couldn't let herself go all mushy over him. She just absolutely couldn't afford it. It would be fruitless pain heaped onto a heart already vulnerable and battered from bad ex-boyfriends. The next time she fell in love it was going to be with a good, Christian, ordinary-looking guy. It was not, not, not going to be with Matt Jarreau.

"Are you married or single?" The middle-aged woman at the church's information desk looked up at Kate inquiringly.

"Single."

"Okay then." She flipped some pages in her binder. "The singles' class meets in room B5. Just take the elevator"—she leaned forward, pointed— "down a floor and it'll be on your left."

Yes! Yes, of course. The basement! Home to many a singles' Sunday school class in many a church. Kate thanked the lady and made her way to the elevator. Darn Gran for insisting on coming to Sunday school today. They'd been attending just the worship hour since arriving in Redbud, which suited Kate perfectly. But today Gran's "Golden Group" was hosting an author who'd written a book about reaching your grandchildren for Christ, and Gran hadn't wanted to miss it. Since they only had one car, it had seemed embarrassingly wimpy for Kate to drop Gran off early and not brave Sunday school herself.

She was already regretting her false bravado.

What was it with churches and single people? In all spheres of life—work, social, athletic, academic—singles mixed with married people. Not so in Sunday school.

What were the married people studying in their classes, anyway? Top secret marriage info? Racy sex tips? What could possibly be so juicy that it merited separating the married and the single adults into two separate areas of the building? Like the *L* sign for loser, she sometimes felt like she wore a big *S* for single on her forehead whenever she set foot on a church campus.

She arrived at the mouth of room B5. A neat, trim, balding guy greeted her, had her fill out paperwork, and made her a stick-on name tag.

"Come on in, I'll introduce you to some people," he said, leading her into the sparsely populated room. He smiled enthusiastically. "We've got a really great group."

How great could any singles group be, Kate wondered darkly, when all of its members were extremely eager to graduate out of it? She clutched her Bible and ventured forward.

It could be worse, she reminded herself. This was a small-town church and all their singles met together. She wasn't going to be treated to that favorite of big-city churches—the divide between twenty-something singles and thirty-and-over singles. Kate, most depressing of all thoughts, now belonged in the latter category. And there was no worse, more pitiable assignment in the entire church than thirty-and-over singles. Even the grief support group was arguably better. The class of shell-shocked divorced people was better!

For pity's sake, the *custodial staff* was better.

Kate kept a close eye on Morty all through Sunday lunch at Peg and William's. Apparently, he hadn't recovered from Friday night's black mood. He was still thunderous, gloomy, and seething with animosity toward Velma.

After the meal, she took him aside to Peg's sunroom, where they stood side by side gazing out the floor-to-ceiling windows, hands in their pockets. Beyond the glass, a view of stunningly vivid orange, red, and yellow fall foliage spread before them. Some of the leaves spun on their limbs while others drifted to the ground like paper airplanes.

"I can't drive my Cadillac," Morty finally said.

"Why not?"

He glanced at her. "You know anything about cars?"

"Not much."

"Well then, this might be hard for you to understand." He ran a hand through his beautiful gel-free silver hair before returning his attention to the woods. "My Cadillac is a classic car. I bought it in '63. I was working on the force then, hadn't made detective yet. Married with two kids. The car was six years old at the time, but the first owner had been an old lady who'd hardly put any miles on it."

Kate nodded. Waited.

"I've always been real practical. Frugal, you know? I didn't make much and my wife was at home raisin' the kids back then, so we had to be careful about money. But when I read that classified ad in the paper, saying that a Cadillac was for sale, I just had to go by and take a look. And as soon as I saw that car, I had to have it. Can't really explain it."

"You don't have to. Some things are just like that. Love at first sight." Against her will, her brain conjured an image of Matt looking slowly up at her from beneath the brim of his baseball cap.

"Exactly," Morty said. "That car's the one—What do you call it? Indulgence? It's the one big indulgence of my life. My wife was mad at me for weeks—" he shook his head ruefully—"*months* over buying that car. I didn't want to drive it much, you see, even back then. So we had to share her car."

Kate could understand why his purchase had gone over like a lead balloon.

"Over the years the kids grew up and left and my wife died, God rest her soul. But I've still got that car."

"I'd like to see it sometime."

"Sure. I've kept it in mint condition. I mean *mint condition.*" He looked at her seriously.

"I believe you."

"The car's perfect. I work on it myself, order parts when I need 'em. A couple times a year I load it onto a flatbed and drive it to car shows. You wouldn't believe the offers I get to buy it. It's worth a fortune."

"I bet it is."

"I won't sell it, of course."

"No."

He sighed, and they watched the leaves together for a few quiet moments.

"I can't just up and start driving it all of a sudden," he said. "It's a collector's item. What if someone runs into me? Where am I going to park it while Velma and I are eating dinner? What if there's a storm? Hail, God forbid? Not to mention just the regular ol' wear and tear of driving it around . . . all those miles I'd be adding."

"I gotcha," Kate said.

"Maybe you could ask Velma to reconsider."

"It wouldn't do any good. She was firm on it, Morty. You know how she is."

He groaned, worked the toe of his shoe into the floor.

"I hesitate to speak for her," Kate said tentatively, "but I think she wants you to drive the car because she thinks you'd get more enjoyment out of it that way. You know, live life to the fullest and all that."

"I couldn't enjoy my car any more than I already do," he answered defensively. "Why does that woman keep wanting to change things about me? When am I gonna be good enough?"

"She indicated that this was her last request."

He scowled. "How'd she like it if I demanded *she* change some things?"

She'd like it like a yeast infection. "Um . . . you could try, I suppose."

"The thing is, Kate, I don't want to change anything about her. I like her just the way she is."

Kate looked at him, this burly man with his new hair and his new clothes and his sad expression. He was trying so hard. "For what it's worth, I think Velma's crazy if she doesn't go out with you."

"And I think that Matt Jarreau fellow is crazy if he doesn't go out with you."

"What?" Kate asked, surprised. "Oh no, we're just friends."

He looked at her with compassion, as if she were the dumbest person alive.

She blinked back at him. What exactly were the seniors talking about when she wasn't around?

"So if I want to go on a date with Velma, it's the car or nothing, huh?" he asked.

"It's the car or nothing, I'm afraid."

"I don't think I can do it, Kate. I just don't think I can do it."

chapter thirteen

Ah, that most glorious of chores. Taking out the trash. The fact that it could pile up with such astonishing, impossible speed depressed Kate. She'd take it out in the morning and, as if by magic, spot it brimming again come noon. She'd tromp out with it at noon and then find herself jamming a box of Cheddar Jack Cheez-Its into a full bin again come bedtime.

But perhaps it wasn't even that—the never endingness of the trash. What bugged her the most was that any person with two brain cells knew that taking out the trash was a man's job. So her failure at finding a husband had, among other things, relegated her to a life of trash handling.

It was Monday morning and she'd woken unusually early. Thoughts of Matt had jumped into her head and prevented her from falling back to sleep.

She padded to the kitchen in her UGG slippers and cotton jammies in search of coffee. Gran was still clunking around upstairs so Kate got the coffee maker going, pulled out the stuffed trash bag with a sigh, and slipped on her quilted trench.

Fog covered the morning in quiet, white, and chilly stillness. She was halfway across the lawn on her way to the trash cans located at the back of the barn when she saw him.

She gasped and stopped, the trash bag swinging.

Matt, leaning against the side of his truck, huddled into his leather coat, watching her with glittering eyes. He didn't look happy.

Her heartbeat kicked at the sight of him. "Hey."

"Hey."

He pushed away from his truck and approached. "Here." He took the Hefty bag from her. "Let me." And exactly as God must have intended for man to do from the beginning of time, he strode into the fog and took out the trash. She could have fainted at the romance of it.

He made his way back a few moments later, materializing suddenly from the mist.

"Did you come to work early this morning to take out my trash?" she asked with a smile.

"Not exactly."

She waited for him to elaborate, but as usual with Matt, no information was forthcoming. On the one morning when a hat would have made sense, he wasn't wearing one. On closer inspection, she saw some other things amiss. His eyes were red, he hadn't shaved, and his hair looked like he'd combed it with chopsticks. Despite all that, or maybe emphasized by it, the lines and contours of his face struck her as starkly, painfully beautiful.

"Hard night?" she asked.

"Yeah."

"Would you like to come inside for coffee?"

"No . . . I . . ." He searched for words, then shook his head. He went to the rear of his truck and unlatched and lowered the back end. "Will you sit with me for a minute?"

"Sure." She walked over, her UGGs squelching on dewy grass, and hoisted herself up to sit on the edge of his truck bed. Her hair was a mess and she didn't have on a bit of makeup, but thankfully she'd washed her face and brushed her teeth.

He lifted himself up beside her. Time stretched. All around them the sounds of Chapel Bluff hushed. It felt, sitting together in the still, pale fog, like they were alone in the world.

Just when she thought he was going to say something, he ground his teeth together, growled, and held his silence.

She sat patiently, the tips of her ears turning chilly, her butt freezing from the cold metal beneath her, trying to imagine what he wanted to talk to her about.

"You said something the other night," he said at last. He spoke low and even, looking down at his hands. "The night we argued."

She watched him.

"You said something about God having blessings He wants to give me. About me not letting Him."

She paused, her thoughts swimming. "I remember."

He met her gaze for a beat, then looked back down. She could see how troubled he was, how torturously hard this was for him. "I just . . . It's been bothering me ever since."

"Oh. I hadn't realized."

"I was happily married once," he said. "God took her away. So if anyone has refused stuff in the relationship between God and me, I guess I just wanted you to know that it wasn't me. It was Him."

She nodded, absorbing that. It was seven in the morning, they were sitting in the driveway of Chapel Bluff in the cold, and after all the weeks of their acquaintance, he was ready to talk to her. She tried to look cool about it, calm. But she could already feel her blood starting to rush. She didn't want to blow this chance with him, to shut him down accidentally, to misrepresent God.

Where to begin? Maybe best to start with easy questions before wading into the hard stuff. "Did you go to church growing up?"

"My mom took us when we were kids."

"And? Tell me more."

"Ah . . . I prayed that prayer you're supposed to pray and was baptized and everything. But when I started playing hockey, I got too busy to go. I was always traveling."

"What about Beth? What was her story?"

"Her whole family, they were big church people. She loved going. Whenever I was in town on Sundays, she made me put on a suit and tie and go with her. I teased her about it, but honestly," he said, looking up toward the tree line, gazing into his past, "I didn't mind it and she knew it. It was the least I could do if it made her happy."

A stab of horrible selfish jealousy caught Kate square in the chest.

He loved Beth. She knew this. Still, the evidence of it stung and stung hard.

"When she was diagnosed with cancer . . . I prayed for her," he said. "It's not like I'd been some great Christian or anything. But I prayed as hard as I could, asking God to save her. Day and night. I actually thought . . ." He shook his head as if furious with himself. "I actually thought between God and the doctors that she'd be okay."

Kate sent up a quick, silent request for insight. She had no wisdom of her own in the face of a beautiful twenty-seven-year-old who'd died of brain cancer.

Matt popped a few knuckles. "Do you know how good she was? She was this, this really good person. Didn't have a mean bone in her body." He looked over at Kate. "Do you believe God could have saved her?"

"Yes," Kate answered.

"So then why, out of all the people on earth, didn't He? Her? Someone who was so sweet and who trusted Him?"

"I don't know."

"Yeah." He scoffed. "Me either."

She chewed on the side of her lip. "This is a fallen world." The words sounded trite, impossibly small. "I hate that it's true, but there are diseases and poverty and suffering. A lot of it's unfair."

His profile hardened.

"He never promised us that we wouldn't suffer. But He's too just not to redeem it. And He does promise us that He won't leave us. That He'll be with us through the worst. That He loves us."

He grunted disdainfully. "He could have saved Beth, and He didn't. Was that love? Because it looked a lot like indifference to me. I can't understand why He didn't let her live. And I don't want to believe in a God that would let that happen to a person like her."

She hugged her coat more tightly around herself. "It's okay, you know, to argue with Him, to confront Him, to scream at Him, whatever. He's big enough. He can handle it. Just so long as you talk to Him."

He released a low, bitter laugh. "No thanks. We're not exactly on speaking terms."

"No?"

"*No.* I wrote Him off when Beth died, and I think we're both fine with the arrangement."

Looking at Matt in that moment—dark windblown hair, distrustful slant to his shoulders, cynical twist to his lips, eyes shadowed with sorrow—a sudden and absolute certainty overcame Kate. Goose bumps lifted down her neck and arms. "Actually," she said slowly, "He's not fine with the arrangement."

Matt turned his attention to her.

Everything clicked sharply into focus. Gran's invitation to come to Chapel Bluff. Kate's easy success in gaining leave from work.

Matt's acceptance of this renovation job. Her recognition of him the first moment she'd spotted him.

She'd recognized him because *he* was the reason God had brought them here. God didn't care about the renovation of old houses. But He did care, very much, about His lost people.

"I think you're the reason I'm here," she said softly, with amazement. "I think that's why Gran and I are both here. For you."

A sense of rightness flooded her. God had meant all along for her and Gran to find Matt in the soundless, touchless cave he'd built for himself. To be God's hands and voice to a man who wouldn't listen any other way.

Inexplicably, tears rushed to her eyes. She blinked them away, hoping he wouldn't notice. He'd probably notice. He was studying her intently.

"That's not right, Kate," he said. "You're here to fix up Chapel Bluff."

"I thought I was. But I just realized there was a bigger plan."

"No, Kate."

"Yes," she said kindly, but with absolute conviction. "I've never been more certain of anything in my life."

He scowled at her.

"He hasn't forgotten you, Matt."

"He should have, Kate."

They sat there, gazes locked, for a long moment. Then, without warning, he reached over and grabbed one of her cold hands. He laced his fingers with hers, holding tightly.

Kate was too stunned to move, to speak.

He looked downward, seemingly riveted by the sight of his rough hockey player's hand engulfing her pale feminine one.

Her heart thundered in her chest, in her ears. A wild reaction all out of proportion to such simple physical contact. They sat together that way for what couldn't have been more than a couple of minutes, her thoughts and her pulse racing crazily the whole time.

Then he squeezed her hand once, tight, and abruptly released her. He pushed himself off the truck, shoved his hands into his coat pockets. "You must be freezing," he said curtly, without meeting her eyes. "Why don't you go in and warm up."

It was her turn to say or do *something*. "Ah . . . sure." She jumped off the edge of the truck with zero grace, but at least she managed it. "You coming in?"

He shook his head. "I'm going home to clean up before work."

"See you later, then."

He dipped his chin, face grim.

Matt went home and stood in his shower under a spray of hot water for endless minutes. Body immobile, thoughts in uproar.

He hadn't been sleeping well. Hadn't been eating well. He'd taken to driving his Lamborghini at ridiculous speeds late into the night, but it didn't help. He couldn't outrace what was happening to him. There was no help for him now. A suit of armor wasn't going to protect him from Kate.

He was defeated. Competitive him, who'd spent most of his life perfecting the art of winning. He'd been trounced by a woman. Killed with one look from those hazel eyes.

Maybe he was even becoming obsessed with her. He could think of little else but Kate and Beth, Beth and Kate, the two of them tangled together in tortured threads of recent and long-past memories. One woman dead. One woman alive. Both of them beyond his reach.

He had thought, for the past three years, that he'd suffered the worst life had to offer. But now he realized that he'd been mostly numb the whole time. It was like when your leg fell asleep. It felt dead and uncomfortable asleep, but it felt far worse when the feeling returned.

He was coming back to life now—feeling returning—and it hurt almost unbearably. He wanted to return to numb. He'd been trying for days now to get back to numb. But numb was gone. He was stuck with all this awful emotion. Inescapable.

After another nearly sleepless night, he'd *had* to talk to Kate about Beth this morning. He'd driven up there at six in the morning in the dark to wait for her. She'd listened and taken it all in without making him feel like an idiot. He'd been handling it okay until she'd looked at him with those eyes. Beautiful, clear, open, and said, *"I think you're the reason I'm here. I think that's why Gran and I are both here. For you."*

Wrong. Crazy to believe God had sent her to Chapel Bluff because of him. Yet that hadn't stopped the hole that had ripped open inside of him, then filled with overwhelming tenderness for her. A few moments later he'd been unable to stop himself from grabbing her hand, which was something he shouldn't have done. *Shouldn't have done.*

On paper it seemed like a harmless thing, holding someone's hand. But it hadn't been. Barriers had crashed to rubble inside him. His body had roared with need.

He'd been a mess around her for a while now. A head case. With this new awkward thing that he'd done between them, he didn't know how he was going to manage.

He put his hands against the tile and leaned into his arms, dropping his head. The spray pounded the back of his neck. He reminded himself of a kid with a security blanket. Stupid, but that's how he felt about Kate. Like he needed her now. Like he wanted to cling to her. The thought sent fear coursing through him.

He wished he were strong, and solid, and normal. But instead he was angry, confused, and hard inside. He was a wreck.

He had nothing, nothing, to offer her.

Matt didn't arrive for work that day until midmorning. Kate heard him the instant he came in. She stilled, holding her breath, but he went upstairs without seeking her out.

What had she expected? Nothing more, and yet she couldn't help but feel . . . what? Even hours later, her mind, her heart, her nerves were still spinning because of those few intense minutes when he'd held her hand. For that short space of time, sitting on his truck bed with him, she'd felt as if he might see her as extraordinary. That didn't seem possible now, in the light of day. Her pragmatic side said it wasn't. But her intuition and the look on his face when he'd held her hand said it was.

Could it be that he actually likes me?

No.

. . . Maybe.

She spent the next hour attempting to concentrate on packaging and addressing items she'd sold on eBay. After discovering that she'd used a permanent marker to write the wrong address on a package she'd spent fifteen minutes wrapping, she put herself out of her misery and went to go find him. She could either break the ice or go insane.

She stopped in the doorway of the bathroom and found him screwing a light fixture into the wall above the mirror. He glanced at her for the space of a heartbeat, then back to his work. He was clean-shaven and he'd changed into a beige waffle-knit henley, a worn pair of jeans, and his boots. The baseball cap—a beaten-up brown one today—that had been absent this morning had returned.

"The bathroom looks great," she said. And it did. The floor was now travertine, the tub and sink clean, simple white. White beadboard wound around the room a third of the way up the wall, ending in molding where the latte-colored walls began. They'd chosen fixtures that were classic, in keeping with the age of the house, but not fussy.

After weeks of using the other upstairs bathroom, the avocado one with appliances circa 1950, this bathroom looked like the spa at the Four Seasons.

"Are you almost done?" she asked.

"This is it. The last thing."

"I'll be able to fire up the bathtub tonight?"

"As promised."

"Yes!" She did a mini fist pump.

He kept right on with the screwdriver.

Self-consciousness hovered between them, but not an unbearable amount. Anything was better than the agonized waiting she'd been putting herself through downstairs.

"What's next?" she asked. "The bathroom down the hall?"

"Yeah."

"Let me know if you need any help in there. That wallpaper is pretty nasty."

"Thanks. I think I'll be all right."

"Catch you later." She made her way back to her wrapping and addressing. Clearly, he'd flipped their relationship switch back to the "reserved and polite" setting.

Though she wanted to be miffed about it, she couldn't quite bring herself to be. He'd opened up to her earlier that morning, trusted her with his thoughts, and that was enough of a breakthrough for one day. For one week, even.

Still, as she took back up her brown packaging paper and clear mailing tape, she indulged herself imagining all the things he could have said just now and hadn't.

Kate, as you could probably tell when I grabbed your hand, I cherish you. You're a queen among women. Let's date exclusively.

Kate, your hand was so soft. You must moisturize. I'd like nothing more than to hold your hand every hour of my waking life.

Kate, touching your hand clarified my emotions. I'm no longer in love with my perfect Miss America wife. I love you now. You!

She laughed out loud at the complete impossibility of that one. "Never gonna happen," she whispered to herself. "You're never going to be his girlfriend. Remember?"

Kate had scheduled a date with Tyler for that very same night. When they'd decided on the night, days ago, she'd picked Monday specifically because Matt didn't stay for dinner on Monday and wouldn't be around to brush shoulders with Tyler. It should have been fine.

Should have been.

However, Matt was working late, most likely because he'd started so late that morning. After what had happened between them on the truck, Kate hated the idea of leaving for a date with Tyler right in front of Matt.

Her very best hope? That Matt wouldn't notice.

Kate was in her bedroom slipping on her shoes when Gran called from downstairs in a loud and ringing voice, "Kate! Tyler's here to pick you up for your date."

The demolition sounds Matt had been making in the bathroom below her room came to an instant and ominous halt.

Kate closed her eyes. So much for her hope that he wouldn't notice.

She felt both embarrassed and guilty, like she'd committed a serious dating foul. But what should she have done? Should she have called Tyler to cancel because "Matt held my hand this morning"? He'd have laughed her out of the building. Matt was just her friend!

When she arrived downstairs she found Tyler occupied with the business of charming Gran. Kate tried to rush him out the door once, then twice, without success. The third time she had him all the way to the threshold when Matt came down the stairs.

Her heart sank.

Matt stopped and stood dead still on the bottom landing of the stairway. He looked dark, rumpled, and foreboding.

Tyler paused with the front door cracked open and smiled in greeting. "Hi, Matt."

"Tyler." Matt's tone could have forced forest animals back into their burrows.

"What's been going on, buddy?"

"Not much."

After a double beat of silence, Tyler chuckled. "Quit talking my ear off, dude!"

Matt didn't so much as flinch.

Kate shuddered inwardly.

"He's wordier than ever, isn't he?" Tyler asked her.

She tugged on Tyler's sleeve. "We'd better go."

"Sure, let's do it."

She glanced back at Matt, who was staring at her with an expression as hard and hot as a branding iron.

Tyler closed the door behind them, cutting Matt from view, then escorted her across the lawn to his car.

chapter fourteen

There were an ocean of things that Kate and Matt could not say to each other. It had been that way since the day they'd met. A vast, wide ocean of things that she was careful never to voice.

As they'd become friends, the ocean had gradually grown smaller. Then wider again when he'd retreated. Smaller the night they'd had their fight. Slightly wider after. Smallest of all when he'd opened up to her about Beth Monday morning. By Wednesday night, after Monday night's debacle with Tyler, the ocean seemed as wide as it had ever been. Wider.

She'd spoken with Matt on and off yesterday and today, keeping things purposefully light. Mostly, though, she'd left him alone because she sensed that was how he wanted it.

She showed up for dinner Wednesday in time to set the table and fill glasses. Gran and Matt had been busy cooking. Gran placed dishes of breaded tilapia covered with mango salsa, new potatoes, and salad on the table.

When Kate slid into her chair beside Matt, she noticed his posture tense.

Her hope dipped. She needed peppermint taffies. And not just a handful.

While Gran said the blessing, Kate snuck a glance at him. His head was bowed, his expression tight. *Are you upset about Tyler?* she wondered. *Do you actually like me? Are you considering going away again inside yourself where I can't find you? Because I won't—I can't—let you.* Her throat clogged with emotion. All those questions were lost in the ocean that separated them, impossible to ask.

The prayer ended and Kate tried to keep relaxed conversation going between the three of them. Gran chatted as happily as always and Matt managed his share, answering in his guarded way.

When she passed him the new potatoes their fingers brushed, sending currents of tingling energy up her arm. He stilled momentarily at the contact, his brows knitting with concentration and displeasure before serving himself.

Help me, God, Kate prayed. *I don't know what to do.*

When Kate returned to the sanctuary of her attic room that night, she went right to her knees beside her bed.

What should I do about him, God? She knew now that God had brought her here to help Matt, but she didn't know what to do next. She wanted to act. Was willing. But what to do? How?

God didn't answer in any clear way. No booming voice. No giant foam finger like fans wore at sporting events to point her in the right direction.

She pulled out her Bible. She'd been given this Bible by her parents when she graduated from high school. It had a soft black leather cover with her name inscribed in gold. Cherished and familiar. Notes and creases and underlined sections in a rainbow of colors marked the inside.

She opened it to the place advised by her "Bible in a Year" plan and began to read a section of Proverbs. A particular verse jumped out and grabbed her by the throat.

16:32. *Better a patient man than a warrior.* She revolved that in her head a few times, read, and reread it. *Better a patient man than a warrior.*

She had her answer. God was calling her, simply, to be patient with Matt.

Patience came hard for her. Especially in a situation like this when her instinct urged her to prod and push.

"I can only do it," she whispered, "with your help."

What did people do before coffee shops? Kate wondered. Where did they go for a little daily treat? A few moments of quiet to unwind? A neutral location where you could either escape from work or get work done?

Her sister Lauren's mother-in-law purported that the whole "pamper yourself" thing hadn't been part of the culture in previous generations. Back then people didn't go around thinking, as a matter of course, that they deserved a manicure at the nail salon, a massage, or a cup of expensive coffee.

Kate acknowledged the current mind-set to be a bit self-indulgent and congratulatory. And yet . . . she *loved* the occasional pedicure, hot stone massage, and venti latte. So what was a girl to do?

Main Street Coffee, located squarely in the middle of Redbud's Main Street, was especially sweet. It held barrels of coffee beans with big silver scoopers wedged into their tops. It had scarred wooden floors, walls covered in folk art and old pictures of Redbud, and a bakery case that could make a follower of the Atkins Diet weep with despair.

Kate and Theresa were splurging on buttery cranberry-orange scones sprinkled with extra big sugar granules. They'd come at midmorning and managed to snag the coveted high round table that sat in the bay window overlooking Main.

"So," Theresa said, stirring her foamy coffee with a wooden stick, "have we known each other long enough for me to delve into your personal life?"

"I suppose so. What do you want to know?"

"I want to know the history of your love life, of course."

Kate made a comical face.

"How many serious boyfriends have you had?"

"Serious as in . . . ?"

"As in multiple year, let's-discuss-marriage type things."

Kate told her in brief brushstrokes about Rick and Trevor. The lack of commitment from the former and the infidelity from the latter.

"Are you lucky enough to have any single girlfriends left these days?" Theresa asked.

"A precious few. Even my younger sister's married now."

"Ouch." Theresa's expression turned sympathetic.

"Three years ago."

"Everyone knows that's against the natural order of things."

"Right."

"In fact, it should be illegal," Theresa pronounced, holding her stir stick aloft, "for younger sisters to marry before older sisters."

"Yes, exactly. Lauren should have postponed her wedding until after I get married. That would only have been polite."

"Only polite!" Theresa echoed, then paused and gave a lopsided smile. "Of course, I married before my older sister."

"Theresa!"

"Well, she's a train wreck. She's never going to find anyone!" She laughed long and deep, and Kate laughed with her.

Outside, the day churned gray and windy. The trees were mostly bare now. Crushed and soggy leaves piled along the curbsides and under the feet of the people who passed, bundled up in neutral-colored jackets and brightly colored scarves.

"Good men," Theresa stated, "are hard to find, girlfriend."

"Very hard to find."

Theresa squinted out the window. "Here comes what might be one."

They both watched a handsome man in a business suit and overcoat walk toward the storefront. He carried a leather brief-case in one hand. As he pulled even with them, he raised his free hand to blow warm air into his fist, clearly displaying a platinum wedding band.

"Uh-huh," Kate said.

"So clearly not him, but there *is* someone out there for you. I'm sure of it."

Matt had said the same thing to her recently. But the words just bounced off her, shoved back by a serious case of doubt.

"What about Matt?" Theresa asked.

"Matt?"

Theresa shrugged. "He's hotness. If you weren't attracted to him you wouldn't have a pulse."

Kate's lips twitched. "I have a pulse."

"Well? Do you think he likes you?"

"There are moments that last about a nanosecond when I think he might."

Her eyebrows shot up. "Seriously? I mean, I'd die of jealousy, but I'd manage."

"I don't know. Ever since I met him, I've simply been trying to be his friend. Most of the time I think that if he'll just let me be that, it'll be a miracle."

"He's hard to talk to, isn't he? Really hard. Every time I've seen him at Chapel Bluff over the past few weeks I've tried. But he intimidates the crap out of me. Those eyes!"

"I know," Kate said sincerely.

"Still." Theresa tilted her head and studied Kate. "If you're willing to put in the effort, he'd be worth it."

"As I said, if he'll just let me be his friend it'll be a miracle."

Something was fishy in Friday Night Poker Land.

When Kate came downstairs on her way to the kitchen, she spotted the seniors in the living room clustered around a retro-looking slide projector.

"Kate, you know anything about these?" Morty asked, gesturing to the projector.

"I'm sorry, I don't."

"I still think it must be that the bulb's burned out," Velma said.

Morty frowned, keeping his gaze averted from Velma, which meant they were still locked in their stalemate. "I don't see how it could be the bulb," Morty answered. "It was working at my place this afternoon."

They'd pointed the projector at an empty wall and elevated the front of it with a hardback book. Kate could see that the On switch had been hit and that they'd plugged the unit into the wall.

"Oh, I know." Kate went to the panel of light switches next to the front door. "You have to turn that outlet on from here." Sure enough, she tripped the switch and the machine came whirring loudly to life, bright light shooting out the front of it.

From the direction of the kitchen she heard the back door open and close.

"Matt," Gran called. "We're in the front of the house."

Moments later, he appeared. His gaze sought out Kate first,

locking on her for a split second that caused her nerves to sizzle. Then his attention skimmed to the others as he nodded in response to their welcomes. His hair shone with dampness. He wore cargo pants and a nubby brown sweater that fit close over the ridges of his shoulders and torso. The color of the sweater made his eyes glitter darkly.

"We decided to do something different tonight," Gran explained to Kate and Matt.

"Got tired of you beating us at poker every week." Morty gave Kate a roguish wink.

"We thought it would be fun to have a little slide show," Gran said. "We're going to look at the slides Morty took at our twentieth high school reunion."

"And then I'm going to show the slides I took on my trip to Cairo in '86," Velma said. "Lots of sand."

Kate regarded them with bewilderment. Why hadn't anyone told her about this torturous change in plan?

"I thought I mentioned this to you." Gran's forehead creased.

"No," Kate said. "What about dinner?"

"We're taking a break from cooking," Gran answered. "We're having frozen pizzas and root beer floats. Isn't that a hoot?" She clapped her hands together, big stone bracelets clicking.

"Just in case you two aren't interested in watching the slide show," Peg said, "I brought a movie for you." She took a DVD out of her Gucci purse and extended it to Kate.

Kate took it. *Notting Hill.*

"William and I like Julia Roberts," Peg said.

"Thank you," Kate replied. "But we don't have a DVD player in the house." DVD players hadn't even been a gleam in the eye of their inventor when the borrowed TV in her room had been manufactured.

"Oh, I didn't realize," Peg said.

"What about you, Matt?" William asked. All the seniors moved their attention to him. "Do you have a DVD player at your house?"

A beat of hesitation, then, "I do."

"Perfect," Peg said. "If you don't want to stay for the slide show, you can both watch the movie there."

This was mutiny, Kate realized suddenly. A setup, when Gran and Velma had both promised her not to attempt any matchmaking! The two of them were both looking at her innocently. Maybe too innocently. "Um . . ." she said, embarrassed.

"That would be fine," Matt said. His voice sounded carefully neutral. Neither grudging nor pleased.

"It's all right, Matt," Kate said. "We don't have to. We can just take the night off. Or . . . stay for the slide show."

"I don't mind."

"Good then!" Gran said. "That's settled." She ushered them into the kitchen, filled a grocery sack with a frozen pizza supreme, a liter of chilled root beer, and a pint of vanilla ice cream. Before Kate could even get her thoughts in order, she and Matt were bundled into their jackets and walking through the drizzly night to his truck.

Kate stopped halfway. "Seriously, I don't want you to feel like you have to have me over."

"I don't."

"Just so you know, I didn't have anything to do with this plan."

"I know you didn't, Kate."

"Good, because it's really not my style to blindside you in front of a group of seniors."

"They're sneaky."

"Do you think all of them were in on it, or just Peg and William?"

"All." He raised the bag of food as proof.

"Yeah, point taken." The wind blew her hair across her face. She reached up to hold a section out of her eyes. "Do you need fifteen minutes to, you know, go home and put the dirty dishes in the dishwasher, pick up socks, that kind of thing?"

His lips curved up a little on one side. "No. It's presentable enough."

"Okay. I'll take my car so you don't have to drive me back later." She walked to the barn, where she'd parked her Explorer.

This was *so* not how she'd wanted her first invitation to his house to go down. It wasn't exactly flattering to be foisted on him against his will by a group of meddling seventy-somethings.

Matt's house was wonderful. She could determine that right away, even peering at it through the damp, cloudy night. Whereas Chapel Bluff had been built in an open meadow, this house had been tucked into acres of densely wooded land without even a strip of lawn, which made it feel like a cabin.

Matt pulled his truck into one half of a double garage, and she parked on the driveway behind him. The porch light and the one light he'd left on inside revealed a craftsman-style bungalow painted in shades of olive, beige, and brown.

He met her on the brick front porch and let her inside. They made their way to the kitchen, with Matt flipping on lights as they went. He set the bag of groceries on a speckled beige granite countertop, then took their coats and hung them on hooks near the back door.

"Wow," she said, taking it all in. "I love your house. Do you mind if I look around?"

"Go ahead." He checked the back of the pizza and set the oven temp.

Clearly, he'd taken out walls, because now the foyer, living room, dining room, and kitchen were all one big space broken only by a kitchen counter and two thick wooden posts that looked like whole tree trunks with the bark stripped off. She made her way from the kitchen into the dining room and then the living room. It was a man's house. He'd painted all the walls a pale tan color. The wood on the floors, baseboards, window trim, and doors had all been lightly stained so that you could still clearly see the grain.

He'd picked mission-style furniture. Leather sofas mixed with dark wooden pieces. A couple of antiques, but mostly new. All of it masculine, clean-lined, and of excellent quality. There were no knickknacks and little art—just a few groups of framed black-and-white photographs of nature.

It might have seemed too spartan to be cozy, except for the sweat shirts thrown over the arm of a chair, the pair of Nikes on the rug, the jumble of newspapers on the kitchen table, and the big stack of mail next to two ball caps on the chest of drawers near the front door.

She glanced up and saw that he hadn't moved from where she'd left him in the kitchen. He was studying her intently.

"Did you renovate it yourself?" she asked.

"Yeah, I did."

"How long did it take you?"

"A year."

"I really like what you did."

"Thanks."

He gave her a tour of the rest of the house. The three bedrooms, including his, were all simply furnished with beds supported by sturdy wooden frames, bedside tables, and wall-mounted flat-screen TVs. The two bathrooms managed to be modern, classic, and deluxe at the same time. She doubted a square inch remained anywhere in the house that he hadn't worked on and improved.

"When was the house built?"

"1932."

"And you lived here growing up?"

"I did. My parents bought it the year my older brother was born. When they were ready to sell it six years ago, I bought it from them."

"Didn't want to let it out of the family?"

"No."

They made their way back to the understated but expensive-looking kitchen. While they waited for the oven to preheat, they leaned against opposite kitchen counters, facing each other. "Gran mentioned that your parents moved to Florida."

He nodded. "We used to go on vacations there every summer. They'd talked for a long time about moving there. After my brother and I left, they finally did it."

"Do they come back often?"

"For visits. They'd like to come up more, but . . ." He shrugged, uncomfortable.

She could read what he wasn't saying. "But they're worried about you and the whole time they're here you feel like they're baby-sitting you?"

He considered her for a moment. "Something like that."

"Are they coming for Thanksgiving or are you going there?"

"So far, neither."

"Neither?"

"Neither."

"Why?"

"What you just said. The baby-sitting thing."

"Okay." Kate folded her arms across her chest in a businesslike manner. "Let me help you sort this out."

He waited, staring at her levelly.

"Which do you want to do least," she asked, "travel to Florida or host your family here for Thanksgiving?"

"Travel to Florida."

"Then you'll have it here. You need to call your parents and tell them they can come."

Matt gave her a small smile. "I do, do I?"

"*Yes*, and if you had any sense you'd know that already. Who else will want to come?"

"My brother and his family."

"Who live where?"

"Philadelphia."

"Who else?" she prompted.

"My grandparents."

"Who else?"

"My aunt's divorced. My mom will want to invite her and her daughter."

"Then tell your mom they're all welcome."

He winced.

"I mean, they won't expect you to do all the cooking or anything will they?"

"No."

"Then invite them."

"Kate," he groaned.

"Look, you can blow off your family for most holidays, but not for Thanksgiving or Christmas."

"Is that the rule?"

"That's the rule. You do it for their sake, no matter how difficult it is for you."

He sighed.

"It's either that or Gran will force you to spend it with us at Velma's. You'll be stuck with Velma and all her loser sons for hours. Is that what you want?"

"Definitely not."

She laughed. "I didn't think so."

The oven beeped, letting them know it had preheated. Matt unwrapped the pizza, slid it in, and set the timer.

"You look like you've done that a few times," Kate commented.

"More than a few." He straightened and stuck his hands in his pockets, seeming uncertain. "Should we watch the movie?"

"Sure."

As Kate followed him she caught sight of a five-by-seven photograph in a silver frame sitting on the bar-height counter between the kitchen and living room. The photograph had captured a black-and-white image of a gorgeous blonde wearing an elegant wedding gown and laughing with joy.

Unable to stop herself, Kate approached the picture and picked it up. Her heart slid slowly downward. She glanced at Matt. He was standing next to the DVD player, arrested, the DVD case open in one hand.

Kate returned her attention to the picture. "She was beautiful," she said, and meant it.

Kate had been smart enough not to go hunting around on the Internet for pictures of Beth, knowing it would be painful to see how perfect she'd been. And, wow, it *was* painful to see a picture of her. She'd been absolutely dazzling. Five times as dazzling as Kate on her best day.

But there were other things in this photo that Kate hadn't expected to see. She'd imagined Beth as a sophisticated, cool, celebrity-type person. But looking out at her from this picture was someone very young. A girl with a lively face, gentle eyes, and an air of trusting vulnerability about her.

It twisted Kate's heart to think that this hopeful girl had died of cancer just a few years after this photo had been taken. Her future, her dreams, her life—all snatched from her tragically early.

Kate was no stranger to feeling jealous of Beth. But she was new to feeling compassion for her. She set the picture carefully back where it had been and settled on one end of the leather sofa.

Matt followed her cue and slid the DVD in without a word, picked up the remote, and turned on the TV. A hockey game came up.

He stilled, his attention honing in sharply on the game. He watched for what couldn't have been more than fifteen seconds—just long enough for Kate to understand a multitude about him, long enough for her to glimpse past all his walls to his heart and mind.

His expression turned grim, and he punched the button to flip the TV into DVD mode.

Wow, Kate thought. Beth and hockey, both in the span of a minute. Two ghosts. One gone. The other gone . . . but not irrevocably. Maybe he could have it back if he wanted it enough.

Based on what Kate had just seen in him, he wanted it. Even if he didn't know it yet.

When the timer went off, Matt paused the movie. He went to work slicing the pizza and setting it on plates. Kate handled her usual responsibility: drinks.

She located two tall glasses, then hesitated. "Are we supposed to drink the root beer floats with dinner or for dessert?"

He lifted his brows. "You're asking me?"

"I say we live a little and have them with the pizza." She moved toward the freezer and hesitated again. "I haven't had one of these since I was like eight. Do you think ice or no ice?"

"Uh . . . no ice?" he guessed.

"Agreed." She fixed the floats and they carried everything to the coffee table in front of the sofa. Without another word, they dug into the food and restarted the movie.

Kate had been working to create a mood of ease between them. But it hadn't been easy for days, and tonight was no exception. A living, breathing force existed between them lately. When he looked at her, he looked at her with an almost predatory gleam. It made her tense and fluttery inside.

Her survival plan for the next two hours was to focus on the movie and try to overlook the hard masculine length of him sitting just inches away.

Matt paid no attention to the movie because his full attention was one hundred percent attuned to Kate. He noticed every bite and sip she took, every shift in her position, every quiet laugh. The movie might as well have been in a foreign language. The food barely registered except that the drink was really sweet and frothy and the pizza was covered in lots of vegetables he didn't usually eat on pizza.

On the drive over from Chapel Bluff, he hadn't been sure how he'd feel about having Kate inside his house. He hardly ever had people here. But as he'd watched her make her way through these rooms that were so personal to him, it had hit him. The pleasure of it. Powerful, dangerous pleasure. It made him greedy. Like he wanted to lock the door behind her and not let her leave.

Beth had never been to this house. His parents had sold it to him right around the time he and Beth started dating. He'd kept the house locked for the next few years, always meaning to drive Beth out to see it, always intending to do something about fixing the place up. But other things had been more urgent or interesting.

He had no memories of Beth here, but already tonight he had dozens of Kate. She'd imprinted herself on his house, and he didn't know how he was going to look at these rooms and not see her in them once she left.

He ran a hand through his hair. He was really losing it. He'd lived in this house three years. Kate hadn't even been here three hours. How could her being here such a short time change anything?

It couldn't. And yet it had. His house had always been familiar and quiet. But it hadn't been warm until she'd come and brought warmth with her.

The movie droned on and on. He sat next to her in the darkened room, his body locked down, his instincts pulling like a dog against a leash. As the minutes ticked by, an ache began inside of him that doubled and redoubled in size. He ached to touch her hair, just a piece of it. To reach for her hand like he had the other morning. To tell her he thought she was beautiful. It scared him that he might not be able to keep himself from doing or saying any of those things. Even though he knew, *he knew*, he'd regret them later.

His entire life he'd been attracted to the kind of girls in Budweiser ads. Blond, big curves on top, mile-long legs.

Kate? Completely different. Not short, but definitely not tall. The top of her head hit him near his chin. She had a slim and delicate body, like a ballet dancer. Her long, straight hair held a dozen shades of dark red. And her eyes ... Lately, those eyes could make his heart pound or his spirits plummet with a glance.

Everything about her brought out the most primitive feelings of protectiveness in him. She made him eager to use his size and muscle to fight for her. Kate would give him flak for it if she knew. But it couldn't be helped. He'd never felt so stupidly possessive of anyone in his life. Which was why he *hated* that she was dating Tyler. Every time he thought about it, it hurt to breathe, and he thought about it almost constantly.

When she shivered he noticed immediately and went to turn up the thermostat. He didn't have any throw blanket things, so he took one of his sweat shirts off the arm of the chair and handed it to her.

She threw him a smile, zipped herself into it, and continued watching the movie.

He forced himself back into his spot on the sofa, a respectable distance between them, and pretended to watch the movie, too. He'd have loved to turn and simply watch her instead. But as soon as he focused his attention on her, she'd be on to him and asking him about it. So he remained rigid, bracing inwardly and outwardly, trying not to feel anything else, working not to notice how much it pleased him to see her wearing his sweat shirt, struggling not to do any of the things he wanted to do.

He couldn't have her.

He didn't deserve her.

She wasn't here to stay.

His head understood how it was, yet his control over the rest of him kept unraveling, deserting him when he needed it most.

After the final scene of *Notting Hill*, with Hugh Grant and a pregnant Julia Roberts together on a park bench, the credits rolled. Kate sighed contentedly. She adored that movie. How could she not? It was a romance with a happy ending—exactly her cup of tea.

Matt hadn't seemed as entertained. He'd barely moved an inch during the entire thing, and he hadn't laughed once. In a way, she understood. He probably hadn't had to sit through a chick flick since Beth died.

They made their way to the kitchen. Matt watched her silently while she rinsed their two dishes. She took off the sweat shirt he'd loaned her with a pang of regret and put on her jacket. Matt followed as she scooped up her purse and let herself out the front door.

She paused on the porch facing him. "Thanks. It was fun."

He dipped his chin.

"I'll be back the next time the seniors force me on you," she said, her smile self-deprecating.

"You can come any time."

"You can invite me any time."

She'd meant the reply to be silly and easy. But in response he kept very still, looked utterly serious. "Would you come?" he asked.

"Of course I'd come."

He nodded.

"Good night, Matt."

"Night."

As she made her way to her car, she glanced back at him. He stood outlined in the light spilling from his front door. Tall, broad shouldered, powerful . . . with a heart exactly as fragile as his body wasn't.

chapter fifteen

Late Monday afternoon, Kate was sitting on her upside-down Home Depot bucket chatting with Matt when her phone beeped to tell her that she'd received a text. She slipped her cell out of her pocket, punched a button, and viewed the message.

"Tyler?" Matt asked, his voice expressionless. He'd learned that Tyler communicated with her mostly by text.

"Yep. Excuse me for a minute." She went downstairs and slid onto the den sofa to reply. While typing her response, she heard Matt come downstairs and make his way out through the kitchen. He shut the back door with a semi-loud bang.

Was he leaving for the day? He always said good-bye.

Slipping her phone into her pocket, she followed the route he'd taken outside and found him slinging some of his tools into the back of his truck.

"You leaving for the day?" she called as she walked over to him.

"Yeah."

"Okay. Well . . ." He looked majorly ticked, and she thought she knew why. Her relationship with Tyler irritated the heck out of him. A fact that irritated the heck out of her. Matt hadn't asked her out and wasn't going to ask her out. So why should he care if someone else did?

"Will you just . . ." When he brushed past her on his way to open his driver's side door, she reached out and laid her hand on his forearm. "Just hold up a second?"

He froze. His gaze fixed on where her hand touched him.

She hadn't meant to grab him. Had put zero thought into it. But now that she had, she couldn't stop her fingers from tightening slightly.

His attention traveled upward until he was looking squarely into her face.

She stared back at him. Attraction swirled through her like molten liquid.

He did nothing. Said nothing. They were only a breath apart.

Finally, his brow knitting, Matt lifted a hand and touched her cheek. His big fingers grazed a slow track to her chin, down her neck, across the top of her shoulder. He took hold of a strand of her hair and rubbed it between his fingers.

Kate's lower abdomen tightened with longing.

Then without warning, without giving her enough time to savor the moment, he dropped his hand and stepped away from her, cutting all contact between them.

No! her body wailed. She held herself still, quaking inside. She wanted to launch herself at him and either kiss him or pummel him with her fists—she wasn't sure which. "What's the matter?" she asked, her tone impressively level. "Why are you in such a hurry to leave here mad?"

He strode away from her, rounded, and faced her. "You really want to know?" he asked.

"I think I already know, but I'd like to hear it from you."

"Okay, here goes. I don't want you to date Tyler anymore."

In the silence that landed between them like an atom bomb,

Matt's expression took on a defiant cast. As if he were saying to her, *You wanted to know and there it is. The truth.*

"Does that surprise you?" he asked.

"No."

"What's going on between you two?" he asked.

"I'm not sure what business that is of yours."

"None, but I'm asking anyway."

The urge to pummel him grew stronger. "We've gone on a few dates, and we might go on a few more."

He waited for her to go into more detail, but she didn't oblige.

"Tyler's full of it," he said. "You can't seriously like him, can you?"

"Maybe I can."

He glowered at her.

She glowered back. "I'm not sure why you care whether I go out with Tyler."

"I care because I can't stand to think about you with him."

"Why?"

He started to speak. Stopped. With a growl, Matt hit the side of his truck with the flat of his hand, then moved toward the door. Kate stepped out of his way. Without another word or glance he started the engine and drove off, vanishing from sight.

Kate stood there for a good long time in a vacuum of astonishment. At length, she realized her jaw was hanging open. She closed it with a stunned click. He liked her! Matt Jarreau actually liked her at least a little bit.

She couldn't believe it. Oh my gosh. He liked her.

It wasn't humanly possible, was it? No.

Yes?

For weeks she'd been telling herself that she wasn't into him romantically. But when he'd been standing close to her and rubbing a strand of her hair, she'd been *dying* inside for him to kiss her. She was such a hypocrite! What in the world was she going to do with herself?

The emotions jangling through her—giddiness, anxiety, excitement, amazement, confusion—wouldn't let her be still a moment longer, so she walked down the driveway. Then she turned back toward the house, reversed herself again, and headed toward the street at the end of the driveway because she had an excess of energy and nowhere else to go. She scrubbed her hands over her face, let them fall.

Her stubborn heart had refused all the practical guys she'd wanted to fall for over the past few years. Now, despite her best efforts, it had come to care deeply for the one guy she'd been trying hard *not* to fall for.

Oh. My. Goodness.

Where to go from here? What to do?

First, she had to acknowledge that all Matt had really done was touch her cheek, touch her hair, and admit that he didn't like her dating Tyler. He hadn't expressed out loud that he himself liked her. And he hadn't asked her out. It was still very likely that he never would.

And maybe—her spirits dropped at the thought—maybe that would be for the best.

She thought of her past relationships, of how devastated she'd been when they'd ended in shreds. By growing more attached to Matt every day, she was headed straight toward devastation again.

Kate neared the place where the driveway intersected the street. A black sports car roared along the road and shot past her, all snarl and gleaming paint. It left nothing in its wake but a flurry of fallen leaves.

Her thoughts were like those leaves, spinning and dipping. She didn't want to go through any more heartache, but she couldn't see her way clear of it. Even if he never asked her out, she was going to miss him badly when she left. If he did ask her out, she wouldn't have the strength to refuse.

It was impossible that he should like her! Too incredible to believe. If he liked her, even a little, how was a regular girl like her supposed to keep herself from tumbling into love with him?

God brought you here, she reminded herself, *to help him, remember? He didn't bring you here to hook up with him!*

If she were a better person, more plugged in to God, maybe she could be more selfless about trying to help Matt through his grief and back toward God. Instead she feared she was helping Matt very little and potentially hurting herself a lot if she lost her head over him.

"What could you be thinking?" she whispered to God, closing her eyes. "Putting me here with him? This is going to cost me." It scared her to think that God had intentionally placed her on a collision course with catastrophe. Yet at the same time, her entire body was still thrumming with delight because she could clearly remember the way he'd looked at her, the way his chest had expanded with his breath, the way his fingertips had slid gently along the surface of her cheek.

Late that night as Kate brushed her teeth, she had to wonder why she was so often using her Sonicare toothbrush manually. Was she *really* too lazy to unearth the charger, plug it into the wall, and stick her toothbrush into it? Really? *That* lazy?

From her bedroom, she faintly heard her cell phone ring. Odd. It was after eleven. She was still up only because she'd been binge-ing on peppermint taffies and thoughts of Matt.

She spit out her toothpaste, did a quick rinse, and hurried to the bedroom. The caller ID read *Unknown*.

Kate hit the Talk button. "Hello?"

"Hey," Matt said.

Her pulse tripped, then started sprinting. "Hey."

He paused. Kate lowered herself to sit on the side of her bed.

"I wanted to . . ." He sounded edgy. "I wanted to say that I'm sorry about today."

"It's all right, Matt."

"No, it's not. I was out of line, and I don't have any excuse."

"Apology accepted."

Silence followed. Kate picked at the nap of her pajama bottoms.

"I like you," he said.

She could barely breathe, much less speak. "You do?"

"Yes. I want to go out with you myself. I do. I just . . . can't."

"I understand," she said quietly. And surprisingly, she thought she did. His head was messed up from Beth's death, and he wasn't ready. He might never be ready.

"Are we still friends?" he asked. "I don't want to lose you as a friend."

"We're still friends."

"Good. Thank you."

"You're welcome."

"Okay," he said. "Then . . . I guess I'll see you tomorrow."

"See you then."

He hung up. Kate set aside the phone, then sat in silence, her hands in her lap, staring at nothing.

So there it was. After all the wild thoughts and wilder feelings that had possessed her this afternoon and evening, he'd called and stated the situation very simply in under a minute.

He liked her but couldn't ask her out and wanted to keep her as a friend. Plain as day.

And probably exactly as it should be, for both their sakes.

So why, oh why, were tears pricking her eyes?

Matt sat alone in one of the wooden deck chairs on his back patio. Dark trees and cold air surrounded him, punctuated only by the frost of his breath. When he'd left Kate earlier that day he'd driven aimlessly, worked out at the gym, paced his house, driven around for a few more hours, and finally returned home before breaking down just now and calling her.

Of all the things that had upset and worried him since he'd left her earlier, what had worried him most was the possibility that she'd want nothing to do with him now. He thought he could maybe bear not to touch her or kiss her, but he knew flat out that he couldn't bear not to see her and talk to her.

She'd assured him just now that they were still friends. He still had that to hold on to. She wasn't going to shut him out. So how come her reassurance didn't make him feel much better?

Because he wanted to be more than just her friend.

Groaning, he fisted his hands.

Half of him still couldn't believe he'd done and said the things he had to Kate earlier. She'd taken hold of his arm as he'd been walking past her and that one small, innocent touch had shut down everything inside of him. All his intentions and defenses had fallen as hard and fast as a heavy curtain dropping onto a stage. He hadn't been able to stop himself from doing what he'd been wanting to do for weeks, from reaching out and touching her.

It had been bliss to feel the smooth skin of her face. His gut ached with pleasure even now, just remembering it.

It had felt almost as good to finally tell her how he felt about Tyler.

For that little gap in time today he'd actually been honest in his actions and his words. Being his true self and touching her, telling her plainly how he felt, had been like eating something forbidden that you'd been starving for day after day. Once you got hold of it, you wanted to gorge on it even though you knew it was wrong.

And it had been wrong. Matt pushed restlessly to his feet and walked toward the back of his property, only vaguely registering the trees that engulfed him.

Before he and Kate had even finished arguing about Tyler, guilt had begun to creep up on him. Beth had been dead three years, but until recently, he'd felt all that time as if he were still married to her. He couldn't shake the idea that he was failing her by indulging his attraction to Kate. Almost as bad, he was failing himself. He knew plainly that he had to resist Kate. He wasn't worthy of her affection, and he sure wasn't whole enough for a relationship with anyone.

His thoughts chased one another through his head. Thoughts of guilt, of longing. Wanting and trying not to want. Regret and hopelessness.

For those few minutes today it had been a tremendous relief to be himself again. Ultimately, though, being himself was a self-indulgence he couldn't afford.

When Matt showed up for work the next morning, Beverly met him in the kitchen before he'd even taken off his coat.

"I have a favor to ask," she said.

"Sure."

"I've decided that I'd like to use the chapel. I have a little daily quiet time, you know, when I read and pray and all, and yesterday it occurred to me that I ought to be spending my quiet times in the chapel. But when I went out there I saw that the floor has some loose nails and one of the pews is broken. I'm sure there are other problems, too." She tilted her head. "Would you mind if I asked you to postpone work in here today and fix the chapel for me instead?"

"Not at all." Though to be honest, he *did* mind. He'd been counting the minutes until he could see Kate again.

You're an idiot, he told himself. It would be far better for him if he spent the next several weeks of this job in the chapel away from her. But he didn't *want* what his head knew was best. And that was the continuing torture of it.

Matt had to assure Beverly a couple more times that the change in plans suited him fine. Then he set out across the meadow toward the chapel with his tool belt in hand.

The small clapboard structure stood at the crest of a rise in the land. He eyed it appraisingly as he approached. The house had been built of stone, but the chapel had been constructed of wooden clapboards that should have decayed and crumbled decades ago. That they hadn't meant that generations of the family had spent time and effort to keep the place up.

He let himself in through the unlocked double doors. The inside smelled like lemon Pine-Sol, which meant that Beverly had done some cleaning yesterday. The small rectangular space held five rows of short wooden pews. At the front, someone had placed a simple cherrywood stand for a Bible. Behind that was a stained-glass window, a big round one that showed a scene of Jesus in a garden with one hand outstretched. The sunlight streaming through the pastel glass fell all across the floor in shades of yellow, green, blue, and pink.

He supposed he'd always known about the window. But from

the outside it looked dark and lifeless. From the inside it was beautiful. Surprisingly bright.

Matt could easily spot the needed repairs that Beverly had mentioned. Rusty nails poked out of the floor. The side piece of one of the pews had come apart and was tilting at an angle. And a pile of debris near the door needed to be cleared out.

He strapped on his tool belt and went to work. It was weirdly quiet. The only sounds came from his muffled movements and the echo of his metal hammer against the wooden floorboards. After everything that had happened with Kate yesterday, the last thing he needed was silence and more time alone to think. He'd been up most of the night thinking.

He glanced at the picture of Jesus, staring calmly out at him from the stained glass. This chapel had the same hushed, holy feeling he always associated with churches.

He tried to pry out a stubborn nail and managed to jam his thumb painfully. He hissed an expletive and shook out his hand. Glanced again at the window. *Look, just back off,* Matt thought. *I never wanted to set foot inside a church again, but I'm here doing a job, so just cut me a break and back off.*

The image in the window seemed to wait patiently. Not offended. Just waiting, with His hand out.

Matt glared at the glass depiction of the face.

I'm angry at you. Unbidden, the words filled his head, his eyes, his ears, his throat. Following closely came a crippling flood of emotion. Endless dark fury. Bitterness. Excruciating sadness. A lust for revenge. Helplessness.

He set aside his hammer and pulled himself onto the nearest pew. His fingers tunneled into his hair and he sat, elbows on his knees, head bent into his hands.

I had everything, and you took it all away and now I have nothing.

Are you satisfied? Is this what you wanted? Tremors ran through him as his body battled to contain the unbearable pressure of his thoughts.

Did you take Beth from me to punish me? What did I do that was so wrong? What possible thing could I have done to you that would have made you take her? She was so young. So young.

Memories of her ripped at his heart. Matt saw her dancing, laughing, flirting with him, cooking in their apartment's kitchen. Colorfully alive. And then he saw her dying, wasted, pale, struggling for breath. And he saw himself, confused and terrified. Not knowing what to do. Struggling to hope that she'd still be okay, that she could still recover from the disease. Even when the doctors told him she wouldn't. And then she was officially gone. Dead. Too late to save, to apologize to, to love.

After all this time, he was still trying to make himself accept what had happened to her. What had happened to his life. One moment he'd had Beth and he'd had his hockey. The next she'd been taken. And then he'd buried the hockey, too. The two biggest parts of his life, gone.

A twenty-seven-year-old dying of brain cancer? How could you let it happen to anyone? But most of all, to her? To her?! She was my wife.

Matt swore aloud, furious. "Your world sucks," he whispered. "I hate the way you've set it up."

The image in the stained-glass window didn't change in the face of his anger. Jesus' hand was still reaching outward.

Kate had told him the other day that God hadn't forgotten about him. For the first time in years, Matt could acknowledge that maybe God hadn't. He didn't know which was worse: being forgotten or being confronted like this with nowhere to turn.

He needed to get out. His heartbeat accelerated. He couldn't do this.

His strides ate the distance to the doors at the back of the chapel. But just as he was about to wrench the doors open, he stopped himself.

What was he going to tell Beverly? Was he willing to explain why he couldn't do these few simple repairs for her?

He was breathing too fast. He tried to slow it down, to calm himself down.

He *could* do this. He had to. He might be a mess, but he wasn't a coward.

Heart still thudding, Matt forced himself to go back to work. He flat-out refused to let himself look at the stained-glass window again. But in the silence, Kate's voice grew harder to ignore.

He'll never leave you.

He loves you.

He hasn't forgotten about you.

He wanted to jeer at her words, to shut her out as surely as he had the stained-glass window.

But he treasured Kate. There were countless things in this life he no longer trusted, but somehow he *did* trust her. Her goodness. Her honesty. Matt let everything she'd said to him revolve in his head while he worked, turning each sentence like a diamond held to the light.

And ever so slowly her words began to do more than circle his memory. They began to penetrate. Past his defenses, his doggedness, and his reluctance to bend.

When Kate returned from a yoga class and some grocery shopping later that afternoon, she heard Matt working upstairs. Which meant he'd finally finished the chapel.

She'd gotten halfway through unloading her eco-friendly

reusable grocery bags when she looked up and saw him standing in the doorway to the dining room. She stilled, surprised. Inside the walls of this house on a workday she was always the one that sought him out. "Hi."

"Hi."

He simply stared at her, so long that she began to wonder if maybe he needed to work on the sink or something and was waiting for her to clear out. "Am I in your way?" she asked.

He shook his head.

"Oh. Well, I'm just . . . just back from the store, trying to get these things put away."

"I'll help you."

"Sure." He took the refrigerated stuff and she took the rest, working together in silence. Every particle of air in the kitchen vibrated with the knowledge of the things they'd said to each other yesterday. All she could hear when she looked at him was his voice on the phone last night. *"I like you. I want to go out with you myself."* He hadn't wanted those admissions to change anything. And she was acting like they hadn't. But actually, for her, they'd changed a lot. The incredible realization that he liked her filled her body with electric tingles she couldn't squelch.

Once she'd finished folding the grocery bags into a neat pile, she leaned her hip against the sink and studied him. He stood with his hands in his pockets, his attention steadily centered on her. "How'd it go in the chapel?" she asked.

"The work went fine, but I was glad to get out of there."

"Haven't been in church for a few years."

"No, and never really planned to go back."

Ah, she thought. God had gone to work on him in there. He looked so miserable about it that she couldn't help but smile.

"Why are you smiling?" he asked.

"Because I'm pleased. It's a start."

Since he didn't seem inclined to say more, she told him about her yoga class and Theresa's progress with their appraisal report, and updated him on the ongoing deep freeze between Velma and Morty. What she didn't say was a single word about the enormous things that had passed between them yesterday.

The next day a miracle happened.

Gran, Velma, and Kate were in the kitchen finishing up a lunch of chicken salad sandwiches and vegetable soup when they heard the deep bass rumble of a car pulling up the drive. It drew closer and closer still.

All three of them lifted their heads, listening. They were used to the sounds of the usual cars that came around. This one sounded totally different. Distinctive.

"Who on earth could that be?" Gran murmured. She bustled to the back door and opened it, peering out. "Well, I'll be." She motioned excitedly to them. "Come see this—hurry!"

They all rushed outside into the cold, bright day. Shielding their eyes with their hands, they watched as an amazing car drew even with them and slid to a stop.

It was Morty, driving what was unmistakably his Cadillac convertible and wearing his new leather jacket, a fedora, and a triumphant grin. The car was low and long. Painted glossy black with glittering silver trim. Twin tail fins in the back. Shiny wheels filled with silver spokes. White leather upholstery trimmed with black. He hadn't been kidding when he'd told Kate that he'd kept the car in mint condition. The entire thing gleamed as if it had just rolled off the showroom floor.

"Morty!" Gran exclaimed, laughing with amazement and admiration. "What a beautiful car."

"Wow, it's *fabulous*," Kate agreed, smiling at him. "Really fabulous."

"Thank you, ladies." He tipped his hat to them, practically glowing with pride.

Kate glanced at Velma. She'd never seen Velma speechless before, but she appeared to be so now. Her mouth opened and closed a few times like a fish gasping on the dry bottom of a fishing boat.

"Well, Velma," Morty said, "hop on in. I'm taking you on a date."

Velma promptly found her voice. "Right this moment, Morty Rittenbower? I'm not dressed for that."

"That's why we're going to swing by your place first. So you can change."

"A woman likes a little advance notice."

"I'll remember that next time."

"Next time?"

"Next time," he assured her.

Velma put her hands on her hips and looked ready to argue. A few tense moments ticked by, sunshine glinting along the contours of the car, before her lips finally bowed into a smile. "I can't believe you actually took this car out of that old garage."

"I actually did." He beckoned with his hand. "Now, c'mon. That's enough fussing. Get on in."

Kate heard the back door open behind her and looked over her shoulder to see Matt walk outside. Something inside her lifted with delight, just like it did every time she saw him. He came to stand next to her as Velma settled herself in the passenger seat.

"Oh! Let me get your things, Velma." Gran dashed into the house and reemerged with Velma's coat and purse.

"Have a good afternoon, ladies. Matt." Morty saluted them and eased the car away, heartily honking the horn a couple of times.

Pleasure rushed through Kate at the sight of the two of them driving away together. She'd actually helped get Velma Armstrong out on a date with Morty! At times it had seemed like winning the lottery would prove more likely. Yet there they were, driving off together.

Gran walked down the driveway after them, clapping and waving.

"He sure didn't look worried about the car," Matt remarked.

"No," Kate answered. "He didn't." He'd looked thrilled with himself. Morty, the old dog, had learned some new tricks and managed to melt the heart of one of the crustiest women on the continent. "You know what this means, don't you?"

"No. What?"

"Well, aside from true love and Morty and Velma's happily-ever-after?"

"Aside from that."

"It means I've got gift certificates to the spa coming my way."

"You don't have the hots for me, do you?" Tyler asked.

Kate glanced at him. They were walking through the club's foyer on their way out. It had been a fun night, just like they all were with him. They'd gone to a pizza place, then to a club where a friend of Tyler's had been playing guitar with his band.

Had she developed hormones for him, however? Either tonight or on any of their other date nights? No.

Tyler regarded her with a resigned half smile.

"Well," Kate replied slowly, "you're illegally charming."

"I am that."

"And *incredibly* handsome."

"Incredibly."

"And I should be wildly infatuated with you."

"Agreed. But you're not, are you?"

They stopped near the rest rooms. People drifted past them.

"No," Kate answered. "But I really do like you, and I'm thankful that we're friends." She flinched a little, gave him an apologetic smile. "Was that patronizing, that last part about being friends?"

"Not patronizing so much as uncreative," he said. "But I guess my ego can take it."

She regarded him sympathetically.

"Quit looking so worried. It's okay."

"Okay."

"You're into Matt, aren't you?"

"Um . . ."

"He's got that whole dark, tortured thing working. Women love that."

Kate thought of Theresa and the rest of the female population of the town, who'd all wholeheartedly agree with Tyler's assessment. "I'm going to top out at friendship with Matt, too."

"Really? The way he was glaring at me the other night when I came to pick you up, I thought there might be more there."

"Nope."

"Well, shoot, little lady. I guess we're both fresh out of luck."

She smiled. "I guess so."

"Here, put on your jacket." He handed hers over, and they both donned their jackets, scarves, and gloves. He took her hand and threaded it through the crook of his arm. They made their way out of the building and through the parking lot toward his car.

"Don't get me wrong, princess," he said. "I wish you were into me."

She nodded.

"But it's all right that you're not."

"Must be rare for you," she commented, "to be on the receiving end of the let's-be-friends thing."

"Oh, extremely rare." He chuckled. "The thing of it is . . ."

"Yeah?"

"I'm glad we're friends, too."

She'd gone on a date with Tyler again. Beverly had spilled Kate's plans to him just as Matt had been leaving work. The news had hit him like a stone to the stomach.

He'd come home, but he hadn't eaten. Hadn't turned on many lights or the TV. All he'd done—all he could bring himself to do—was pace.

Why was she still seeing Tyler? Did she care about him? She must, to keep going out with him. Tyler definitely cared about her. Matt would have staked anything on it.

With a growl, he finally quit his pacing, grabbed up his car keys, and headed . . . again . . . for the empty solace of his Lamborghini.

chapter sixteen

It really wasn't fair that Matt should be *so* gorgeous. I mean, really. It was just wrong. Nice-looking was one thing. But over-the-top beautiful?

They were halfway through their Friday night poker and were taking their customary break. Kate and Matt had made their way into the kitchen together for dessert. He was chewing a bite of pecan pie. She'd mostly been chewing on resentment over his looks.

His beauty wasn't like that of, say, a statue of a Greek god. Matt had scars under his lip and near his eyebrow, after all. And a nose that had been broken. But somehow those things plus the long-lashed eyes, plus the serious mouth, plus the dark hair, plus his sheer size equaled IRRESISTIBLE. Even today, when he'd seemed especially guarded and upset about something, he struck her as painfully handsome.

And *this* was the person who'd looked at her with heat in his eyes and told her he couldn't stand to think about her dating other people. *This* was the person she was supposed to be immune to.

What a joke! She sure wasn't succeeding at developing immunity toward him. If anything, her feelings for him kept sending roots deeper and reaching up higher, despite her best intentions.

She was caught in purgatory—constantly trying to talk herself out of her attraction to him even though goose bumps pebbled her skin every time he so much as looked in her direction. It was terrible. It was wonderful.

"Okay," she said, finishing her pie and setting aside her plate. "So I was supposed to go antiquing tomorrow with Theresa, but her daughter's sick and so she can't go. Would you like to come with me instead?" Now that they'd mutually agreed to be friends, she thought she might have the right to ask him that kind of thing. The difficult part would be avoiding hurt if—when—he turned her down.

"Antiquing?" he asked her skeptically.

"Yep. Gran needs some things to finish out the house. Rugs, lamps, and a couple of sofas. I'm planning to hit the flea market, one estate sale, and maybe an antique store or two just for fun."

"Right," he said slowly. "Just for fun."

She laughed. "That sounds like a man's idea of cruel and unusual punishment, doesn't it? I don't know what I was thinking. Look, forget I said anything—"

"I'll go."

She blinked up at him. "You will?"

"Yeah. What time?"

"Nine?"

"I'll pick you up in the truck."

His words had been easily spoken, but there was something in his expression as he gazed down at her. A troubled, dangerous, almost haunted light that made her chest hurt.

She desperately wanted to see something better and clearer in his face before she left and went home to Dallas. But instead of improving, in some ways he seemed worse lately. And she was running out of time.

Morty and Velma drifted into the kitchen. Morty had on his Tommy Bahama shirt, despite the frigid weather outside. Velma had on a lime green velour sweat suit with a white ribbon stitched across the top in what looked like the pattern of a heartbeat on a monitor. Velma's astute eyes flicked over Kate to Matt. "How you doing, hottie?"

"Um . . ."

"You don't mind me calling you that, do you?" Velma asked him.

"Actually—"

"Aw, get over it." She swatted a hand at him.

Morty chuckled. "She's a spitfire, isn't she?" He eyed Velma with lovestruck admiration.

"I most certainly am," she replied, "and don't you be forgetting it."

"Now, how could I," Morty asked her, "even for a second?"

She lifted penciled eyebrows behind the spheres of her glasses. "Well, you've got a point there." She poured iced tea into three glasses, then glanced up at Matt. "Mind helping me carry these in to the others?"

"I can do it," Morty said.

"If I wanted you to do it, I would have asked you. I want the hottie's help."

Matt groaned but picked up two of the glasses and followed her out of the room.

"I'm glad I've got you alone," Morty said to Kate. He reached inside the pocket of his jeans and pulled out an envelope. "I've been on an official date with Velma and you haven't asked me about the spa certificates."

"I didn't want to be crass."

He smiled and handed the envelope over to her. "Good thing then that I never welsh on a deal."

Kate accepted the envelope. "Thank you. Really. I'll enjoy this."

"You earned it."

"I don't know if I did that much—"

"Yeah, you did, kid. You helped a heck of a lot."

"If I did, I'm glad. Would you like some pie?"

"Sure."

She served him a wedge. "Listen, I've been wondering about something."

"Shoot."

"What made you decide to take your car out of storage?"

He held his fork in his knobby hands while he chewed pensively. "It was something you said. About how you thought Velma wanted me to drive the car because she wanted me to enjoy life more. I went and visited the car a few times last week. You know what? That ol' garage was cold. Damp. Lonely. That car wasn't enjoying itself in there and neither was I. I finally thought, what am I waiting for? The Lord to come for me? That car is old, like me, but she can take a few miles. And I've really been wantin' that date with Velma. *Really* wantin' it. For years."

Kate nodded. "Will there be more dates?"

"She's lettin' me have one date a week. So that means you'll be getting a few more certificates before you leave town. Good thing you're leaving, too, or you'd drain me dry." He winked at her.

"I'm sure Velma's worth every penny," she lied.

"Every penny," he vowed.

"I'd love a ride in your car myself sometime if it's not too much trouble."

"You would?"

"Definitely."

He reached out and squeezed her hand affectionately. She squeezed back.

"On the next pretty day, then," he said. "You, me, and the Cadillac."

"You, me, and the Cadillac," she agreed.

Astonishingly, Matt turned out to be the ideal antiquing partner. He didn't shove his opinion at her. But when she asked him for it, he gave her thoughtful answers. And after seeing the way he'd decorated the inside of his own house, she found it easy to respect his taste. He never complained, never rushed her, never looked pained. He never asked to use the bathroom, like a girlfriend would have. He handled the driving and the parking. He carried all the stuff. And—*and*—he was eye candy to look at.

Together, they had a very successful morning. They scored three lamps and a set of lithographs at the flea market. At the estate sale they decided on a chocolate-colored leather sofa and chair, and two beautiful beige, brown, and sage-green oriental rugs. After a pit stop at a deli for sandwiches, they parked near the center of town so that Kate could revisit a few of Redbud's antique shops.

Everywhere they went people recognized Matt. A few acquaintances greeted him by name and with a handshake. The rest, strangers, whispered about him and watched him with avid interest when they thought he wasn't looking. Kate could easily read the speculation in their faces. They were all wondering what this very average woman was doing with their town celebrity.

Before subjecting him to more antiques, Kate insisted on buying him coffee. Main Street Coffee was crowded, so they took their drinks, a latte with lots of whip and chocolate sprinkles for her, and a plain coffee with low-fat milk for him, to one of the black iron benches positioned along the street.

Kate settled in with a contented sigh. Sitting here with him felt right. Better than that. Perfect.

She squinted upward through the barren tree branches to the swath of sky. The temperature hovered in the mid-fifties, but the day was sunny and windless. Her quilted trench coat and leather gloves were keeping her plenty warm.

She glanced over at Matt, who was wearing a well-worn pair of jeans and a black North Face jacket. He met and held her gaze, utterly still but tense with that awareness that lived between them now.

She sipped her latte. "I want to ask you about something, and I already know you're not going to want to talk about it."

He raised an eyebrow.

"But it's been on my mind a lot lately, so I'm going to ask you about it anyway."

"Uh-oh."

"What happened with your hockey?"

He winced, his lips setting into a firm, hard line.

"Will you tell me?" she asked. "Or is it totally off-limits?"

"I'll tell you." Several cars hummed by before he said more. "Beth died during the hockey season. Did you know that?"

"No."

"The coach and the GM met with me afterward, told me to take a few weeks off. So I did." Slowly, he lowered his coffee cup to his knee and turned it around and around. "Those were bad days—with the funeral and all the family, the reporters. Every day of those two weeks I wished I could go back to practice. I was sorry I'd taken any time off at all. I thought that when I got back on the ice at least something in my life would be right again." He kept silent a long time.

"But it wasn't right?" Kate asked.

"No. It was meaningless. I'd thought the hard work would help. But instead it was just . . . empty." He frowned. "Beth knew what was important in life, and it became clear to me that hockey wasn't it."

"I'm sorry," Kate said.

"Yeah. It's pretty bad when you suddenly hate something you've always loved."

Kate nodded. "Drink something," she gently reminded him.

"Oh." He took a sip. His posture, which had tightened, visibly relaxed.

"So you left the team?"

"Not at first. I forced myself to play for another month and a half out of nothing but discipline. Then one day at practice . . . I was playing fine and everything was normal . . . but on that day I just—I just suddenly couldn't make myself do it anymore. I walked off the ice."

Kate watched the muscles in his jaw turn stone hard. "And that was it," he said. "The end of my hockey career. I was done."

He looked at her, and she returned his attention evenly. She thought she saw regret in his expression. Waste. Loss. "And then you came to Redbud," she said.

"Yeah." He watched a group of teenagers pass, clearly finding it easier to talk to her while looking at the bustle surrounding them. "I only took two things out of the New York apartment and then I moved—"

"What two things?"

He tilted his head, quizzical.

"What two things did you take out of the New York apartment?"

He paused. "Remember that picture of Beth you saw at my house?"

"Yes."

"That and . . . well." He hesitated again, seeming embarrassed. "A hairbrush of hers with a silver back on it."

Kate pretended extreme interest in an approaching mother and toddler so that Matt wouldn't see her lips tremble. Emotion pressed against her from the inside as she fought back the urge to cry for him. He might have been a big-time hockey star once, but on the inside, he'd always been this quiet, intense person whose feelings ran deep. The kind of person who'd want to keep his wife's hairbrush to remember her by.

She kept her gaze sternly focused on the toddler and waited to speak until she could be certain her voice would sound normal. "What did you do with the rest of your stuff from New York?"

"I had it put in storage."

"And then you moved into your house here."

"Yeah."

"Which was in pretty bad shape at the time."

"Right. I didn't mind, though. Working on it, making it better, gave me something to do, something else to think about."

She could see how the process of repairing old houses had been good for him. Therapeutic. Sort of a metaphor for what she wished he could do with his heart. "How did it become your business?"

"By the time I finished my house I had several other offers, people around here who wanted me to come work on their houses. So I took a few of them up on it." He shrugged.

"Are you involved with hockey at all anymore?"

"Not at all."

"Why?"

Silence. "Kate," he groaned.

"I know, I'm torturing you. Just go ahead and get it over with and tell me."

"Man, you're persistent." But he didn't look annoyed. He regarded her with tenderness.

Tiny shivers raced between her shoulder blades in response. "I'm horribly persistent, aren't I? I'm sorry. It's terrible! I wish I could be more—"

"I'm not involved with hockey anymore because it's painful. That's the short answer, I guess." He ran a hand through his hair. "How do I explain this? I hardly even like to think about it."

She waited.

"I used to love hockey. It was my life. It's difficult to be reminded of it now, because every time I see it on TV or hear about it or think about it I remember that it's over for me and that it's continuing on without me."

Since that moment at his house when she'd seen the look on his face when hockey had come on TV, she'd been thinking about Matt and his sport. She could almost hear God whispering to her, saying, **He needs to return to it, Kate. He's not done.**

This conversation had only cemented the idea in her head. Matt Jarreau, hockey legend, needed to make phone calls, train, play the minor circuit if there was one, audition if they did that, and whatever else was necessary to get himself back into the NHL. He was never going to have closure or peace about it until he finished his career on his own terms.

Could he find the same passion for it that he'd had before Beth died? She'd bet that it had already returned. Otherwise, accidentally catching a glimpse of it on TV wouldn't have the power to hurt him like it did now.

"Thank you for telling me," she said, and left it at that. This wasn't the time or place to share her revelation with him. She needed to think and pray about it. To sort out everything clearly in her own head.

"Are you cold?" he asked with a trace of worry.

"Not at all."

"Sure?"

"Sure." She drank down the last of her latte and licked her upper lip.

His gaze followed the movement. "Can I ask you a question?"

"Of course. Anything."

"I want to know about your job," he said.

"What would you like to know?"

"How you feel about it."

"Well . . ." Over the weeks, they'd often talked about her job, but their discussions had only touched on things like her day-to-day duties, what the complex was like, her co-workers. That he'd ask her this made her wonder if he could read what she didn't say, the same way she was learning to read him. "I used to feel really confident about my job. I enjoyed it, I got a lot of satisfaction from it. But more than that . . . This is going to sound weird to you."

"Try me."

"I felt like it was exactly what God wanted me to be doing."

"You're right. That *is* weird."

She balled up the napkin she'd wrapped around her coffee cup and threw it at him. He caught it effortlessly one-handed. Grinned.

"You're such a joker," she said.

"Yeah, I'm full of laughs. Here." He took her cup and threw all their trash in a nearby garbage can. When he returned he asked, "So how do you feel about it now?"

"Like maybe I've done the job too long." She struggled to be as truthful with him as he'd just been with her. "One of my kids, a teenage girl, committed suicide about six months ago."

Matt's breath hissed inward at the news.

"After that happened my job started giving me this sad, hopeless feeling. I always used to be so optimistic about the kids, about their futures, but now I don't know. I was having a hard time finding any joy in it for those last few months before I left."

"You're planning to go back to it when you return to Dallas."

"Yes. Although, if nothing's changed, then I'm going to have to think about looking for another job, which scares me."

"When are you leaving Redbud?"

"In about a month."

He scowled. "That soon? I didn't know."

"Thanksgiving is next week. We'll stay a week or two into December, but no more than that. Gran and I both need to get back for the holidays. Will you be finished working on Chapel Bluff by then?"

"Yeah, I'll be done."

A beat of quiet. "Ready to look at a few more antiques?" she asked.

He nodded, and they made their way side by side down Main.

"Listen," he said. "About Thanksgiving. I'd really like for you and Beverly to come over to my house and spend it with us. You owe me that after forcing me to invite my whole family."

That he wanted her to join him for Thanksgiving pleased her inordinately. "We've already told Velma we'll do Thanksgiving dinner with her, but we could probably come over to your house that evening if you want us to."

"I want you to."

"Then we'll be there. What can we bring?"

"Nothing. We'll have too much food as it is."

"Gran will insist on cooking and bringing something. Just tell her to do a pie—that'll make her happy."

They reached the nearest of the shops. Matt held the door for her as Kate entered into an environment brimming with classy accessories, expensive British antiques, and the smell of cloves. Kate weaved her way along, appreciating the various pieces, until she came to a table that stopped her in her tracks. It wasn't large. It was dainty, in fact, with a satinwood rectangular top and two satinwood sides that folded down. Its graceful cabriole legs ended in worn brass casters. The top and sides of the table had been skillfully painted with swags of leaves and wreaths accented with fluttering white ribbons.

"You like it," Matt said.

"I do." The piece clutched at her heart in the way that antiques sometimes did. "It's a Pembroke table." She checked the dangling white price tag. Five thousand dollars.

The owner of the store, a ruddy-faced older gentleman, approached them with a smile. He did a double take when he recognized Matt. "Are you Matt Jarreau?"

"I am."

He extended his hand and introduced himself. "Henry Vernon. I watched every televised game you ever played. I'm a big fan."

"Thank you."

"It's a real pleasure to meet you." He glanced from Matt to Kate to the table. Cleared his throat. "I bought that on my last trip to London. Just came in on the container I had shipped over. It's a beauty, isn't it?"

"Yes, it is," Kate said.

"It's a George the Third Pembroke table. Made around 1780."

They chatted about the table, some of the other finds he'd made on his trip, and about the delights of antiquing in England. When a trio of new customers came in, he excused himself to greet them.

"This is too expensive for Beverly's budget," Matt said.

"Way too expensive, and she doesn't need anything quite like this. But it *is* pretty." Kate admired it for a few more moments and then reluctantly moved on.

"Kate," Matt said.

She turned.

"I just wanted to say thank you."

"What for?"

"For today. I've enjoyed it."

"You have?" She found it hard to believe.

"Yes."

"I should be the one thanking you. You've been a big help and really patient, even though most of what we've done must have bored you to death."

He gazed at her levelly. "I wasn't bored."

"Good, I'm glad." She started forward. "C'mon, almost done here. Then one more store and I'll let you off the hook."

Matt followed her, his thoughts churning. He'd been completely serious when he'd told her he'd enjoyed their day. Actually, if anything, it had been an understatement. Today had been the best day he'd had in years because he'd been near her.

Inside Chapel Bluff's chapel, he'd railed at God because this world could be so incredibly rotten. But today had reminded him that there was good in it, too. There was still beauty here and there was still kindness and maybe . . . maybe there was even still hope.

chapter seventeen

Kate was in serious trouble. She knew it almost instantly. She'd lived with asthma long enough to differentiate between her regular symptoms and a severe attack. This was a severe attack, and it had come on suddenly and hit her like a freight train.

She paused, leaning her hand against the trunk of a tree. She tried to relax. Hard to do with her heart rate surging, pounding fast in her ears. *Calm down*, she told herself. But her airways only constricted more, and the wheezing sound of her breath grew louder, more labored.

She pushed away from the tree and continued up the driveway to Chapel Bluff. She'd woken up restless this Sunday morning. . . . A walk had seemed like a good idea. She coughed repeatedly. It had turned out to be a bad idea. A really bad idea. It shouldn't have been. She'd checked the weather online before she'd left, thinking it'd be okay. But the air was much colder than she'd expected. And cold air combined with exercise could sometimes trigger her asthma. But rarely—so rarely—did it ever get this bad.

Desperation rose inside her. She kept her focus forward, on where the house would be when she rounded the bend. How much farther? How many more steps until she could get herself inside? Gran was there. Her inhaler was there.

Help me, God.

She was struggling to get any air at all now, her chest unbearably tight. *You'll be okay*, she told herself. *You'll be okay. You'll be okay.* But the house was still far away and the panic was rising, overwhelming her. She wheezed in and out, drowning without a drop of water anywhere in sight.

"Matt?" Beverly said.

The tone of her voice over the phone caused Matt to still immediately. "Yes."

"I've just brought Kate to the hospital, to—to the emergency room."

A bolt of pure fear tore into him, deep and deadly. He couldn't bring himself to speak. His fingers clenched the phone.

"She had a terrible asthma attack. They've taken her away to treat her. I'm sure she'll be fine but I'm worried. . . . Her lips were turning blue."

"You're at the ER at Redbud General?"

"Yes. I'm about to call Peg and Velma but I felt—I felt like I should call you first."

"I'm on my way."

"That's probably not necessary—"

"I'm on my way." He clicked off the phone and tossed it on the kitchen countertop. His body was hot and cold at once, and he thought he might be sick. *Kate is in the emergency room. Kate. Oh, God.* He knew he needed to get a grip but couldn't quite manage it.

He rushed into the living room, pushed his feet into his Adidas, palmed his car keys, then bolted out the back door toward the garage.

Near-death experiences took a lot out of a girl.

Once the doctors had stabilized Kate—her breathing passages open, her chest loose—her mind had washed clean with relief and her body had turned heavy and relaxed. They'd wheeled her to an upper floor, and she'd simply let herself sink into the hospital bed and drop into sleep.

Sometime later, a deep drum roll of thunder penetrated her dreams. Half conscious and eager for more sleep, she screwed her eyes shut tighter and tried to shift onto her side. The IV in her wrist pulled uncomfortably, so she returned to her back with a sigh.

What exactly had happened? She went back over her memories of the day, starting with the walk, the attack, Gran's frantic drive to the hospital, the blur of doctors, nurses, faces, medicines, and finally—blessedly—the ability to breathe freely. How bizarre that all of it had happened so quickly. The morning had started in the same normal way that all of her mornings at Chapel Bluff had started. But between then and now she'd nearly suffocated, been rushed to the ER, and was currently tucked into one of those mechanical hospital beds with the top half raised at a forty-five-degree angle.

Rain pattered against the glass. Blearily, she cracked open her eyes and looked toward the windows—

Matt was leaning against them. In the room's corner, where the windows met the wall.

Matt? Goose bumps flowed down her arms. How long had he been there? She struggled to fight past the last of the grogginess and the beginnings of embarrassment. She didn't exactly want him seeing her like this.

He said nothing, just stared at her with burning brown eyes.

His arms were crossed and his face was grim. Something like anger radiated from him in waves.

She wasn't sure exactly why he'd be angry—and then it hit her. Hospitals. After everything he'd gone through with his wife, he must hate these places. He looked like a lion in the far corner of its cage, defiant but trapped all the same.

She honestly wouldn't have imagined he'd come here. If she'd been conscious, she would have stopped him from coming to spare him the reminders.

He pushed off the wall and approached her. He had on jeans and a frayed gray Abercrombie sweat shirt. "How are you feeling?" he asked.

"Pretty good."

She must look atrocious. She had an oxygen tube running under her nose. Her hair and face were probably a mess. And under the flannel sheets she was dressed in nothing but one of those white and blue hospital gowns.

Maybe she should blow off those worries, however, because for once Matt himself looked horrible. His expression was gaunt, his skin pale, and his hair stuck up in tufts.

"What time is it?" she asked.

"Three o'clock."

"Where's my grandmother?"

"They're all waiting down the hall. They were scared of waking you."

"Oh."

"I promised to go and get them as soon as you woke up." He made a move toward the door. "Do you want me to—"

"No. Just give me a couple of minutes first."

He paused, watching her intently.

She yawned, stretched a little under the covers. Her attention panned around the small room, so similar to every other hospital room she'd ever been in. TV hanging from a big metal arm that bolted into the wall. Sink and cabinets opposite the windows and beyond that, the bathroom.

"Can I get you anything?" he asked.

"Maybe just some water."

A nurse had left a cup with a straw and a pink pitcher on a tray next to the sink. He filled the cup and handed it to her. She took some long draws through the straw. Thanks to the round ice pellets, the water tasted blessedly cold.

"What is this they're giving you?" he asked, gesturing to the IV stand.

She glanced at the tubing running from the bag into her wrist. "Some kind of corticosteroid."

"And oxygen." His gaze moved to the line beneath her nose.

"Right."

"What happened, Kate?"

She took one more sip of water and handed the cup back to him. He placed it back on the tray.

"I went for a walk this morning," she said. "When I felt my asthma start to kick in, I turned around and headed home. At first I thought it was going to be fine. Manageable. But then it got worse fast, before I could get back to the house. It was pretty bad by the time I reached Gran."

He frowned. "Beverly said your lips were turning blue."

"Hmm." She made a face. "That must have been lovely."

"This isn't your first time to be hospitalized for this," he stated. While she'd been sleeping, Gran had obviously filled him in on her history with asthma.

"No. I've had some attacks like this before, but the last one was five years ago. I've kept it really well under control since then."

"Until today."

"Until today," she acknowledged. He was inexplicably furious. She could read it in every rigid line of him, but mostly she could see it seething in his eyes.

Good grief. He didn't exactly have a warm bedside manner. "Matt," she said gently, "I get that this probably isn't your favorite place. Thank you for coming to check on me, but it won't hurt my feelings if you want to go home. This is your day off. I'm sure you'd rather be at home taking it easy."

"I'm not leaving."

And he didn't. He stayed and stayed. All through the hours that the seniors kept her company. All through dinner, which he went out and brought back for her from her favorite salad place. All through two really bad reality TV shows.

When she couldn't hold her eyes open another second, she drifted off to sleep. Much later, when a nurse roused her in the middle of the night to check her temperature and blood pressure, Matt was still there. Back in his spot in the corner of the room by the wall and the windows. His arms crossed, his face foreboding.

A caged lion.

Matt drove his Lamborghini home from the hospital in the wee hours of the morning, hardly aware of the road in front of him.

From the little he'd been able to pick up from the doctor, Kate might have been able to curb her asthma attack if she'd had her inhaler with her or if she'd avoided exercising in the cold. Simple precautions. Easy. And yet she'd ignored them and gone and gotten herself into a seriously dangerous situation. Just thinking about her alone, away from the house, and fighting for breath made him stiff with dread.

His irrational fear for her pissed him off. But what pissed him off more was that she'd put her life at risk out of sheer carelessness.

He wanted to kill her himself, he was so angry.

He reached home, eased his car into his garage, and hit the button that closed the door behind him. But he didn't move. He just sat there in the dark, holding on to the steering wheel.

When he'd arrived at the ER, the doctors and nurses had restricted him and Beverly to the waiting room. The other seniors had arrived gradually. Their small group had been surrounded by sick adults, fussing kids, and worried family members. He'd sat there the whole time, waiting, with his heart thudding dully, his thoughts a chaos of panic.

After what seemed an eternity, the doctor had come out and explained how they'd gotten Kate's attack under control. An orderly had escorted them up to her room. By the time he'd arrived she'd already been fast asleep.

He'd expected her to look terrible, but she'd actually looked beautiful. Her skin had been smooth and clear like white china, her hair blazing dark red. She'd reminded him of a doll tucked smoothly into its doll bed—except for the lifeless gown, the dripping IV, and the oxygen tube.

It reminded him powerfully of Beth. There had been times during her fight against cancer when she'd looked deceptively beautiful, too, and he'd wanted to believe she wasn't as sick as they'd said. But there had been evidence of reality those times, too. Endless doctors, nurses, hospitals, machines, medicines. Eventually she'd begun to look every bit as seriously ill as she was.

He'd *never* wanted to stand by the bedside of another woman at another hospital, feeling as powerless and scared as he had the first time. But that's exactly what he'd just spent the past sixteen hours doing.

The fact that Kate was recovering well and would be released tomorrow didn't ease his mind at all. People were fragile. You couldn't count on them not to die.

Kate had an acute case of bliss brought on by spa immersion.

The pedicurist had just exfoliated her legs from the knees down and then wrapped them in hot towels. Kate was reclining in her chair, eyes closed, listening to the spa's soft music. It sounded like rain and wind chimes.

She had to admit that she felt slightly guilty for taking Morty's spa gift certificates. He was retired and short on funds, after all. She probably *should* have been noble and humble and refused payment. She probably *should* have said something about how furthering the cause of love was reward enough.

But then she recalled in gory detail what she'd gone through to un-dye Morty's hair. Aw, to heck with guilt. She'd earned this.

She sighed, relaxed all her muscle groups, and wondered what Matt was doing. After that marathon vigil he'd kept in her hospital room, she'd expected to see him again the next day. Hour after hour at the hospital had passed. Without wanting to, she'd caught herself waiting for him, looking for him every time she heard footsteps in the hallway, every time someone knocked on her door. She'd been discharged around noon, and Gran had brought her home to Chapel Bluff where Matt should have been busy working. Instead the house had greeted them with emptiness. Gran told her that Matt had been there earlier but had left to make a Home Depot run. Kate had spent the remainder of the afternoon waiting for him to return and the remainder of the evening waiting for the phone to ring. He hadn't come back and he hadn't called.

As usual, she didn't know what to make of him or what to do

about him. She wasn't sure if she should be thankful for the time at the hospital or miffed that he'd been avoiding her since. Or both. Or maybe she had the right to feel neither.

When Matt still hadn't returned to Chapel Bluff by ten thirty this morning, she'd decided that between her asthma attack, her hospital stay, and her frazzled emotional state over Matt's absence, she needed a trip to the spa.

And what a good idea *that* had been. Her thoughts drifted in delirious patterns. This was so relaxing. And she'd have such pretty toes when she left. There'd be plenty of time later to angst over the man with the heartbreaking brown eyes.

After her pedicure, Kate took herself and her novel out for a long, leisurely lunch. When she finally returned to Chapel Bluff that afternoon, she immediately spotted Matt's truck parked near the barn. The sight of it almost sent her straight into another red-alert asthma attack.

She sat in her car for a few minutes, lecturing herself about being calm, about how she was his friend, about how she was a grown woman and could easily handle this situation.

Gran had left a note for her on the kitchen table, saying that she and "the girls" had gone to a matinee.

Kate paused, listening. From the second floor, where she knew Matt would be working, she could hear nothing. She made her way up the stairs.

She'd worn her black flip-flops home from the spa. They made a faint slapping sound against her heels as she approached the bathroom. She'd chosen a glossy lollipop pink polish for her toes, which coordinated with the pale pink turtleneck she had on. Her jeans, she noticed, were still rolled up one tuck at the cuffs.

She reached the doorway to the bathroom. Usually she found Matt working and he'd continue working while they chatted. But today he was standing immobile at his full height, as if he'd stopped what he'd been doing the moment she'd entered the house and had been waiting for her to find him. And he was staring at her like a gladiator would stare at its mortal enemy—in a way that promised her he was about to take her apart limb by limb.

She'd had a greeting ready in her head, but it evaporated like a plume of steam. "Are you . . . mad at me?"

"You know, Kate, I am," he said, voice tight. "I've been waiting for it to go away, but I don't think it's going anywhere."

"Why?" she asked, stunned. "What did I do?"

"You nearly killed yourself."

She fumbled around mentally, trying to understand. "My asthma attack?"

"You knew you shouldn't exercise out in the cold like that."

"I . . . I checked the weather online before I left. They forecasted a high of sixty-two."

"You went out early for your walk. It wasn't going to reach that for hours."

Her lips opened, but no words came out.

"And where was your inhaler? You had it with you that other day when I saw you walking."

"I just forgot it. It's . . . it's one of those things I usually take with me, but not every time. I'm almost always fine without it."

"You obviously weren't fine without it this time." The bigness of him and his emotion pushed against her like a storm cloud.

Her own irritation started to rise and grow to meet his, to push back. "Well, maybe you're perfect and never forget things, but I admit that I did this time, okay? I've already paid for my mistake physically, and when the hospital bill arrives I'm sure that I'll pay for it with my wallet, too. So maybe you can cut me some slack and spare me the lecture."

His chest rose and fell with his angry breath.

"A little sympathy would be nice," she said.

"Sympathy?" His features twisted in disbelief. "That's what you want from me? A little sympathy?"

"Yes!"

"Unfortunately, when I saw you in the hospital with a tube in your arm, my feelings went way deeper than sympathy."

She struggled to think past the pulse pounding in her temples. "Is this why you were angry in the hospital? You were mad at me for what I'd done? I thought it was because you were back in a hospital again after what you'd gone through with your wife. I thought it was memories."

"My memories didn't exactly put me in a better mood."

"But mostly it was me?"

"Mostly it was you. Mostly it still *is* you. It makes me crazy," he said, making a sharp gesture with his hands, "to think that you'd be—so careless."

Her hands curled into fists. "What else do you want me to say, Matt? That I'm sorry? I'm sorry. How's that? Better?" She turned on her heel and took off down the hallway.

His footfalls pounded behind her. She sped toward the stairs, but he caught up, his hand wrapping around her upper arm. His strong fingers held her with careful pressure, staying her but not hurting her.

She turned toward him, and they were suddenly very close. Almost chest to chest.

"Why do you have the right to be so angry, exactly?" she asked.

"I don't."

"Did I worry you? Is that it? If so, I am sorry for what I put you and Gran and the others through."

He moved forward, even nearer. "What they feel for you and what I feel for you are nothing alike."

She ought to step away. She was angry. Wasn't she? She had been two seconds ago. But her anger had scattered in the face of his glorious nearness.

They breathed together, their exhales and inhales fast. She gazed into his eyes, and he gazed back without shields. She saw vulnerability, frustration, desire.

"Promise me you'll be more careful with yourself," he whispered roughly. His forehead came to rest against hers. "I don't want anything to happen to you."

The words hit her with physical force, stabbing a direct hit to her heart.

He changed the angle of his head so that their lips were close. Closer. His hands brushed up the sides of her neck and tunneled into her hair, holding the back of her head. His mouth moved even closer, until it pressed against hers and he was kissing her.

Kate kissed him back, straining into him, arching up onto her tiptoes. Her arms came around his neck, grabbing fistfuls of shirt against his nape.

She adored him with that kiss, while her brain spun with the impossibility and magnitude of it, and her body reveled in the touch and feel of him.

He made a growling noise and his thumbs moved possessively against her jaw. He kissed her and kissed her and kissed her and she kissed him back, until she was forced to come up for air. She broke contact, tilting her face back. He stayed right where he was, watching her, his hands cradling her head.

Kate breathed unevenly, looking into his eyes.

She loved him.

She absolutely, no-going-back-now, one hundred percent loved him. She couldn't trust him to return her love. Wasn't sure God intended for her to love him at all. But she couldn't help it.

Kate released the handfuls of his shirt she'd been gripping, smoothed the fabric, then flattened her palms on his chest. Every molecule she had screamed at her to grab him close and beg him to kiss her until she couldn't breathe again. Instead, she forced herself to gently push him away.

He took a step back, his arms falling to his sides.

"I thought," she said, swiping a lock of hair out of her eyes, "you said that we were just friends."

"I want to be more than just your friend, Kate."

The heater made its familiar *clunk* and *whir* as it roused to life. She could smell the subtly masculine scent of his soap.

"Do you feel the same way about me?" he asked. Doubt clouded his expression.

She almost laughed. She could hardly deny that she did after the way she'd just kissed him. "Yes. But . . ."

"But what?"

But it probably spells disaster for me because I love you. She shrugged helplessly, unable to think of anything suitable to say. Her lips felt swollen from his kisses, and she couldn't seem to put two coherent thoughts together.

He reached for her hand. He gazed at it, kissed the inside of her palm, then threaded his fingers through hers and held firmly. His attention returned to her face.

She simply looked back at him. Silent.

They stayed that way as the seconds stretched.

"I have something I have to do," he finally said.

She nodded.

"I'll be back."

"All right."

He gave her such a smoldering look of longing that her heart took up its pounding again. Before she could melt into a puddle, he walked away and down the stairs. From below, she heard the kitchen door close behind him, then his car's engine as he drove away.

Kate pressed both hands against the bottom half of her face. Oh. Heaven. Above.

She loved him.

She couldn't love him!

But she did.

chapter eighteen

Matt had a ghost to confront. Or, more accurately, a gigantic storage unit full of Beth's possessions to confront. After leaving Kate he drove straight for the place.

He'd never visited the storage facility that stored his old life. Not once. He'd arranged for the space over the phone, and he'd had their Manhattan apartment packed and transported by a moving company. Frequently over the years, though, he'd thought about all the things that were sitting in the dark, shut away, and waiting for him. He'd always known that he needed to sort through it all. Until now he'd never had the motivation to face it, so he'd avoided it.

After kissing Kate—

He probably shouldn't have done that. He'd managed to resist kissing her for weeks, and he certainly hadn't planned to kiss her today. But now that he had . . .

He couldn't make himself be sorry.

A dizzy kind of emotion—happiness?—was still buzzing through him. Man, he was rusty at happiness. It felt light, foreign, addictively good. Even the promise of future pain couldn't faze him at the moment. Like a junkie shooting cocaine, he knew what he felt for her was bad for him, but he couldn't make himself stop. If she let him, he'd kiss Kate every chance he got right up until she left.

He flipped on his blinker and exited the freeway. He'd never in his life felt such power in a kiss.

In the quiet moments that had followed it, though, the thought of this storage unit had slithered into his head. Of all things, he didn't want to think about this storage unit when he was with Kate. So here he was.

He steered his truck through the gates that surrounded the facility. Quickly, he checked the number on the key he'd stopped at home to retrieve. He located his unit and turned off the engine. It looked just like all the others. Brightly painted door. Industrial.

He exited the truck, wind raking him as he worked his key into the unit's lock. The clouds hung low, covering the sun and making the day cold and gray. He could hear only the muffled drone of the nearby freeway. As far as he could see, no other person had come out today to check on their belongings, which suited him fine.

The slotted door rose with a soft whine. Behind it, new-looking cardboard boxes filled the space. Toward the front they'd been stacked on top of one another. Further back, the boxes became larger, and further back still he could make out the shape of furniture, which had been wrapped with some kind of heavy plastic to protect it.

The moving company had done a tidy job. They'd left a pathway from the front to the rear. Each box had been secured with thick clear packing tape. And everywhere he looked block handwriting in permanent marker told him what the boxes held.

Resistance struck him with thudding force. He didn't want to do this. He didn't want to open any of these boxes and look inside and remember. He only wanted to shut the door, get back in his truck, and drive.

Tamping down on the instinct, he walked the length of the space and back again, taking it all in. He didn't know where to begin. There were so many boxes. He stopped near the mouth of the unit and used one of his keys to slit the tape across the top of the nearest box. He lifted the flaps. Inside he saw Beth's clothes, precisely folded in stacks.

He remembered these shirts. Could picture her wearing them.

Grief hit him like a wave crashing. He stood frozen, chin down, memories of her cycling through his brain.

They don't smell like her, he thought. He'd have thought they would. But this box and its contents smelled like everything else in the space, like cardboard and dust.

Without touching so much as a fingertip to even one shirt, he made himself move to the next box. More things from her closet. Scarves, gloves, hats.

He'd loved her. She'd been a wonderful, wonderful girl.

He wished for the thousandth time that he'd taken care of her better during the last months of her life. When she'd been diagnosed, he'd sat her down and they'd talked about the possibility of his giving up hockey so that he could be with her full time. He'd known—absolutely known—that stopping was the right thing to do. But when she'd refused to let him quit, when she'd urged him to continue playing, he'd let himself be persuaded. A small part of him had even been secretly relieved, a truth that shamed him to this day.

He'd brought up quitting a few more times with her over the coming months. Each time she'd grown agitated until she'd finally, earnestly, asked him to stop suggesting it.

Beth had preferred to deal with cancer by continuing on with life as if everything were normal. She'd been in denial, and he'd been in denial right along with her. It was only during that final month that it had really sunk in for him that she might not beat it. Dazed, he'd lived each day just going through the motions, and then—before he could grasp her to him tightly enough—she'd died.

He couldn't forgive himself for playing through her illness. For the past three years, guilt had dogged him mercilessly, kept him up at night, made him hate himself for the way he'd treated her. Regret was a bitter thing. Horribly bitter, because he couldn't go back and change a single thing that he'd done.

He opened a box that contained her jewelry. Then a box of her jeans.

He'd been a lousy husband to Beth in life, and he was being a lousy husband to her in death, too, because he was falling hard for someone else. His affections were moving on, when hers never would or could.

"I want you to go on with your life," Beth had said to him once, late at night in their bed. She'd turned on the lamp and grabbed his hand and looked at him with urgency. *"I want you to find someone, after me. Someone to love you."* Her blue eyes had filled with tears. *"Someone you can love. I want you to have a family and to be happy. I need for you to promise me that you will. I can't face this if I'm having to worry about you every minute."* He'd promised her, but only because it was what she'd wanted to hear. He hadn't had the slightest hope that he'd ever care about another woman.

"I'm sorry, Beth," he whispered into the silence, meaning it with his whole heart, standing there alone in the storage unit. "I'm sorry." The sorrow went deeper than tears. He'd never been able to cry, though he'd often wished he could.

Beth hadn't deserved what happened to her. He looked upward. *She didn't deserve this!*

His only consolation had always been that Beth wasn't in any current pain. Despite his hostility toward God, he believed in heaven and he had no doubt at all that Beth was there.

Right?

This time a reply did come. He heard a steady voice deep inside himself speak for the first time in a long time. **She's with me now,** it assured him. **I've got her.**

Amazingly, tears did come to him then, blurring his vision. "Good," he managed to say. "Good, then."

He locked his jaw and moved on, opening one box after another after another, cutting through all the items that belonged to his old life, to his dead wife. There was no running away anymore from what had happened to Beth and to him, no matter how fast his car.

He'd gone about a quarter of the way through the unit when he opened a box that contained some of his hockey memorabilia. Trophies, certificates, framed photos, jerseys. A sense of loss stung him, a fresh sadness layered on top of all the other sadnesses of this place.

Faced with the proof of his past accomplishments, he realized that he couldn't go on with this chore. Or maybe it wasn't that he couldn't. It was that he realized there was no point. He wasn't going to bring any of these things home with him. He didn't want any of them in his new life. Not a single item.

He dug his smartphone out of his pocket and started to search for local charities. He'd contact one of the agencies Beth had supported. He'd tell them they could have it all.

But as the first screen of results appeared, he reconsidered. Some of these boxes contained picture albums, childhood keepsakes, wedding china, and all kinds of other things that Beth's parents, or his own parents, might want. Before he gave it away, he needed to offer it to them.

He called his mom. He lucked out when she didn't answer and he was able to simply leave a message. Then he scrolled through his phone's contact list and found Beth's parents' number. He'd seldom spoken to them since Beth's death, but he got them on the line, explained the situation, and heard himself say that he'd fly down tomorrow and bring whatever they wanted with him. Beth's mother knew exactly which things she wanted and exactly the things Beth's siblings wanted, as if she'd made a mental list long ago and had only been waiting for him to ask.

Once he got off the phone with Beth's parents, he dialed the airlines and booked a trip to Georgia.

Lastly, he called Kate. She sounded like light to him. Just the tone of her voice eased him. He tried to tell her what he'd been doing and why he'd be gone tomorrow, but he knew he was screwing it up. "I need to take some of Beth's stuff . . . the stuff that her parents want to keep, down to them in Atlanta, and then I can get this storage area cleaned out."

She didn't ask him why he'd raced away from her to visit a storage unit and open boxes of his dead wife's stuff. In a way, Kate already seemed to know why he'd done it. "Okay," she said, and by the tone of her voice, he could tell it really was.

"Maybe I should talk to Beverly," he said, "and ask her for the day off."

"No, I'll talk to her. Listen, it's fine. Take as much time as you need. The work will still be waiting when you get back."

"I'll just be gone tomorrow. I fly down in the morning and back tomorrow night." He didn't say that he couldn't stand to be away from her for more than a day. "So I'll see you Thursday."

"Sounds good."

"I'll miss you." It slipped out before he could stop it.

A split second of quiet, then, "I'll miss you, too."

"I'll be back soon."

"Safe travels."

Beth had inherited her mother's beautiful blond looks and her father's soft and sentimental personality. Matt could remember the two of them talking about it, Beth chuckling over the way the genetics had filtered down. Looking across the coffee table at her parents now, Matt could easily see the evidence of it again. Looks from Mom. Personality straight from Dad.

The three of them sat in Beth's parents' classy living room, in their big classy house with the white columns, in their classy Atlanta neighborhood. Beth's mother, Anne, had a slim frame, stylishly cut short hair, and almond-shaped blue eyes. Her father looked exactly like what he was—a southern gentleman and a successful businessman half retired now so that he could play golf three times a week.

When Matt had spared a thought for them in the past few years, he'd always pictured them the way he'd last seen them the week of Beth's funeral—pale and devastated.

But they weren't that way anymore. They looked tan and healthy. They showed him pictures of the five grandchildren Beth's brother and sister had now given them. They talked about their vacation home in Costa Rica and their upcoming trip to Switzerland in the spring.

They brought up memories of Beth easily, as if they were used to talking about her. They went back over childhood stories about her he'd heard before. They talked about the pageants, Matt and Beth's wedding, and holidays he'd spent with their family. They reminisced about all her best qualities. And they reminisced about her weaknesses, too. How she'd burst into tears sometimes when she got too stressed. Her outright terror of flying on airplanes. Her anxiety over her weight even though her weight had always been perfect. It made Matt feel uncomfortable, but her parents smiled over those traits just as fondly as all the others.

Matt had never known Beth's father not to choke up with emotion at a family gathering, and their visit turned out to be no exception. Talking about Beth caused his eyes to fill with tears a few times, and he got emotional all over again when Matt stood up to leave. He embraced Matt in a bear hug. "We visit New York about once a year. Would it be all right if we made a side trip to Pennsylvania to see you next time?"

"Sure," Matt said. The two men shook hands and then Anne walked him out to his rental car.

"Thank you," she said, "for making the effort to bring Beth's things to us."

"You're welcome."

They stopped on the lawn next to the car. She wrapped her long light-blue sweater tight around herself and studied him.

"She was a great person," Matt said. He'd been wanting all day to say that to her, at least.

"And you were a great husband to her."

He winced a little. Right away, he could tell that she'd noticed his reaction. Unlike her husband, Anne had a very practical, steely, commonsense kind of personality and could be as observant as a hawk.

"*You were,*" she insisted, her gaze unflinching. "You made her extremely happy. No one else could have made her as happy as you did, and we'll always be grateful to you for it."

"No, I—"

"Never doubt that you were a wonderful, *wonderful* husband to her, Matt."

He regarded her painfully.

"It's certainly none of my business," Anne said, "but have you by any chance . . . found someone?"

"There is," he said slowly, "someone."

"Good." She reached out and briefly squeezed his shoulder. "*Good*. I've been concerned about you. Beth told me more than once that she wanted you to move on someday. I'm sure she told you, too."

"She did."

"Well. Maybe it's up to you now to accept that she meant what she said, to give her that much credit, and to respect her wishes." She watched his face. "She didn't want you to go through life lonely, Matt. She was much too softhearted, and she loved you too much to ever want that. Let go of the guilt. You understand me?"

He didn't know what to say, so he nodded.

She hugged him, then gestured toward the rental car. "Go on now. It's chilly out here."

He got in the car and reversed down their driveway. The visit had been rough on him, but not as rough as he'd thought it would be. He'd done the right thing, and found satisfaction in that.

His last image of Beth's childhood house was of her mother, who looked so much like her, standing in front of it and waving good-bye as he drove out of sight.

"Cream or sugar?" Gran asked Kate and Theresa, motioning to the little china bowl and pitcher she used whenever she served high tea.

"Don't mind if I do," Theresa answered, helping herself to both and to two snickerdoodles.

Ah, Kate thought, looking at the fresh-out-of-the-oven

cookies and the steaming cup of tea. When they left Chapel Bluff, she was really, seriously going to miss the food. She'd actually put on a little bit of weight here, which she almost never did, and it might be her imagination but her boobs seemed incrementally bigger because of it. How depressing it was going to be to return to Dallas, frozen food, a life without Matt, *and* smaller boobs.

"I've been waiting to get you both sitting down," Theresa said. "Now that you are, I think the moment's suitably dramatic."

"Especially since we're all wearing hats as big as punch bowls," Kate said.

Theresa laughed and pulled a folder from her bag. "Ta da!" She presented it to them as if on a silver platter. "The official appraisal report for the contents of Chapel Bluff."

"Theresa!" Gran exclaimed. "Oh, how wonderful." She took the folder and began eagerly thumbing through it with hands so weighted down by two enormous turquoise rings it was a wonder she had any dexterity in them at all.

"So you really did finish it." Kate grinned at her friend.

"It's a miracle. Between PTA meetings, indoor soccer practices, The Plaid Attic, and trying to take care of my two wayward children, I actually, finally, did it. I'm surprised at myself."

"I'm not a bit surprised," Gran answered. "I knew you were the right person for the job."

"Me too," Kate said.

"Well," Theresa replied, her corkscrew yellow hair puffing out wildly from under the brim of her hat, "I guess I was the only doubter, then."

"Have the antiques made Gran enormously rich?" Kate asked.

"Enormously, as we all already suspected. You'll see." She nodded toward the folder. "I was able to authenticate most of the pieces, and the others all have value in their own right." She patted Gran's hand. "You'll need to look into some security, a home alarm system at least, and have everything insured."

"Well, I'll be," Gran murmured. "Thank you, Theresa."

"Thank *you*, Beverly."

"To Chapel Bluff," Gran said, raising her teacup. Kate and Theresa clicked the rims of their cups with hers.

Theresa chased her sip of tea with half a snickerdoodle. "Is Matt around?"

Kate's nerves jumped at the mere sound of his name. Since their kiss he'd been on her mind constantly.

"Not today," Gran answered.

"Bummer," Theresa said. "I made sure I looked presentable, just in case. Where is he?"

"He flew to Atlanta," Gran said.

"Why? What's in Atlanta?"

"Beth's parents," Kate answered.

Theresa's head lolled forward. "No way. Really?"

"Really."

"Why did he go to see them?"

"Apparently he has a storage unit where he's kept stuff from the apartment he shared with Beth," Kate said. "He went through it all yesterday, and then he flew down to see her parents today so he could bring them some of her things."

"He told you all of this?" Theresa asked.

"Yeah."

"What's going on between you two?" Theresa asked. Both she and Gran regarded her with sharp curiosity as they waited for her answer.

Kate wasn't anywhere near ready to divulge the truth. She shrugged and tried not to look guilty. "We're friends."

"What was the catalyst?" Theresa asked. "What made him suddenly want to clean out her stuff after all this time?"

Another sham look of innocence. "I don't know."

"What does it mean?" Theresa gazed at Kate, then moved her inquiring look to Gran.

"I think it means something very good," Gran ventured. "I think it means closure."

"You think he's finally ready to move on? That he'll start dating again?" Theresa laid a hand on her heart. "You think we women of the world are going to get another shot at him?"

"Well, not you, Theresa," Gran said, laughing. "You, dear, are married."

"A girl can dream, Beverly. Don't you have a celebrity crush?"

"Me?" Gran asked.

"Yes, you."

"I . . . I . . ."

"C'mon," Theresa prodded, "fess up."

"For many years it was Michael Landon."

"He's dead, Beverly! You're going to have to do better than that."

Gran pursed her lips. She took off her glasses and fidgeted with the beaded string that held them around her neck. "Well, if you must know, I have a little, um, soft spot for Patrick Dempsey."

"McDreamy? Do you watch *Grey's*?"

"I'm embarrassed to admit it," Gran said. "It's terrible of me, but yes, I do."

Theresa and Kate both laughed.

"And you, Kate?" Theresa asked. "Who's yours?"

Matt Jarreau. But Theresa would squawk at her for copying. "David Beckham, of course. But not so much when he's talking. Mostly just when he's posing for photographs."

"Hear, hear!"

While Theresa brought Gran up to date with the most recent plot twists on *Grey's*, Kate's thoughts drifted predictably to Matt.

Since their kiss, part of her—the biggest part—had been stunned, giddy, and euphoric. He actually had the hots for her! He—gorgeous, famous, craveable him—had the hots for ordinary, mortal, civilian her! He'd said, *"I want to be more than just your friend, Kate,"* and she could remember every exact detail of how he'd looked when he'd said it. She'd been going over and back over each millisecond of their fight and their kiss and his words, hugging the memories to herself.

But another part of herself—the tiniest part—had been turning with uneasiness ever since. She'd spent time praying last night and this morning about Matt. Thanking God, asking Him for a future for their relationship. In response, she'd felt no answering peace or sense of rightness. On the contrary, a foreboding shadow had fallen over her. As if, should she dare to ask God directly if a romance with Matt was what He wanted, He might say no. She couldn't bear to risk that, so she hadn't asked and wasn't planning on asking.

She loved Matt. She'd tried so hard not to love him. But maybe some things in life, some loves, just couldn't be stopped.

She had no intention of blurting out her feelings to him and every intention of playing it cool. She'd been scrupulously careful not to let herself indulge in fantasies about his following her to Dallas, about a proposal, about a wedding and babies. She hadn't completely lost her mind. She knew not to go there.

Her plan? To take whatever he was willing to give her for the days that she had left in Redbud. He meant too much to her to even *contemplate* the idea of giving him up. No way. Not now, with so little time remaining.

chapter nineteen

Kate's heart leapt when she heard Matt's truck pull up the next morning. He'd arrived right on time, and as usual for his weekday arrivals, she and Gran were in the kitchen cleaning up breakfast. She scrubbed the countertop with extra gusto. When he walked in she wanted to look both industrious and simultaneously like someone who hadn't gotten up extra early to shower, do makeup, and use both a blow-dryer and straightener on her hair.

He came in with a gust of crisp morning air wearing jeans, his North Face jacket over a gray cotton shirt that fit close to his body, and his work boots. Pleasure soared through her at the sight of him, as if it had been days instead of hours since she'd seen him.

"Matt!" Gran cried and rushed over to greet him.

As he spoke with Gran, he met Kate's gaze for a long moment. Obediently, he handed Gran his jacket, answered her questions, and took the cup of coffee she foisted on him.

"Better get to work," he finally told her. As he was walking out of the room, he glanced at Kate and tilted his head meaningfully, asking her without words to follow. She did, and as soon as they were out of Gran's sight he reached for her hand. "Hi." Without breaking pace, he smiled at her, a smile that could have melted butter from a hundred yards.

"Hi, yourself."

He set his cup on a side table in the living room and drew her into the library. Once he'd shut the door behind them, they were alone in the quiet with sunlight streaming all around.

His attention roamed over her as if to assure himself that she really was standing in front of him all in one piece.

"How was your trip?" she asked.

"It was fine."

"Really?" She used the single word to confirm that it actually had been fine for him, emotionally.

"Yes." He kept a firm grip on her hand, his thumb rubbing over her knuckles. Oddly, he seemed content just to look at her.

She raised her brows and waited for him to say something.

"Would you be willing to help me work today?" he asked.

"You hardly ever let me help you work."

His mouth quirked up. "Things change."

"Gran and I are going shopping together this afternoon, but I'd love to help you this morning."

"You're dressed too nice to lay tile."

"I'll put on my work clothes."

"That black and white outfit with the ballet shoes?" Humor shone in his eyes.

"Ballet flats, you mean." She tilted her head. "Are you making fun of my work clothes?"

"I guess I am."

"My work clothes are perfectly fine!"

"They make you look like you're ready to star in an Audrey Hepburn movie."

"How on earth do you know about Audrey Hepburn movies?"

He shrugged a muscular shoulder. "I'm well-rounded."

"Right," she said with heavy skepticism.

He smiled and she smiled back at him.

"It's really good to see you," he said.

"It's really good to see *you*."

"If you're free, I'd like to cook dinner for you tonight at my house."

"I'm free."

He squeezed her hand and gave her such a look of tenderness that her insides jumbled together with absolute, chaotic, and crazy joy.

That night he made her steak, salad, and baked potatoes. Kate had never, in the whole of her life, seen anything quite so handsome as Matt Jarreau cooking her dinner.

They ate at the little table in the kitchen's breakfast nook, while the overhead fixture bathed them in light and the house's sound system played something bluesy. They talked easily about Chapel Bluff, poker, and the seniors.

Whenever she glanced away and glanced back, there seemed to be either more sour cream or more butter on her potato. Finally, she purposefully looked away and then almost instantly looked back and caught him red-handed, with a spoonful of sour cream suspended over her potato. His eyes sparkled like a six-year-old's at his practical joke.

She laughed and mock scolded him. He grinned back at her, unrepentant. To see him this way—so relaxed and charming—was more than she'd dared to hope.

After dinner, they straightened up the kitchen and moved to the sofa in the living room. Matt leaned over and pulled a newspaper off a side table. Underneath, he'd hidden a bag of peppermint taffies. Exactly the ones she liked.

He handed them to her.

Kate looked down at the familiar package with complete sur-prise. "How did you know?"

"I noticed some of these in your room when I was up there touching up the paint on the baseboards."

"And you remembered?"

He nodded.

"Thank you."

"You like peppermint?"

"I love—majorly love—this particular kind of peppermint taffy. Here. Try." She pulled the bag open and tossed him one.

They both chewed a piece.

"Pretty good," he said.

"Could you eat, say, half a package in one sitting?"

"No. Two will probably do me."

She made a scoffing sound. "Then you're not in my league." She tossed him another.

Before he opened it, he reached down and swooped up both her feet. "May I?" he asked, but didn't wait for permission before shifting so that he could drop her lower legs across his lap. He opened and ate his taffy, relaxed, as if little intimacies like her legs across his lap were common between them.

"So," he said, after a pause punctuated only by the sound of candy wrappers.

"So?"

"What about Tyler?"

"What about him?" She smiled.

"You know what. Is he out of the picture?"

"We talked the last time we went out and decided to keep things friendly."

"He decided or you decided?"

"I did."

"You're not into him?"

"We get along great. But no, I'm not into him like that." *Not like I'm into you.*

"Kate," he said, grinning at her, "that is seriously good news."

They talked about everything under the sun until one in the morning. She noticed at some point during their conversation that the framed picture of Beth had disappeared from its spot on the bar.

As he walked her to her car at the end of the night, he tugged her to him. He gathered her to his body and held her tightly against him. He kissed her forehead, her cheek, the corner of her lips. Their breath mingled for a suspended moment and then they were kissing.

Despite her very best efforts, the freezing temperature eventually caused her to shiver. Just as she'd known he would, Matt noticed, and bundled her into her car so she could warm up.

Darn, she thought as she drove off. Darn that shiver! She could gladly have kissed him for hours.

Two nights later, Matt drove his Lamborghini to Chapel Bluff to take Kate out on a date. As they made their way from the house toward the driveway, she stumbled to a stop at the sight of his car. "What's this?"

"My car."

"You drive a truck."

"This is my *other* car."

"You're kidding."

"Nope."

Her eyes went big and round. "Seriously?"

He laughed. Kate never failed to amuse him. He loved to watch her face. Loved the things she said to him. She could make him smile just by walking into a room.

Kate circled the car, taking it in. "What is it?"

"A Lamborghini Murcielago."

"It's beautiful."

"Thanks."

She looked at him. "What are you, some big hockey star or something?"

"Used to be."

Kate smiled. "I guess so."

He opened the door for her, and she slid in. He'd been looking forward to tonight for the past two days. He was going to take her three towns over to a restaurant his brother had told him about. He had a few reasons for picking the place: the drive would make the date last longer; the food was supposed to be good; and it was fancy, so he'd get to look at her all night in the snug black dress and high-heeled black boots she was wearing.

Kate chuckled and pointed toward Chapel Bluff's kitchen window. "Looks like we have spectators."

He saw both Beverly and Peg peering out at them, their faces practically pressed to the glass. He lifted a hand toward them in greeting, then took off down the driveway.

"Feel a need for speed?" he asked her a few miles later as he steered onto the highway.

"I don't know. How fast are we talking?"

"Not fast enough to put you in danger."

"Okay, then. Let 'er rip."

He grinned and hit the gas.

Every night leading up to Thanksgiving, Matt either stayed for dinner at Chapel Bluff or invited Kate to eat dinner with him at his house. Kate accepted his invitations more than she declined them because she wanted, desperately wanted, to spend every moment she had with him. But a sliver of herself continued to urge caution.

She knew she was mostly stupid over him, but she didn't want to be completely stupid. She needed to preserve an escape rope of independence, some small amount of distance. Sanity. Protection. A piece of herself held back.

So she declined a few of his invitations, too. On those occasions she sat in her room at Chapel Bluff, watching her little TV, missing Matt, and wishing she'd chosen to spend the evening with him instead.

His family arrived from out of town the day before Thanksgiving. She didn't see Matt at all that day, but he called her three times from his cell. Each time he wanted to tell her he was thinking about her, to ask what she was doing, and to make certain that she was still planning to come by his house the next afternoon once she and Gran finished celebrating Thanksgiving at Velma's.

She assured him all three times that she'd be there.

Kate and Gran arrived at Matt's house around five o'clock on Thanksgiving Day. He opened the door for them even before they had a chance to knock. His attention went straight to Kate, taking her in. He gave her the same warmly assessing look he gave her every time he saw her after time apart. She gazed back at him, her lips pulling into a smile, her insides tingling. This would go down as her best Thanksgiving ever simply because he was a part of it.

"Hello, hello!" Gran greeted him. "We're so glad to be here. Thank you for having us."

"You're welcome. Let me take that from you." He lifted the homemade pumpkin pie from her hands. "Come on in."

Gran sailed inside.

"Happy Thanksgiving," Kate said to him softly.

"It is now that you're here," he grumbled. "I've been waiting for hours."

"We're here exactly when I said we'd be."

"Seemed like forever."

"Is the day going all right?"

"It's going fine." He motioned with his head. "Follow me."

Inside, the house was cozy, cheerily lit, and filled with the scent of turkey and cranberries. Matt's family rose to their feet and crowded around Gran and Kate for introductions.

Matt's dad had dressed in an organic knit sweater, beige pants with pockets and zippers on the sides, and hiking shoes. He looked like the kind of guy who routinely trekked through the wilderness and ran marathons. All sinew and lean muscle.

Matt's mom, Elaine, had brown hair cut at chin length, parted on the side, and tucked behind both ears. She wore a Florida tan, tasteful diamond stud earrings, and an outfit straight out of a Land's End catalog.

Matt's brother was an older and shorter version of Matt. He had the same dark hair and eyes, but he wore glasses, carried an extra fifteen pounds around the middle, and had a businessman's demeanor. He, his wife, and their four-year-old and infant sons were all dressed and groomed in the style of a successful yuppie family.

Matt also introduced them to three sweet-faced grandparents, one intellectual-looking aunt, and the aunt's awkward and nerdy college-aged daughter.

Once they'd met everyone, all the men except Matt went back to the sofa and chairs. They unpaused the TiVo and picked up their football game where they'd left it.

One of the grandmothers and the nerdy cousin took the four-year-old to the kitchen table, where they had a game of Candy Land going. The rest of them settled around the dining room table, which had been extended as far as possible for the occasion. A centerpiece of greenery, orange gourds, thick white candles, and sprays of yellow berries had been arranged by someone female who had great taste. At one end, Rummikub tiles lay face down, at rest in between rounds.

They spent an hour talking and visiting, getting to know each other. Matt didn't return to the football, but instead sat next to Kate, answering questions when asked, listening. She felt almost sorry for him when Gran suggested they play Rummikub.

"You can go watch football if you want," she murmured to him. "Gran and I are okay here."

"No, I'm good."

He stayed and played with them, even though she could tell he thought Rummikub was a slow-moving, sissy game.

When dinnertime rolled around everyone declared themselves still half full from the enormous meal they'd eaten earlier. But saying it was a Thanksgiving night tradition, Matt's mom, grandmother, and aunt assembled sandwiches for everyone on paper plates. Toasted white bread with mayonnaise, iceberg lettuce, and slabs of leftover turkey liberally sprinkled with salt and pepper. They cut Kate's sandwich on the diagonal and served it to her with potato chips. Kate hadn't had much of an appetite before she started on the food, but the sandwich tasted absolutely delicious and she ended up eating everything on her plate, then chasing it with Gran's pumpkin pie and coffee.

"I feel like I should warn you," Matt said to her. "Every Thanksgiving night they play Trivial Pursuit, men against women."

"Tell me it's one of the newer versions."

"You wish. It's the original version. The same one they've been playing for decades."

"Maybe Gran and I should make our exit."

"Nope, you're staying till the bitter end."

"I'm going to embarrass myself."

He regarded her with amusement. "So? You embarrass me every week at poker."

"I wouldn't have to embarrass you if you had an ounce of skill."

He laughed and Kate saw his mom, Elaine, look alertly toward the sound.

"Kate," Elaine said, "if you have a minute, I'd like to show you some portraits I had made."

"Sure." Kate followed her to one of the guest bedrooms. Elaine opened her suitcase, took out a flat box, and motioned for Kate to sit near her on the edge of the bed. One by one, she showed Kate beautiful shots of her family on the beach surrounded by dunes, white sand, and clear water.

"I convinced Matt to come and see us for a week this past August," Elaine said. "These were taken then. I brought copies and gave them out to everyone earlier."

Kate nodded. "They're gorgeous." There were mostly group shots, then some of just Matt's brother's family, some of just the two grandchildren together, some of Matt's mom and dad. The final picture was a candid of Matt. The photographer had captured him from the side, standing with his hands in his pockets.

"Matt doesn't know I had that one taken. He wouldn't pose for it, of course, but I wanted . . ." Elaine's voice trailed off. "I wanted one of him."

In the shot, Matt looked starkly handsome and achingly alone. He was staring moodily out at the ocean while the wind ruffled his hair and pressed his shirt against his chest.

"It captures him well, and yet it makes me sad every time I look at it," Elaine said.

Kate could see why. It made her sad to look at it, too.

"He's been through an awful time." Elaine's kind, vividly bright brown eyes filled with a sheen of tears. Sniffing a little, she surveyed the portrait for a moment more, then put it back into its box with all the others and set it aside. She swiped beneath her eyes with her fingers. "I'm sorry to get emotional on you like this."

"It's really okay," Kate assured her.

"It's just that I've been worried about him for so long. This trip he seems better. For the first time in years, I see improvement in him and I'm just so *relieved*."

"I understand."

"You've known him for a few months."

"I have."

"Does he seem better to you, too?"

"Yes."

She angled her head slightly. "What do you think's helped him?"

What could she say? She didn't want to speculate, and she really didn't want to betray his confidence. "I don't know for sure."

"Are you a praying person?" Elaine asked.

"I am."

"I knew it!" She reached over and gave Kate's hand an impulsive squeeze. "I'm a praying person, too, and I've been praying like crazy for Matt for a long time. I've been praying that someone would be able to get through to him. None of us could seem to do it. We kept trying and trying, and he kept shutting us out."

"Yeah, he's good at that."

"But you've managed to do it, I think. He must have looked out the window a dozen times while he was waiting for you to arrive. You've been able to get through to him."

Kate hesitated. "Maybe," she allowed.

"I want to thank you. I'm so grateful."

·"No thanks needed." She'd never had the ability or strength to heal Matt on her own. "God's been working on him."

Elaine nodded. "Well, praise God. He really does answer prayers."

"Yes, He really does."

A pulse of understanding, agreement, and common belief passed between them. It was that recognition of a friend, of someone like-minded, that spurred Kate to ask Elaine what she'd been wanting to ask. "I have a question for you."

"Sure."

"What are your thoughts about Matt's hockey?" She hadn't said a word to Matt about it yet, but the career he'd walked away from hovered near her thoughts all the time. Nearer as the days passed.

Elaine's expression softened with memory. "Did you ever see him play?"

"No."

"He was amazing to watch. This perfect combination of power and coordination and grace. He wasn't one to throw off the gloves and fight. He was always very calm, cool, and collected. Absolutely lethal. You wouldn't have believed it to see him. I didn't." She smiled. "He played on the American Olympic team, you know. And he was the Barons' leading scorer the year they won the Cup. So you see, I'm not just another mother boasting about her child when I say that he was one of the world's very best."

One of the world's very best hockey players was currently laying tile in Kate's grandmother's bathroom. It no longer felt quite right. The work of restoring old homes was respectable work. For anyone else, it might have been perfectly in line with God's plan. But not for Matt. God had bigger plans for him.

"I try to talk to him about hockey now and then," Elaine continued. "You'd think that would be healthy for him, right? To talk about something that was such a big part of his life? I mean, if you knew all the hours, the traveling, the practicing. But he won't discuss it with me. Won't watch it with his dad. Nothing."

"I've noticed that, too," Kate said.

"For it to have ended that way . . ." Elaine clucked her tongue. "For it to have been left so unfinished. I don't know if it's good for Matt to have to live with that." She gave Kate a sad, confiding smile. "I know he'd never consider it, that it's impossible, but I sometimes dream of him going back to it, being able to end his career the way that other athletes do."

Her words so echoed Kate's own feelings on the subject that chills raced all the way down her arms. It wasn't really Elaine who'd just confirmed it for her. It was God. His plan was for Matt to go back to his hockey.

Just like with Matt's emotional scars, she had no power in and of herself to make him return to hockey. But she was willing to let God use her.

He needs to return to it, she could sense God saying. It was a refrain He'd been whispering to her repeatedly lately. **He's not done.**

Oh, heaven, she thought. Matt wasn't going to be happy about it.

chapter twenty

On Sunday night, Kate finished her dinner of microwaved leftovers and curled up on the sofa in the den with her novel. Halfway through chapter three, a knock sounded at the front door. She jumped at the sound, startled, because she wasn't expecting anyone.

She padded to the door and peered through the peephole.

Matt stood on the other side, framed by darkness. Her stomach did a euphoric flip. She unlocked and opened the door, grinning at him.

He had on the brown sweater she loved, the one with the short zipper at the front of the neck. His family had remained in town all weekend, and though he'd snuck away to call her often, she hadn't seen him since Thanksgiving.

He smiled. "Rumor has it that the seniors are out of the house tonight."

"Rumor's correct. They're at a piano concert."

He came forward, so close he was almost on top of her. She gave a half yelp, half giggle and started backing up. He kept coming. She kept retreating.

"Someone from Ireland, I think," she said. "Playing the piano, that is." *You're babbling, Kate!* She couldn't help it; his nearness made her head spin. Her rear hit the nearest wall. "The seniors have a more active social life than I do."

"Is your social life so bad?" he murmured. He trapped her body with his, then angled his head down for a wickedly good kiss.

Kate's heart thumped wildly. It didn't take much of him to set her off. Just looking at his hands, or catching a whiff of his soap could make her body hum. Much less his kisses! *Oh, his kisses.* She'd experienced a few kisses from a few different boyfriends in her time, but never like this. *His* kisses blanked out her mind and flushed her with heat.

"I missed you," he whispered.

"I missed you, too."

He held her face in his hands and gave her another gentle kiss. Pulling back, he gazed down at her with one side of his mouth curling upward.

She led him to the sofa. William had started a fire in the room's rock fireplace earlier. It flickered and popped sedately.

Matt did his usual thing, scooping up her legs and depositing them in his lap. "You look beautiful."

"I do?" She glanced down at herself. She was wearing an ivory velour sweat suit, her pink UGGs, and her hair in a ponytail.

His eyes sparked with humor. "You're supposed to just say thanks."

"Thanks. You look beautiful, too."

"I do?" he asked, mimicking her, and they both smiled.

"Your family's all gone?"

"Yes, thank God. I just dropped my parents off at the airport."

"Oh, come on," she said, in response to his agonized expression. "The weekend wasn't that painful, was it?"

"It was painful, Kate."

"Well, at least you have the satisfaction of knowing you did the right thing."

He grunted and stretched his arm along the back of the sofa.

Gently, he took hold of a tendril of hair that had fallen out of her ponytail. He rubbed it between his callused fingertips.

Oh boy. She didn't want to do *anything* to rock this boat, to jeopardize the easiness between them. But she was going to have to. The hockey thing had become a pressure inside her.

While they talked, he continued to toy with her hair. When she got up to get them both bowls of Cherry Garcia ice cream, he stole more kisses from her in the kitchen. Back in the den, he poked at the fire and added a few pieces of wood to it. They ate their ice cream side by side on the sofa, admiring the new flames and laughing over the quirks his family members had displayed over the weekend.

"What's that about?" he asked her during a pause in the conversation when they set aside their empty bowls.

"What?"

"That frown thing. You keep doing it tonight. Like you're distracted by something that's worrying you."

That he'd noticed took her aback. "When did you get to be so observant?"

"Where you're concerned, Kate, I don't miss much."

She bit the side of her lip.

"What is it?" he asked.

She couldn't bring herself to say anything.

"Just tell me," he said quietly.

"It's . . ." She sighed. "It's about you and your hockey."

"There is no me and hockey anymore."

"But there could be."

"No."

"Hear me out." She sat up straighter, her brows knitting as she tried to order her words. "I think that anyone who loves their job, who's amazingly good at it, always hopes to leave that job when they're ready, on their own terms."

"I did leave it on my own terms."

"Yes, but that was then. If you had a second chance, would you do it differently?"

"It doesn't matter. I won't have a second chance."

"Why not?"

A log broke apart and fell with a cracking sound into the fire. "*Why not?* Because I quit it. I quit it years ago."

"But if you wanted, you could go back and finish."

He looked incredulous. "That's impossible."

"Why?"

"Because I haven't played hockey in years."

"But you've stayed in amazing shape. You could train to get yourself ready to play hockey again. What would a comeback take? I don't know. Tell me."

He pushed to his feet and went to stand by the window. He braced one hand against the frame and stared out at the black sky. He didn't answer.

"You must know a coach who could help you, right? And a trainer. You must've had a sports agent. You could call him, too, see what he says."

"I don't want to talk about this." Every word came out cold and hard.

She rose to her feet, felt her limbs tremble. "I know you don't."

"Then drop it."

"I can't because I have this sense that you're never going to be completely happy unless you go back and finish what you started the right way."

He faced her. "What exactly do you know about what would make me happy?"

"Nothing," she said, stung. "Because you haven't told me. But you're not the only one who's observant. I've watched you, and I've seen how painful it is for you when anyone so much as mentions hockey. I've seen how your face looks when you see a hockey game on TV. It wouldn't have the power to hurt you anymore unless you still loved it. Unless you regret how it ended."

"What more do you want from me, Kate?" His eyes blazed. "I'm already giving you all I've got."

She drew herself up, steel in her spine. "I want you to play professional hockey again."

A growl rumbled in his throat. "If you were anyone else I'd tell you exactly what you could do with that suggestion."

"But you won't tell me that because you know I only want what's best for you. Right?"

He grabbed up his keys and stalked out the front door without once looking back.

Congratulations, Kate. She sunk onto the sofa. *That went well.* She took deep breaths and willed herself not to cry.

Kate spent a miserable hour trying to read, failing at that. Trying to watch TV in her room, failing at that. Trying to surf the Internet, failing at that. Finally, she went downstairs and cleaned everything that needed cleaning because at least it kept her hands busy. She'd unloaded the dishwasher and was turning out the kitchen light when she glanced out the window—

And saw him.

Matt, standing in the night air outside, leaning against the side of his truck, watching her through the window. Her emotions, already churning close to the surface, pushed against their thin barriers. Trying to stay calm, she reached for her jacket, buttoned it slowly, then let herself out.

He pushed away from his truck and met her halfway. They stopped a few feet from each other.

"I can't stand for you to be mad at me," he said. "It makes me sick to my stomach."

Her heart eased. She hadn't driven him away irretrievably. "I feel the exact same way."

He frowned, gazing at her with troubled eyes.

"Look," she said, "I'm sorry I upset you. That was a lot to spring on you like that, and I'm sure I didn't do it the best possible way."

A muscle ticked along his jaw. "I'm not going back to hockey."

She wasn't going to be content with that. But she knew he'd heard all he could stand for one night, and that she needed to back off. "At this point I just want you to promise me that you'll think about it."

"There's nothing to think about."

"For me?" she asked, "Can you agree just to think about it?"

He groaned as he enfolded her ferociously tight in his arms. He buried his nose in her hair as if he wanted to inhale her, to take her into himself. "I'd do anything for you," he said fervently against the top of her head. "I'd buy you anything, take you anywhere."

"So you'll think about it," she whispered into his jacket.

He clasped her even tighter to him.

She waited.

"I'll think about it," he said.

By unspoken agreement, neither Kate nor Matt mentioned the fact that she would be leaving town soon. Matt thought about it constantly, though. He thought about hockey, too, just as he'd promised her he would.

He'd even made himself sit through an entire game on TV. It

had been strange and difficult to watch his sport again after so long. He'd looked at it with a critical, educated, and experienced eye. He wished cold analysis had been the only thing going on inside him. But the whole time he'd been sitting there alone in his house, the TV screen glowing in front of him, emotions had eaten at him, too. Bitterness. Jealousy. And worst of all, a lousy kind of longing.

As usual, Kate was making him do and feel things he didn't want to. But he'd told her he'd consider it, even though she was nuts to think he could go back to it now. Never going to happen.

"So," Beverly said. They were cooking dinner together. Chicken Cor Don something. "Kate and I have set a firm departure date."

Matt's grip on the knife he was using tightened.

"We're going to start our drive back a week from Saturday," she said. "That's just ten days away, and oh my, am I *ever* going to miss you! What am I going to do without my cooking apprentice?"

He couldn't seem to breathe. His throat closed up, and he couldn't swallow, either. He didn't have enough time left with Kate.

What was he going to do? He didn't know—really didn't know— if he could live without her. He'd been trying to act the way a normal boyfriend would act. To say and do normal things so he wouldn't completely freak her out. But he knew he wasn't normal. He needed her too much. During the months that he'd known her, she'd slowly but surely become everything to him.

"Matt?" Beverly asked. "Are you all right?"

He realized he'd been standing motionless. He glanced at her. "Yeah. Yeah, I'm fine." He resumed his job of slicing the vegetables she'd placed on a cutting board before him.

Ten days? His mind and heart reeled. Ten days.

He could have finished his work at Chapel Bluff a week ago, but he didn't want to be away from Kate, so he'd been inventing more work for himself and doing that work *very* slowly. If he hated to be away from her for an hour, how was he going to cope when she moved back to Dallas?

He looked down at whatever he was chopping—What was it? A zucchini? Another kind of squash?—and realized that he'd rather move to Dallas than live apart from her. Or maybe she'd be willing to stay here in Redbud if he asked her to, if he helped her find a job she could love.

The worry banding around his chest loosened a little.

He'd need to be smart about it and pick his moment to talk with her and not frighten her by letting her see how much he cared. But maybe if he played it just right, he could convince her not to let him go.

"You in the mood for a movie tonight?" Kate asked him a couple days later. Matt was working, and she was sitting on her customary bucket taking a break, drinking bottled water, and surreptitiously admiring him from every angle. "I could pick something up on my way over tonight."

"Sure."

"How about *Pride and Prejudice*?"

"What's that?" he asked warily. "It's not one of those movies where they all wear old-fashioned clothes and walk around talking in British accents, is it?"

"That's exactly what it is."

Matt groaned.

"It's romantic! Maybe one of the most romantic stories ever."

He paused to study her. "What do you think is romantic?"

"Seriously?"

"Yes. What's romantic? To you."

She took some time to consider. "Okay," she said when she had it.

"If it's an English guy," he said, "wearing a top hat and tight pants, then you're fresh out of luck."

Kate laughed. "No. There's this couple who live in my neighborhood at home. They're old. Really old. And I think the wife might have Alzheimer's. They go on walks together every morning. I get the feeling that her husband buttons her into her coat, picks out her shoes, combs her hair. And then the whole time they're walking, he's supporting her, kind of holding her up." She couldn't help it, she got teary.

Matt watched her with concentrated attention.

"That's romantic," she said. " 'Till death do us part' is romantic."

Silence and dust motes drifted between them. Matt unbuckled and set down his tool belt. "Come to my house with me."

"It's one-thirty in the afternoon."

"Which means we can watch your movie and hang out together for the rest of the day."

"What about your work?"

"Screw it."

"Gran will wonder where I've gone."

"Leave her a note."

She gaped at him for a surprised moment, then chuckled. "All right, let's do it."

When they got outside, she headed toward her Explorer.

"I can drive you home tonight, Kate," he said. "I want to drive you home. Let me."

But she held firm and took her own car to the video store. As she steered from there through the now familiar streets toward Matt's house, she called herself every kind of idiot.

Here she was, in love with him. She. Loved. Him. And yet she kept holding like a life preserver to a couple of things: (a) she always drove herself to and from his house in her own car, and (b) she still occasionally turned down his invitations and stayed home in the evenings with Gran. As if either of those strategies could protect her heart now! And yet she continued to cling to them. She clung to them because she couldn't shake the feeling that things weren't going to end well for her and Matt. It had become a persistent, gnawing, unsettled ache that lived all day beneath her other thoughts and emotions.

Things aren't going to end well.

She shoved the worry aside.

Problem was, the more she shoved it aside, the more aware she became of its silent and ominous presence.

The days she had left with Matt began to escape Kate's reach like a smooth stone skating away from her down the glinting surface of a playground slide. She couldn't stop or catch back her time with him, which filled her with helplessness.

Just five days before she was to leave, she met Matt in town. They had dinner reservations, and any sane person would have gone straight to the restaurant on such a cold, snowy evening. But it hardly ever snowed in Dallas, and Kate loved walking through the falling flakes. So like a good sport, Matt had agreed to meet her early so that they could walk along Main Street together to window-shop and marvel at all the Christmas lights that had been strung on trees and along storefronts.

She'd just locked her car door behind her when she spotted him, big, muscular, and darkly handsome, walking toward her through the snow. Carefully, she memorized the image: his long dark dress coat, his flashing eyes, the serious cast of his jaw.

When he was a few feet away she noticed that he was carrying a coffee cup from Main Street Coffee. He extended it to her. "For you."

"Wow, thank you."

"You're welcome. I don't want you to get cold."

She took a sip. He'd ordered her a latte with extra whip and, she'd bet, chocolate sprinkles. "Exactly how I like it."

"I'm good, aren't I?"

"Very good."

The coffee was perfect, she thought. Just like him. And she almost burst into tears right then and there. To keep herself from doing so, she slid her arm through his and they set off down the street.

"Listen," he said. "I'm worried about you breathing in this freezing air. That's one of the things that can set off your asthma, right?"

"Yes, but I have my inhaler."

He gave her a concerned look. "I don't want it to come to that."

"It won't."

"If I hear so much as a cough, Kate, we're going to the restaurant."

"Okay."

"I mean it."

She hid a smile behind the guise of another sip of latte. It was nice—really, really nice—to have a manly tough guy fussing over you.

They shared a leisurely and delicious dinner at the restaurant, then went to Matt's house for dessert.

Kate had discovered from Matt's mom that Matt loved chocolate chip cookies. Plain ones, without nuts or oatmeal or any other imaginative ingredient. Kate had asked Elaine to write her recipe down, and Elaine had scribbled it off for her gladly, from memory.

Kate, who almost never cooked, had followed the recipe religiously that afternoon. However, either Chapel Bluff's ancient cookie sheet or its ancient oven hadn't functioned quite right. The cookies had come out too brown on the bottom. They'd tasted okay enough, though, that she'd boldly announced to Matt earlier that she'd made dessert for him. Now that they were at his house and she was about to uncover her simple, oddly shaped cookies, she had to wonder what she'd been thinking.

"Let's see what you've got." He rubbed his hands together.

She peeled back the foil. "I made your mother's chocolate chip cookies."

"You made these for me?" Matt looked genuinely pleased. "I love these."

"That's what she said."

They both took one and ate, leaning against opposing granite countertops. "These are incredible," he said. "The best ones I've ever tasted."

Kate let out a peal of laughter. "Liar. They're too brown on the bottom, and they're really cold from my car."

"The best ones ever," he insisted.

"Maybe we should microwave them."

"No, I like 'em just the way they are." He palmed two more.

She could remember times, early in their acquaintance, when she'd thought him rude, indifferent, unkind. She'd been dead wrong. All that had been a shield. Underneath it, he was the opposite of every one of those things.

"Before you and Beverly came I never ate dessert," he said.

"That's pitiful, Matt."

"I guess I won't be eating it after you leave, either."

"Well, we can't have you missing out on dessert! I guess we're going to have to stay."

"I'd like that."

"Nah, you just like chocolate chip cookies. That's all." She picked up her second cookie, an embarrassingly deformed one, and took a bite.

"Actually," he said, "I'm serious."

She almost choked.

His expression turned solemn, his attention steady and determined. He curled his hands around the edge of the granite on either side of his hips.

Trying to look composed, she set aside her cookie, finished chewing, and swallowed.

"I don't want you to go," he said.

She only stared at him, tasting chocolate and hope.

"I want this thing between us to continue," he said. "I'm not ready to pack up your car and say good-bye to you."

Her pulse thrummed fast through her veins. "I . . . I have a job I have to go back to."

"I know. I'd never ask you to leave it unless you wanted to."

She chose her words cautiously. "Even if I wanted to leave it, I couldn't. Not at the moment, anyway. I don't have another job lined up."

"I could help you find one here, if you wanted to stay. Maybe an antique shop of your own. I could get you set up somewhere, buy all the furniture you'd need to get started."

She let out her breath in a soft, admiring whistle. He'd offered her something almost unbearably tempting. Except . . . What was she going to do? Accept capital from him, someone she hadn't even had a define-the-relationship talk with? "That sounds amazing," she said truthfully. "But I couldn't accept money from you."

"A job then at one of the antiques places that are already here? Theresa's, maybe? Or we could find you something completely different. Something where you could use your social work degree."

She couldn't believe they were even *having* this discussion. She'd known he liked her, cared about her, but she'd thought he'd accepted the fact that she was moving home in a few days. She'd had no clue that he'd been thinking along these lines. That he was serious enough about her that he wanted her to remain in Redbud.

"Or if you return to Dallas," he continued, "and keep the job you have, I was thinking . . ."

She waited, resisted the urge to bite her lip.

"I don't know." He shifted uncomfortably. "I was just thinking that I could use a change of scenery. I wouldn't mind moving down to Dallas, giving it a try."

He's willing to move to Dallas? His offer was an over-the-moon miracle, something she'd only dreamed of, *more* than she'd dreamed of. She wanted to shriek and throw herself into his arms.

Except that same sense of uneasiness that had been dogging her for days intensified right alongside her excitement. Matched enemies, wrestling inside her. "You have a house here," she said.

He shrugged. "I'll hold on to the house."

"What . . . what kind of work would you do in Dallas?"

"Same as here. They must have old houses there, too, right?"

"They do." She could see the vulnerability in the depths of his brown eyes. This was costing him, to put himself out here like this, and she didn't want to hurt him. Not for the world. "What about your hockey?"

"Hockey's not a factor. I've been thinking about it like I told you I would, but it's just not going to happen, Kate."

"Why not?"

"Too much time has passed. It's not the kind of thing you can just pick back up and put on again like an old coat."

"I know it won't be easy. But I have—" she pursed her lips— "I just have this gut instinct that you can do it."

"Kate. Do you know how hard it is to get yourself to a level where you can compete in the NHL?"

"No."

"Nearly impossible. I look back at my career and sometimes I can't believe that I managed it." She could see tension gathering across his shoulders, near the edges of his mouth. "I can't get myself there again."

He was being practical, and she couldn't blame him. He was also worried about failing, and she couldn't blame him for that, either. To make it so big, to fall from grace, to attempt a comeback, and to blow it would be horrible. Worse than never trying to mount a comeback in the first place.

Kate sighed. "I want to say one more thing about it, okay?"

His forehead grooved. He looked away.

"I don't know anything about hockey, but I do know a little about you. And I think you still have the talent and the determination that you had before. Will you look at me?"

Matt returned his attention to her.

She put all her feeling into her words. "I believe that you can do this."

"Kate—"

"Matt," she said sincerely. "Sometimes you just have to take a leap of faith."

They looked at each other searchingly. She could guess how hard this was for him. His belief and optimism had been battered by life. It would take tremendous courage to overcome that and try again.

"About the other," she said quietly. "About me staying in Red-bud or you coming to Dallas . . ." She closed the distance between them. Lifting up one of his hands, she threaded her fingers with his. She kissed a knuckle. "Nothing in the world would make me happier. But I need time to consider it. Okay?"

"Okay."

Kate knew she needed to hit her knees in prayer. But that night, after some more cookies, some kissing, some laughing, and some soft-spoken conversation while cuddling, her spinning mind would hardly settle enough to put toothpaste on her toothbrush, much less to pray.

He wanted her to stay in Redbud! He was willing to move to Dallas! Those ecstatic revelations had tipped her world on its axis.

First thing the next morning, she took a hot shower, dressed, and spent time reading her "Bible in a Year" passage. Then she knelt beside her bed, her hands laced tightly together on top of the quilt, her head bent. She felt equal parts hopeful and concerned. This had *magnitude*. This discussion with God would mark a turning point, and she knew it.

She started her prayer with jumbled happy words of thanks and praise for Matt and their relationship. He was what she'd always, always wanted. She'd been asking God for *the one* all these years, and if Matt was him—and she was starting to think that he was!—then he'd been worth the wait, the heartache, the loneliness, the doubt. He was the answer to all of that. He was wonderful. He was way too good for her. He was, very simply, the deepest and dearest desire of her heart.

She paused.

No sense of rightness fell upon her. No assurance. Only odd, stilted silence.

Disquiet wormed upward inside of her, expanding.

She gathered all her nerve and made herself ask, *Do you want our relationship to continue?*

Part of her struggled to hear God's answer, and part of her struggled not to. She made herself clear her thoughts and listen.

And into that still place came a certainty.

No.

No was His answer. He didn't want their relationship to continue.

Tears rushed instantly to her eyes. *Oh, God. Please. I want this so much.*

She had the terrible feeling that not only was God saying no now, but that He'd *been* saying it for days, since their first kiss. Ice slid through her chest right down to her fingertips and toes. She began to tremble with fear and crushing sadness.

Please let me have him. Please! I'll do anything.

No audible response came. She understood, however, His kind, loving, and yet unyielding answer.

Still no.

She rushed to her feet, pushing away from the bed as if it had burned her. Hurriedly and by rote, she went through the motions of putting on her makeup, brushing her hair. Unable to stand being trapped indoors, she told Gran she had errands to run, grabbed her jacket, and hurried to her car. She drove downtown. Not many people were out. The stores hadn't opened yet. She got out and aimlessly walked the cold streets, her mind blank and dull.

Walked. Walked.

In the tumble of her thoughts, she explained to God how she

felt about Matt. As if He didn't already know. She went on and on about how good she thought they could be for each other. As if He didn't already know. She pleaded with Him. As if He hadn't already answered her.

Her chest began to constrict. She honestly wasn't sure if it was heartache or asthma. Just in case, she used her inhaler. Matt worried about her and would be furious if she had another attack.

More aimless walking, more fruitless begging.

At length, she stopped on a bridge that arched over a stream. Looking down into the passing water, she saw instead an image of Matt. He was decked out in his hockey uniform and gear. Skating breathtakingly fast across the ice, aiming and shooting the puck with deadly precision. The puck sailed into the goal, and she saw him lift his fists and grin with triumph.

Tears slipped over her lashes. She took deep breaths, mopped away the wetness with her fingers.

I can't have him, can I? she asked God.

Matt needed to play hockey again, and he'd never do it in Dallas. He'd never do it in Redbud, either, if he let himself continue with his current job, if he chose to replace hockey with her, if he settled.

What had Matt's mom said about him? That he was one of the world's very best hockey players. *One of the world's very best.* It was mind-blowing to even think about being that good at something. But Matt was. He was too extraordinary, too rare, too wildly gifted to be held back by his current job, by the little town of Redbud, or by her.

She wasn't a beauty, a genius, a talented artist, or an incredible athlete. How was she supposed to hold on to him once he returned to hockey and that whole glittering world of fame and professional sports and money?

The answer? She wasn't. She'd had a role in his life these past three months. But her part was ending. And what was best for him now was for her to let him go.

She didn't know if she could make herself do it.

She envisioned him skating again, fast and smooth. His face flushed with life, determination, concentration. He was in his element. And Kate understood, looking down into the water beneath the bridge, that she *could* let him go.

For his sake, she could.

chapter twenty-one

She told herself that she'd tell Matt her decision that very night, which was supposed to be one of Gran and Matt's cooking nights. But when Kate came downstairs at dinnertime, she found Gran sitting at the kitchen table alone eating a bowl of leftover vegetable soup and reading a *People* magazine with Patrick Dempsey on the cover.

"What's up?" Kate asked.

"Matt told me to tell you that he has something planned for you tonight. He'll be by to pick you up," she said, glancing at the clock on the wall, "any minute."

"What kind of plans?"

"A surprise." Gran did a double eyebrow lift.

"A surprise that I need to get more dressed up for? Or is this all right?" Kate motioned to her black turtleneck, jeans, and sneakers.

"You're perfect. It'll be very casual."

Just then she heard a car pull up. Kate went to work donning her jacket, scarf, and hat. Gran bustled over to assist, handing Kate her purse and gloves.

Matt stuck his head in the door. "Ready?"

"Ready."

"Have fun!" Gran said.

"Thanks." Kate kissed her on the cheek. "G'night."

"Good night." Gran gave them both a cheerful wave.

Outside, gleaming gloriously in the moonlight, Morty's Cadillac waited.

"Brace yourself, Kate," Matt said. "We're going on a double date."

Despite the lead ball of dread that had been lodged inside her stomach all day, Kate's spirits lifted a little. "With Morty and Velma?"

"Right."

"In the Cadillac."

"And my car both."

Velma exited the Cadillac and watched them approach. "This was Morty's idea," she said to Kate. "I'm surprised that hottie here agreed to it."

Matt shot Velma a warning glance.

"But I sure am glad he did," Velma continued. "Now I can spend the whole evening checking him out."

"Velma," Matt growled.

Velma chuckled gleefully. "Morty wanted to give you a spin in his car, and since there's just the two seats, I'm going to ride with Matt on the way to dinner and the movie."

"Sounds good."

Velma held the door for her, and Kate slid onto the Cadillac's passenger seat.

"Just don't get too comfortable in my seat, you hear?"

"Your seat, is it?" Morty asked Velma, beaming at her.

"Yes," Velma replied, with bite to her tone, "that seat is mine, and if I see any other females sitting in it while we're dating, I won't think twice about taking a wooden paddle to your behind."

"Wouldn't dream of letting anyone else sit there, honey." Morty grinned.

Velma huffed.

Morty put the car in gear and they took off. Kate enjoyed the fresh air, the car, their chitchat, and the ride, but mostly she felt relieved. This double date meant she didn't have to talk to Matt about her decision tonight. She was only delaying the inevitable. Still, she was a wuss, and she'd take the stay of execution gladly.

With Matt and Velma following in the Lamborghini, they drove to a ramshackle roadside joint that served hot dogs, chili, and chili on top of hot dogs. The diner had been in business since Morty and Velma's high-school days, and the two of them told stories from way back when. In addition to the chili dogs, the four of them shared a red leather booth, a pitcher of Diet Coke, and a plate of onion rings.

After dinner, they drove to Redbud's movie theater. Kate had a moment of panic and took Matt aside right before they reached the ticket line. "This isn't R-rated, is it? I can't handle language or nudity while I'm sitting next to Morty and Velma."

He winked down at her, amused. "Strictly PG, babe."

"Ah, thank you."

Inside the theater she sat with Matt's arm around her and a bag of popcorn and a box of Junior Mints between them. It had been a great date, original and quirky and memorable. If Kate had been able to concentrate on it, she probably would have found the movie enjoyable, too. Instead, all she could think about were squirrels.

Squirrels.

Many hundreds of them lived in Dallas. They had an unceasing longing, perhaps wired into their biology, to want to cross streets. Because of this dangerous desire, coupled with a lack of any actual brainpower, they frequently ran right out in front of Kate's car.

Sometimes the squirrels stayed on a straight course, crossing the street in a mad dash. Sometimes, though, they'd turn back in the middle and bolt back the way they'd come. Often that decision, to stay straight or to turn back, made the difference between life and death. It was hard for the poor squirrel and the poor driver to know which choice meant life. Which death. It just depended.

Tonight, she felt like one of those squirrels. She had two choices facing her: to ignore God and keep Matt, or to listen to God and lose Matt. She knew, in her head, which choice meant life and which death. But it felt the opposite way to her heart. She'd never before been so tempted to turn her back on God. She longed to do what she wanted instead.

She was just being a stupid squirrel, she told herself. Overwhelmed by a dangerous desire and a lack of brainpower. And yet, *oh*. She squeezed her eyes closed, feeling the warmth of Matt's arm around her, his bulk beside her. She really really wanted to cross the street.

She barely slept that night.

Kate wasn't ordinarily an early riser, but it was easy to get out of bed at the crack of dawn when the alternative was lying there racked with misery and insomnia. She'd showered and dressed by six thirty.

She knew that Matt went to the gym at seven almost every day of the week, and she wanted to catch him at home before he left. Had to catch him. She couldn't stand to keep her decision to herself for a second longer.

Feeling destructive, she hit the donut shop on her way to his place and bought twelve of the most sinful donuts they had. Way more than the two of them could eat. Way more than her nervous stomach wanted.

Mist swirled around her, damp and fragrant, as she stood on his doorstep and knocked.

His face broke into a grin at the sight of her.

"Good morning," she said.

"It is now." He leaned in and kissed her.

She followed him inside, set the box of donuts on the chest of drawers near the front door, and shed her jacket. "Last time it was cookies," she said. "I brought another vice with me this time." She motioned to the donuts.

He flipped up the lid and had a look. "You're determined to corrupt me, aren't you?"

"Determined."

He wore a faded white T-shirt that said *Nike* across the front in gray letters. Its thin fabric revealed the hard contours of his shoulders, chest, and abs beneath. His track pants were black and unzipped on the sides at the bottom, revealing bare feet. She could smell the sport soap he'd used in the shower. His dark hair had only half dried.

He looked incredibly hot. She wanted to wrap her arms around him, nuzzle him, and cling to him for the remainder of the day.

He was studying her closely, eyes narrowing. "How much sleep did you get last night?"

She was *so* busted. "A little."

"It looks like a very little. What's the matter?"

She looked at him helplessly, unsure where to begin.

He sighed, jerked two chairs out from the dining room table, and led Kate to the first one. He lowered into the second. "I'm not going to like it, am I?"

"It's not terrible," she rushed to say. Which was a laugh, considering she'd been in agony over this for the past twenty-four hours.

"No?" She could see him bracing for bad news.

He'd come so far during the time she'd known him. He trusted her. It seemed worse than cruel to do this to him when he was just beginning to heal. "I've been thinking about me staying here or you coming to Dallas."

"You don't want to do either one," he said slowly, "do you?"

"It's not that I don't want to. I do. Either one would be wonderful."

"But?"

"But . . . I'm just not ready yet." She knew instinctively not to blame her decision on God or on hockey, which left her with nothing to give him but vague half-truths.

He looked at her, those beautiful, sad eyes framed with dark lashes.

She bit the inside of her cheek to keep herself from babbling a hundred useless things.

"But I can still talk to you after you go," he said. "Email, text. All that."

"Sure."

"And we'll see each other. I mean, we can take trips back and forth."

She nodded, though inwardly she knew it was going to be impossible for her to see him. Too painful.

Matt watched a shadow cross over Kate. He could see her withdrawing. He didn't know what to say to keep her, to convince her to change her mind.

His stomach felt hollow, his throat tight, his heartbeat loud in his ears. He could accept that she didn't want to quit her job and move here. That was a lot to ask of anyone, especially when they'd been together such a short time. But she didn't want to let him come with her, either, something that would cost her nothing. He didn't have the balls to ask her why. He didn't want to know why.

He just . . . he just wanted to be near her. His instincts urged him to grab hold of the shirt she was wearing, to curl his fingers into it with all his strength, and not let go. She was his life. He couldn't face going on without her.

"What're you thinking?" she asked.

"That I . . ." *love you.* His pride stopped him from saying it. Idiot pride. After everything he'd been through, it came as a surprise to discover he still had some of it left. "Nothing." Dizziness came over him, as if he couldn't trust the earth to stay solid beneath him. With extreme force of will, he tried for a casual shrug. "I understand."

"You do?" Her face softened, hopeful.

"Yeah. It's too soon. Too fast. I get it."

She leaned across the space that separated them and pressed her lips to his. "Thank you," she whispered against his mouth before leaning back. She pushed a piece of her shiny red hair behind her ear. "I've been so worried. I don't want to hurt you, ever."

"It's cool," he said. "Really." He felt exposed, and he didn't think he could sit here like this much longer. He wasn't that good an actor.

"I just want you to know," she said, "that if things had been different, I'd have loved to move here."

He needed to get up now and escape from her inspection. His chest was on fire.

"If I could have . . ." She lifted one shoulder awkwardly. "Well. If things had been different, I would have."

He rushed to his feet. "I'm just going to go finish getting dressed. Be right back." He left her and closed himself into his bedroom, leaning against the door. Harshly, he scrubbed his hands over his

302

face, raked them through his hair. He was shaking. The shudders began way down in the core of him and radiated outward.

He needed time to get control of himself. Except that Kate was out there, probably staring toward where he'd disappeared, confused, waiting.

He made himself put on socks, his Adidas, a hooded sweat shirt. Then he forced himself to return to the front of the house.

She looked at him quizzically.

"You want to come work out with me?" He asked her only because he could see she wasn't dressed for it and would have to turn him down.

"No thanks. I think I'm going to go back and see if I can get some sleep."

"Good idea."

"I'll see you up at the house later?"

"Yeah."

She lifted a hand to his face. Her fingertips skimmed across his cheek, jaw, and then rubbed along his lower lip.

He almost lost it then. He nearly caved under the rush of longing that howled through him.

She gave him an affectionate smile and turned toward the door.

As he let them both out of the house, the last thing he saw was the box of donuts sitting untouched. Their enjoyment, sweetness, promise . . .

Wasted.

Once alone in his car, Matt debated going to the gym. He felt too raw to be surrounded by people. But what else was he going to do with himself? Hide at home alone? Drive the highways too fast? He made himself go and proceeded to push his body with such bruising force that everyone in the place cut a wide path around him.

Repeatedly, as he worked out, he told himself to quit panicking. Kate wasn't cutting him off completely. They had a couple more days together before she left, and she'd said they could continue long-distance. Except that his own hopes for their future had been so drastically different. Her choice struck him like an outright rejection, a crushing disappointment.

He'd thought she felt the same way about him that he did about her. He'd thought that she'd stay or that she'd want him to move there. He'd been way off. Once again, his perceptions were out of whack. He was a man out of touch with what was normal, with what everyone else already understood.

Why did you think she'd want you? he asked himself. *What exactly do you have to offer her?*

He wasn't a hockey player anymore. He wasn't famous anymore. No doubt she hoped to find someone to date who, like her, hadn't been knocked around by life. He'd been married before, which no girl in her right mind would want in a boyfriend. And he had a truckload of baggage, which he knew had been a big pain for her to deal with.

Of course she wanted to take things slow. He should be overcome with gratitude that she wanted to continue with him at all.

But he didn't feel grateful. He felt like his anchor had been ripped away. Aimless, unsure of himself, worried.

Kate noticed right away that Matt wasn't the same.

She'd thought, or maybe she'd just wanted to think, that he'd taken her decision to return to Dallas really well. But the very next time she saw him she could tell that she'd hurt him.

To give him credit, he worked hard to keep up appearances. Over their final few days, they still spent almost all of their time together, he was still attentive toward her, he still looked at her with the same fiery intensity.

But something had changed. Diminished. There was a gauntness in his face. His smiles weren't as sincere. And he was too . . . careful. As if, when he was near her, he had to think about everything he said and did before he let himself say or do it.

He'd trusted her, and she'd dealt him a blow. She knew she deserved whatever he dished out. Even so, his reaction devastated her. She'd treasured how easy he'd been with her. The way he'd let her inside himself. She'd lost that now. She told herself it shouldn't make any difference. She was about to lose him entirely anyway. But it *did* matter. It mattered desperately.

Around midday on the day before their departure, Matt officially finished the last of his work at Chapel Bluff. Gran and Kate made a huge fuss over him, thanking him, repeating over and over what an amazing job he'd done and how much they appreciated it.

When he went home, Kate and Gran walked through the house arm in arm.

The grande dame looked beautiful. They'd finished what they'd come here to do, and Kate couldn't have been prouder of their work. The honey-colored hardwood floors gleamed. The creamy paint looked rich and tasteful and also perfectly complemented the patina of the wood at the windows, moldings, and baseboards. Everywhere you looked, family antiques preened. The long-forgotten paintings had been mounted, the Depression glass displayed, the old quilts pressed back into service as bedcovers. All of the new pieces they'd acquired had been carefully chosen to flatter instead of detract from the old. They'd added simple furniture with clean, bright lines. Rugs. Throw pillows. Curtains. Tasteful lamps.

Chapel Bluff had become a home again. Warm and inviting, stately and charming, restored to its former glory. Gran had announced that from now on she'd be spending about half of every year here, and Kate herself was determined to come back often and bring the rest of their family along. This house had woken from its decades of sleep.

The two of them were slightly tearful and wholly sentimental by the time they finished their tour. Unfortunately, there wasn't time to sit around reminiscing about the past three months. They had to run errands in preparation for their trip. And they needed to finish the sad, sad business of packing their suitcases.

That night, Kate's last night in Redbud, fell on a Friday. Poker night.

Had it been any other night of the week, Kate and Matt could have spent it alone. But in honor of Gran and Kate's departure, the seniors had planned a special poker night celebration.

Velma and Peg brought over dish after dish of their homemade specialties. They arranged a centerpiece of evergreen and gold ribbons and served dinner on festive Christmas plates with matching napkins. Gran poured sparkling cider in champagne flutes and everyone took turns making toasts before dinner and again before the gingerbread cake dessert. When it came time for poker, Morty was delighted when the others, in deference to the occasion, let him raise the buy-in from five to ten dollars.

Kate and Matt had decided ahead of time to bow out of the poker early so they wouldn't have to spend all of their final night with the others. According to plan, they both faked a respectable showing before losing big.

By the looks on the faces of the seniors, not a single one of them had been fooled.

Kate stuck her hands in the pockets of her jeans. "I guess we'll just go up and watch some TV," she said.

The seniors gave them knowing smiles.

When they got up to Kate's attic room, they propped pillows against her headboard and reclined facing each other with their legs stretched out, feet tangled together, and their fingers intertwined. Her suitcases sat around them on the floor, filled but not yet zipped. Neither of them made any move to turn on the TV.

A weight settled squarely on top of Kate's heart, and it was all she could do not to break down and cry. They talked quietly about the drive back to Dallas, about what she would do when she got home, friends she'd see, family, restaurants, and shops she'd missed. They talked about him and which job on which house he might want to do next. She laid out, again, her reasons for wanting him to pursue hockey. Matt deflected her gently. And the entire time, every second, she wanted to tell him that she'd changed her mind. That she wasn't leaving. Ever. She wanted to plead for his forgiveness and beg him to trust her again.

Yet the words, jumbled together with her own selfish needs, were held back by what she knew—*knew*—to be right.

You'd never believe me, she thought, looking at his face. *But I'm doing this for you. You don't know it yet, but you're going to play hockey again, Matt Jarreau. And you're going to be great. I'm only holding you back.*

When the seniors finally called upstairs to say they were wrapping things up for the evening, Kate was almost relieved. She truly didn't think she could bear another instant of being with him and knowing their time was running out.

Kate and Matt went downstairs and said good-night to the

others. His truck was the only vehicle left on the drive when Kate bundled herself up and walked him out. Stars gleamed above them, hard and bright.

"So you're leaving around nine in the morning?" Matt asked. "I'll come an hour ahead to load up your car."

They'd reached the side of his truck. "Actually . . ." She took both of his hands in hers. Neither had put on gloves and already their skin was turning cold. She gripped hard. "I think it would be better if we made this good-bye."

His face registered blank surprise. "What? No . . . I—"

"Matt," she whispered, "I can't stand it." Moisture did pool in her eyes then, wavering her view of him. "I can't stand to say good-bye to you again tomorrow, especially not with everyone watching."

He looked stunned, unwilling.

"Take pity on me." She attempted a smile, failed. Her heart twisted with sharp pain. "Take pity on me, okay? This is really hard."

He hugged her tight, cradling the back of her head against his chest. "Don't look like that," he murmured. "Don't, Kate. I'll do whatever you want."

She released a trembling breath that frosted the air.

He rocked her in silence. When he pulled away, he frowned down at her, visibly upset. "Are you all right?"

No. No! "Yes. You?"

He nodded, but his face was ashen, and she knew he was lying.

"Look," she said, past the painful lump in her throat and the nauseous pounding of her blood. "I know you've been disappointed in life before. And I know that I've disappointed you. I didn't want to. I'm so sorry—" Her voice broke. "Even though you can't trust this world, or our relationship, or me to be perfect, I just wanted to say that you *can* trust God."

"Kate."

"I had to say it." She squeezed his hands, brought one up, and kissed it. "And I want you to remember it."

He groaned and dragged her to him for a kiss that held an edge of desperation and cascades of sadness. When they broke apart they rested their foreheads together, breathing hard.

"Don't forget me," he said, so low she barely heard.

"I won't."

He pulled back, chest heaving, and she saw the turmoil in his face.

Walk away, Kate. He needs you to go now. He's struggling, and he doesn't want you to see.

She lifted on tiptoes for one last fierce hug. One last press of lips. Then she turned and walked fast, head down, toward Chapel Bluff. She let herself in and sat heavily in the empty, darkened dining room. Her energy had gone, drained away.

She sagged against the chair's back, waiting, listening. Minutes ticked by. *Don't come in after me,* she silently pleaded with him. *I can't handle it. I won't be able to resist. I'll do what I know is wrong and stay. Don't come in.*

Finally, she heard his truck engine turn over and the sound of wheels crunching rocks as he drove away from her into the night.

Matt got up the next morning, dressed warmly in workout clothes, and set off from his house at a run. He ran off the roads, then off the footpaths and directly through the icy December woods. He finally reached the edge of trees surrounding Chapel Bluff. He paused. He'd purposely arrived early so that Kate and Beverly wouldn't see him, and as he'd planned, he could see no evidence that anyone inside the house had woken. He continued quietly across the meadow to the clapboard chapel.

Beverly had asked him to watch over Chapel Bluff while she was gone, so she'd left him his own set of keys. He used them now to open the chapel's door and steal inside the small building.

He waited for a few hours, freezing his butt off, leaning against an inner wall of the chapel. He had a good view out a small side window toward the place where they'd load Kate's car.

She'd asked him not to come back today. He wasn't going to intrude, or bother her, or ignore her request. But she was leaving, and he flat couldn't let her go without at least *being* here.

At last, the seniors began arriving. Kate's friend Theresa and Theresa's kids also came.

He waited for a glimpse of Kate, impatiently shifting his weight from one foot to the other and blowing warm air into his gloves. When she finally emerged from the house, wearing her familiar quilted jacket and her red hair in a ponytail, his heart hitched at the sight of her. She pulled her car near the back door, then opened her trunk. Morty and William carried suitcases, bags, and boxes from the house to her Explorer, and the three of them worked together to make everything fit. He wanted to be the one to do that for her—carry her stuff, pack her car.

The process of leaving took a long time. Everyone came out and went in again numerous times. After Beverly had locked, checked, and rechecked the back door, the group stood around talking. Despite the cold morning, they talked for quite a while, reluctant, he figured, to say good-bye. Whenever Theresa wasn't looking, her kids took turns shoving each other.

At last, Kate and Beverly moved around the circle giving everyone a hug, then they climbed into the car.

Matt set his jaw. His fisted hands buried deep in the pockets of his sweat shirt. He loved her. He desperately wanted her to stay. He hadn't slept last night. He'd only paced, driven his car, paced. His body was half sick, half numb.

Beverly and Kate rolled down the car's windows and waved. Everyone waved back. As Kate drove off, he could hear the calls back and forth between the two groups—the one leaving and the one left behind. He watched intently as she steered her car slowly away, then disappeared.

Gone.

For long moments he looked at the place where her car had vanished, making himself believe that she'd left. The other cars belonging to the other people gradually left, too.

Loss settled over him with crushing weight. Sadness. Anger at her for going and leaving him behind with nothing. He couldn't deal with all the emotions inside him. He didn't know what he was going to do, how he was going to hold himself together without her.

At length, he turned and sat in the pew where he'd sat the last time he'd been in the chapel, the day he'd come to repair the place. He regarded the stained-glass window and the artist's rendering of Jesus.

He remembered how Kate had told him that God had brought her to Redbud and Chapel Bluff for him.

What bull. Why would God do that only to take her away again? It was cruel to finally give him something that mattered only to take it—and whatever peace he'd found with Kate—away again.

"Thanks a lot," he growled at the stained-glass window. He pushed to his feet and locked the door behind him on his way out.

chapter twenty-two

What was that thing people liked to say? That "if you love something let it go" thing?

Ah. Kate remembered. If you love something, let it go. If it comes back to you, it's yours. If it doesn't, it never was.

That philosophy was absolute unadulterated crap. Someone should wipe that saying out, delete it entirely from America's consciousness. If you loved something you should—*obviously*—dig your nails into it and never let it go.

Kate smiled without joy, in the way of someone who was exhausted, frayed, and on the verge of a meltdown into tears.

She'd been home for almost a week, safely back in her two-bedroom Dallas duplex next door to Judy of the plants and cats. During these last few days before Christmas, before she was expected back at work, she'd envisioned herself being industrious. Shopping, sending out cards, catching up with friends.

Instead, since returning home, she'd done nothing.

Nothing.

Today she had on drawstring pajama bottoms, an old sorority sweat shirt, and an ugly pair of ski socks. It was Sunday, and she should have gone to church. But the thought of church, just like the thought of nearly everything else these days, depressed her.

She didn't feel like praising God or being surrounded by a lot of other people praising Him. Honestly, she didn't feel like talking to God, either. Or even thinking about Him.

From the top shelf of a hall closet, she pulled down her box of Christmas decorations. She lugged it to the living room and set it on the coffee table.

Sighing, her hands motionless on top of the box, she surveyed her surroundings. She'd always loved decorating, and the interior of her duplex was exactly as she'd left it in September, not a picture askew or a throw blanket out of place. She'd done a great job, she thought dispassionately. The color scheme of ivory, pale blue, and brown soothed. The mix of antiques, art, and comfortable furniture hit just the right note of coziness balanced with sophistication.

So why didn't it stir her? Why didn't her house bring her any pleasure anymore?

Forcing down a niggle of panic, she opened the box. Yep, there they were. The same familiar Christmas decorations that she set out year after year.

She lifted a carved wooden nativity set from the box. The three containers of tree ornaments she set aside. She wouldn't be using them this time around—too close to Christmas to hassle with a tree. She made piles of the white lights she usually strung on the bushes outside. Wrinkling her nose, she decided to pass on those, too. The winter wreath with fake greenery and red ribbon looked crimped and lopsided. She hung it on her front door knocker without bothering to fuss with it. Finally, she displayed her collection of glass snowflakes on the mantel above the fireplace and set out the Santa mugs that her aunt Sally gave her every year.

Several items still waited at the bottom of the box, but Kate had run out of steam and didn't feel like putting the rest of them out.

She laid the ornaments and lights back in the box and returned the whole thing to the hall closet.

She padded into her bedroom and slipped back under the covers of her unmade bed. Lying in a fetal position, she thought of Matt. Saw him running toward her shirtless, with his iPod strapped to his bicep. Saw his face above hers in the hallway the day he'd kissed her, his eyes a dark, fiery brown. Saw him sitting barefoot in his apartment, his hair wet, his expression shuttered after she'd told him she was leaving without him.

What had she done?

She'd been obedient to God, that's what. Yet she felt no peace in it. No joy or contentment. Only heartbreak and emptiness and yawning loneliness. This wasn't the first time her heart had been broken, but it was the worst time. Never had she been knocked this low.

Matt called her every night, and thank goodness he did, because she was living to hear his voice. Even though she spent the entire conversation pretending to be fine. Even though her spirits plummeted the second the call ended.

Already he'd asked her when he could come see her. She yearned to see him, and yet she knew it wouldn't change anything, that it would only make it all more brutally painful. So whenever he asked, she put him off by making up excuses, or changing the subject, or lightly saying they'd plan a date later.

He wouldn't stand for it forever, and she knew it. One of these days he was going to write her off entirely.

She probably should have broken up with him cleanly back in Redbud. Maybe it would have been better that way, easier than this slow death of their relationship that she was putting them both through. But she hadn't broken up with him then. And she didn't have the guts to ask him to stop calling now. Her stubborn heart was determined to cling to the slender thread that remained between them for as long as she possibly could.

Two days before Christmas, Matt returned to the chapel at Chapel Bluff. He sat again in the same spot in the same pew looking at the same stained-glass window.

Kate didn't want to see him. He'd sensed her hesitation before she'd left, when he'd mentioned commuting to visit each other, but he'd convinced himself it would be all right. Then he'd tried to wait a couple of weeks before saying anything about flying to Dallas to see her. But he'd been so lost without her that he'd brought it up just days after she'd gone.

Every time he mentioned it, she shot him down.

She didn't want him to come. He couldn't *believe* she didn't want him to come. But clearly, she didn't. She was cutting him loose.

Sickness rolled in his stomach.

"I know that I've disappointed you." Her words whispered out at him from the freezing silence of the chapel. *"Even though you can't trust this world, or our relationship, or me to be perfect, I just wanted to say that you can trust God."*

God. *God.* He had the sense that he'd been running and that he'd finally come to the end of that running. No further to go, no more energy, no more options to try, nothing left to hope in.

The figure of Jesus in the pastel glass window was still waiting patiently, arm outstretched.

The wooden pew creaked as Matt pushed to his feet. He walked to the open space at the front of the chapel and lowered onto one knee. He leaned over, pressing his palms into the floor.

His mind went frighteningly blank. Where to start? He tried the Lord's Prayer but only got halfway, then realized he didn't remember the rest. So screw it, he was just going to have to let his mind be blank for a minute until something came to him.

What came to him was Beth. It surprised him and he almost, reflexively, shoved the thought of her away. Almost, but not quite. He fought back the barriers that he'd developed and let the memories come. Guilt pressed in on him, just like it always did when he thought of Beth.

Forgive me, he silently prayed. It was all he could manage, two small words that encompassed so much. Everything he wished he'd done for her, should have done, regretted. All the ways he'd screwed up.

In answer, a clean wind blew through his chest.

He thought back over the past years and how angry at God he'd been. The ways he'd ignored Him, hated Him, insulted Him.

Forgive me.

More wind. More space inside himself opening up. Freeing.

Things came into his head that he'd never even considered before. The way he'd broken his word and his contract when he'd left his hockey career. How he'd injured his family and friends by pushing them away. The selfishness and pride he'd been holding on to and using like a weapon. His shame over loving Kate when he should have loved Beth forever. All of it came bubbling up like bad sewage, and he just kept letting it come. On and on and on. Until he'd emptied himself and there was nothing left.

Forgive me.

It seemed impossible, but he felt God's response immediately. **You're forgiven.**

Just that quickly and simply. No lectures or blame. Only the feeling that God had heard everything and forgiven everything in one fell swoop. Just like that.

Gratitude filled him. He stayed exactly where he was, unsure what to pray next. Except that it was more than that. He was unsure what to do with *his life* next.

Over the past week he'd purposely taken a short and easy job, something he'd already started and finished. He'd hated it. The house hadn't been Chapel Bluff, and Kate hadn't been there.

Since Kate had gone, he'd been letting himself into Chapel Bluff night after night, staring at the bare places where she'd been, missing her. He couldn't keep this up. He had to do something.

"I want you to play professional hockey again." He could clearly remember the way she'd looked—standing tall and determined—when she'd said those words to him. *"You're never going to be completely happy unless you can go back and finish what you started the right way."*

Matt shook his head. Anything but that. Maybe he should go away and travel for a while. Or take college courses. Or meet with one of those people who helped you figure out what career would be best for you.

"I believe that you can do this. Sometimes you just have to take a leap of faith." Kate's words were every bit as persistent as the woman herself had been in the flesh. *"Hockey wouldn't have the power to hurt you anymore unless you still loved it."*

Did he? Did he still love it?

It didn't matter. He couldn't go back now. Chances are he no longer had what it would take and he'd blow it—

He stopped himself. Underneath his automatic denial, underneath his fear of failing, did he still love it? And if he did, did he have enough faith in himself and in God to try to get it back? It would take more than just a little faith to put himself out there and face the overwhelming odds that he'd humiliate himself.

No, he didn't have that much faith. He was new at this God

thing and what had happened with Beth and Kate hadn't exactly increased his ability to trust people. . . .

Maybe that was the point, though. God wasn't a person. He was God. And just like Kate had said to him, that made God way more worthy of trust.

His brain staggered. He couldn't believe he was even considering this.

He wasn't considering this.

Was he?

How much did it cost to have an enormous box delivered to someone on Christmas Eve? Kate wondered. Lots. Crazy money. Money that Matt had apparently paid.

The UPS guy wheeled the package into her duplex on a dolly, had her sign her name on his handheld computer, and wished her a merry Christmas before leaving.

She blinked at the rectangular cardboard box. It stood waist high and about four feet wide. Thank goodness she was running late for the family dinner her parents hosted every Christmas Eve. If she'd been on time, she'd have missed this.

Quickly, Kate got her scissors and went to work unwrapping. Whatever it was had been professionally and carefully packed. It took her a few minutes to slice away the sides of the box and wrestle off the Styrofoam padding. Finally, she pulled off the last slab of bubble wrap and uncovered an antique table. A very particular Pembroke table with a satinwood top, cabriole legs, and paintings of green garlands and white ribbons. She recognized it instantly from the day she and Matt had gone antiquing together. She'd seen it in one of the shops on Main and loved it, but it had been *so* expensive. . . .

Matt had remembered and bought it for her.

A big red bow with a little white tag attached to it stretched around the top of the table. She angled the tag toward her.

Merry Christmas, Kate.
-Matt

She pressed a hand to her mouth. Tears filled her eyes, ran down her cheeks. The delicate table gleamed in the light from the overhead fixture, every bit as gorgeous as she remembered.

She loved him. And somehow, against all odds, he cared about her. What had she been thinking? She was going to call him this minute and tell him that if he'd have her, she was moving back to Redbud for him.

Kate sniffed and wiped away tears as she dialed his cell phone number with shaking fingers.

He picked up on the third ring. "Hello?"

"It's me. I just got the table and I can't believe it. Oh my gosh, thank you! Thank you so much. It's beautiful! I'm just—I'm speechless."

"Are you crying?" he asked suspiciously.

"Yes."

"And that's a good thing?"

"Yes."

"Then I'm glad you like it."

"I love it. I really do. It's the best present I've ever been given. I can't *believe* you bought it for me."

"I wanted to surprise you."

"You did!" She breathed unevenly, crying with happiness, overwhelmed.

"Are you heading over to your parents'?" he asked.

"About to. Are you at your brother's?"

"I'm still in the car. Almost there."

She was ready to blurt out the rest, about moving back—

"I'm glad you called," he said. "I want to tell you something."

"Sure."

He paused, and she could hear his exhale. "I've decided to give hockey another try."

Oh. Her euphoria circled downward, crashing hard into reality. "That's great!" she said, hoping she sounded like she meant it.

"You think so?" He sounded doubtful.

"Yes, of course I think so. What made you change your mind?"

"You and everything you said before you left. Couldn't get it out of my head."

Which meant that God had kept it in his head. "What's the first step?"

"Back when I was sixteen up until I started playing for the Barons, I was coached by this guy named Jim Gray. Best coach I ever had. I called him this morning. He's retired now, but he said he'd work with me."

"Where does he live?"

"New York."

"Wow, so you're going to close up your house and move there?"

"Yeah. I'll find somewhere temporary to live while I train."

"That's wonderful, Matt. Really wonderful." And it was wonderful for him. It was exactly what she'd been hoping for and wanting and expecting, because it would make him happy, give him closure. "I don't have a single doubt that you'll succeed."

"That makes one of us."

She gave a soft laugh. "You'll see."

"I don't know, Kate. Like I told you before, it's going to be tough."

"*You're* tough. You can do it."

Quiet answered while he seemed to weigh her words.

"I better go," she said, needing to get herself together mentally and emotionally. "I'm going to be seriously late and I'm bringing an appetizer."

"You cooked?"

"I know, scary, isn't it? Did you remember to bring my gift with you?"

"I have it."

"And you'll open it tomorrow?"

"Yes, but not in front of everybody. When they let me alone for a second I'll open it and call you."

"Sounds good." Before leaving Redbud, she'd taken a black-and-white photo of Chapel Bluff. She'd had it mounted and framed in the same way as the photographs he had hanging in his house. Not that she aspired to the level of those. Nor the level of his amazing gift to her. "Thank you for the table. I love it. Thank you."

"You're welcome."

"And I'm thrilled about the hockey. Merry Christmas until tomorrow."

"Merry Christmas until then."

She clicked the phone off and stood staring at the wall. The man she'd met when she arrived in Redbud—the injured, bitter, reclusive Matt—was gone. He was healing, growing stronger, and heading back into the limelight. He was, she was positive to the marrow of her bones, going to make it and make it big. Hockey had always been God's plan for him. She'd known it. She'd left because she'd known it. God had used her to help him find his way out of his grief, back to his hockey…and maybe, in the process, back to Him. That was the sum total of her role. She wasn't going to have a place in Matt's future.

She felt as if she were standing on a shoreline watching him become smaller and smaller as he swept out to sea on a boat she couldn't board.

Oh, she missed him. Wanted him.

With tears stinging her eyes again—all the stupid tears!—she glanced at the Pembroke table. Foolishly, futilely, she wished she could marry Matt, keep him forever, and put the table in a house they shared. Instead, the table would have to live here, in the duplex of a woman who was on her way to celebrate Christmas Eve again this year as the family's odd, only, and much-to-be-pitied single girl.

December slid into January and Kate returned to work. It wasn't awful to go back and it wasn't great, either. She no longer found the pleasure in it that she once had, but at least it got her out of the house and gave her something worthwhile to do with her days. Also, the kids constantly recalibrated her perspective. It was hard to feel sorry for yourself when you worked day in and day out with kids so neglected or abused that they'd been removed from their homes.

In the evenings she watched HGTV and *Antiques Roadshow* and read library book after library book about hockey.

Church? She wasn't going.

January gave way to February and Matt spent his days pushing himself to his physical limits and beyond. He arrived at the gym by six in the morning, where he worked with the team of trainers he'd hired. After two hours at the gym, he drove to the rink and logged four more on the ice with his coach. After lunch, he did physical therapy, consulted with a nutritionist, sometimes talked to his agent, and then headed back to the ice for the scrimmages his coach had arranged to return him to his previous form. At night he drove to the soulless furnished apartment he rented by the month.

Through it all, he thought of Kate.

In the early weeks it had been hard to suck at hockey. He'd been horrible and rusty and he'd wanted to throw in the towel. Kate had stopped him. Not because she encouraged him to continue every night when they talked on the phone, even though she did. What had stopped him wasn't pretty, and he wasn't proud of it. What had stopped him from quitting was a desire to make her sorry for leaving him. To show her how good he could be at something. To make her love him back.

That motivation had kept him going when nothing else could have, when his body screamed at him to give up.

And slowly, the tide turned. He began to improve. He started to regain his old form. His skills and instincts sharpened.

Over time, he got good.

February eased into March. Matt's coach and trainers insisted that he rest and let his body recuperate on the weekends. So on Sundays, he started attending a church down the street from his apartment. He arrived a few minutes after the service started and left right when it ended, which allowed him the luxury of having to talk to almost no one.

He liked church. The singing, praying, offering, and preaching filled him with quiet and stirred him at the same time.

On his own during the week he discovered that prayer came easier with practice. Trusting God also came easier with practice. Every time he took a step forward with his hockey, putting himself out there to face disaster on nothing but blind hope, God calmly met him. And somehow, so far, it had been okay.

He'd told Kate about that day in the chapel when he'd decided to play hockey again, and he'd told her about going to church on Sundays. She was cool with it, excited for him, without making him feel awkward.

In fact, she supported him in everything *except* coming to see her. Matt tried not to bring it up. Honestly, he tried. But in weak moments, when he missed her so much that he couldn't stand it, he'd cave and he'd ask her if he could come.

She kept saying no. The reasons why kept piling up. Twice after she'd turned him down, his confusion and hurt had boiled over and he'd gotten seriously mad at her. He hadn't called for two days after the first time. The second time he hadn't called for a week. But every minute during those times when they weren't talking, his gut had been tight with anxiety. Talking to her, having her in his life at least through their phone calls, meant too much to him to give up.

So he pressed on with his hockey in the idiotic hope that once he'd succeeded, once he was back on a team playing in the NHL, that maybe *then* she'd agree to see him.

In mid-March Matt returned to professional hockey and to the New York Barons as a mid-season signer. His comeback was big news.

Kate started watching ESPN, reading the sports pages of local and national newspapers, and buying *Sports Illustrated*. Like a proud mother cutting clippings for a scrapbook, she didn't want to miss a single mention of him. It proved difficult to hear and read *everything* because the story was so widely covered. Nonetheless, she tried.

Gran was over the moon about Matt's comeback. She'd been telling everyone she knew about it for weeks on end. To celebrate, she'd planned a game-watching party at her house. The rooms would be bursting at the seams with food, people, and black-and-red decorations. She'd assumed, of course, that Kate would attend and had been shocked when Kate turned her down. But Kate didn't want to be surrounded by a crowd while she watched Matt play. She wanted to be alone with her TV so she could focus on every single second of action without distraction and without having to worry the whole time about what her face might be giving away.

On her way home from work the night of the big game, Kate ran over a squirrel. *Fitting*, she thought. The darned thing would have been fine if it had continued across the street at a sprint. But it had paused, swiveled, and tried to run back to where it had started. Instead, it had run directly under her Explorer's tire.

Not the greatest of omens.

Feeling bad about the squirrel and conflicted over Matt's return to fame, she let herself into her duplex. She changed into jeans and the Barons' jersey Matt had sent her, then microwaved and ate a single portion of Stouffer's lasagna for dinner. She settled herself and a quarter bag of peppermint taffies on her sofa in front of the television with time to spare before even the pregame show began.

Much later, when he finally skated onto the ice for warm-up, the sight of him literally took her breath away. She gazed at the TV screen, eyes wide. She'd seen him tersely answering questions this past week on news shows, but this was different. He was decked out in the full uniform, pads, skates, whirling across the ice, completely in his element. During the national anthem, they gave him a long close-up, and Kate's heart pounded nearly out of her chest.

For the next few hours she got up only once, for a furtive trip to the bathroom during a commercial break. Because of all the reading she'd done, she understood exactly what the commentators were talking about when they mentioned positions and strategy. She knew all the penalties and what they meant.

Matt skated the way his mother had described. He wasn't a bruiser out there, he was a surgeon. All focus, precision, and steely calm. Kate was completely in awe.

Several times, they cut to shots of Matt's family in the stands. His mother, father, brother, and sister-in-law were there, all of them grinning broadly and cheering wildly. He'd invited her to be there, too. And every time they showed his family, she wished she'd taken him up on his offer.

The station also treated her to frequent shots of Matt's female fans. Most had gorgeous faces, dangly earrings, long stylish hair, tight designer jeans, and jerseys branded with his number and *Jarreau* across the back. One foursome had even penned a poster that said *WE'RE MAD FOR* and then each one sported a letter spelling *M- A- T- T* across the fronts of their snug shirts.

She should have expected the women. Stupidly, though, she hadn't.

Before the game tonight, her worst fear had been that Matt wouldn't live up to the hype. So many of the experts had predicted that he wouldn't be as good as he'd once been. That he was older, that the years away would have eroded his abilities.

This performance was going to shut them all up. He wouldn't top his best performances, but he was going to come close enough. He scored two of the team's three goals, one in the waning minutes of the third period to edge ahead for the win. When the final buzzer sounded, Kate relaxed, unclenched her hands, and took some deep breaths. She hadn't realized until then how tense and nervous she'd been for him, how desperately she'd wanted him to succeed.

Reporters clamored to interview Matt in the tunnel that led to the locker rooms. Obliging them, he took off his helmet and paused to answer questions. His hair was fully wet with sweat, his face flushed, his eyes very dark. His pads made his shoulders look even more enormous than they were.

"How was it to be back out there tonight wearing a Barons' uniform?" the reporter asked.

"It was good, it felt really good," he answered, slightly out of breath.

The reporter rattled off Matt's game stats. Matt inclined his head downward to listen. "You've got to be pleased with those numbers," the reporter said.

"Yeah, I am. There's room for improvement, and I'll be working to get better. But this first game back, I just wanted to play solid so I could be an asset to the team."

"You scored the game-winning goal with just two minutes forty seconds on the clock. How'd you manage it?"

"Barkov set me up with a great pass. I saw an opening and managed to angle it up into the top right corner of the goal."

"Congratulations on your first game back, and thanks for talking with us."

"Thank you." Matt ducked out of the shot and disappeared.

Kate watched the rest of the post-game coverage and then clicked off the TV. She could still go to Gran's. There'd be people there for the next hour or two. If she went, she could at least have company, someone to talk to and laugh with. But honestly . . . she didn't have the energy.

She did her bedtime skin care and teeth care routine, then slipped on a tank top and pajama bottoms, which were baggier than they'd once been because she'd lost weight. She frowned. Skinny girls couldn't afford to lose weight! She didn't even want to think about what was happening with her cup size.

She toed off her pink UGGs, leaving them beside her bed in their usual spot, and nuzzled under the covers. She tried to read the latest nonfiction hockey book that she'd checked out from the library, but all she could see was Matt skating and all she could think was that he'd been hers for a little while. It seemed impossible, almost surreal, that he had been.

She set the book aside, turned off the light, and tried to consider sleep. Sleep hadn't come easily since she'd left Redbud.

The house wrapped her in overwhelming and stifling silence. So empty. So painfully, heavily quiet.

The phone rang, causing her to jolt with surprise. Squinting, she grabbed the handheld unit off her bedside table and read the digital letters on the tiny screen.

JARREAU, MATT.

"Oh my gosh!" She almost dropped the thing in her scramble to sit up, push the right button, and answer. "Hello?"

"Kate."

"Matt," she said. "Hi." She'd just seen him on TV and now here he was, calling her—*her!*—tonight, when he must have a thousand people wanting his attention and time.

"Did you see the game?"

"Every second." She turned on the bedside light, bathing the room with color. "You were amazing. You were really, really amazing. I was so nervous watching it that I probably shaved a year off my life, but it was worth it."

"So you liked it?" She could hear the smile in his voice.

"I loved it!"

"All your studying help you know what was going on?"

"How did you know about my studying?"

"You mentioned it to me."

"I did?"

He chuckled. "Yeah."

"I knew exactly what was going on the whole time. I even understood that whole 'icing' thing."

"You'd be one of the few. Did I look like a dork in the interview afterward?"

He'd looked like a shoo-in for *People* magazine's World's Most Beautiful issue. "No, you did well. I was glad you didn't use a lot of sports clichés like most athletes." She could hear voices drawing near on his end.

"Shoot," he said. "I've got to go."

"Okay. Good game."

"Thanks. Talk tomorrow?"

"Sure."

"Good night, Kate."

"Night, Matt."

He clicked off and she was left holding a dial tone to her ear.

Without warning, her aloneness rushed back, surrounding and suffocating her. After thirty seconds of silence, she put the phone back on its stand, clicked off the light, and stretched out on her back, staring up into darkness.

Since leaving Redbud, there had been many, many times when she'd almost agreed to let him come and visit her. She'd been tempted by the possibility of seeing him almost more than she could bear. But every time she'd leaned over that cliff, God had whispered **no** and pulled her back.

Ultimately, she'd kept herself away from him for his own good, and his success tonight showed her clearly that she'd made the right decision. He'd succeeded without her as he never would have if she—and he—had stayed in Redbud.

His phone calls were no substitute for the real thing. For him in the flesh. But they were something. He'd gotten angry with her a few times when she'd shot down his requests to visit. Without his phone calls, those days had been the longest and most depressing of her life.

She'd completed the job God had set before her, and by all accounts ought to close the case file titled *Matt Jarreau*. But she *still* couldn't stop herself from clinging to their phone conversations. They were her final link to him. Matt had it all now, and in time he was going to move on, forget her, and fall for someone in his own league. Which was exactly what God had determined for him all along.

The thought of her future without him caused her stomach to clench with dread. She loved him. And she wasn't doing so well without him. And yet she knew to her toes that sooner or later she was going to have to find a way to let him go for good.

chapter twenty-three

Matt stood in his hotel room, scowling at his cell phone. With a curse, he threw the thing. It beelined through the air, hit a wall, and thudded to the floor.

He'd just told Kate he was coming to see her, and she'd just told him no. For what felt like the five hundredth time.

He began to pace, his strides eating up the beige carpet. Forward. Back. Forward. Back. The curtains were drawn against the cold afternoon outside, but he could hear the wind sailing past the building, causing the brick and mortar and glass to shudder.

After his comeback game and another at home, he'd been traveling with the team for the last six days on a three-game stretch away. Five games back, now. Five games. It was time to admit that his egotistical hope that she'd warm to him once he'd returned to hockey had been shot to smithereens. Women were supposed to like professional athletes! That should have been something he could take to the bank. But this one redheaded Texan wasn't bending.

Kate, his Kate, with the ballerina's body and the hazel eyes, the trash-talking poker habit and an old woman's fondness for antiques . . . it didn't matter to her that he wasn't a small-town contractor anymore. That he'd become a professional hockey player

331

again. It didn't matter because she didn't want him. Period. How much clearer could she make it? She didn't want him, and she'd made it plenty clear enough. And yet he'd have sworn, *he'd have sworn*, that she cared and cared deeply for him.

He didn't get it!

Their separation had made him absolutely certain of how he felt about her. Every hour had cemented her more firmly into his heart. His head was clear. His emotions fixed.

But hers?

He eyed the confines of the hotel room with contempt. He'd practically killed himself to get here. And she didn't want him.

Well, you know what? That wasn't going to fly.

On a wave of restlessness, he went to the closet and yanked out his duffel. Started stuffing his clothes into it. He was done. Done calling her. Done asking to see her.

Done.

Kate had an *Amazing Race* habit. For years she'd been watching the show on Sunday nights with her friend Brian. They had a standing date. She'd record the show. Around seven thirty he'd walk over from his house four doors down. They'd eat whatever snacks Kate happened to have on hand while they cheered for their favorite contestants and booed their least favorites.

There had been a time, a few years back, when Brian had had a small case of the hots for her. She'd fended him off. He had the kind of blond good looks that had probably made him the heartthrob of the first grade, but now just made him look overly young and freshly scrubbed. The fact that he was gainfully employed as an accountant and thoughtful and friendly had not been enough to convince her body to have hormones for him. So she was his friend, dating advisor, and *Amazing Race*–watching partner.

After the way her phone conversation with Matt had ended earlier in the day, Kate was in a funk and had tried to back out of watching the show tonight. No go. Brian had replied to her text saying that they *were* watching it, he *was* coming, and too bad for her if she didn't want to. So here she was on an ordinary Sunday night, eating Chex party mix with Brian, listening to an occasional clap of thunder from the spring storm rolling over them, and worrying about the nice sister team on the show who'd lost their lead.

Someone knocked on her door.

Kate frowned at Brian and he frowned back. "Expecting someone?" he asked.

"Nope." She paused the show and brushed her hands off on her pants as she went to the door. She freed the lock and opened it—

Matt was standing on her porch.

A jolt of pure, undiluted energy struck through her, pebbling her skin, freezing her to the spot.

Her porch light illuminated one side of him, revealing his rain-spattered shoulders and damp hair. He was wearing a familiar pair of jeans and a thin dark-gray sweater with a shallow V at the throat. The sweater clung to him just enough to hint at the muscle beneath.

He . . . he was so much bigger than she remembered. So much more handsome. His eyes so much angrier.

Kate couldn't seem to get her mind to turn over.

Vaguely, she heard Brian behind her. "Kate?"

Matt stared at her, unmoving, unblinking.

"Kate?" Brian called, louder.

Matt's focus cut behind her to where Brian was sitting. His eyes narrowed.

"It's okay," Kate said, half turning to Brian. "It's a friend of mine."

Her attention swung back to Matt. She felt like she was going to have an asthma attack—chest tight, heart thundering, mouth cotton dry.

"Can I come in?" he asked.

"Yes—yes, of course." She moved out of the way to let him pass.

He turned to wave off a taxi idling at the curb, its headlights spearing through the dark and the rain. After picking up the duffel bag at his feet, he walked inside. The living room of the duplex seemed tiny with him in it, everything—including her bravery—shrinking in the face of his size and presence.

Brian pushed to his feet and the two men sized each other up while Kate stood between them. The silence lengthened, awkward, yet she was still so rattled that she didn't know what to say. Where was her inhaler?

Matt shifted his grip on his duffel.

"Here," she said, motioning toward an empty stretch of floor. "You can set that down if you'd like."

He did so, his movements tense.

Brian came forward. "I'm Brian Lufkin."

"Matt Jarreau." The two shook hands.

"The Matt Jarreau that plays for the Barons?" Brian asked, eyes rounding with surprise.

Matt nodded.

"Wow!" Brian grinned with amazement, glanced at Kate. "I didn't know the two of you knew each other."

Kate flinched inwardly. She might be his dating advisor, but he wasn't hers. "Yeah," she said lamely, "we met when I was up in Pennsylvania."

"Very cool, very cool." Brian gave Matt a brief clap on the

shoulder. "I've been following your story on ESPN, caught most of your comeback game. Congratulations, man."

"Thank you." Matt moved his gaze to Kate. His eyes—oh, those eyes—sizzled with foreboding.

She cleared her throat. "Would you excuse us, Brian? I'm sorry about the show. . . . It's taped, though. So maybe tomorrow? Could we finish it tomorrow?"

Brian's face slackened with surprise. "Sure." He scratched his head and gave her a long, inquiring look before finally moving for his coat. "Uh, no problem." He paused on the threshold as he was leaving. "Nice to meet you, Matt. Good luck with the hockey."

Matt dipped his chin.

"See you tomorrow, Kate."

"Bye."

Brian closed the door behind him, trapping Kate and Matt alone together. The only sound was the hum of central heat.

Matt was watching her like a tiger would a deer. "Who was that?"

"A friend."

"A friend?"

"Yes."

"You didn't tell him about me?"

"No," she said. "I didn't." Avoiding his gaze, she glanced down at her hip-hugging beige corduroys, her chocolate brown boat-neck cotton shirt, and pink UGGs. Not what she'd have chosen if she'd known he was coming, but at least it was passable. Nervously, she smoothed an imaginary wrinkle out of her sleeve.

He turned and strode to the window that overlooked the street. He stared out at the night and the storm, his hands jammed in his pockets.

Why was he here? *Why are you here?* she wanted to shriek.

She'd talked to him just a few hours ago. He'd been in Chicago. She'd told him not to come. Yet here he was.

She hungrily catalogued all the details about him that she'd begun to forget. The straightness of his dark eyebrows. The way his hair curled just a little bit at the nape of his neck. His clean smell. The powerful line of his wide shoulders.

It was bliss, singing bliss, to see him again in person. But it was also like an excruciating punch to the gut. He'd probably come to break up with her to her face. They'd fought and he was honorable enough to tell her in person that they were through.

Except . . .

Except, really? Would he fly across the country for that? To break her heart at close range?

"Stormy here in Dallas," he said.

"Yep."

"Is it always this . . ." He shifted uncomfortably. "Stormy?"

"We get a lot of severe weather in the spring. It's just so flat. The fronts barrel over us." She had to intentionally stop herself from babbling.

"How's Beverly?" He was still staring out the window.

"She's doing great."

"And Velma?"

"I got a letter from her last week. She and Morty are taking his Cadillac to a classic car show soon. All the seniors are doing just fine."

He nodded. "And your family? Are they well?"

"They are."

There was a long silence. "And *your* family?" she asked, desperate.

"Fine."

More silence. More humming of the heater.

Suddenly Matt groaned with frustration and raked his hands through his hair. He looked at her. Looked away. Looked back. "Here's the thing," he said. "I'm sick of pretending I don't love you."

All the air left her lungs on a wheeze.

"I'm beginning to feel like I felt when I was playing hockey after Beth died. Like the whole thing is stupid and pointless. I'm out there on the ice every day when all I really want—" his lips set in a hard line—"is you."

She blinked at him, her throat clogging with emotion, moisture rushing to her eyes.

"You've told me over and over not to come see you," he said, "and I know you don't want me. But I . . . I had to come. I thought maybe . . ."

"I do, actually."

"Do what?"

"Want you."

It was his turn to lose his words. She closed the distance between them. Slowly, reverently, she reached up and smoothed a lock of his hair into place.

He grabbed her hand and pressed a kiss into her palm.

She smiled at him, her vision misty.

"Then why did you leave Redbud?" he asked.

"Because it was obvious to me that you were meant to return to hockey. I didn't think you would if I stayed."

"Why wouldn't you let me visit you at least?"

"Same reason. I thought it would just prolong the inevitable and make everything more painful. I didn't want to hold you back."

"Kate."

"It worked," she whispered. "Look at you now."

"Yeah, look at me now. I'm a mess."

"You're a superstar."

"I'm a mess," he insisted, "without you." Fiercely, he hugged her to him, burying his face in the side of her neck. She could feel him shaking.

Joy opened like a rose inside of her. It grew and expanded, making her almost dizzy. A few tears slipped over her lashes. "I love you," she said.

He pulled back to look at her face.

"I love you," she repeated.

"Then why are you crying?"

"I'm happy."

He rubbed the tears away with the pads of his thumbs. "I love you, Kate."

She gave him another wobbly, beaming smile. "I love you, Matt."

"You'll let me stay or you'll come back with me?"

"You can't stay here. You play hockey in New York, and you're definitely *not* quitting."

"Then you'll move to New York?"

"Yes."

"And I can see you all the time?"

"Yes." *So many yeses*, Kate thought. A thousand yeses wouldn't be enough.

"Thank God." He kissed her, long and deep, then scooped her up in his arms and carried her to the sofa, where he sat back into the cushions with her stretched across his lap, held in an iron grip. They stayed that way together for a long time, just drinking each other in, sharing breath and whispering kisses. He twined her hair between his fingers. She touched his face—couldn't stop touching his face.

Kate waited to feel guilty. She'd gone against God's will just now, accepting Matt. But strangely, in this soft space in time, there was no guilt. Only a soaring rightness that went on and on.

God? she asked. She could sense His nearness, and yet she felt no shame or discomfort in what had just happened. Only this rich sense of overwhelming blessing. And God's pleasure.

She saw it then. The full perspective of the road she and Matt had taken together. The truth clicked into place. "Oh," she breathed.

"Oh?" Matt asked.

"Oh," she answered, and cuddled deeper into his embrace.

He chuckled. "You're beautiful to me," he said.

She'd heard God say no back in Redbud.

But what God had actually been saying to her was no and then not yet.

His plan had been for Matt to return to his hockey, which meant that three months ago had been the wrong time for them. God had needed these past months to work on them both. To get them where He wanted them to be.

But now—*now*—was the time for them. *Yes, God? Am I understanding you?*

Yes.

How like God to bless Matt with hockey and to bless her with him. It was far more than she'd hoped for and far more than she deserved. She'd had so little faith. When she'd left Matt behind, she'd stopped trusting God, been willing to turn her back on Him. While God had only, ever, this whole time, been working for her good.

The thought humbled her deeply. Even in the face of her rebellion, He'd still given her this gift. Matt. The best of all gifts. *I'm sorry*, she prayed. Followed by, *Thank you, thank you, thank you,* her heart filling to bursting with gratitude.

"Remember what you told me about that little old couple who go on walks together in your neighborhood?" Matt asked. "The man whose wife has Alzheimer's?"

"I remember."

"I've thought about that so many times."

Kate studied him.

"I want to be that guy."

She smiled. "Are you sure? He's bald as a cue ball."

Matt grinned, a rugged, slightly uneven grin that took her breath away. "I'm sure. I want to be that guy for you. Your forever guy."

"A 'till death do us part' kind of thing?"

"Yes."

What had she ever done to get so lucky? Nothing. Yet here he was, saying these amazing things to her, things to build her future on. "I don't believe I've mentioned this yet, but I love you." She let a beat of quiet pass. "Even if you can't play poker."

He threw back his head and laughed. When he looked back at her, his once wounded brown eyes shone bright with humor and affection. "And I love you, even though you have asthma attacks just walking around the block."

She laughed. "Then I guess we'll be okay."

"Yeah," he said, his expression warm, "I think we will."

epilogue

The girl who'd been praying for a husband since the fourth grade was married that fall in the chapel at Chapel Bluff.

The light that poured through the round stained-glass window drenched the space in gold, pink, pale green, and peach. It haloed the couple who stood at the front of the building, holding hands while they spoke their vows.

The bride wore an elegant, straight, strapless white gown. Her red hair had been caught at the back of her neck in an elaborate knot. Diamond teardrops, a gift from her husband, glinted from her ears. The bouquet she held had been artfully created out of white roses and hydrangeas, because they reminded her of the first bouquet Matt had given to her.

The groom wore a stunning black tuxedo, a white rose boutonniere, and a persistent smile.

When the ceremony concluded, the close-knit group of family and friends made their way across the meadow beneath a sunset sky the color of honey and past a tapestry of trees brightly colored orange, yellow, and red.

After milling about inside the house to congratulate the couple, hug one another, and eat appetizers carried on silver trays, the party settled themselves at the round tables dotted through Chapel Bluff's first floor. White linens drifted downward from round tables while tall, thin candles reached upward from the floral centerpieces, their flames casting romantic light on the diners. Elegantly dressed waiters and waitresses moved through the group, bringing course after course of extravagant food. It was the first wedding the old walls had seen in decades, and those who knew the house well could sense the grande dame's delight.

Velma and Morty were spotted holding hands under the table, and once, sharing an affectionate peck. Beverly reveled in her role as hostess, her blue eyes sparkling, her smile quick, her house and her heart full. Matt's mother spent the evening alternately wiping away tears and beaming at her son, well aware every moment that she was witnessing a miracle. God had heard and generously answered her most fervent prayer.

Kate's prayer, too, He had heard and answered. Her long wait for *the one* was over. He'd come. And he'd been worth the wait. She would have wept with joy and appreciation and wonder, except that she was too busy laughing and trying to imprint every detail of the evening into her memory for always.

As for Matt, he couldn't claim that Kate had been an answer to prayer. He hadn't asked for a wife because he'd been too far from God and too cold and grief-stricken even to consider such a thing back then.

No, for him Kate had been a blinding surprise. Unexpected. *Treasured.* The best thing that could have happened to him had been God's answer to a prayer he'd never prayed.

As he sat at their wedding dinner next to her—sharing words, cradling her hand in his, kissing her, smiling—emotion expanded inside of him, constricting his throat and stealing his voice. Huge and overwhelming.

It was love for her. Deep and fierce and true.
It was love.
Heaven sent.
Perfect.

"Now to him who is able to do immeasurably more
than all we ask or imagine,
according to his power that is at work within us,
to him be glory."
—Ephesians 3:20–21a

Book Club Discussion Questions

1. What do you think of when you hear the term *romance novel*? Is your immediate reaction positive or negative?

2. What are some of your favorite romantic movies, books, or TV shows? Why do you think those particular ones stand out so strongly in your memory?

3. Can you remember some of the first romances that you ever read? Can you remember some of the first Christian novels that you ever read?

4. What challenges do you think Becky Wade faced when she set out to write a book that would be on one hand a romance novel and on the other hand a Christian novel?

5. While she's writing, Becky boils the theme of her book down to one word. That one word describes what her book is really about. What do you think that word was for *My Stubborn Heart*?

6. Consider the humor in the book. Where did it come from? Did any one element in the book strike you as particularly funny?

7. Becky uses a few metaphors in *My Stubborn Heart* to

represent the changing state of Matt's character. Can you think what those might be?

8. Over the course of the book, Becky writes from both Kate's and Matt's point of view. Did Matt's point of view feel authentic to you? Why or why not? How were Matt's sections written differently than Kate's sections?

9. Do you know anyone who's experienced the loss of their spouse? Did they remain alone? Or did they move on and find a new relationship?

10. What did you like or dislike about Kate's character? What particular facets of her personality were used by God to bring Matt "back to life"?

11. At one point in the novel, Matt goes to his knees in the chapel before God and asks for forgiveness. If you found that scene moving, why did it strike you that way?

12. Near the end of the book, Kate hears God say no to something she dearly longs for. Has God ever said no to you over something you desperately wanted? How was your relationship with God affected in the season that followed?

13. How would you characterize Becky Wade's writer's voice? What elements of her storytelling style did or didn't work for you?

14. Which scenes did you enjoy the most in *My Stubborn Heart*? Why?

Becky Wade is a graduate of Baylor University. As a newlywed, she lived for three years in a home overlooking the turquoise waters of the Caribbean, as well as in Australia, before returning to the States. A mom of three young children, Becky and her family now live in Dallas, Texas. Visit *www.beckywade.com* to learn more about Becky, her writing, and a behind-the-scenes look at the creation of *My Stubborn Heart*.

If you enjoyed *My Stubborn Heart*, you may also like…